THE DISCIPLES

Contents

Prologue

Janice Longman didn't even flinch when the stranger's hands encircled her throat. She did what she always did on these occasions: switched off her mind from the actualities and focused on the five twenty pound notes nestling in her handbag.

Janice was a prostitute, and, although she didn't really enjoy her life on the streets, she had to admit that at times it was pretty easy money. There were other times when it became downright dangerous, and she had experienced a few beatings. Some of the punters were quite obnoxious whilst one or two were even quite fanciable. With experience she learnt how to satisfy the sexual demands of the quirky ones.

Janice hadn't set out to become a prostitute, it had just happened. She had become pregnant at fifteen and was booted out of home by her furious father after refusing to help her sick step-mother with the household chores. She had lived for a time with the baby's father, a no-good waster who frequently beat her up. Janice stoically endured the beatings but all that changed when one day she had caught him slapping the child for interrupting his drunken slumber. In a fit of violent rage she had seized a kitchen knife and thrust it into his chest, narrowly missing his heart. She had then calmly phoned for an ambulance, and for a while it was touch and go as to whether he lived or died, but he eventually pulled through and was discharged from hospital. By this time Janice had served a term of imprisonment and had had her baby taken into care.

On her release from prison she had been unable to find work, except for one opportunity to become a waitress, which she declined because she regarded it as 'skivvying'. She had no home to go to so she had lived rough on the streets. She dossed down in numerous squats together with a motley collection of disillusioned teenagers and drug addicts. Inevitably she began experimenting with drugs herself, marijuana cigarettes at first, progressing steadily down the well-worn path to crack cocaine. Unable to fund her growing habit, she turned to selling her body.

She picked up a few punters on Forest Road but incurred the wrath of the regular girls who attacked her for poaching on their territory. It was during one of these altercations that she was forcibly introduced to the local black pimp who controlled most of the area. She was given an ultimatum which left her with no option but to agree to his terms. She was given the lease of a flat and agreed to hand over a large percentage of her earnings to the pimp in return.

After a good hot bath and the acquisition of some new clothes, Janice soon settled into her new mode of life. She even deluded herself into believing that after a couple of years she would have earned enough money to be able to give it all up and reclaim her child. Some nights were better than others, but this particular night had started out very badly.

She had stood, together with two other girls, for three hours on Forest Road, enticing only one punter between them in that time.

It was a bitterly cold night and Janice decided that she had had enough. She knew that her pimp would be far from pleased and had resigned herself to the prospect of a beating. She trooped wearily down Noel Street and was startled when a light blue Ford Escort pulled up alongside her. As she bent down to address the driver, he leaned forward and opened the passenger door.

"Get in," he said curtly.

Janice did as he asked. Feeling a little apprehensive she said, "Don't you want to know how much? And while we're at it just where the bloody hell are we going?"

She glanced at the driver, whose features were hard to discern, half hidden behind his turned-up collar and cap pulled well down over his head.

He stared straight ahead as if concentrating on his driving before he replied gruffly, "You ask a lot of questions. I'm taking you to Colwick Park to meet my friend who is a bit kinky, but don't worry – you will be well paid for your services."

Janice felt the first pangs of alarm. "Now look here, mate, no funny business, and if your oppo wants kinky sex then I'll warn you I don't come cheap."

The driver smiled to himself at Janice's unintentional pun. He reached inside his coat and produced his wallet, which he handed to Janice. "Open that and take out the notes. I think you'll find they add up to one hundred pounds."

Janice swiftly extracted the notes and passed the wallet back to the driver. "Yeah, okay, but what exactly does your friend expect me to do for this?" she asked.

"You'll soon find out," came the reply.

They continued the journey in silence for the next ten minutes until the Escort entered the deserted car park of Colwick Park near the racecourse.

The car's headlights illuminated a green Kawasaki motorcycle on which sat a helmeted rider clad in black leathers. The car drew up alongside the motorbike and the driver turned to Janice, who still could not clearly see his face, which was covered in thick stubble. "Okay, girlie, this is where you earn your brass. Get in the back seat and take all your clothes off."

"Right you are, sir," said Janice, touching her forehead in a mock salute.

She got out of the vehicle on one side whilst the driver exited the other. Janice got in the back seat and pushed forward the two front seats to give herself more room to undress. She swiftly divested herself of her clothing, placing them neatly folded on the front seat. She wound down the car window and addressed the driver who was standing nearby. "Tell your mate to hurry up and get on with it – it's bloody cold in here! I suppose you'll get your kicks out of watching. I don't mind if you want to join in but it'll cost you!"

The driver ignored Janice and shouted at the motorcyclist, "She's ready, all yours, mate."

The motorcyclist dismounted from his machine and, opening the rear door of the car, he knelt at Janice's side, as she was stretched out along the back seat. Without saying a word the motorcyclist placed his hands around her throat. Janice looked up at him. She could see only his eyes beneath his visor. She grinned up at him.

"Come on, mate, I know you're probably shy but at least take that bloody helmet off."

These were the last words Janice Longman uttered on this earth. Whilst she was speaking the rider's hands suddenly tightened. Janice, panic coursing through her body like a tidal wave, desperately tried to throw off the rider's grip. Her eyes bulged as his grip tightened still further, her limbs thrashing around in a vain attempt to dislodge her assailant. With a strength born of sheer desperation, she managed to move her head over the edge of the seat, but this last-gasp resistance further angered her attacker, who redoubled his efforts. Tidal waves of red mist engulfed Janice as her life ebbed away and soon her head hung loosely from her dead body. The leather-clad assailant released his grip and sat back on the car seat, panting from his efforts.

The car driver opened the rear door and peered in.

"All done, mate? I bet that makes you feel better."

He studied Janice's lifeless shape. "Bit of a waste that. She's not too bad-looking under all that make-up, nice body too!"

The motorcyclist snarled, "Bloody thieving useless whore, just like all the rest of them. You're right, I do feel good now. One down, three to go. Give me a hand to dump her and if we hurry we might get a pint in before closing time with fish and chips to follow."

"You callous bastard," said the driver.

Stumbling a little in the darkness, they carried Janice's body to the corner of the car park and propped her up against the locked door of the gents' toilet.

The motorcyclist grinned at his companion.

"I expect the milkman will get a shock when he goes for his early morning piss!"

After retrieving the notes from Janice's handbag, they flung it, together with her clothes, into a waste bin. The driver poured lighter fuel into the bin and tossed in a lighted match. The resultant blaze illuminated the bizarre scene.

Fifteen minutes later a passing motorist received the shock of his life when he stopped to investigate the cause of the blaze.

The Meeting Place

Matthew knew the day, already a bad one, was not going to improve even before the trouble with the Irishmen. He pushed open the door of Yates' Wine Lodge and entered the famous hostelry. He immediately became aware of the warmth and intimate atmosphere in spite of the raucous but not intimidating music of some long-gone country and western band.

The Disciples, as they were known in the office, met at Yates' every Wednesday afternoon. It gave them a chance to wind down and forget the worry and stress of their work. Three of them, Luke Tomey, Mark Daley and Matthew Haines, were agents for the Birmingham and Nottingham Assurance Company. The fourth member of The Disciples, though formerly in insurance, was now the sales manager of the highly successful Briars Garden Centre. Tall, good-looking John Rawson eagerly looked forward to the regular Wednesday meetings with his former workmates. Matthew Haines, the senior member of the insurance trio, was smartly dressed and immaculate-looking as always, save for the recalcitrant lock of dark hair which flopped over his forehead. He pushed his way through a throng of mainly university students before taking his place at the bar.

He was on the point of ordering his drink when he was startled by a fierce slap on the back. Turning abruptly, he was confronted by John Rawson, whose six foot frame towered over the smaller Matthew. His handsome rugged features creased in a smile as he addressed Matthew with, "A pint of the usual and a red biddy chaser if you please, as you appear to have won the race to the bar."

"Cheeky bleeder," said Matthew. "I never even saw you. I bet you have been waiting for me to pay your round."

"Sorry, old son, but I've already had one drink. I've been here since half eleven. I got away early today and I was going to volunteer to be 'in the chair', but I won't argue as you seem to have beaten me to it," laughed John.

Matthew placed the drinks on a tray and followed his friend to look for a table. This task proved difficult as the office workers and shop assistants, on their lunch breaks, had increased the already large throng of jostling people. Eventually Matthew espied two vacant high stools situated around a pillar. Gratefully the two men laid claim to the seats, sniffing the air suspiciously. The seats on the other side of the pillar were occupied by two very rough-looking individuals imbibing pints of Guinness. A rancid foul body odour filled the air and John wrinkled his nose in distaste.

"Cor, what a pong. No wonder nobody wanted to park their bums here!"

Matthew eyed the jostling throng and replied, "Beggars can't be choosers. It's either stay here and put up with the pong or join that lot and lose your drink."

"What sort of a mood was your favourite manager, old Mooney, in this morning?" asked John.

"Oh, still moaning as usual despite the fact that I had a bloody good sales week. Mind you, he's a bit uptight because of his monthly meeting with the area manager tomorrow. Personally I hope he gets a right bollocking – he certainly deserves one for all the stick he hands out to us. Although that could prove to be a double-edged sword as he's bound to take it out on us afterwards."

"You just can't win, Matt. Anyway, forget work, sup up and eye the talent all around us. Hey, isn't that the new bit of stuff from the office?" John gestured towards the main door as three girls came in.

All were attractive but one in particular had an outstanding figure, long black hair and a short leather mini skirt which drew admiring glances from the male drinkers.

"Yeah, that's young Jane Milford," said Matthew. "Quite a looker isn't she? But eyes off, mate, or you'll be in trouble with your Marilyn."

Marilyn Watkins was personal secretary to Area Manager Frederick Coombs, and she had been engaged to John for three months.

Glancing around the bar, Jane's face lit up when she recognised Matthew. "Hiyah, Matty, fancy meeting you here!"

"Come here, gorgeous," said Matthew, his arm encircling Jane's waist as he drew her towards him.

"Hey, keep your hands to yourself," protested Jane in mock horror, her smile indicating that she didn't really mind at all. She picked up Matthew's glass of red biddy and took a sip. "Ooh, that's lovely and warm as it goes down. How about buying me one?" she asked.

"I'll buy you one and give you something warm for afters!" laughed John.

This remark provoked a bout of unrestrained giggling amongst all three girls.

"Right then, girls, what are you all drinking?" asked John.

"Three of them biddies please," said Jane. "Who's your good-looking friend then?" she asked of Matthew, who slowly shook his head as he replied, "His name is John, but steer well clear because he's engaged to Marilyn."

"Don't let that put you off," said John, turning as he pushed his way to the bar.

Matthew asked Jane, "Did you spot Luke or young Mark on your way here?"

"No, they were both still in old Mooney's office waiting to present their accounts when I left," said Jane. She eased herself on to the high stool vacated by John by resting one elbow on Matthew's shoulders and the other on one of her friend's. As she completed this manoeuvre, her already revealing mini skirt moved further up her leg, displaying a shapely thigh.

This proved too much for one of the two scruffy Irishmen seated on the other side of the pillar. Goggle-eyed, he reached out and caressed Jane's thigh muttering, "Ooh, lovely bit of leg that, so it is."

Jane screamed loudly as the Irishman squeezed her thigh with his none too clean hands, his fingers probing ever upwards. Her two friends recoiled in horror at the suddenness of the assault and Jane made frantic efforts to dislodge his hand. Momentarily taken aback, Matthew decided that it was time he took a hand in the proceedings.

He thrust out an arm towards the Irishman's throat, exclaiming, "Take your filthy hands off her, you bastard!"

The Irishman released his grip on Jane but lost his balance on the high stool, falling backwards and scattering the contents of a nearby table. Matthew followed up his initial attack by grabbing the Irishman's shirt with the intention of inflicting further punishment on him. Before he could achieve this, the second Irishman reacted violently to the attack on his friend. He grasped an empty lager bottle and brought it crashing down on Matthew's head with considerable force. Matthew staggered forward, dazed and gasping in pain from the blow. The excited chatter from the crowded bar temporarily quietened, then became more intense as people pushed forward to discover the cause of the disturbance.

John had reached the bar before he became aware of the rumpus. He quickly pushed his way back through the throng of people and managed to grasp hold of the stumbling Matthew before he collapsed altogether.

"Just what the bloody hell is going on?" asked John.

Matthew put his hand to his head and gasped, "Oh Christ, it's bleeding!"

John put his arm around his friend and half dragged him towards the bar, the crowd parting as if in sympathy for

Matthew's plight. A man bedecked in Yates' uniform grasped Matthew's waist and assisted John in taking him behind the bar.

They settled Matthew down on to a rather comfortable-looking red leather seat, as two more of Yates' staff looked on with concern.

They were joined by a thin young man in a lounge suit who introduced himself as Tom Coyne, the manager.

"By the look of that head wound it'll need stitching," said Coyne. He turned to address one of his staff. "Lucy, ring for an ambulance and the police."

Matthew groaned, "No, mate, please, no fuss, just put a plaster on my head and I'll be on my way."

"You can't be too careful with head wounds," said Coyne. "Besides you may develop delayed concussion and as for the police, I have a statutory duty to report all disturbances to them."

"Just my bloody luck!" groaned Matthew.

John sighed in agreement.

"I dunno, I can't leave you alone for five minutes before you get involved in a punch-up. By the way who was the other geezer?"

"Some bog-eyed paddy, you know, the one with the smell. Besides I was only rescuing young Jane. Do you know the dirty sod had his hand up her skirt?"

At the scene of the disturbance, Jane was surrounded by a crowd of mainly male sympathisers to whom she was vividly recounting her version of events.

The two Irishmen, realising they were not eliciting any sympathy, decided that they would be better off well away from the scene. Taking full advantage of the general confusion, they pushed their way steadily through the crowd of curious onlookers, pausing only to finish off any half drunk glasses of beer or Australian wine temporarily relinquished by the drinkers. When they reached the main door they merged into the crowds in Slab Square.

This proved perfect timing for, within seconds, flashing blue lights and beeping sirens heralded the arrival of a police patrol car from Market Street, closely followed by an ambulance diverted en route to the Queen's Medical Centre. Two police officers emerged from their patrol car and were met at the door by Tom Coyne.

"What's the damage this time?" enquired the first police officer. "Surely not another punch-up this early in the day?"

"Come on through," said Coyne. "One chap has had his head bashed in by a bottle; it's bleeding rather badly, but my staff are attending to it. As for the other guy, well, there were two of them, but from all accounts they have now scarpered leaving a load of empty glasses in their wake."

"Aha," said the second policeman. "That sounds like our good friends the brothers Devlin."

The two policemen were closely followed by two ambulance medics who carefully examined Matthew's head wound and replaced the large white towel that enveloped it with a neatly wound bandage. They escorted the still-protesting Matthew to the ambulance for conveyance back to the hospital for a more thorough assessment of his wound. John accompanied his friend to the door of the ambulance and assured Matthew that he would contact his wife Elizabeth, let her know he was okay and try not to alarm her unduly.

The two policemen were eliciting statements from those people prepared to give them. The bulk of the information on the assault was gleaned from Jane, who revelled in all the attention heaped upon her. John told the policemen all he knew, which unfortunately didn't amount to much. They informed him that they would be visiting the Queen's Medical Centre to take a statement from the unfortunate Matthew.

Recumbent on a stretcher inside the ambulance, Matthew ruefully reflected that it had just not been his day. Things had progressed from bad to worse. The day had started badly with a row with wife Liz followed by a sharp reprimand from his

20

manager at the office – and now this! Some days were just not worth the effort of getting out of bed!

The Office

Reginald 'Mooney' Malone frowned as he rectified yet another error in his young agent's collecting book. Malone's neat crossings out and adjustments in red and green ink were liberally scattered throughout the pages of the oblong-shaped book.

Fresh-faced Mark Daley shifted uncomfortably on his chair wondering how much longer he would be detained on this particular Wednesday, not only from the chance of a good natter and a drink with his fellow agents, but also from the opportunity of meeting up with the vivacious Jane in surroundings away from the restrictive confines of the office. Mark had joined the insurance firm straight from school and was, even now, barely out of his teens. Keen and raring to go, his boyish charm had proved infectious and, after a spell in the office learning the basics, he had progressed to fieldwork and an agency to the north of the city. His progress, though not spectacular, was steady. His affable nature and 'little boy' smile brought out the maternal instinct in many a woman, which in turn resulted in buoyant sales. Not so his bookkeeping, which was untidy and inaccurate.

He dreaded this weekly meeting with his district manager, whose main purpose in life (or so it seemed to Mark) was to be highly critical of his work. Malone's sardonic remarks made Mark feel unworthy and placed doubts in his mind as to whether he really was cut out to be an insurance agent.

After what seemed an interminable length of time to Mark, Malone snapped shut the collecting book and shoved it across the table towards him. He pushed his corpulent body back into the tubular office chair, intertwined his pudgy fingers on his protruding pot belly, and regarded Mark through his pig-like eyes. "I regret to say, Daley, there is not much, if any improvement in your work over the past month. Though your sales figures are better than average, your bookwork remains slovenly and your accounting inaccurate. Also, your general appearance leaves a lot to be desired. Please remember that a suit complete with collar and tie should be worn when you are dealing with the public. Bear in mind that out on your debit round you personally reflect the company's image. In conclusion I want to see an all-round improvement by next week, otherwise I shall be reviewing your position with the company."

Malone flicked open the green cover of his office diary and said to Mark, "Tonight is a free night for me. I can meet you at 6 p.m. so I want you to select six suitable prospects for me to canvass for new business."

Mark's glum face reflected his feelings. "But Mr Malone, I have made arrangements to go out with my friends tonight; after all, it is my half day."

"Mr Daley," said Malone, "may I remind you that a half day is a privilege not an entitlement in this office. You have to earn time off and, quite frankly, in view of your recent performance you will not be enjoying a half day for some time yet. So don't forget to meet me at the Vale Hotel, Daybrook, at 6 p.m. tonight, and don't be late. Now send in Tomey right away."

As Mark opened the office door he couldn't help smiling as he regarded the semi-recumbent figure of Luke Tomey, long legs stretched out on the second of two tubular chairs. 'Cool Hand Luke', as he was known in the office, certainly lived up to his nickname. Luke was a twenty-seven year old black man with natural business acumen, ideal material for the most demanding agency in the district. Luke's area encompassed a run-down inner city labyrinth of streets peopled with the usual ethnic mix of races living side by side with white locals in an uneasy alliance akin to the situation in so many of Britain's cities.

From the mean backstreets of back-to-back houses of Radford and Hyson Green had emerged many of Nottingham's famous sons, among them world-renowned author Alan Sillitoe. Luke, together with his wife and childhood sweetheart Myra, had been brought up in the area, and both were well liked by all. Allied to his natural business skills, Luke's knowledge of the area and its inhabitants combined to give him a good living in his chosen profession.

Another of Luke's assets was the instinctive ability to keep calm in times of crisis, a quality that had provided him with his nickname. Unlike his fellow agents, he was immune to the barbs of Malone; indeed he had developed an innate ability to rub him up the wrong way. Whilst respecting Malone's undoubted knowledge of insurance, Luke was contemptuous of the rotund manager's treatment of his staff. He strongly suspected that Malone took a perverse pleasure in making them appear inadequate.

Malone was unpopular with both field and office staff. The female staff were particularly wary of him and always referred to him by his nickname. This was acquired when he had been caught *in flagrante delicto* over his office desk with a young typist, his ample posterior exposed for all to see. It had been seen on this occasion by Marilyn Watkins. Despite being the object of office gossip for some time after this, Malone had continued his sexual harassment of the younger female staff who were too much in awe of him to complain.

Luke smiled back at Mark. "Cheer up young 'un," he said. "It's about time you were finished. I thought you had taken root in there!"

"Watch your step," replied Mark. "I've just had a right bollocking as usual and I've got to work with him tonight."

"He can't do that!" exclaimed Luke. "You're entitled to a half day same as everybody else."

"You try telling old Mooney that," said Matthew. "I did and he just kept harping on about me not having earned the right to have time off."

Luke rose to his feet, picked up his briefcase and ruffled Mark's hair. "Don't let him get to you, Mark. Remember the old adage, 'Don't let the bastards grind you down'!"

He pushed open the door of his manager's office and entered without bothering to knock.

"Good morning," he said brightly.

Malone, head down, deep in his correspondence, emitted a grunt in reply.

Luke settled himself on the tubular chair opposite his manager, opened his briefcase and arranged his papers in neat chronological order on the desk top for perusal by Malone. He gazed around the walls of the office, which were tastefully decorated in lime green, a colour which strangely blended in with the pink of the fitted carpet. The wall behind Malone's bald pate was dominated by a large framed picture depicting a smiling Malone receiving a cup from the company chairman Charles Haines. Underneath, the inscription read, *The National Sales Cup being presented to Mr Reginald Alfred Malone, manager of the country's most improved district, December 1978.*

Malone looked up from his papers and regarded Luke with a fishy stare.

"Sit up straight, Tomey, don't lounge about."

"Sorry Mr Malone, I wasn't aware I was lounging," replied the ever-smiling Luke. "I don't suppose you could rush me through? It's rather late and I am supposed to be meeting up with the lads at Yates'."

Malone scowled. Tomey always got under his skin. He disliked him intensely and he had a feeling that this was reciprocated. He longed to find fault with Luke, whose grinning features further irritated him, but his work was faultless. Grudgingly he reached out for Luke's forms, earnestly scanning the details hoping to find a fault, but, with a sinking heart, he realised they were as perfect as usual.

"I suppose you have collected the first premiums on all these new proposals, Tomey?" he asked hopefully.

"You suppose correctly," replied Luke.

Malone grunted, pushing aside the green life assurance forms. He proceeded to peruse the blue personal accident forms.

Suddenly, jabbing his pudgy finger on the form with a cry of triumph, he exclaimed, "Aha, Tomey, you have omitted to enter the policyholder's full occupation. It reads 'Business Manager'. Head office will not accept such a vague description, in view of the risk involved."

Luke leaned over the desk.

"Ah yes, that particular proposal refers to a Mr Dawson. I guess you could best describe him as being in the entertainment business."

"Well why not say so?" snapped Malone, deleting Luke's entry and writing in red ink, 'Showbusiness Manager'. He examined every page of Luke's collecting book, hoping to find a discrepancy; by taking his time, he hoped to delay Luke from his meeting with his friends.

He finally handed back the book to an uncomplaining Luke, grudgingly conceding, "Good work, Tomey. Don't forget to see Mrs Compton before you leave the office. She will give you details of the annual audit of your book, which this year will be conducted by Mr Allis."

Luke groaned inwardly at this last remark. He was certainly not looking forward to working with company auditor George Allis, who was better known throughout the district as 'The Ferret'. He had earned his nickname from his investigative prying methods, which he applied to root out financial discrepancies in the agents' accounts. Many an agent lived in fear and trembling on hearing of an impending visit from The Ferret.

Further down the corridor the *click-clack* sounds of an electric typewriter emanated from a room marked AGENTS. Inside this room, hunched over her machine, was Mrs Janet Compton. This plump, pleasant-faced, forty-two year old woman was universally popular with agents and office staff alike. She was particularly valued by the agents, on whose behalf she toiled ceaselessly, dealing with their endless correspondence. She adopted the guise of agony aunt to the younger agents, to whom she appeared a maternal figure, listening with a sympathetic ear to their problems and providing a buffer to the obnoxious Malone.

She greeted Luke as he entered the agents' office, "Hullo Luke. You looked quite cheerful when you came in this morning. But I can see from your face all that's changed. Now I don't suppose that's got anything to do with dear old Reggie, has it?"

"Hi Janet," said Luke, brightening visibly. "How about cheering me up by agreeing to come away with me for a dirty weekend? I'm sure your hubby wouldn't mind!"

"I'm quite sure he would," replied a blushing Janet, secretly flattered by Luke's remark. "And I daresay Myra would have a thing or two to say on the subject!" She selected a blue folder from the many on her desk and handed it to Luke. "That's all your correspondence up to date including arrangements for your audit; there are also four cheques for you to deliver."

"Thanks Janet. What would we do without you?" said Luke.

"Oh, one more thing before you go," said Janet. "There was a call for you about an hour ago from a bloke who would only give his name as Bo. He sounded a bit sinister – said you would know him and asked me to tell you to meet him tonight at The Cricketers to discuss business."

Luke frowned slightly before replying. "Oh yeah, he's a friend of mine and he also happens to be Myra's cousin. I really—"

Further conversation was interrupted by the *buzz-buzz* of the telephone. Janet answered the phone, her face expressing some concern as she listened to the caller. She passed the phone to Luke.

"You had better take this. It's John phoning from the Queen's Medical."

"Bloody hell," said Luke taking the receiver. "Hullo John, old lad, what's the score then?" He listened for some minutes, his face expressing the anxiety he felt. "Okay, John, stay there with him for a bit longer. I'll handle things from this end. I'll nip straight along to Boots and let Liz know about Matthew and tell her not to panic as he should be home later today. Cheerio mate."

He replaced the receiver and turned to Janet. "Poor old Matthew – seems he's had four stitches in a head wound. He has been involved in a punch-up at Yates' defending young Jane's honour."

"Oh dear," said Janet. "We will have to keep this under our hats because if Mr Malone finds out there will be hell to pay. Reputation of the company and all that. I suppose I had better let Marilyn know that John is all right. I'll ask her to be very discreet."

"I don't think there will be any problem with Marilyn," said Luke. "Young Jane will be full of it in the morning and it's bound to be all over the office. Try and speak to her first thing and nip it in the bud. Now it's high time I was out of here. Cheers for now, Janet."

Luke ran along the corridor and down the stairs, taking them two at a time. On reaching the main office he was met by an impatient Mark.

"About bloody time," said Mark, frowning when he saw his friend's glum expression. "What's the matter with you? You don't look too full of the joys of spring."

He hurried after Luke, who was already pushing his way through the swing doors of reception.

"Don't ask," replied Luke. "Forget all about Yates'. I've got to get to Boots in a hurry. It's a long story. I'll tell you all about it on the way."

On the Debit

Mark Daley visibly relaxed as he contentedly sipped his second pint of lager, easing his sparse frame back on to the green leather bench seat in the lounge bar of The Vale Hotel. The events of the morning had precluded his usual lunchtime drinking session with his friends and, more importantly for Mark, another chance of chatting up the enchanting Jane. He had arrived home from the office and, after having a quick bite to eat, had changed into his suit and left for The Vale at 5 p.m. He found to his delight that the lounge bar was practically deserted save for one or two lone drinkers. He was able to spread out his large client register on the table and peruse the contents without fear of interruption. He chuckled to himself as he deliberately selected calls to cause maximum embarrassment to his manager.

Draining his pint, he glanced up at the large clock at the rear of the bar and realised with a start that it was nearly six o'clock. Nodding his thanks to the barman, he made a hurried exit through the swing doors. He fumbled in his pocket for the half tube of strong peppermints, hastily cramming two in his mouth, fearful lest Malone smelt his beery breath. He had scarcely closed the door of his Mini when a swish of tyres announced the arrival of his manager. It was exactly 6 p.m. You certainly couldn't fault old Mooney for punctuality. Malone opened the door of his gleaming Rover saloon and made his way towards Mark's Mini. He made a point of always using his agents' cars whilst engaged on business, fearing they would spoil the spotless interior of his own car. He opened the door of the Mini and settled his bulk uncomfortably in the seat remarking, "Pokey little motor, Daley, far too cramped for my liking. It's about time you bought yourself something more suitable, in keeping with the company's image."

"It's the best I can afford at the moment," replied Mark.

He started up the Mini and eased it forward towards the busy Mansfield Road. The first of his calls was to Bestwood Park, a dilapidated council estate on the northern fringe of the city.

Ten minutes later he halted the Mini halfway along a street of scruffy council houses whose front gardens were mostly overgrown with grass and weeds. Broken milk bottles, discarded fast food cartons and garish wrappers littered the pavements. Most of the street lights were smashed, and the pavements were deserted save for a group of youths and girls gathered outside a block of boarded-up shops.

Malone surveyed the gloomy scene and remarked, "Very salubrious place to start, Daley. Who exactly do you wish me to see?"

Mark passed him the register of clients and indicated the entry referring to the Gardiner family.

"We're right outside the house now," said Mark. "I thought you ought to canvass the eldest son Brian, who is nineteen next birthday and has a policy maturing next year. He has got a job and earns a reasonable wage."

"Are the premiums up to date?" asked Malone.

"About a month's arrears owing," replied Mark.

"Far too much," said Malone. "Anyway, let's make a start. Lead on, introduce me and I'll do all the talking."

Mark pushed open the sagging wooden gate, brushed aside the overgrown branches of a tired-looking lilac bush and knocked hard on the battered front door. This was devoid of paint save for a few crumbling flakes. Originally it had contained four glass panels but now two were replaced by cardboard, one was open to the elements and the fourth badly cracked.

A child's high-pitched voice answered Mark's knock.

"Who is it?" screeched the voice.

"Insurance man," shouted Mark, lifting the flap of the letterbox.

There was a sound of hurried footsteps running away from the door, returning seconds later. The door opened very slowly and the insurance men peered down on the chubby features of a small dirty-faced boy.

"Me Mam says to tell you she's norrin," piped the boy.

From within the house a much deeper voice roared, "Stupid little bogger, open the bloody door and lerr' 'em in!"

Mark smiled, Malone frowned and the pair entered the house. Their nostrils were assailed with the lived-in aroma of stale cooking, cigarette smoke, sweaty socks and other unmentionables. From the living room emanated the sound of a TV set at full volume.

Mrs Gardiner met them at the door of the living room. They saw a large-bosomed forty-two year old woman whose straggly hair framed a lined face devoid of make-up. Her flower-patterned dress was none too clean, she wore laddered tights and her feet were encased in trodden-down slippers.

"Oh, it's young Mr Daley," she said. "Come in, me duck, and bring your friend with you. I'll see if I can find you summat to sit on."

They entered a room dominated by a huge thirty-two inch television set in almost new condition, in sharp contrast to the contents of the rest of the room. The carpet was badly worn, the three piece suite threadbare. Slumped in one of the armchairs was a large man displaying a beer paunch. Face upturned towards the ceiling, he snored contentedly. Seated on the couch was a young couple, arms entwined around one another. The young man's right hand was inserted beneath the jumper of his female companion. In the centre of the room a little girl was busily playing with her toys whilst the young lad who had admitted them to the house stared at the visitors and picked his nose.

Mark smiled at Mrs Gardiner. "This is my manager, Mr Malone."

"Pleased to meet you, my dear," smirked Malone, extending his hand.

Mrs Gardiner hastily wiped her hands on her dress before shaking hands with Malone. She smiled falsely. "I expect you'll be wanting to see the books. I know there's a bit owing but I am paying off the arrears wi' a bit extra each week, just as the young mester told me."

"Don't trouble yourself, dear lady," said Malone. "I have not come to inspect your books, though I have a suggestion to put to you enabling you to clear your arrears entirely as well as leaving you with some cash to spare." This brought a rare smile from Mrs Gardiner. "However," continued Malone, "the main purpose of my visit is to have a word with your son, Brian."

Mrs Gardiner indicated the couch. "Move up, our Brian, bloody leave that lass alone and listen to what this gentleman 'as to say."

Without any warning Mr Gardiner suddenly stirred from his slumbers and noisily broke wind, which provoked a fit of giggling from the girl on the couch. Malone eased himself gingerly next to Brian, whilst Mark, unable to find a seat, stood by the wall. Malone politely requested that the volume be turned down on the television. Before Mrs Gardiner could comply with this request, Brian said, "Leave it alone Mam, we're watching this."

Mrs Gardiner shouted at him in exasperation, "Don't be so bloody mardy, our Brian, you've 'ad nowt but eyes for that lass this last hour. Straighten yoursen up and listen to what this gentleman 'as to say."

She made for the kitchen door. "I'll get some tea on now. I'm sure you two gentlemen must be gasping for a cuppa."

"Er, yes please," said Mark, restraining the urge to shudder as he recalled the many occasions he had gulped down Mrs Gardiner's oversweet tea served with sickly condensed milk in dirty cracked cups.

Malone made a great effort to attract Brian's attention to a host of facts and figures with the aid of his folder. "Now then, young man, for the price of a packet of cigarettes I can secure your future for you. Doubtless you have your dreams but with the aid of this plan I can make them come true for you. What are your plans? Marriage to this young lady perhaps? A nice car? Why not both? Which is quite possible if you put a little aside each week with this scheme."

"I don't reckon on saving 'owt," said Brian. "Be time I've paid for me fags, paid me board, 'ad a few pints and took Jenny out there's nowt left. In fact I 'ave to borrow off me mates as often as not."

"What exactly do you do for a living?" asked Malone.

"I wok on t'bins," said Brian.

"Now that's a well-paid job," said Malone, smiling. "I am quite sure you could easily put away two pounds a week and not even miss it. With our present bonus rates you could he drawing about three and a half thousand pounds out in fifteen years' time."

"Sounds a bloody lifetime does that," said Brian.

Malone nodded in agreement. "At your age it must seem like a long time but—"

He was interrupted by the arrival of Mrs Gardiner bearing a tray of steaming mugs of tea, some of which had spilt on the tray, which was now slopping around in a milky brown lake of liquid.

"'Ere y'are duck" she said handing Malone a cup of the sickly concoction.

Everybody else was served mugs of the steaming brew, except for the two children who were given plastic beakers. Mrs Gardiner carried the one remaining giant-sized mug over to her husband, whom she roused with a none too gentle prod to his large stomach.

"Wek up Fred, we've got company though I don't know what they think about you snoring and farting in your sleep."

Fred grunted, wriggled himself into a sitting position and took an almighty gulp of his tea, belched loudly, rubbed his eyes and glared at the visitors. "Bloody death hunters. What the 'ell do they want? More bloody money I bet. Never catch the buggers paying any out!"

"Now that's just where you are wrong," said Malone triumphantly.

Turning away from Fred, he addressed Mrs Gardiner, sensing a weak link in the defensive armour. "I see that you have a couple of long-term policies on hubby. After doing my sums I reckon we could raise two hundred pounds plus if you were to cash them in right now. You could then pay off all your arrears and still be left with at least one hundred and fifty pounds to spend on yourself. Now, how does that sound?"

"Ooh, that sounds lovely, duck!" said Mrs Gardiner with a broad smile.

"Righto," replied Malone. "Mr Daley will see to all the paperwork and he'll make out a new proposal for your son."

"Hey! I 'aven't said I want one yet," protested Brian.

"Now you listen to what this nice gentleman says, it's for your own good, our Brian," said Mrs Malone, who had mentally already spent the money on new curtains and a bit extra on the bingo.

Mark clipped the forms together and handed them to his manager.

"Aren't we forgetting a little matter of the first payment?" prompted Malone.

"Ooh, 'eck, do we 'ave to pay now?" asked a crestfallen Mrs Gardiner.

"I'm afraid so," replied Malone. "As soon as you pay your first premium, the policy comes into immediate effect, meaning if, God forbid, anything were to happen to your husband, then the whole sum would be payable to you immediately."

Mrs Gardiner's eyes gleamed at the thought of all that money.

Fred scowled, "Typical bloody death hunters. You'll be encouraging her to grease the bloody stairs next!"

"Shurrup Fred!" exclaimed Mrs Gardiner. "Get yer 'and in yer pocket for a change and gimme some money – I've only got a couple of quid in me puss."

Fred produced two pound coins from the depths of his pocket and thrust them at his wife. "'Ere, that's all you're having. I'm off down the pub to spend what's left before these con men rob me blind!"

He pushed past the insurance men and strode angrily out of the house. Mrs Gardiner stood, hands on hips, snorting defiantly after him.

"Just like a bloody man – ask 'im for money and 'e's away like a shot. Now then, our Brian, I don't suppose I've a hope in hell of gerrin' any money out of your pocket either?"

Jenny disengaged herself from Brian's clutches, located her handbag from beneath the settee and proffered a further pound coin to ease the burden. Mrs Gardiner smiled in relief. "Ee, bless you, duck. I'll let you 'ave it back at the weekend. I'll raid the kids' money boxes for the last quid."

Mark made as if to stop her but was restrained by Malone. He whispered in Mark's ear. "It doesn't matter where it comes from so long as you always collect the first premium."

Mrs Gardiner returned clutching a handful of small change, which she gave to Mark. He counted it out and entered the details of the new policies in the premium receipt book which he handed to Mrs Gardiner.

Malone, beaming broadly, extended his pudgy hand to Mrs Gardiner.

"Goodbye dear lady, it's been a pleasure and thank you so much for a refreshing cup of tea."

"I'll make you another if you've got time, duck," said Mrs Gardiner.

Malone politely declined her offer, almost knocking over a chair in his haste to reach the door.

Once outside the house he turned to Mark. "I hope the rest of your calls are of higher quality than that, Daley. I trust you have learnt the lesson that with a little forethought even the most hopeless of calls can be made profitable for all concerned. You might have warned me about that foul tea though!"

The remaining calls were successfully negotiated by the pair and the efficient Malone proved his worth by completing further new business. Mark was absolutely delighted with the night's work and he had to admit that although Malone was a pig to work with, he had at least earned him a tidy sum in commission. When he finally pulled up in the car park of The Vale Hotel, he felt in such a generous mood that he even asked Malone to accompany him in a celebratory drink by way of a thank you for his efforts. Malone declined and Mark was secretly relieved.

After-Dark Recreations

Malone almost had second thoughts about Mark's offer as he watched the young agent disappearing through the swing doors of the pub. He felt the need for a large whiskey to wash away all traces of that dreadful tea which had left him with a queasy stomach. But this urge was tempered by the distinct feeling of unease he felt in the presence of his agents other than on business ventures.

It had been a very successful evening's work but he now felt the need for a little winding down to relax after a trying day. Malone's version of relaxing was a yearning for female company and young females in particular. At forty-eight years of age, the spice had evaporated from his marriage. His daughters had both married at a young age and were living away from home. His wife Betty immersed herself in local charity work and endured his occasional lovemaking with a patience acquired with much practice. His numerous discreet affairs had petered out with the onset of advancing years. A vain man at heart, Malone was loath to admit that his once handsome features were in decline. He had tried, and was indeed still trying, his hand with various females in the office. But his efforts of late had been rebuffed; all the staff were by now well aware of his reputation and the source of his nickname. The memory of this infamous episode still rankled with Malone and he was now obliged to confine his liaisons to furtive meetings with prostitutes to satisfy his lust.

He reached into the glove compartment and produced a dark-haired wig which he pulled over his bald head, adjusting it carefully in the car mirror. From the inner pocket of his coat he produced a pair of horn-rimmed spectacles and finally a pair of leather gloves. Starting up his dark blue Rover, he eased it smoothly out of the pub yard, expertly timing the lights on green to swiftly traverse Mansfield Road and ease on to the ring road towards his Wollaton home. Except that it was not the leafy reaches of Wollaton for which Malone was making for. On reaching Basford, he turned off the ring road and took a left towards Hyson Green.

Soon the large tower blocks of flats loomed into view. As he entered Noel Street, the sight of several scantily clad girls caused him to slow down. He particularly attracted the attention of one large-bosomed girl who, to gain his interest, opened her coat to reveal her pendulous assets.

"Like what you see, duck?" she shouted.

Malone gave a cursory glance and decided that the area was a bit too public for his liking. As he increased the speed of his car, the girl shouted after him, "Fuck off then! I hope your wheels fall off!" This remark provoked peals of laughter from her companions.

Malone negotiated the junction with Radford Boulevard and sped up the hill towards the traffic lights. Turning into Forest Road, he saw, directly under a street light, three prostitutes deep in conversation. One striking-looking girl had a coffee complexion and her tall lithe figure was encased in a black leather mini skirt and thigh boots. The other two girls, though young-looking and attractive, paled in comparison with the dark beauty.

All three girls were controlled by local pimp Bo 'Dangles' Dawson, whose colourful name enhanced his reputation. The tall black girl was Angie McPherson. Her mother had moved down from Glasgow some twenty years previously and was herself still occasionally 'on the game'. Her two companions, both in their early twenties, were Christine Delaney and Jacqui Reid. Malone slowed down on seeing the trio, uncomfortable with their number as he much preferred to approach solitary women, considering that the fewest number of people who observed his nefarious activities the better.

He peered out of the car window, immediately drawn to the lithe figure of the tall black girl. Angie's image, attractively enhanced under a street light, was more akin to that of a catwalk model than a streetwalker. Malone stopped his car after taking a cursory glance in his rear mirror to check for the presence of a police patrol car. He wound down the car window and waited with growing excitement the expected approach of one of the girls. His arrival broke up the animated conversation of the three girls.

"Punter!" said Jacqui to her two companions.

Angie shrugged her shoulders. "He's all yours, Jacqui. I've had four already tonight and I could do with a rest."

Nevertheless she accompanied Jacqui on her walk to the car, eyeing the occupant. One glance was enough for her. Laughing, she turned to Jacqui. "He looks an old geezer. I can't do with all that huffing and puffing before they come. You can have him, Jacqui – he'll never wear you out!"

"Cheeky bleeder," said Jacqui as Angie retraced her steps.

Jacqui sauntered towards the car and, puffing on her cigarette, she leaned nonchalantly on the wound-down car window. "'Ello, darling, looking for business, are we?"

"Er, what about your tall friend there?" asked Malone, nodding his head towards the retreating figure of Angie.

"No go, darling," said Jacqui. "She's bloody wore out she is. What about me then? I'll give you a really good time!"

Though he felt a little disappointed, Malone opened the car door and Jacqui slid into the seat alongside him. Settling herself down on the plush leather seat, she exclaimed, "Ooh it's a bit cold on me bum!"

Her short skirt rode up her thighs and received an appreciative glance from Malone.

"I take it we are going back to your place?" he said.

"Ooh, no darling, my old man would have a thing or two to say about that," laughed Jacqui. "No, I do all my business in punters' cars. Take a right at the lights across Radford Boulevard and on to the waste ground back of Players' factory that was."

Malone glanced at Jacqui with some distaste because she was still puffing away at her cigarette. "Do you mind getting rid of that cigarette? I don't allow smoking in my car," he said.

"Ooh, fussy old bugger you are," said Jacqui, taking one last puff before discarding the cigarette through the car window and replacing it with a stick of chewing gum.

Remembering Jacqui's directions, Malone soon found the waste ground and drove the car over a bumpy surface of crumbling bricks and broken glass crunched into a well-worn surface of muddy grass. He took great care parking his car as far away as possible from the glare of the street lights.

Jacqui leaned provocatively towards Malone in a deliberate move designed to reveal that she was not wearing a bra. Confident that she now had his full attention, she launched into her sales pitch. "Straight sex is £20, I do hand relief for a tenner and oral sex for a fiver extra."

Malone, by now fully aroused, leaned over her and released the lever which made her seat recline.

"Take your clothes off," he said.

"Hold your horses, big boy! Money first then business," said Jacqui. "And by the way, it's extra for a complete strip."

Malone reached into his jacket, produced his wallet and extracted from it two £20 notes which he gave to Jacqui.

"Ta love," she said, quickly slipping off her jumper and wriggling out of her skirt with practised ease.

Malone, excited by the sight of her nudity, reached out for her.

"Easy, darling, give me time to get me skirt off!" exclaimed Jacqui.

Fumbling in his eagerness, Malone struggled to remove his trousers and underpants.

"Let's not forget the rubber, love," said Jacqui, reaching for him.

The sex act was soon completed and the red-faced Malone lay back on the seat breathing heavily.

"Ooh, you needed that! Are you going to drive me back then?" said Jacqui, hastily dressing herself.

"Don't put your skirt back on, I haven't finished yet. I want my money's worth – I did pay you extra," said an indignant Malone.

"Listen mate," said Jacqui testily, "if you want more action then you'll have to bloody well pay for it!"

Malone grabbed her by the shoulders. "You cheap tart, I want my money's worth!"

"Take your hands off me!" Jacqui shouted.

She leaned towards Malone, grabbed his testicles and squeezed hard. Malone cried out in pain, releasing her instantly.

Whilst he was thus distracted Jacqui opened the car door, got out and ran across the waste ground.

Malone clutched his genitals in pain for five minutes until he could compose himself. He was furious and annoyed with himself for being so easily conned and more so when he realised that his wallet was missing. "Thieving little whore," mused Malone. "I'll get even with the bitch."

He started his car and drove slowly towards the entrance, leaving his headlights unlit in order to draw no attention to himself.

In the far corner of the waste ground was parked a car displaying no lights. Its occupant was visible only by the glow from the end of his cigarette.

Inner City Lifestyle

At half past eight that same evening Luke Tomey turned his car into Noel Street and glanced at his watch. He realised that he was already half an hour late. It had been that sort of day, with everything going wrong. Luke pondered, not for the first time, just what it was that Bo wanted from him.

The two young men, though not exactly bosom pals, had been educated at the same Radford school together. That was about all they had in common, though, apart from being distantly related. In those early schooldays Bo had emerged as one to be wary of in playground scuffles, which he often started and ended. Fellow pupils developed a healthy respect for him and avoided him when they could. At the age of eleven he was caught pilfering from a local shop.

Undeterred by warnings from his headmaster and his first encounter with the law, he had continued his thefts from local shops, openly selling stolen cigarettes to his schoolmates. Next he embarked on house burglaries and street muggings. After one particularly brutal attack on an old lady, a spell of approved school did nothing to quell his criminal activities. He joined a local street gang, and, after a series of violent episodes punctuated by a six month Borstal sentence, he emerged as their natural leader. He became well known in the Hyson Green area as a pimp who 'ran' some half dozen girls.

Surrounded by a bodyguard of local hard men, Bo did more or less as he wanted.

Although he acquired a considerable income from the activities of his street girls, Bo had increased his income threefold by becoming a drug dealer, the run-down streets being a fertile breeding ground for this activity.

Conversely Luke's path after leaving school had taken a different direction from that of his half-cousin. Hard working in his early school days, he could have progressed to university in the opinion of his teachers. Instead he had opted for a career in insurance. He had been married for two years to his childhood sweetheart Myra, who was a nurse at the Queen's Medical Centre.

Luke and Bo had met up sporadically over the years, each possessing a healthy respect for the other.

Luke parked his car in the car park of the pub directly under the huge tower block, a monument to the disastrous building policies of the Sixties.

On entering the pub his ears were assailed by the jerky reggae music emanating from a huge jukebox. The bar was full of mainly black youths, many of them sporting dreadlocked hairstyles which hung like knotted ropes from their heads. He soon located Bo, who was sitting at a corner table surrounded by his cronies and two white girls who, judging by their appearance, were prostitutes. Bo greeted Luke profusely.

"Over here Lukey boy," he said in his curiously high-pitched voice, a fascinating mixture of Jamaican patois and his natural Nottingham accent. "Grab yourself a pint at the bar or you can have a can of Red Stripe."

He indicated a pile of beer cans on the table, most of which were empty. Luke ordered himself a pint of bitter, and, glass in hand, sought out a seat next to Bo. This was soon possible due to the quick exit of a blonde-haired girl, assisted on her way by a slap from Bo.

"Park your arse here," said Bo, patting the seat so recently vacated.

"What's your problem, Bo?" asked Luke. "Surely you haven't got a claim on that policy I sold you last week because it's not even been issued yet!"

"No man," replied Bo. "Well, maybe in a vague way perhaps but I've thought up a little scheme of benefit to both of us."

"I don't like the sound of that," observed Luke.

"Easy man," said Bo. "Relax, enjoy your beer, the night is young. Take some pleasure before business. How about a freebie with one of the girls? No problem, it can be arranged. Me and you go back a long way, Lukey boy!"

Luke, wary of upsetting Bo, politely declined his offer of sexual dalliance, but gradually relaxed as the beer took effect.

Minutes before closing time the tall figure of Angie McPherson entered the bar, accompanied by her friend Christine Delaney. They made straight for Bo's table, both in apparent distress.

"Hallo girls, what's all this then?" said Bo, indicating his watch. "Get back on your beat – you're missing out on the golden hour."

A worried-looking Angie leaned over the table.

"Bo, I'm scared shitless. Jacqui has gone missing. She went off with a punter at half past eight and she ain't come back. She always reckons to come back to Forest Road after seeing a punter in his car. And you know Jacqui's style, she doesn't hang about – wham bam, thank you mam, that's our Jacqui. I'm really worried, Bo, especially after the way Janice was done in a couple of months ago."

Bo reached out for Angie and pulled her on to his knee. "Now listen darling," he said reassuringly, "don't you go worrying your pretty little head about the likes of Jacqui. She's been on the game long enough to look after herself. Perhaps she's gone back to a punter's house for a long session. Always had an eye for a quick buck, has our Jacqui. Anyway, leave the worrying to me, I'll check with that no-good husband of hers, Charlie; that's if he's managed to drag his arse out of the bookies! It could be the tart has decided to have an early night without checking in. In the meantime get back on the beat, you two. The streets will be swarming with randy punters by now."

Angie stroked Bo's face. "I thought maybe me and you could have an early night for once."

"On your way," laughed Bo, pushing her off him, and slapping her behind. "Come back to the flat in about an hour. I should be finished with Luke by then."

Half an hour later Luke sat uneasily on a white leather sofa in Bo's flat which belied its council flat status by resembling a millionaire's luxury pad. The entire interior was carpeted with thick black and white luxurious shag pile. The centrepiece of the living room was a dazzling white four piece leather suite. Reggae music pounded out from four speakers connected to a state-of-the-art stereo system. In one corner of the room was a small bar complete with illuminated drinks cabinet, whose shelves were stocked with every conceivable type of drink.

Luke sipped cautiously on a double Bacardi and coke, aware that he was very near being drunk. The potent mixture of beer and spirits was beginning to take its toll of him and he realised that he was in no fit state to drive home. He experienced a distinct feeling of unease when Bo outlined his 'business' proposition. Much to Luke's surprise, Bo revealed that he had arranged a discreet surveillance to be placed on his movements. This came as a complete shock to Luke, who had been totally unaware of his 'shadow' over the past few weeks. He was even more amazed when Bo explained it was due to the presence of his unseen minder that he had not been challenged or mugged. By way of a 'thank you' for this service Luke was expected to reciprocate by agreeing to 'an arrangement' of mutual benefit.

Bo wanted him to deliver small envelopes containing crack cocaine to various of the households he already called upon for insurance. Though this proposition greatly alarmed Luke, Bo argued that it would be the perfect set-up. Who would ever suspect the insurance man going about his daily business?

As a reward for carrying out these deliveries Luke would be given £100 a week, plus, of course, the protection service from his minders. Luke was outraged at this proposal and testily enquired his fate if he were to refuse. Bo's mood changed totally on hearing Luke's lack of enthusiasm and apparent rejection of his generous offer. Bo was used to getting his own way and was intolerant of any opposition to his plans. Luke was warned that if he didn't go along with the plan his 'protection' would immediately be withdrawn, leaving him wide open to being mugged and his insurance monies stolen. Worse still, Bo hinted that he would apply a little pressure on Luke's established clients to change their allegiance.

Luke began to realise that he had no option but to go along with the preposterous plan and agreed to meet Bo again in one week's time to collect his supplies for the first delivery. He rose, a little unsteady on his feet, brushing aside offers of further drinks. Bo, now that he had got his own way, was in a generous mood and phoned for a taxi to take Luke home, assuring him that he would arrange for his car to be driven back to his house by the morning in good time for him to start work.

During the journey home in the taxi, a bleary-eyed Luke noticed that there was an unusual amount of police activity in the area of Radford Boulevard.

The Morning After the Night Before

Malone braked sharply as the morning rush hour traffic came to yet another temporary halt at the Derby Road traffic lights. He was in an increasingly irritable mood, after a restless night of tossing and turning in his bed, his mind disturbed by the events of the previous night. Eventually sleep overcame him at 6 a.m. and at a quarter past eight he was rudely awoken by his wife. He rose from his bed bleary-eyed, his head throbbing with a pain born of his sudden awakening. As he collected his thoughts he realised the unpalatable fact that, for the first time in his life, he would be late for the office. An unthinkable thought to a man who prided himself on his punctuality and who was only too ready to chide others for lacking this compulsion.

After a snatched breakfast of tea and half-eaten toast, he rounded on his long-suffering wife and blamed her for not setting the alarm clock. She stoutly denied this unfair charge, reminding him that he always insisted on setting the alarm himself. His main worry was the loss of his wallet and the resulting inconvenience it would cause. He would have to notify the bank without delay regarding the loss of his credit cards. Even more worrying was the loss of his driving licence and the membership cards of several sleazy clubs, the identity of which would raise a few eyebrows, to say the least.

At last the lights changed to green and the traffic edged forward. Malone's Rover neared the lights, with only one car in front of him, when they changed to red. He cursed loudly and reflected miserably that, once late in the morning, everything conspired to make you later.

Partly to relieve the boredom, he switched on his car radio hoping to hear a traffic update. The Radio Nottingham newsman's voice droned on with Malone only half-listening: "And finally an update on our main story. Police have confirmed the identity of a woman found strangled on waste ground near Hartley Road late last night. Details are being withheld until relatives have been informed. Further news of this and other stories will be given in our later bulletins."

An icy chill gripped Malone and his fingers tightened on the steering wheel. He stared ahead, oblivious of the flickering traffic lights changing to green. The frantic blaring of a car horn from the vehicle directly behind him pierced his reverie, causing him to grate the gears as he slammed in the gear stick. He was very badly shaken and barely recalled the rest of the journey. His mind was in complete turmoil. The loss of his wallet was now a major crisis. Fearing the discovery of his wallet by the police, he envisaged court appearances and newspaper headlines. The utter shame of it all! Why oh why had he not been more careful? Could he be connected to the murdered girl on the news bulletin? Was it the same girl with whom he had sex? He recalled that he had used a condom, but where was it now? He remembered reading about the latest testing of criminal evidence which had been gathered by the police and the use of specialised techniques to identify suspect DNA. What if they tested his semen in this way? His eyes darted to the well of the car searching unsuccessfully for the used condom. A sixth sense caused him to avert his gaze to the windscreen and he only just avoided a collision with the car in front of him by a frantic application of his brakes, causing the car to slew slightly sideways.

Stationary at the next set of lights, he glanced out of his offside window at a bus drawn alongside him. The driver pointed at his head and mouthed the word 'nutter' at him. Beads of sweat trickled down Malone's face. He switched off the car heater but still felt warm despite the chilly morning.

With a supreme effort of will he banished all negative thoughts and switched his mind to concentrating on behaving rationally, reasoning that his first priority must be to establish an alibi to account for his movements after he had left Mark Daley. He parked his car in the Fletcher Gate Car Park, for which he had a season ticket. He then spent several minutes in a public call box, firstly contacting his bank and then making three further calls concerning the losses of his various cards.

By the time he had completed this very necessary task, his lateness had reached the embarrassing stage. At five minutes past ten he was already sixty-five minutes late for work.

Head down, he entered the main office of the insurance building with a hurried step, muttering a cursory good morning to the staff at the reception desk. Janet Compton paused in her task of collecting the late mail delivery and exchanged knowing looks with her two companions.

"It's his poor wife I feel sorry for," she said. "By the look of him, he's had a night on the tiles. It must have been some night, because I can't recall him ever being late for work."

"Yeah," nodded Jane Milford in agreement. "I feel sorry for her too – imagine having to sleep with that slimy toad!"

As Malone entered his second floor office, Marilyn Watkins hastily put down her cup of coffee. "Oh, Mr Malone, there have been several urgent calls for you, including one man who refused to leave his name or message."

She gathered up the details of the calls, clipped them together and handed them to him. She reddened as she perceived Malone staring at her breasts, which were sharply outlined under a pale pink blouse. She felt distinctly uncomfortable in his presence and, although he had never made any sexual advances towards her, she felt as if Malone's eyes were mentally undressing her at every opportunity. She stared challengingly at him.

"And Mr Coombs asked that you go up to see him as soon as you arrive." She glanced meaningfully at the office clock.

Malone averted his gaze from Marilyn's bosom and mentally changed gear, reverting to his efficient business-like manner. He briefly thanked Marilyn and began the task of replying to the most urgent of the calls.

Fifteen minutes later he emerged from his office and ascended the stairs to the top floor office of Area Manager Frederick Coombs. The Area Manager was a very large man, a veritable giant in fact. His height of six foot four inches and weight of over sixteen stones made him seem akin to a heavyweight wrestler, but his imposing figure and deep voice combined to exude an air of supreme authority. In common with other large men he had a gentle manner, but was capable of extreme anger when provoked. He respected Malone's undoubted skill as an insurance manager but disliked him personally, being well aware of his manager's obsession with the opposite sex.

"Morning Reg," he boomed. "You are more than an hour late for our meeting, most unlike you, I must say. Still, let's proceed with the agenda as I have a working lunch in Birmingham today and I'm running late."

"I am so dreadfully sorry for being late, Mr Coombs," fawned Malone. "No real excuses for my tardiness, except I'm sorry to say that I overslept, which resulted in my being caught up in rush-hour traffic. However, here are my figures for the past month. You will see that we are well up on target sales figures, the only disappointing figures being the arrears, which remain stubbornly high despite my constant exhortations to the agents."

Malone passed over his file to Coombs who perused the figures for several minutes. Glancing up at his manager, he said, "Yes, Reg, very good figures indeed. The state of the arrears, though worrying, nevertheless reflects a situation that is prevalent throughout the country. In fact this very subject is the main topic to be discussed at the meeting in Birmingham this morning. I want you to organise a meeting with all the agents for Wednesday of next week. We will try and instil some commitment to reducing the arrears with each and every one of them."

This remark pleased Malone, who enjoyed exercising his authority over his agents and he relished the thought of the forthcoming campaign. Coombs brought their meeting to a speedy end in his haste to be in good time for his lunchtime meeting in Birmingham.

Malone returned to his office and dictated details of next week's proposed meeting and replies to other letters to the efficient Marilyn. Ten minutes later he was in contemplative mood as he pondered as to just who would provide his alibi. He drew comfort from his mid-morning cup of strong coffee while he considered the options. The sudden jarring buzz of the telephone interrupted his chain of thought. He picked up the receiver.

"Malone here."

There was a click and a slight pause before a muffled voice began, "Malone, you dirty old bastard. Did you enjoy yourself last night?"

"Who am I speaking to?" rasped Malone, aware of a vague familiarity in the voice.

"That's for me to know and for you to find out, pal," said the voice, chuckling at first, then adopting a more sinister tone. "I expect the police would like to know all about your wallet being clutched in a dead girl's hand, and I expect that you would like to have it back, wouldn't you? Well, you'll just have to sweat awhile. But don't worry too much. I will be contacting you again very shortly."

There was an ominous click as the unnamed caller replaced the receiver. Malone sat dumbstruck, feeling the cold chill of fear yet sweating profusely.

The Investigation Commences

The intensive police hunt for the killer of Jacqui Reid began at 2 p.m. on Thursday in an untidy conference room at the rear of Radford Road Police Station. The small team of detectives was headed by Detective Chief Inspector Peter Hutchinson, an experienced officer who had been involved in several successful murder investigations. His second in command was Detective Sergeant Brian Mulraney, a long-serving officer who provided excellent back-up to his chief. The trio of detectives was completed by Woman Detective Constable Jackie Harper, a rising star of CID. Added to the investigation team were two members of the city vice squad, Sergeant John Mabbutt and Woman Police Constable Lisa Harris.

It was with some reluctance that Hutchinson had included the vice squad duo in his investigative team. His reservations were due to the animosity between his sergeant Brian Mulraney and John Mabbutt of the vice squad. Both men were in love with the same woman, Detective Constable Jackie Harper. Her blonde hair, long legs and exquisite English rose looks ensured that she received many a second glance from police officers of all ranks and incurred the envy of her female colleagues.

When she had first appeared as a police probationer, she had been inundated with requests for a date. Seemingly unaware of the furore she was creating, she had turned them all down, focusing instead on pursuing a successful career in the force. She had certainly achieved this aim and pleased her superiors with her cheerful but efficient attitude in performing her routine duties, her willingness to learn and to act upon the advice given to her.

She was relentlessly pursued for both romantic and personal reasons by John Mabbutt. He kept pestering her for a date whilst simultaneously trying to persuade her to join the vice squad. Jackie's foremost ambition was to be a detective, but for her first move up the career ladder she was offered the choice of the vice squad or an attachment to the Rape Crisis Unit. She had chosen the former, and had eventually succumbed to the pressure exerted upon her by John Mabbutt by finally agreeing to meet him outside work.

For several weeks they were embroiled in a brief but passionate affair, aided by the release of simmering emotions in both of them. Apart from her ambition, Jackie had joined the police force to flush from her mind the memory of her first real romantic affair with a much older married man which had left her with bitter-sweet memories when he returned to his wife and family. In similar vein John Mabbutt was licking his wounds at the end of a stormy five year marriage which had ended in acrimonious divorce.

Though they tried to be discreet in their liaisons, it became virtually impossible to keep their affair hidden, given their close working relations and the friendly atmosphere of the police force. The officer in charge of the vice squad interviewed them both separately and in the end fate decreed that Jackie was transferred to CID.

Well aware of her enthusiasm, Hutchinson allowed her to accompany him on numerous investigations and was pleased with the progress and tigerish persistence she used in even the most routine investigations. Jackie put in a lot of overtime in her new role and this resulted in her meetings with Mabbutt becoming fewer and fewer. Their brief affair was now ended, at least as far as Jackie was concerned, and Mabbutt feared the worst as she seemed bored and disinterested. The reason for this was that she was now heavily involved with Hutchinson's second in command, Brian Mulraney.

Forty-three year old Mulraney was a seasoned veteran of the force. By no stretch of the imagination could his craggy features be deemed good-looking. He was a man's man, solid, dependable, cool in a crisis, and it was these attributes which had first attracted Jackie, who felt secure in his company. Unlike her last affair, this was not an instant romance, more a slow gradual awareness of each other. Mulraney regarded Jackie as the kind of girl he had always longed to meet but never had; now, incredibly, despite an age gap of twenty years, this girl was actually in love with him.

Mulraney's marriage was all but over, but his wife was reluctant to divorce him, one eye on his pension which loomed nearer. Jackie, well aware of the ripples caused by her former relationship, was ultra careful in her meetings with Mulraney. They met only once a week at a prearranged out-of-town rendezvous. By mutual consent they gave no hint of their relationship during working hours. The one person, apart from Mabbutt, who was aware of their relationship was Hutchinson, who experienced misgivings over his decision to include the vice squad in his investigative team.

Hutchinson addressed the group with the aid of a blackboard, attached to which were enlarged street maps of the inner city area.

"I would like to say that this is a particularly nasty killing of a young woman who we know for certain was engaged in prostitution, and, according to our friends in the vice squad, she had been an active prostitute for some five years previous to her death. This is the second murder involving a prostitute during the last three months. The purpose of this meeting is to prepare for a thorough hunt for this killer and to this end I have enlisted the services of the city's vice squad, whose detailed knowledge will prove invaluable.

"Now we know there are something like three hundred prostitutes in Nottingham today. The majority of these work the streets but there are some who operate from private houses, brothels, massage parlours and drinking clubs. The vast majority who work the streets do so for their own benefit. However, there are two main pimps, both known to us, who control the main inner city area. The first of these controls girls in the Hyson Green and Radford areas. He is one Archibald Dawson, of Caribbean origin, commonly known as Bo. His counterpart or rival working the St Ann's and Sneinton areas is also of Caribbean origin and his name is Benjamin 'Rasta' Alexander.

"There has been the odd clash between these two and we strongly suspect that both of them are engaged in the distribution of drugs. So I suggest we commence this investigation by questioning these two to confirm or eliminate the number one theory in this case, that the murder was carried out as an act of revenge. I concede that as of this moment there is not a shred of evidence to support this theory. All that is known for certain is that the dead girl worked for Dawson. I have already sent out a team of officers to detain Dawson and Alexander and bring them back for questioning. Now are there any questions so far?"

"Yes, sir," said WPC Lisa Harris. "Whilst on patrol with the vice squad I noticed that the dead girl was usually accompanied by two girls in particular, namely Christine Delaney and Angie McPherson, who is currently the girlfriend of Dawson. Should we not be questioning these two also?"

"Good point indeed," said Hutchinson. "I'll arrange for them to be apprehended and brought back to the station."

Several more routine points were dealt with by Hutchinson who then assigned each one of the team to interview the various suspects. Jackie Harper drew the short straw by being selected to question Bo Dawson, Hutchinson theorising that her terrier-like questioning would wear Bo down whilst her good looks would keep him interested. They all trooped into the canteen for a short coffee break whilst they awaited the arrival of the suspects. Jackie sat next to her best friend Lisa

Harris, whilst John Mabbutt hovered uncomfortably close by, unsure whether he should sit next to the two women. Anxious to speak to Jackie, yet unsure of her reaction, finally he pulled up a chair and sat down next to her, but she deliberately averted her face and pointedly resumed her conversation with Lisa. Mabbutt tentatively tapped her on the shoulder.

"Er, Jackie love, I see that Hutchinson's landed you with Dawson. Now he can be one very tacky character in the presence of women, so would you like me to sit in with you on the interview?"

Jackie's eyes flashed with anger. "No, I bloody wouldn't! Don't be so patronising! Your macho attitude makes me sick. Do me a favour and clear off to another table."

Mabbutt reddened, for Jackie's angry retort, delivered in a raised voice, was heard by most of those present in the canteen.

Brian Mulraney made his way, precariously balancing two cups of tea in each hand, towards a table at which sat his chief in deep conversation with the police surgeon. Mabbutt, face flushed with anger, strode towards the swing doors of the canteen. His path crossed that of Mulraney and he deliberately flicked out his elbow causing one of the cups of tea to crash to the floor, closely followed by the second cup as Mulraney desperately tried to retrieve it. He angrily made as if to follow the departing figure of Mabbutt, but was stopped in his tracks by a warning shout by Hutchinson.

"Leave it, Brian."

Feeling somewhat shamefaced but still angry, Mulraney ordered two more teas from the counter and brought them over to Hutchinson, who resumed his conversation with him as if nothing had happened. Feeling as if she were the focus of attention, Jackie left the canteen in the company of her loyal friend Lisa, who had her own reasons for disliking Mabbutt.

An hour later all four detainees were consigned to separate interview rooms prior to questioning. In one of them was Bo

Dawson, his lean frame supported by a tubular chair. He leant backwards, his right heel resting on his left knee, hands behind his head as he chewed steadily on a matchstick. He looked challengingly at the uniformed constable who stood, hands behind his back, at the door. His eyes lit up when the attractive Jackie Harper entered the room. She sat down opposite him and switched on a tape recorder.

Bo leered at her. "Only the best for Bo. You're a cracker, darling, but with a figure like yours you could be earning a fortune working for me!"

"Oh, so you admit you are a pimp?" said Jackie.

"No, darlin', 'course not. What I meant was I could get you a job as an exotic dancer," said Bo, smiling.

"Right, let's get down to business," said Jackie. "I should first of all tell you this is an informal interview. To begin with I'd like to establish that you knew Jacqui Reid and in fact that she actually worked for you as a prostitute. Can you confirm these facts?"

Bo's leering features changed to anger. "Whoa, hold your horses a minute, darlin'. No, she never worked for me, as you put it, and you can ask her old man Charlie to confirm that. But, yes, 'course I knew her. After all, she's a mate of my girlfriend Angie."

"And talking of your girlfriend Angie – she is a prostitute, isn't she? And what's more she works for you too," said Jackie.

"Nah darlin', you've got it all wrong. Sure, Angie turns a few tricks now and again but that's strictly her business, nothing to do with me. She comes to my bed quite willing and for free. In fact she loves it, as do all the girls," said Bo, now openly leering at Jackie, who reacted by pointing a finger at him.

"I would remind you that this is a murder inquiry. Now I want you to give me an exact account of your movements last night from 8 p.m. onwards."

Bo dropped his gaze, sat upright and opened his hands palm uppermost.

"Easy darlin'. I spent the entire evening in The Cricketers pub, left there about 11.30 p.m. and went back to my flat until breakfast this morning and I can give you the names of at least a dozen people who'll tell you the same."

"Did you see Jacqui Reid after 8 p.m. last night?" asked Jackie.

"No darlin', I did not," said Bo.

"Interview suspended," said Jackie, switching off the tape recorder.

In an adjacent interview room valuable information was obtained from an interview of Angie McPherson conducted by Hutchinson. At first Angie had been reluctant to recount the events of the previous evening as she was fearful that the police would charge her with soliciting. Hutchinson reassured her that, due to the very serious nature of the crime, all other violations of the law alleged to have been committed by her would be overlooked in this particular case, as long as she gave the police her version of the events.

Hutchinson looked closely at Angie across the desk. There was no doubting that she was an attractive girl, but what a waste of talent. With her looks alone she should be able to make a small fortune in showbusiness. Why on earth did she need to sell her body for a living? Worse still, why was she under the spell of that odious pimp Dawson? Despite skilful questioning, Hutchinson could not get her to admit that Dawson was her pimp. She insisted repeatedly that he was her boyfriend and that her immoral earnings were purely for her own benefit. Not wishing to antagonise Angie by pursuing the matter, Hutchinson resumed his questioning about the events of the previous evening.

"Okay, Angie, cast your mind back to the very last time you saw Jacqui on Forest Road last night. Tell me in detail exactly what you can remember."

Angie drew nervously on her cigarette before replying.

"Well, me, Chris and Jacqui was stood around having a chat like, waiting for punters, when this big blue car pulls up."

"Let's stop you there," said Hutchinson. "Can you remember what make of car it was?"

"Ooh, I'm not very good on cars. But Chris reckoned it could have been a Rover or some British car. It were definitely newish looking and in good nick."

"Could you recall any of the numbers or part of the numbers on the number plate?"

"Naw, I didn't really look. Well, you don't usually bother with things like that, do you? Oh, I suppose you do all the time though, you being a bloody copper!"

Angie giggled unrestrainedly at her own riposte.

Hutchinson, keeping a straight face, continued, "Did you get a good look at this punter? Think back very carefully and try and give me a very thorough description of him."

Angie's brow furrowed and she scratched her head before continuing, "As I remember, Jacqui went over to the car and I tagged along behind her. I wasn't really interested as I'd only just finished with one old geezer. I glanced casual like at this one and I remember thinking, 'Oh God, not another old fart.' I didn't fancy him one bit and said to Jacqui, 'He's all yours.' He looked kinda thickset. He had on them very thick horn-rimmed specs and his hair didn't look right, as if it was a wig like."

'Shrewd observation,' thought Hutchinson. If only some of his officers were quite so perceptive. He continued the questioning. "How old do you reckon he was then, Angie?"

"Ooh, hard to say, duck. Middle-aged I reckon. Fifty, sixty maybe, you can't always tell. Do you reckon it was 'im that did Jacqui in then?"

"We don't know yet, Angie. We still have very many more inquiries to make. But thank you, you have been very helpful. That will be all for now."

Hutchinson switched off his tape recorder and, as Angie made her way out of the room, he suddenly stopped her. "One more thing, Angie, I very nearly forgot. I would like you to assist the police artist in drawing up a likeness to the man you have just described."

Angie grinned at Hutchinson. "Can't say I enjoy obliging you coppers, but I'll make an exception in this case if it helps to nail the bastard who did Jacqui."

By 8 p.m. all the interviews had been completed and the four interviewees left the police station. A brief flare-up occurred when Bo almost collided with Rasta Alexander on exiting the building. Threatening words and gestures were exchanged by the two rivals, and Alexander had to be forcibly restrained by two police officers before Bo left via a side entrance.

The whole team retired to the canteen for a welcome break of tea and sandwiches. The tireless Hutchinson retired to his office and played back all the taped interviews, stopping the tapes at intervals and making copious notes. An hour later he rejoined the others in the canteen.

"Well, troops, I've heard all the interviews and despite the obvious antagonism between the two pimps that we all witnessed, I think we can rule that out as a motive for the killing, though I wouldn't dismiss it completely.

"There appears to be no obvious motive for the killing. From an examination of the body by the police surgeon it has been established that she had had protected sex prior to her death and, as there were no marks on her body with the exception of her throat, we assume she was not raped. Her purse, containing some eighty pounds, was found untouched in her shoulder bag, so no robbery motive. We do have an excellent description of the man in whose company she was last seen. With the help of one of our witnesses a shadow profile has been drawn up and this will be distributed to the media and be on show to the public by tomorrow morning. Another significant clue was that he was driving what we assume was a nearly new dark blue Rover car. I want you all to check with local dealers the exact location of any such car distributed over the last two years.

"I have concluded that this murder has several similarities to that of Janice Longman, some three months ago. Not least of which is the fact that both girls worked for Dawson. The chief, in fact the only suspect in the Longman case is a motorcyclist, who is apparently a young man. Which, on the surface, rules him out of this murder, except that there is no obvious motive for either murder. Finally, thank you for your efforts. I would now like you all to go home and get a good night's sleep, because we have got an awful lot of hard work ahead of us. We must catch this character before he attacks any more unfortunate victims. The media boys, especially the gutter press, must be already licking their lips at the prospect of a serial killer on the loose whose target is prostitutes."

The police officers trooped out of the building, deep in conversation, oblivious to the familiar surroundings. Not one of them even bothered to glance across the street where a leather-clad motorcyclist sat astride his bike, arms folded and his visor pushed upwards. Shivering slightly in the chilly night air, the officers disappeared around the back of the station in search of their cars. The motorcyclist pulled down his visor, kick-started his powerful machine and roared away up Radford Road, his exhaust scattering the autumn leaves from the gutter.

Unwelcome Visitors for Charlie

For the third time that morning Charlie Reid was interrupted preparing his obligatory heroin injection. The harsh rattle of the door knocker caused string of profanities to fall from his thin lips.

Charlie was a shambles of a man, and though only thirty-five years of age he looked nearer sixty. His sparse frame and bony drooping shoulders gave him a gaunt appearance. His hair was fast receding, he always looked badly in need of a shave and his general hygiene was poor. He would certainly not look out of place amongst the human flotsam found daily sprawled on the steps of the Council House.

Earlier that morning the police had had to resort to breaking into his house and shaking him out of his drunken and drug-aided slumber in order to inform him of his wife's untimely demise. They had bundled the confused Charlie into a car and driven him to the morgue to identify Jacqui. Bleary-eyed, he had shaken his throbbing head in an effort to clear it before nodding recognition of the corpse. Charlie felt no sudden remorse; he was numb to the loss of anything save his meal ticket.

The day dragged interminably on as Charlie's head slowly cleared and shadowy hallucinations were replaced by the grim reality of his daily existence. His stomach ached from lack of food, his head still throbbed, his mouth was dry, his skin felt itchy and he trembled at the onset of that all too familiar craving. He felt the need to clamber aboard the magic carpet that made his mind drift from everything unpleasant.

Charlie gathered his confused thoughts together and attempted to make some sort of sense of what he could remember of the events of the last twelve hours. He recalled the coppers with their stupid questions, on and on: 'Did you know your wife was on the game? Did you profit from her immoral earnings? Did you know that Bo Dawson was your wife's pimp?'

''Course I knew she was on the game, the bloody stupid cow! Didn't I warn her to be careful with all the nutters that are about these days? Did she take any notice of me? Not bloody likely mate! No, she knew it all, reckoned all men were alike, letting their pricks rule their brain. As for money, well, that nearly all went to her bleeding sister and that spoilt kid of hers. That was her one big regret – she couldn't have kids, not that it bothered me,' reflected Charlie. 'Don't like the little bastards anyhow!'

Still she had had her good points, for at least he got a good regular supply of smack from Bo who regarded Jacqui as one of his best girls. Also she did slip him the odd twenty pound note or two if she had had a good night.

These thoughts reminded Charlie of the £400 in notes underneath the floorboard in the bathroom, which he had discovered only last week. At least there wouldn't be a row when she discovered that they were no longer there.

Charlie had made several attempts to inject himself with the mind-numbing drug, but was constantly being thwarted by interruptions. First there was that nosy fat cow from next door, then Jacqui's sister Pauline, whom Charlie disliked intensely as she made no secret of the fact that she regarded Charlie as a waste of space and held him responsible for her sister's occupation.

Between bouts of copious weeping she needled Charlie with her barbed comments. "She was so good to me and the kid. I don't know how I'm going to manage without the money she gave me every week. She always insisted that I bring him up proper. He's going to need new shoes, not to

64

mention a new school uniform when he starts his new school early next year. Then there's Christmas coming up—"

"Stop right there!" interrupted Charlie, distinctly annoyed. "I know bloody well what you're leading up to and you can forget it. There is no way I am going to subsidise that bloody kid. Whatever Jacqui did was her business, though I never did agree with it and I told her so! I haven't got enough money to support meself let alone your kid!"

Pauline glowered at Charlie. "I might have known it was a waste of time appealing to your better instincts – you haven't bloody got any! You always were a mean selfish bastard. Exactly what Jacqui ever saw in you I shall never ever know. At least she's rid of you now."

"Listen, you!" shouted Charlie, now so angry that the bile rose in his throat. "For Chrissake shut up, get out of my house and leave me to grieve in peace for my Jacqui. She's scarcely cold on the slab and all you care about is the money you won't be getting any more."

Charlie reinforced his argument by steering Pauline towards the front door. But Pauline was not yet finished. Pausing at the door, she delivered her parting shot. "You lying bastard! You never cared for our Jacqui. All you ever think about is your next fix. Why don't you do us all a favour and take a bloody overdose!"

With that she slammed the front door with such force that it rattled the windows.

Though she had similar features to her sister, Pauline was much taller and fatter. Her short skirt was incongruous and did nothing to hide her meaty thighs as she strode angrily down the street. The twitching curtains were a sure sign that her shouted last remark to Charlie had been heard by a few of the street's residents.

Charlie's next visitor was Christine Delaney, who was one of the few people who actually liked Charlie, and the feeling was mutual. This was probably due to the fact that they shared a common interest: they were both heroin addicts.

Christine supported her habit from her street earnings and Charlie had on two occasions in the past, though unbeknown to Jacqui, spent an hour or two in the afternoon locked in amoral embrace with her.

For a few seconds they clung to each other, each seeking solace in one another; Christine tearful and mournful for her good friend Jacqui, Charlie feeling slightly aroused by the close contact of a friendly female body, mindful of the fact that it was nearly a month since his sexual needs had been sated.

Christine, becoming aware of his arousal, pushed him firmly but gently away from her. "Not now, Charlie love. It don't seem right with Jacqui only just gone."

She burst into a fit of renewed sobbing as Charlie gently steered her towards the couch.

Christine was a small, delicately-featured, doll-like girl. Her short black hair seemed moulded around her face in the mode of a Twenties flapper. Her pleasant easy-going nature was incongruous with her chosen profession. She had failed as a drama student and had taken her disappointment badly, allowing herself to drift aimlessly and mix with the wrong crowd of people. She had dabbled with drug-taking and soon the 'bit of fun' had turned into an uncontrollable habit. She had encountered Angie McPherson and her two friends at a Hyson Green rave party and had followed them into prostitution. Jacqui's murder had shocked and frightened her, especially as she had not yet recovered from the shock of her friend Janice being similarly murdered. She felt in need of comfort but had guilty thoughts about the two occasions she had betrayed Jacqui by allowing Charlie to make love to her. Deep down she knew that Charlie was a worthless so-and-so but she couldn't resist a lame dog. Charlie comforted her on the couch, but, with his desire unfulfilled, he soon became aroused and slid his hand up her skirt. She pushed his wrist away.

"No, Charlie! I really mean it!"

"Okay doll," said Charlie shrugging his shoulders resignedly. "Tell you what, let's comfort ourselves with a little mind-blowing relaxation. I was just about to shoot up when you arrived."

"Now you're talking," replied Christine, dabbing at her eyes with a small handkerchief.

She followed Charlie into the small kitchen, wrinkling her nose in distaste at the unsavoury smells emanating from the unwashed pots, intermingling with stale beer fumes and the unmistakable sweet cloying aroma of marijuana. Rolling up her sleeve, she sat alongside Charlie at the kitchen table and allowed him to place the red home-made tourniquet around her arm. Charlie tightened it and searched for an unused portion of vein, no easy task as her lower arm was a veritable mass of purple and red pinpricks. At last he found a minute space amidst the plethora of mini eruptions and was about to plunge the syringe in when he was interrupted by the sudden opening of the front door. Into the kitchen burst Bo Dawson accompanied by his 'bodyguard' of two expressionless black youths.

He took in the scene at a glance, then, shaking his head, he said, "I dunno, Charlie. I've just been talking to your sister-in-law and she's right – you have got the morals of a pig. No sooner is Jacqui out the way than you're leaping on her mate!"

Charlie spluttered, "It's not like that, Bo, honest. Chris came round to cheer me up and we both thought that we'd ease our grief by indulging in a little smack."

Bo strode over to the table and, leaning down, he pushed his face up to Charlie's, their noses almost touching.

"How very very cosy. Well, from now on, Charlie boy, things are going to change. You are going to have to earn your keep. In case you have already forgotten your provider and my best working girl aren't around any more. No more free smack for you, my lad!"

Charlie, by now thoroughly alarmed, made as if to rise from the table but was prevented by Bo's right hand pushing him firmly back in his seat. With his left hand he grabbed what was left of Charlie's hair and once again confronted him face-to-face.

"Now listen good, Charlie. Your first job starts tonight. I want you to break into old Suleiman's surgery and load yourself up with every bottle and every capsule of methadone you can lay your hands on, and while you're at it grab a few bottles of amphetamines as well. Make sure you do it quietly and cleanly, no cock-ups, and if you do get caught by the filth I know nothing about it. Got it?"

He poked Charlie in the chest to emphasise the point. He next turned his attention to Christine, an uncomfortable observer of the events. "And as for you, you slag, get your arse out of here and get back on the street. Angie tells me she hasn't seen you all day. No wonder when you're entertaining this useless piece of shit! With Jacqui gone, we're all losing money so get out there and bloody earn some!"

Christine, wary of Bo's fearsome reputation, rose swiftly to her feet, skilfully evading a blow delivered by him. She ran out of the kitchen so fast that she tripped up on the metal door strip, sprawling ungracefully on the linoleum floor. She was helped to her feet by one of Bo's grinning aides who unashamedly groped her breast before she angrily wriggled free from his grasp and left the front door open in her haste to get away from the house.

Bo continued his verbal onslaught on the unfortunate Charlie.

"I've had one grilling from the filth about Jacqui working for me. I hope for your sake you haven't been blabbing your stupid mouth off."

Despite Bo's painful grip on his hair Charlie rose to his feet in protest. "No, Bo! I would never ever shoot my mouth off to the filth about anybody, least of all you. Do you really want me to do this job tonight? I mean, I don't feel too good, especially with all that's happened lately. Couldn't I at least do it tomorrow night instead?"

In reply, Bo struck Charlie a fearsome blow with the back of his hand which sent him reeling towards the couch, blood beginning to ooze from a split lip.

"Pull your bloody self together and get out there! When you've done the job put all the gear in a hold-all and bring it round to my flat later and if you're caught, remember I don't bloody know you!"

Dr Raschid Suleiman's surgery was located halfway down a Radford backstreet of unpretentious *Coronation Street* style terrace houses. The short drab street was blocked off at one end by a high brick wall behind which was Shipstone's Brewery. The forty or so houses were occupied by a pot-pourri of inhabitants, comprising in the main, older retired long-standing residents, young unemployed families, at least a dozen Pakistani families, and two Hindu and one Polish family completed the ethnic mix. Several of the residents added to their meagre incomes by letting out a room or two to students.

The surgery was contained in an amalgamation of two houses. Despite being involved in two medical inquiries, from which he had emerged untarnished, Dr Suleiman's reputation was a little murky, at least to his fellow doctors. Shunned by the local group practices, he had been forced to go it alone and to this end he had proved successful. He was well liked by the local populace, mainly due to his dispensing of drugs both legally and illegally, the latter proving a profitable sideline. His nightly surgery was scheduled to end at 6.30. p.m. but a steady stream of after-hours patients was seen until 7.30 or even sometimes until 8 p.m.

On this particular Friday night a thin drizzle enveloped the drab street and the earthy smell of the brewery pervaded the night air, causing the hunched figure of Charlie Reid to shiver in the autumn cold. Charlie had positioned himself at the end of the street, observing the comings and goings from the surgery, easily located by the green illuminated globe above the main door. Impatient after a twenty minute wait, Charlie glanced again at his wristwatch.

'Bloody old Paki! What the hell is he doing at this hour? Dishing out drugs like sweets and making a packet,' thought Charlie, conveniently forgetting the numerous occasions he himself had been helped out by the popular doctor. He sighed with relief when at last the squat figure of Dr Suleiman appeared underneath the green globe, slamming the surgery door firmly shut and hurrying across the street to locate his dark blue Renault car.

The car's security system emitted a brief screech as the doctor disconnected it before he entered the vehicle. The sleek Renault soon purred into life and the doctor perfected a three point turn at the end of the street and passed the hunched figure of Charlie, who averted his face as the car passed him at the road junction before turning left and roaring away up Radford Road.

Charlie shuffled hurriedly up the street until he reached the passageway between the surgery and the next door house. His entrance was barred by a green painted door secured by a Yale lock. This proved to be no problem for Charlie. Glancing briefly left and right to ensure he was unobserved, he expertly slid a plastic card under the base of the Yale lock lever. A quick wiggle or two and the lock snapped back.

Charlie slipped inside the passageway and snapped shut the door. Halfway down the passage was a blue stained toilet window. Charlie reached into his holdall and produced a pair of glass cutters with which he inscribed a small circle on the thick glass of the pane. Next he attached a piece of brown sticky paper to the marked glass. From his voluminous holdall he produced a small silver hammer with which he struck two sharp blows to the glass. Though the sound was muffled, the tinkle of falling glass was unmistakable. He paused for a few moments before carefully removing the sticky paper which had large slivers of glass attached to it, the remaining glass having fallen on to the toilet floor. The meticulous Charlie carefully dropped the sticky paper into a Sainsbury's paper bag, disposing of this tidily in his holdall.

Next he very carefully slid his hand through the circular hole and opened the window after locating the catch. The toilet was halfway down a corridor at the end of which was the surgery.

After opening the glass door, Charlie's ferret-like eyes soon located the drugs cupboard, situated in an alcove to the right of the surgery. He took from his pocket a large bunch of assorted keys of all sizes. It took him a full five minutes before he found one that snapped free the lock. But here Charlie was in his element, inserting the keys with practised ease and the maximum of patience. His eyes lit up when he observed the contents of the large drug cupboard. There were at least three dozen bottles of methadone which he grasped and eagerly thrust into his holdall. He grabbed bottles of amphetamines and greedily snatched up bottles of sleeping tablets, ampoules of morphine and even antibiotics.

Soon the holdall was crammed to capacity. Charlie, gingerly testing its weight, suddenly realised that perhaps he had overdone it a bit. Still, he reflected, he could make a packet flogging some of these drugs. Some of the youngsters would take anything these days. He would make sure that he kept Bo happy by giving him most of the methadone and amphetamines. The rest he'd flog and make plenty of dosh for himself and Christine. He had decided that he might as well shack up with her; after all, he could ponce off her earnings and now, he came to think of it, he had always fancied her more than Jacqui. These pleasant thoughts made Charlie feel quite euphoric.

So heavy was his bulging holdall that he needed two hands to carry it. He knew that he really should unload some of the bottles but greed caused him to persevere. However, he displayed extreme caution as he slowly released the Yale lock on the street door. Half-opening the door, he peered gingerly out into the street.

The thin miserly drizzle had increased in intensity, enough to form small puddles of rainwater glinting under the macabre orange glow of the street lighting. Save for a bedraggled ginger cat returning from a nightly foray, the street was deserted. Charlie slid awkwardly through the door dragging the holdall behind him, just remembering in time to snap shut the door. He made slow progress down the street and his arms ached with the effort of keeping the holdall from dragging on the pavement.

Breathing hard with the exertion of dragging his heavy load, he paused at the junction with Radford Boulevard and decided to hail a taxi. Common sense had prevailed as Charlie began to realise his predicament should he be challenged by the police.

Ten minutes later he was dropped off directly outside his home and he even tipped the taxi driver in a fit of rare generosity. Still in euphoric mood, Charlie hummed contentedly to himself as he bent down to rummage through the side pockets of his holdall in search of his door keys. As his fingers probed the pocket he became aware of the presence of two shadowy figures either side of him. He turned his head to confront them and received a crashing blow to the side of his head, rapidly followed by two more. Charlie sank to the ground, vaguely aware of a sticky substance trickling down his face. Puzzled now, his last thoughts before lapsing into unconsciousness were of his hand encountering a reddy-green liquid oozing from his head. The latter stages of the attack on Charlie were witnessed by Luke Tomey, who had emerged from a house two doors away from Charlie's, nearing the end of his Friday night collection round.

Due to an unlit street light, Luke could only make out the vague outline of two men raining blows on another lying helpless on the ground.

"Hey you!" he yelled, running towards the incident, "What's your game then?"

The two men, realising they had been spotted, reacted instantly by throwing bottles from Charlie's holdall at the oncoming Luke. Three of the bottles missed their mark and splintered on the pavement. A fourth struck Luke on the side of the forehead, causing him to literally stop in his tracks and instinctively throw up his hands to deflect further missiles. The two men continued to hurl bottles at Luke as they made their way to two motorcycles parked at the side of the road. Luke, having halted temporarily under the deluge of missiles, broke into a run as the men mounted the two motorcycles and roared off into the night.

The sound of breaking glass had persuaded some of the streets residents to forsake their nightly television-watching to satisfy their curiosity about the sounds of a fracas. Luke examined the fallen figure of Charlie whose head was actually resting on his own doorstep. A trickle of blood oozed steadily from a head wound; the blood was liberally mixed with the contents of two bottles of methadone poured over his head by his attackers. All around Charlie were scattered broken bottles of methadone and numerous white, blue, yellow and black capsules strewn along the path like confetti.

Luke located Charlie's pulse, turned to a curious neighbour and said, "Ring for an ambulance, mate. He's still with us but only just, and while you're at it ring for the police as well."

The Drugs Connection

Brian Mulraney was on his way back to Radford Road and five minutes away from the end of his shift when he heard the first news of the incident on his police radio. He responded immediately to what appeared at first to be a run-of-the-mill Friday night mugging, his gut instinct telling him that there was more to it. He waited impatiently in the traffic for a gap to turn round his Escort and spotted the slim figure of a uniformed Jackie Harper on patrol with a male colleague. He experienced the familiar tightening in the throat, the quickening of his pulse. He grinned wryly. There's no fool like an old fool, but what the hell, she was so damned attractive and he couldn't help himself.

Manoeuvring his car to the opposite side of the road, he glided to a halt alongside the police patrol pair. Winding down his window, he said, "Hop in, Jackie, we're off to Wiverton Road."

Looking slightly puzzled, Jackie opened the rear door of the vehicle and climbed inside whilst Mulraney addressed her companion. "Radio in to your superior that WPC Harper is accompanying Detective Sergeant Mulraney on an urgent CID inquiry. Do it *now*, son." He emphasised the last point.

The startled constable was on his radio immediately, Mulraney possessing that air of authority which warranted instant obedience.

Leaning over from the back seat, Jackie nuzzled Mulraney's ear with the practised ease of a familiar lover.

"What exactly is this all about, Brian? It's not some cunning ruse to get me on my own, is it?" She laughed gaily.

"There really is no need for all this subterfuge – I'll come with you quite willingly!"

Mulraney felt her sweet breath on his ear and her soft feminine presence excited him, but with an effort he controlled himself and when he spoke to Jackie his words were delivered in an authoritative tone, adopted in an attempt to disguise his true feelings.

"There's been a nasty assault in Wiverton Road on a yet unnamed man. The attackers have made off on two motorbikes, green in colour, and I've got a funny feeling that this incident could tie up with the two murders we're investigating."

Despite rapid progress, Mulraney's Escort was not the first police car on the scene, which was a hive of activity by the time he screeched to a halt. The flashing lights of two police cars and an ambulance indicated the prompt response of the emergency services. The immediate area around Charlie's house had already been cordoned off with the familiar blue and white tape. Two blue painted boards, displaying in white letters the words SLOW – POLICE INCIDENT, were placed one hundred yards either side of the scene.

Mulraney was soon deep in conversation with a uniformed sergeant whilst Jackie Harper sought out Luke to interview him in his role as principal witness. Two paramedics were administering first aid to Charlie and indicated to Mulraney that the patient had to be removed to hospital immediately as his life was in imminent danger. Mulraney nodded assent and a police photographer hurriedly snapped a shot of Charlie before he was placed on a stretcher and conveyed to the ambulance.

Fifteen minutes after Mulraney's arrival, Hutchinson joined the ever-increasing police presence which denoted a major incident. He was dressed incongruously in evening dress, his night out as guest speaker at a convention of local businessmen having been rudely interrupted by a message from Mulraney. The sergeant considered the incident to be of such importance as to warrant interrupting one of his chief's rare evenings out. He needn't have worried overmuch as, truth to tell, Hutchinson was immensely relieved at the sudden recall to duty which relieved him from delivering his ill-prepared speech and answering the inevitable awkward questions common at these gatherings. Charlie's identity had now been established and Mulraney expertly brought his chief up to date with all the relevant details of the incident.

"Hmm," murmured Hutchinson, stroking his chin reflectively. "This is a bit of a strange one, Brian. On the surface it appears as if Charlie Reid was attacked because he was in possession of a large quantity of drugs. But then why didn't the attackers take the drugs? Why destroy them and scatter the tablets willy-nilly? It could be drug rivalry."

Mulraney interrupted his chief. "We do actually have a witness who saw Dawson leave Charlie's house earlier this evening."

"Okay, pull him in again," said Hutchinson. "But you know, Brian, these two bikers worry me. I mean, are they the same two from the Janice Longman case? And if so what is the connection between Janice Longman and Charlie Reid, other than prostitution? Come to think of it, where does the middle-aged man in the blue Rover fit into all this?"

Mulraney was about to reply to his chief's comments when he was interrupted by the arrival of Jackie Harper, who had completed her witness statements and was awaiting further instructions. Hutchinson's eyebrows were raised at the sudden appearance of the attractive woman constable.

"I thought you would like to know, sir," she said, addressing Hutchinson, "that the principal witness to this incident, one Luke Tomey, is related by marriage to Dawson."

"Hmm, odd coincidence," replied Hutchinson. "Correct me if I'm wrong but aren't you supposed to be on routine patrol tonight, Constable?"

"Yes sir, that's correct," said Jackie, "but Sergeant Mulraney met me en route to the incident and requested my assistance."

"No matter," said Hutchinson, "but I'd like you to return to the station right away and resume your normal duties after seeing that your witness statements are typed up."

"Right away, sir," replied a somewhat chastened Jackie, turning on her heel and leaving the two senior detectives.

Hutchinson placed a hand on Mulraney's shoulder and led him to the side of the house. "A cautionary word in your ear, Brian. I know young Jackie is very fanciable and I don't blame you for trying your luck, but just be a little more discreet. She is only probationary in CID at the moment and you had absolutely no right to pull her off routine patrol duties on your say so alone. In future consult me before you nominate your assistants. Favouritism has no part in the police force, as well you know. I've already got Mabbutt on my back over her, now I'll have to explain your latest action to Inspector Renfrew and we all know what a fussy old bugger he is!"

Mulraney's craggy features creased into a sympathetic grin.

"Sorry, sir. I really have dropped you in it, haven't I? I just didn't think. Yeah, of course I fancy her but, believe it or not, nothing was planned. I really did bump into her on my way here and decided on the spur of the moment to bring her along. She really does have a knack of eliciting thorough statements from witnesses."

"Okay, Brian, nuff said for now," said Hutchinson. "For the moment let's get our teeth into this case. For starters organise an immediate check on all green-painted motorcycles, especially Kawasakis. All such owners must be quizzed on their whereabouts over the last few hours. Also, I want you to bring in Dawson again and question him particularly as to his friendship or otherwise with Charlie Reid and find out exactly what he was doing in Charlie's house earlier tonight."

A thorough search of the immediate area surrounding Charlie's house had revealed one item of real significance, namely the silver hammer, which had been removed from Charlie's holdall and, judging by the bloodstains, had been used to batter his skull. This was placed carefully in a polythene bag and removed for forensic examination at the police laboratory. There were still some unbroken bottles of methadone scattered on Charlie's front lawn. These, together with all the scattered tablets, were removed from the scene before the police were satisfied and the incident tapes removed. Charlie Reid had been allocated VIP status in one of the twelve precious intensive care beds in the Queen's Medical Centre.

WPC Harris from the vice squad had been chosen to keep a vigil at Charlie's bedside in the hope of gaining an interview with him if he should regain consciousness. Lisa had been specially selected as she knew Charlie and his late departed wife extremely well, having interviewed them both at length on more than one occasion.

Charlie's chances of ever regaining consciousness were extremely slim. He was on a ventilator and his bed was surrounded by a mass of equipment and tubes. A nursing sister paused from her ministration of Charlie to talk to Lisa Harris. The dumpy dark-haired WPC was seated demurely by Charlie's bed ploughing her way through a paperback thriller.

"You're in for a long wait, my dear," said the sister.

"Will he ever come out of it?" asked Lisa.

"Hard to say, dear," said the sister, peering at the reading on one of the numerous instruments surrounding Charlie. "They are all at death's door when they come in here, but roughly sixty per cent pull through. What's so special about this particular fellow?"

"Well, put it this way," said Lisa. "If he doesn't make it, then someone will be up on a murder charge."

"We'll do our very best," smiled the sister, withdrawing through the bedside screen to check on her next patient.

At 11.30 p.m. that same evening Luke Tomey arrived at his Mapperley home to be confronted by his unhappy wife. Myra Tomey was a small, neat, well-proportioned black woman. She was very industrious, indeed she had to be as her daily schedule was very tight and any deviation from it annoyed her intensely. She was a ward sister at the Queen's during most of the day and the mother of two small children, so she had organised her life down to the last detail. Her house was spotless and she preferred life to be orderly and smooth running.

Luke frequently spoilt her schedule and tonight he was definitely in the doghouse. Last night he had returned in the early hours much the worse for drink, having spent the evening in the company of her notorious cousin Bo. A furious argument had ensued, continuing into the wee small hours, after which they had both relapsed into troubled sleep, missing the morning alarm call and being awakened only by the arrival of the daily babysitter. In consequence Myra had been late for work, since Luke always drove her there and she returned via taxi in the evening. On this particular evening he had not arrived home at his usual time of eight thirty and Myra became increasingly agitated, presumed the worst and thought that he had embarked on another binge with Bo in retaliation for her tirade against him on the previous occasion. He had only just come through the door when Myra delivered her opening salvo.

"What bloody time do you call this then? Really, Luke, you are too bad, after all your promises last night. I just can't understand you lately! I—"

"Myra!" shouted Luke. "Bloody shut up a minute will you and let me get a word in edgeways! The reason I am late tonight is that I have been involved in a police inquiry. I was witness to a violent attack."

"Oh no," moaned Myra. "I told you to stay well clear of Bo."

"It's absolutely nothing to do with Bo," said Luke, frowning slightly, "At least I don't think so! I saw two blokes setting about Charlie Reid who happens to be the husband of that murdered prozzie."

Myra's eyes opened wide. "Oh Luke, what on earth have you got mixed up with? You do realise it will be in all the papers?"

"Don't be silly, Myra. I'm not involved, I was coming out of my client's house when I saw the whole thing. By the time I realised what was going on the two blokes had scarpered, but not before they had pelted me with bottles."

"Ooh, Luke, they might come after you, especially if you were the only witness," said Myra.

"Naw," said Luke, laughing. "It's not exactly Chicago round here, is it?"

"It won't do your business any good if it is in the papers," said Myra.

"Myra," said Luke reaching out for his wife and clasping her to him, "I keep on telling you I am a witness, not a criminal, and even if my name does get in *The Post* it will provide a good talking point for me and the clients when I'm out trawling for new business. Now enough of this. What have you got for my supper? I'm bloody starving. I fancy a good nosh-up then straight to bed with you." He squeezed her meaningfully.

"Your dinner is ruined, it's been too long in the oven. In fact I threw it out half an hour ago. So you had better nip round to Gino's for a pizza and while you're at it bring me one too."

Fifteen minutes later they were snuggled up together on the sofa devouring their takeaway pizzas, a Caribbean special for Luke and a ham and pineapple for Myra.

She had mellowed by now, her anger abated and was impressed that Luke had remembered her favourite pizza without any prompting on her part. She nuzzled the nape of his neck contentedly before a sudden thought entered her mind.

"Before I get too carried away, Matthew rang you earlier this evening with a reminder to you to meet up with the usual gang at The Midland at one o'clock tomorrow prior to the match."

"Great news," said Luke. "He must be feeling a lot better now. I didn't give much for his chances when I saw him yesterday."

"You lot are all the same," said Myra. "Mention booze and football and you all effect the most amazing recoveries!"

"Shuttup you," said Luke affectionately.

Slipping his arms under Myra's thighs, he swept her up in one movement.

"It's high time we got to bed!"

A Face from the Past

Matthew Haines took a long swig of his pint before leaning back with a sigh of satisfaction, enjoying the Saturday morning scenario in the busy public bar of The Midland Hotel. Matthew adored Saturday match-day mornings, which encompassed all the gathering excitement of the forthcoming match and the high expectations of a Forest win, defeat being unthinkable. The increasing buzz of animated conversation amongst the eager fans, the genial company of his mates, the pre-match pints which somehow always seemed to taste better on Saturday mornings – all these things made Saturday the best day of the week as far as Matthew was concerned. He pushed back the annoying lock of hair which always seemed to flop over his face, wincing slightly as his fingers encountered the site of the four stitches, a constant reminder of Wednesday's ill-fated fracas. He glanced at his watch and realised that there was still some fifteen minutes before the arrival of his friends, who usually caught the same bus to town.

The bar was populated well-nigh exclusively by Forest fans, sporting their familiar red and white colours and Matthew was surprised at the entry of some half dozen youths bedecked in the blue and white colours of Sheffield Wednesday. The incoming youths paused when they glanced around the bar and took in the massed presence of the Forest supporters. The barman, anxious to quell any hint of trouble, smiled reassuringly in welcome, "What'll it be, lads?"

The Wednesday followers proceeded cautiously to the bar, nervously glancing left and right as the hum of conversation,

82

temporarily lulled by their arrival, now resumed its normal level.

Matthew glanced curiously at the rival fans, their crew-cropped heads indistinguishable in their uniformity. One of their number removed his bobble hat and, as he bent his head to quaff his pint, Matthew noticed his stubble of red hair. He felt a glimmer of recognition and rose to his feet to approach the youth and tap him on the shoulder. The red-haired youth turned angrily to confront Matthew and his companions, sensing trouble, glared hostilely at the newcomer.

Matthew grinned in recognition at an old friend. "Hello Ginger, you old reprobate! What's with the Wednesday colours then? Have you deserted the Reds? And what the hell have you done to your hair? Don't tell me you have joined the marines!"

Ginger grinned back as recognition dawned on him.

"Hallo Matty. Nice to see you again. No, I haven't joined the marines. I live in Worksop now and as all my mates are Wednesdayites, you know the old saying – when in Rome et cetera!"

"Come and join me for a pint," said Matthew. "We can have a good old natter about old times. The other two will be along any minute."

Ginger glanced briefly at his companions before replying, "I can't stop long, Matt, as my mates are only stopping here for one pint, but I'll give you a couple of minutes."

He picked up his pint and joined Matthew at his table.

"Well now," said Matthew, rubbing his hands together. "Give me all your news. There's been a fair bit of water under the bridge since you left Nottingham."

"You can say that again!" laughed Ginger. "Just after I left the firm I had to sell the house because, as you know, I no longer had a job and Karen had left me so I thought I might as well make a fresh start. I'm living at my sister's now and have got a good job with a security firm, hence the haircut.

How are things back at the sharp end? Still knocking about with the same motley crew?"

Matthew smiled. "Yeah, some things never change, although we do have one new lad in tow. I'm sure you'll like young Mark. They'll be along any minute now."

"It'll be nice to see the lads again," said Ginger. "Is John coming this afternoon?"

"No, he's working," said Matthew. "He's been promoted to sales manager, so he's going up in the world, but he can only manage to see midweek matches now. I'll remember you to him though."

Ginger was about to reply when he was interrupted by one of his crop-haired mates, who addressed him in a broad Yorkshire accent. "Come on, Pete lad, sup up, there's too many Red buggers in here for my liking."

Ginger shrugged his shoulders resignedly, grinned at Matthew and said, "Sorry, Matt, I'd best be moving on. Give my best regards to the lads."

"Give it another couple of minutes, Ginge, they'll be here any time now."

Ginger drained the dregs of his pint and clasped Matthew's hand in a farewell handshake.

"Must rush, Matty. I'll probably be seeing you all in the not too distant future. Enjoy the match."

With this parting rejoinder he disappeared through the swing doors on the heels of his companions.

It seemed only seconds later when the swing doors opened once more and Matthew was joined by a rather breathless-looking Luke and a jovial Mark.

"About bloody time," said Matthew, handing his empty pint glass to Mark. "Get 'em in, kiddo, that'll wipe the smile off your face!"

Mark's grin widened as he uncomplainingly collected Matthew's glass and made for the bar.

"Blimey, what's up with him?" asked Matthew. "He looks like the cat that's got the cream!"

"Well, I suppose he has as far as he is concerned," laughed Luke. "He finally managed to get a date with young Jane last night and he's full of it. He hasn't even mentioned old Mooney's name once this morning! But I have got some other quite exciting news to tell you. I was principal witness to a possible murder last night and I had to give a full statement to the coppers."

"Tell me more," said an eager Matthew.

By the time Luke had regaled his friends with a rather lurid account of the evening's events, two more rounds of drinks had been imbibed by the trio. Luke glanced at his watch. "Come on, lads, it's high time we were heading for Trentside. There's only half an hour to kick-off."

"Two minutes while I finish this," said Matthew, indicating his half empty glass. "Besides, there is something I've got to tell. Two minutes before you arrived I was chatting to an old friend of ours."

"Who?" chorused Luke and Mark together.

"Ginger Tomlinson," said Matthew.

"Bloody hell!" said Luke. "And there was me thinking he'd joined the Foreign Legion!"

"I've never even heard of him," complained Mark.

"No, he was a bit before your time," said Matthew. "Three years to be precise. His full name is Peter Tomlinson, but we all know him as Ginger, for obvious reasons. Nice enough bloke, a little naive maybe. He was always on the wrong side of old Mooney, which as we all know isn't hard to do! He was continually picking on poor old Ginger and it got to him. His sales went all to pot, and when he had his audit discrepancies totalling about a thousand quid were found and he got the obligatory chop. Mind you, he did have some things going for him. He had a beautiful missus by the name of Karen – and she was something else!"

"Yeah," agreed Luke with a wistful look in his eyes before scowling at Matthew. "For Chrissake, Matt, get that bloody pint down your neck before it solidifies!"

Five minutes later the trio had crossed Station Street and joined the jostling throng of supporters en route to the ground. Crossing Trent Bridge, they turned left and joined the long queue alongside the river patiently awaiting entry to the Trent End turnstiles.

After negotiating the turnstiles they joined yet another long queue for the gents' toilets. Several youths were either too impatient or had been plain taken short and had ignored the queue, relieving themselves against the wall or the stanchions of the stand. The cold autumnal afternoon produced wisps of swirling mist over the ground from the river. This was enhanced by the steam from the urine of those unable to make the toilets, provoking giggles from young ladies about to enter the stand and downright disgust from older ladies.

After emerging from the crush of the toilets, the trio pushed their way into the packed terraces of the Trent End, whose pre-war structure was totally out of character with the rest of the ground, which was undergoing a slow process of modernisation. It remained, however, the spiritual home of all loyal Forest fans and soon the trio was lustily joining in the pre-match chants and songs so beloved of modern-day football followers.

The biggest roar of all was reserved for the arrival of the two teams.

Early Forest pressure and a near miss prompted the inevitable surging forward of the crowd on the packed terracing, resulting in the trio being pushed down several of the concrete steps. As he was lighter than either of his two friends, Mark was pushed further and faster. His forward momentum was abruptly halted by impact with human flesh, female at that.

'What a nice feeling!' thought Mark as his outstretched hand encountered a soft female breast.

"Sorry," gasped Mark, looking up into the startled features of Angie McPherson and being immediately smitten.

Angie's initial surprise soon turned to anger and she glared at Mark, slapping him sharply on the side of his face. "Let go of my tit, you dirty little bugger!"

Three black youths to the left of Mark seized hold of him and he cried out in pain as his arm was twisted, none too gently, up his back. Another youth punched him in the stomach and another much larger youth, noticeable for a deep indentation across his left cheek, grasped Mark by his hair and raised his fist as if to strike him.

Luke, recognising the youths, stepped in quickly, seizing the upraised fist of the scar-faced youth. "Easy, brother, he's a mate of mine. He didn't mean anything. We were all pushed forward in the surge."

Scarface scowled at Luke, angrily shaking off his intervening hand. "And who the fuck are you?"

"I'm related to Bo. My wife is his cousin actually."

"Oh, she is actually," mimicked Scarface, leering at Luke but breaking into a grin when he saw the fear reflected on his face. "You just saved this pretty boy's life, brother, but nobody messes with Bo's bird and gets away with it."

He kneed Mark in the groin, causing him to cry out in agony, then he pushed him away. "Don't cross my path again, pretty boy, or you'll be sorry!"

A much chastened Mark was half pulled and half pushed back up the steps by his two friends.

Matthew grinned down at him.

"You don't do things by half, do you, mate? Fancy having a feel of the girlfriend of the leader of the Hyson Green boot boys."

"I didn't mean it," protested Mark. "It all happened so fast. One minute I was flying down the terraces, next thing I'm crushed up against this gorgeous black girl. I'd give my right arm for a taste of that!"

"You very nearly did just that, mate!" said Luke. "Anyway take my tip and steer well clear of that crowd. They are trouble with a capital 'T'. But if you really fancy Angie, she comes at a price."

"You don't mean she's a pro, surely!" said a disbelieving Mark.

"'Fraid so, mate, and she isn't cheap either, so you had better save your pennies, but if I were in your shoes I would stick with young Jane. She's far less trouble!"

"Oh please don't tell her about this," said Mark, his conscience belatedly troubling him.

The remainder of the match passed without incident save for a solitary Forest goal, which Mark missed because he was vomiting at the rear of the stand at the time.

The Pressure Mounts

Due to the ever-increasing complexity of the murders, extra police from the county force were drafted into assist in the routine checking of all local garages in the search for the blue Rover car and green Kawasaki motorbikes. A thorough fingertip search of the wasteland scene of Jacqui Reid's murder had revealed few clues other than the unearthing of a plethora of used condoms.

In a surprise move, instigated by Hutchinson, small snatch squads of police were despatched in the early hours of Saturday morning to the homes of known drug pushers and addicts, and considerable quantities of drugs were seized. Extra interview rooms had been hastily set up at both Radford Road and Central Police Stations to accommodate the unusually large haul of suspects brought in for questioning. Prior to this Hutchinson had consulted his team as to which direction the investigation would take after the attempted murder of Charlie Reid.

They decided first and foremost that no restrictions should be placed on the red-light area in a deliberate attempt to entice the killer into the open. However, a very discreet undercover surveillance team had been instructed to keep a watching brief on the activities of the prostitutes and their clients.

Next on the agenda was the requisite full briefing of the media, both national and local. The two prostitute murders had, as expected, attracted lurid headlines ranging from *The Sun*'s RED LIGHT STRANGLER STRIKES AGAIN, *The Mirror*'s KILLER STALKS VICE GIRLS to the more sober *Evening Post*'s POLICE SEEK DRIVER OF BLUE ROVER.

Hutchinson sighed as he replaced the receiver of his desk telephone after concluding a one-sided conversation with his immediate superior, Chief Superintendent Harold 'The Hawk' Maudsley. The Chief Super was extremely angry at the amount of flak directed at the police over the murders and he was anxious for an early arrest, fearful that any further killings would enhance the reputation of a possible serial killer, who appeared contemptuous of the police efforts to capture him.

Hutchinson was disappointed but not surprised at his chief's attitude, as he already had the reputation of a perfectionist. Taking advantage of a slight pause in his diatribe, Hutchinson had seized the opportunity to inform his chief of exactly what action he had already initiated. Maudsley was singularly unimpressed; indeed Hutchinson's remarks seemed to incense him further. He ranted on and on and muttered veiled threats that heads would roll if no arrest was imminent. Hutchinson rode the storm well, taking comfort in the fact that on past occasions Maudsley had acted in a similar fashion, his bark being worse than his bite.

Hutchinson's office door opened to reveal a young, fresh-faced constable sporting an unruly mop of red hair. He was nervous in appearance and peered apologetically at Hutchinson.

"Come in, Walker," said Hutchinson. "Don't look so terrified. Say what you've got to say, then get out. I don't suppose one more interruption will spoil my day."

"Er, sorry, sir," said PC Walker, swallowing in an effort to contain his nervousness. Hutchinson's aquiline nose and sharp piercing eyes exuded authority, which he found made him very nervous. "There is a rather irate lady at the desk who insists on seeing you. I told her that you were extremely busy but she says she won't take any flannel as she knows all about police procedures. In fact she says if you won't see her then she'll go straight to Chief Superintendent Maudsley."

Hutchinson raised his eyebrows at the mention of his chief. "Heaven forbid. Who exactly is this woman?"

"Mrs Mulraney," said PC Walker.

Hutchinson snorted angrily. "Why didn't you say so in the first place! Send her right in."

'It's just not my day,' moaned Hutchinson to himself. It had started with a call from Lisa Harris, reporting in after her all-night vigil at Queens. Her depressing news revealed that although Charlie Reid had survived the night his condition had worsened still further and hope was fast ebbing away. Hutchinson's gloom had deepened following his twenty-five minute conversation with Maudsley – and now Brian's wife. What on earth had prompted her to come to the station? He could only hazard a guess and he hoped that he was wrong.

Caroline Mulraney opened his office door without knocking and strode purposefully across the floor. Without saying a word she sat on the swivel chair facing Hutchinson, her eyes seeking out his in a challenging stare.

She was an overweight, blowsy-looking woman whose once attractive features were now bloated and made to look still worse by a layer of excessive make-up. Though she dressed expensively, her attire was ugly and unfashionable.

Hutchinson repressed an urge to shudder as he returned her stare, tensing himself for her expected outburst. When it didn't arrive, Hutchinson initiated the conversation with a smile.

"Hallo Caroline. What brings you to the office? I'm afraid Brian is over at Central conducting questioning."

"I know damn well where Brian is and it's you I came to see, not him," said Caroline, lighting a cigarette and angrily puffing out the smoke. "Don't give me all the polite bullshit. I know all about Brian screwing that little blonde tart. I know exactly what he wants. He wants a divorce and I'll tell you what I told him – he's not bloody getting one!"

"Now just a minute, Caroline," said Hutchinson. "Before you go—"

"Don't bloody interrupt me, Pete!" screeched Caroline, her voice increasing in decibels. "Listen to what I have got to say. I know you're bloody busy and in the middle of a murder investigation and you haven't got time for the likes of me. I mean, that's exactly what *he* says all the time. Well, you're going to bloody hear me whether you like it or not. I want that blonde tart Harper posted away from my Brian. She's nothing but a brazen hussy flaunting herself in front of married officers. Brian isn't the first – I know all about John Mabbutt. When she'd finished with him, she dropped him like a used johnny. Why, only last night she was seen in the back of a police car with Brian and they were both hard at it only two streets from where we live."

"Did you see them yourself?" asked Hutchinson.

"No, but my neighbour did. If I had caught them at it you would have another woman's body to add to your list."

"Now, Caroline, surely you realise it isn't within my power to organise postings of any police officer away from this area. After all, this isn't the army, you know."

Caroline gasped in exasperation at Hutchinson. "If you don't do something about that woman, then I'll go straight to Maudsley."

"Please calm down, Caroline. I'm sure this is only a brief period of infatuation on Brian's part. He's been under a lot of stress recently, indeed we all have. I know that we policemen are difficult to live with – all the long hours and overtime – but it works both ways, you know. Why not try being nice to him and making an extra effort to make him feel welcome when he comes home?"

"I might have known you would take his side!" sneered Caroline. "It's bloody obvious he's been bleating to you!"

She rose to her feet and strode angrily towards the door, pausing briefly to deliver her final remark. "You haven't heard the last of this. I shall be informing Chief Superintendent Maudsley about your one-sided attitude over this affair and I can promise you here and now that I'll move heaven and earth to get that bitch away from here."

Hutchinson sighed as he considered his next step. Pressing the buttons on his phone, he decided to contact his wife directly to ensure that his conversations would not he heard by the WPC telephonist, aware that the grapevine was already buzzing with the latest juicy gossip.

"Hello darling! ...Yes, up to the eyes in it as usual. ...I've had an unexpected visitor and I need your help... Caroline Mulraney... Not half so surprised as I was... Well, Brian has been having a bit of a fling with one of our WPCs... Jackie Harper actually... Look, I can't go into detail right now but you'll be doing me an awfully big favour if you could pop round and have a word with her. ...Of course I've tried but I only made it worse. She's such a foul-mouthed bitch, I find it hard to have any sympathy for her. You're so good at that sort of thing... Of course I'll have a word with Brian, but try and calm her down and, above all, dissuade her from contacting Maudsley or the shit will really hit the fan. I've already had a run-in with him about my handling of the latest cases. ...Good! ...God bless, darling. Must go now, I'll see you tonight but don't ask what time. 'Bye."

Over at Central Police Station the object of Caroline's hatred was in the middle of her second interview with Bo Dawson in forty-eight hours. Jackie Harper's persistent questioning was beginning to pierce the defensive wall Bo threw up in all his dealings with the police, whom he regarded with contempt.

"It's no use you denying you were at Charlie Reid's house last night – we have three independent witnesses who saw you there," said Jackie.

"Are you deaf, darlin'?" said Bo. "I have at least a dozen witnesses to prove I wasn't!"

"Why don't you come clean and admit that your supply of drugs was dangerously low and you ordered Charlie to break into Dr Suleiman's surgery to snatch some methadone and whatever else he could lay his hands on?"

"I admit fuck all!" roared Bo. "You filth have got nothing on me and I'm not saying another word until my solicitor gets here."

"You watch your filthy mouth in the presence of a lady!" shouted Brian Mulraney, seated alongside Jackie, until now happy to let her continue with questions that obviously riled the pimp.

"It's okay, Brian," said Jackie quietly.

"Oh, touched a raw nerve there, did we?" sneered Bo. "Fancy her do you, copper? I must admit I wouldn't mind giving her one myself!"

Sensing the charged atmosphere, Jackie switched off the tape recorder. "Interview suspended," she said before leaving the interview room.

Mulraney was now alone in the room with Bo, save for the presence of a uniformed constable standing with his hands behind his back near the door. Mulraney glared at Bo and rounded the desk. He clasped Bo by his shirt front, hauled him to his feet and thrust him against the wall. He knocked Bo's head backwards and forwards, the rear of his head bouncing off the wall.

"Listen, you useless blood-sucking piece of shit! I know all about your drug pushing, your exploitation of young girls, your beatings-up and your blackmail threats. Do you really think you are so big that you can get away with murder? Well, I don't care what your brief says or doesn't say and even if you walk out of this station without any charges proved against you, I want you to keep one thing in your mind crystal-clear and that is that I will personally hunt you down! I don't care if it's next week or next year but I'll nail you, you bastard, and that's a promise!"

Mulraney thrust Bo back in his chair, breathing heavily with the exertion of the assault.

Bo, though trying hard to appear unruffled, was nevertheless shaken up and he felt gingerly around the back of his head, hoping to detect some blood.

"Did you see that, mate?" he shouted to the uniformed policeman, who remained unmoving at the door. "That's a clear case of police brutality and intimidation right in front of your eyes and I want a statement from you to that effect. My solicitor should be here any minute now. Can't think what's keeping the bastard!"

"I didn't see anything," said the constable, trying hard not to break into a smile.

Bo's solicitor arrived five minutes later and the interview was resumed. Mr Sornsen was a balding, stooped, angular-looking man, well versed in criminal law and popular among those members of the criminal fraternity who could afford his exorbitant fees. He did, however, earn his fee and had already been at work on Bo's behalf. The proof of Bo's involvement with Charlie Reid hinged on the evidence of the three eyewitnesses. All three were interviewed for a second time, with the result that one of them denied ever identifying Bo whilst the other two admitted that they could have been mistaken. Mr Sornsen reinforced Bo's claim of a dozen witnesses placing him well away from the scene.

Though reluctant to do so, the police had no alternative but to release Bo Dawson, as no charges could be made to stick against him. Mulraney was personally convinced that Bo was deeply involved in the two murders of his working girls and had ordered the attack on Charlie Reid.

Before Bo reached the main entrance on his way out of the station, he turned towards Mulraney with a smirk on his face, then he slowly jerked his left index finger upwards in a crude gesture of farewell. Mulraney, arms folded, looked on expressionless, though he was inwardly seething.

The Screws Are Tightened

Malone's hands trembled as he read and reread the headlines in *The Evening Post*: POLICE SEEK DRIVER OF BLUE ROVER.

He looked forward every week to his leisurely Saturday morning fry-up, but so great was his anxiety that he had been unable to eat most of it. He was at a loss as to what to do with himself and spent a restless morning pottering aimlessly in the large garden of his Wollaton home.

He felt very much on edge and trembled every time the telephone rang. On every occasion the calls had been answered by his wife Betty and he was relieved that the calls concerned her charitable activities. Even Betty was aware of his constant edginess and irritable mood but put it down to overwork. On this particular Saturday, she was looking forward to a rare evening out with her husband. Malone had obtained two tickets for a performance of *La Bohème* at the Royal Concert Hall. A love of the opera was one of the few passions they had in common. Until quite recently they had both been actively involved in the local amateur operatic society. The night out at the opera would be further enhanced by a late dinner, to be taken at one of the restaurants in the Royal Hotel complex. Betty had been eagerly anticipating this night out with her husband and was confident that his mood would change once they arrived at the Royal Concert Hall.

A taxi had been booked to pick them up at 6.30 p.m., an arrangement which suited Malone as it enabled him to indulge himself with a drink or two during the evening without the worry of driving home. He spent the best part of the afternoon fastidiously cleaning the interior of his car, a routine task he performed most weekends. On this occasion, however, he took more care than usual, scrupulously covering every square inch with the aid of his portable vacuum cleaner, determined to eliminate the slightest trace of the murdered girl. He knew full well that the police would commandeer his vehicle and go over it with a fine-tooth comb, and even a small hair from the girl would prove her presence in his car. After finishing the vacuuming, he vigorously scrubbed the seats and rubber mats with carpet shampoo and hot water.

Five minutes before the taxi was due, he stood at the foot of his stairs nervously drumming his fingers on the hall table. Betty, in the manner of all women, was not yet ready and was busily applying last-minute touches to her make-up. His reverie was interrupted by the jangling of the telephone, causing him to twitch with startled anticipation.

"Hullo," he snapped into the receiver.

"Hullo Malone, you creep."

The voice sent a chill through him as he instantly recognised the mystery caller from Thursday.

"It's you again," answered Malone, talking quietly, fearful that Betty would overhear his conversation. "Who the hell are you and what exactly do you want?"

"Like I said before, that's for you to find out," said the voice with a chuckle. "Now listen very carefully. I'm going to give you some instructions and I want them carried out to the letter at the precise time I tell you. If you fail to comply with these instructions then I shall have no alternative than to inform the police that you murdered that girl and explain how she came to have your wallet clutched in her hand."

"Listen, whoever you are," snapped Malone. "I didn't kill her! And how do you know so much about it?"

"Shut up!" said the voice with a hint of anger. "I know exactly what occurred so save your story for the police. If you want your wallet returned and not a hint given to the police, then you must comply with the following instructions.

First and foremost you must pay an early visit to your bank on Monday morning. Draw out the sum of five thousand pounds in cash, the higher the note denomination the better. At 1 p.m. proceed to the Arboretum. Between the bandstand and the pond you will see a litter bin. Place an envelope containing the cash on the top of the contents of the litter bin. Walk away and do not look back. Remember, I will be watching your every move. Next go to the telephone kiosk at the corner of Raleigh Street. The phone will ring. Answer it and I will give you instructions for the retrieval of your wallet.

"This is preposterous!" exclaimed Malone. "I haven't got that sort of money! This is sheer blackmail! I'll go straight to the police!"

"Oh, I don't think you will. What exactly will you tell them anyway? Now listen, Malone, I am not prepared to argue with you any longer. Just be there with the money or you will soon find yourself in the dock facing a murder charge."

There was a click which signified the termination of the conversation by the mystery caller.

Malone shakily replaced his receiver. He felt absolutely dreadful; all his worst fears were becoming reality.

Betty leaned over the banisters. "Who was that, darling? You sounded rather cross?"

"Oh, nobody you know, dear," replied Malone. "Just a disgruntled client moaning about his claim settlement."

The arrival of the taxi prevented any further conversation, much to the relief of Malone.

The ensuing evening's entertainment did little to ease his troubled mind. Although he was passionate about the opera, on this particular evening the sight of heaving female bosoms failed to gain his full attention.

Betty sensed there was something troubling him, for it was most unlike Reggie to be so quiet. Her instinct warned her to leave well alone, as a quiet subdued Reggie was preferable to an angry one. She did not allow his morose mood to spoil her enjoyment. Later in bed that same night, stirred by the music and emboldened by the effects of a few drinks, she made a rare overture to her husband. She did her level best to arouse him, a task which usually required no effort on her part; quite the reverse of normal, when Malone invariably seized the initiative in their lovemaking.

'That was very hard work,' reflected Betty as she pushed away her recumbent husband. Curiously she felt satisfied for once, but not so Malone, who remained unsated.

Sunday was a day of agonising slowness for Malone as he pored over the Sunday papers in a fruitless attempt to divert his mind from his predicament.

At long last Monday dawned and Malone threw himself into his work. After making suitable excuses he left the office about mid-morning and, despite feelings of great reluctance, he withdrew the sum of five thousand pounds from his bank account. He returned to his office, locking the door to prevent any intrusion, where he stuffed the notes into the largest brown envelope he could find.

Despite the mild autumnal day there was a slight drizzle in the air as he entered the gates of the Arboretum. This charming park, set but a stone's throw from the hustle and bustle of the city centre, was a haven for all types of people who snatched moments of happiness within its tranquil surroundings. Not so Malone, who glanced furtively around observing the usual crowd of students from the nearby college. There was a cluster of young mothers proudly wheeling their newly acquired offspring in prams. Small boys emitted excited shrieks as they chased one another hither and thither up and down the paths. The odd vagrant was stretched out on a park bench sleeping off the effects of the contents of the empty wine bottles discarded beneath. Young lovers, arms entwined, stared with wondrous gaze at each other, oblivious to all around them.

Malone scanned all these people in a desperate search to identify his tormentor. He knew that it could be any one of these people. The nagging thought remained that he had previously heard that voice in the not too distant past – but where and who? Try as he might, he could not find an answer.

He was but yards from the litter bin when he paused in dismay at the sight of an old tramp rifling through the contents of the litter bin. Eventually the tramp fished out the remains of somebody's half-eaten sandwich lunch and, stuffing it into the pockets of his voluminous overcoat, he shuffled off up the path.

Malone hurried up to the litter bin and glanced furtively around before hastily stuffing the brown envelope in the bin, covering it with a discarded copy of last Friday's *Post*. He hastened away from the scene but slowed his pace as he neared the park gates, unable to resist sneaking a backward glance towards the litter bin; but there was nobody within yards of it.

He crossed Waverley Street and reached the corner of Raleigh Street but was disappointed to find that the telephone kiosk was occupied by a teenage girl who appeared to be in ardent conversation. Malone strode up and down the street impatiently, reflecting on the folly of actually placing five thousand pounds of his hard-earned cash in a litter bin of all places. What a fool he was! Supposing that old tramp returned and departed with renewed faith in miracles, heaven forbid!

He was able to hear the sound of pips emanating from the kiosk and saw the girl rummaging unsuccessfully in her handbag for coins to renew her call. Groaning with disappointment, she reluctantly vacated the booth.

Malone hovered anxiously, almost willing the phone to ring, fearful lest anyone else entered the kiosk. After what seemed an endless period of time but was actually only two minutes, the phone rang at last.

He snatched open the door and seized the receiver. His whole body was trembling with the tension of the moment as he gasped into the mouthpiece, "Hallo! Is that you?"

"Hallo Malone," said the familiar voice. "I see that you have been a good boy and done as you were told, so now for your reward. Look down at the telephone directories in front of you; there are three. Take out the bottom one and inside it you will find your wallet. 'Bye for now."

Malone didn't bother to replace the receiver, which he left dangling on its cord as he snatched at the third directory, knocking the other two to the floor in his haste. Between the pages he found his wallet, opened outwards.

A check of the contents revealed that they were intact, with the exception of the sixty pounds he had been carrying in notes. He was about to vacate the booth when he saw a patrolling policeman halfway up Raleigh Street. A sense of overwhelming guilt engulfed him and he realised that he must do nothing to attract the policeman's attention. He replaced the dangling receiver, picked up the telephone directories and tidily replaced them. Head down, he left the booth. Turning right down Waverley Street, he made an effort to moderate his quickening step as he made for the city centre.

About the same time, from another telephone kiosk further up Waverley Street, at its junction with Forest Road, a leather-clad motorcyclist emerged. He mounted his 750cc Kawasaki motorcycle and roared off up Forest Road.

Bo's Startling Discovery

Bo Dawson was not a happy man and it showed. Since returning to his flat on Archer Walk he had been in a foul mood. Those closest to him had seen this mood on past occasions and knew full well that this was a time to steer well clear of him.

His three henchmen, Hector Bart-Williams, Johnny Renton and Winston Benjamin, felt the full force of his fury from the second he crashed open the door of his flat to discover them lounging on his luxurious furniture, inhaling marijuana cigarettes, their arms draped around three half-dressed young females, two of whom were school age. The monotonous jerky beat of reggae music boomed out its melancholy message. A torrent of foul language erupted from Bo's lips as he unceremoniously dragged the girls to their feet.

"Get these slags out of here!" he yelled at Bart-Williams.

He yanked the plug from the stereo, causing a rare silence, broken only by the quickened breathing of the terrified girls, who stood open-mouthed and trembling like startled deer. They were transfixed by fear and unable to move. Bo lashed out with his fists at the one nearest to him. She screamed as his powerful blow split open her lip.

"Are you fucking deaf?" he yelled. "Get out now!"

The three girls didn't require further persuasion as they almost fell over one another in their rush to the door. Bart-Williams made as if to follow them but was restrained by Bo, who shot out an arm to stop him in his tracks. Bo glared menacingly at his three cohorts.

"And as for you idle layabouts! Do you think I pay you for using my flat to smoke pot and screw schoolgirls? Don't you lot realise just what has been going on behind our backs? Whilst you have been enjoying yourselves and allowing things to plod on as usual, we've been shafted good and proper by that pervert Alexander and the St Ann's lot! Just consider what's happened lately. Two of my best tarts have been knocked off, making the filth to suspect me, of all people! My drugs courier is practically beaten to death and all the drugs destroyed. I've been questioned by the filth twice in forty-eight hours and that bastard Mulraney has singled me out for special treatment. All of a sudden the filth are very interested in me and my business. Now why the sudden interest? And more importantly, who put 'em up to it?"

Hector Bart-Williams eased his huge bulk from the white leather armchair. He was an ex-professional boxer and, though still powerfully built, he displayed considerable flab around his middle. Weighing in at nineteen stone, he was not a man with whom to pick an argument. His hair was cropped so short that it gave the impression he was bald. He knew only too well the vagaries of Bo's demonic mind and he sought to calm him down before things went too far. The other two men had wisely left the room and busied themselves in the kitchen hastily tidying up the leftovers and repairing the ravages of their recent party.

Hector patted Bo reassuringly on the shoulder. "You're right, Bo, we have all been too bloody easy-going recently – we've let things slide. And I reckon you've hit the nail on the head mentioning Alexander. That bastard has always been number two in Nottingham and he's jealous so he has decided to take you down a peg or two, but I don't like his methods. I reckon we should all get together and raid his premises before he gets too big for his boots!"

"Yeah, now you're talking my language," said Bo. "That's what I want to hear. But let's plan carefully, let's be as crafty as those slimy bastards. It's no use rushing in willy-nilly. I reckon we should make a night raid on their warehouse and grab their drugs. Where do they stash their stuff nowadays?"

"Funny you should mention that," said Hector. "I was talking to that skinny little queer Martin the other night after I caught him loitering near Angie's patch on Forest Road. I tweaked his tabs and roughed him up a little before he told me that Lover Boy Rasta had chucked him out for two-timing. So he thought he might try and peddle his wares on our territory. Anyway he handed over the few quid he'd made and I relented and said he could hang around our patch provided he didn't poach on the girls' territory. And that he gave us thirty per cent. He wanted to give us only ten per cent but after I threatened to cut his balls off, he came round to my way of thinking!"

Bo's face at last relaxed into a smile on hearing this last remark.

"Anyway I pumped him about Rasta's latest plans and he told me that he has only just moved their valuables into an old disused church on some waste ground just off Woodborough Road."

"Yeah, I know the place," nodded Bo. "But it will be difficult to break into without being spotted – it's very open ground."

"Shouldn't be too bad at night," said Hector. "Particularly if we take out the bulbs from the street lights. He does leave a couple of guys inside the building to guard the place at night but that shouldn't pose a problem."

"Okay," said Bo, "let's get to it right away. For a start organise those two idle bastards to do something useful in the kitchen and cook up some saltfish and rice. We'll all need full bellies tonight."

Hector was pleased that he had alleviated some of Bo's anger at least and turned his thoughts towards a more positive frame of mind. He reached for his coat and turned to Bo.

"Give me an hour, Bo, and I'll round up some of our finest. I'll organise the blue transit, and make sure the lads are tooled up." His eyes shone with enthusiasm. "Do you know, Bo, this reminds me of the old days! You're dead right – we have gone soft lately."

Bo literally cooled himself down by taking a shower, the tension easing out of his body with the soothing effect of the hot water. He twisted the control knob towards the blue dot and gasped with shock as the icy needles of water quickly turned his skin to goose pimples.

Later, as he towelled himself down, his body took on a warm glow, making him feel vibrant and full of confidence. He entered his living room and was pleased to see that his aides had busied themselves in his absence by preparing his favourite meal. A large plate of rice was topped with two saltfish over which was poured a delicious sauce of tomatoes, chillies and onions. In addition there were dishes of lentils, black-eyed peas and beans to supplement the main dish.

Bo came to the sudden realisation that he was very hungry and attacked the meal with gusto. He pushed away a proffered glass of white rum.

"Nah, not now. I want my mind to be clear and uncluttered tonight, and you boys should do the same. I don't want any of you piss-artists slipping up."

One hour later Hector returned with some half dozen youths he had pressed into action. Hector had a way about him of persuading even the most uncommitted.

"These are the best I can come up with at short notice," said Hector.

Bo gave them a cursory glance before delivering his briefing. "Okay, you lot, we're making a raid on Rasta's store tonight. Now I don't want any cock-ups so listen carefully while I tell you what you should and shouldn't do. First of all, timing is most important so we'll get there about two thirty in the morning, when hopefully the only people prowling around will be cats. We'll actually park the van round about midnight, well off the road so we don't attract the filth. Then we'll lie low in the van for a couple of hours. Next one of you will approach the church with care and you'll signal back to the van with a torch once you find out how many men are inside. We'll come running and deliberately attract the attention of those inside to make 'em open the door. Once they do that, we'll rush 'em and give 'em a good going-over. Nothing too serious, just enough so Rasta gets the message. Then we'll loot the stores and for good measure torch the premises."

"Don't you think that's going a bit too far?" interjected Hector.

"No, I bloody don't," said Bo. "It's about time we put that queer bastard in his place and gave him something to think about for a change."

The remainder of the evening soon passed with Bo's troops making full use of their time by preparing thoroughly for the raid. They were all dressed in similar blue or black clothing, their head covered by balaclavas with crudely cut eyeholes. A collection of baseball hats was placed in the van together with two large rubber torches and a sinister-looking object wrapped in a blanket, which was a sawn-off double-barrelled shotgun.

Bo and Hector took up their positions in the front of the battered blue transit van and the rest of them piled into the rear of the vehicle. Bo meticulously checked that all the lights and indicators were working before he fired the engine into life and drove the van at a very sedate pace towards St Ann's.

Ten minutes later he eased the transit van between two lorries parked for the night on the edge of waste ground, facing the old church, giving a good view of their target area. A dull glow could barely be seen through one of the side windows of the church, indicating a light from either a low wattage bulb or a battery lamp.

The two hours from midnight to 2 a.m. seemed an interminable age to the youths crammed into the back of the van. They conversed in low voices, occasionally raising them in heated argument. These lapses were soon silenced by Bo who reminded them of the need not to draw attention to themselves. Much to the consternation of the rest of them, one of their number broke wind, befouling the cramped atmosphere of the van's interior.

A furious Bo hauled out the culprit, cuffed him about the head and volunteered him for the dangerous task of reconnoitring the disused church and then reporting back his findings. The youth shuffled reluctantly over the waste ground, pausing every now and again to see if he had been observed. An occasional lorry rumbled down the Woodborough Road and one solitary police patrol car passed the line of lorries, causing Bo and Hector to crouch down as its headlights swept past. The youth dropped instantly to the ground before resuming his slow progress on all fours. Reaching the church at last he crouched beneath the small side window and listened intently. He could hear a rasping intermittent sound which he recognised as snoring. Feeling more confident now, he slowly raised his head and peered through the window.

He found it difficult to see through the filthy dirt-encrusted window, which was bespattered by the bodies of various squashed insects. He spat on his handkerchief and rubbed vigorously at the window exposing a small circular patch. He pressed his face against the window and peered in. Directly under the window was a blown-up mattress on which lay a black youth, face upturned, snoring loudly. In the crook of his outstretched arm lay a blonde-haired girl whom the youth recognised as a familiar sight on Woodborough Road. There was a small wooden table alongside the bed, on which were a baseball hat, a Stanley knife and what looked like a handgun, though whether this was real or imitation was impossible to discern. He eased himself back below the level of the window and produced from his pocket a small hand-torch which he switched rapidly on and off in three quick flashes to alert the occupants of the transit van.

Bo had been observing his every move with interest and sighed with satisfaction. "Good, let's get cracking."

He turned in his seat to address the waiting youths.

"Right, you lot, this is it. Remember, bags of hush and remember what you were told."

The youths were relieved to get away from the fetid atmosphere of the van and relished the feel of the cool night air. One of their number remained as a lookout. They fanned out approaching the old church but on reaching their objective encircled it in order to cut off any escape route for the occupants.

Bo held a brief whispered conversation with the first youth, his face brightening on hearing that there were only two people in the building. Rubbing his hands with glee, he turned to Hector.

"Piece of cake, mate. There's only two of 'em and one's a girl. Start a rumpus and we'll soon flush this bastard out."

Hector grinned and from his pocket he produced a blue package which he ignited with his cigarette lighter. He waited seconds for the blue paper to flare up, then he carefully thrust the firework under a crack in the door.

Bo gestured for the youths to step back a pace or two, but before they could comply there was a loud bang from inside of the church as the firework exploded.

"That should wake the fucking dead!" exclaimed a grinning Hector.

Inside the building the sleeping man woke with a start, pushing aside his terrified companion who screamed at the sudden interruption of her slumber. He struggled into his jeans as the girl clutched the bed sheets to her, shivering in the early morning air. The man armed himself with a handgun and snatched up a torch. He paused on his way to the door and kicked out the still-smouldering remains of the firework.

"Some bastard's idea of a joke," he grumbled. "I'd better see if they are still around. Probably some bloody kids."

He slid open two bolts before opening the large mortise lock. He peered cautiously through a crack in the door before opening it fully. He stepped out into the darkness, flashing his torch to the left then gasping in pain as a baseball bat crashed down upon his right arm, causing him to drop the handgun. The muscular arm of Hector encircled his throat in a vice-like grip and lifted him bodily in the air, his legs thrashing wildly.

Bo and the remaining youths entered the church, flashing their torches to the left and right, their beams picking out the terrified girl. Her screams increased in intensity at the sight of the intruders.

"Shut that bitch up," motioned Bo. "She'll wake up half of Nottingham."

A grinning Johnny Renton was only too happy to comply. He slapped the screaming girl viciously twice in the face and her screams ceased instantly. He pulled the sheet away from the terrified girl, enjoying the sight of her nudity.

"Ah, I know you," he said. "You reckon to stand at the corner of Cranmer Street most nights." He grabbed at her breast. "Don't fancy paying for it so I'll have you for free!"

"No, you bloody won't," said Bo. "Get that cow dressed and tie her up. We haven't got time for distractions now. Maybe later, who knows!"

Hector brought the struggling man inside and slapped him around a little before tying him up with rope and silencing his groans by sealing his mouth with brown sticky tape. Johnny wrapped the sheet around the girl before encircling her body with rope and trussing her up like a mummy. For the next ten minutes the interior of the dusty church was systematically stripped in the search for drugs or other incriminating material but with disappointing results. Apart from two baseball hats and an assortment of knives, nothing was found.

"It looks like we've been given a bum steer," said Bo. "Where the bloody hell does that queer bastard stash his drugs?"

"Let's ask this dickhead," said Hector, indicating his prisoner.

At the far end of the church Winston Benjamin had painstakingly removed a pile of old church pews dumped unceremoniously in a heap. Beneath the pile of pews was a large dusty tarpaulin. He hauled this to one side and shouted in triumph, "Bloody hell, Bo, come and take a look at this!"

Bo and the rest of the youths converged on Winston, eager to discover the reason for his excitement. The removal of the tarpaulin revealed two shining green 750cc Kawasaki motorbikes.

"The crafty bastard!" exclaimed Bo, feeling his anger rising. "So it was that queer Rasta all along. He knocked off Janice and Jacqui, clobbered Charlie and dobbed me into the filth. I was right all along. Well, this puts a different complexion on things – we'll torch this lot and then we'll crucify the bastard!"

"Wait a minute, Bo," said Hector. "Let's just think this through. If we do Rasta in, you'll be number one suspect. The filth will come down on us like a ton of bricks. We'd be playing right into their hands. Why not play Rasta at his own game? After all, he dobbed us in, let's do the same to him. We haven't murdered anybody – he has."

Bo considered the suggestion thoughtfully. "Yeah, I suppose you're right, though I don't like the idea of dobbing anyone in."

"Well, he didn't think twice, did he?" said Hector.

"Okay," said Bo, now warming to the idea. "Put everything back where you found it and we'll all go straight back home as if we'd never been here."

"But what about these two?" asked Hector, indicating the two gagged and bound prisoners.

Bo's eyes gleamed. "Oh, I think a little gentle persuasion will make sure they don't say anything."

He grinned at the leering Winston and Johnny. "Enjoy yourselves, boys, and don't do anything I wouldn't do!"

On the return journey to Hyson Green through the deserted streets Bo halted the van next to an unvandalised phone box. He dialled the number of the Radford Road Police Station, then, placing a handkerchief over the receiver, he spoke into it in measured tones.

"Hallo. This is a message for Detective Sergeant Mulraney concerning the prostitute murders. The bloke that did the murders is Rasta Alexander. You know where to find him. If you want proof the evidence is under a tarpaulin at the rear of the old church on the waste ground off Woodborough Road."

Bo replaced the receiver, smiling smugly to himself.

Mulraney's Problems Increase

Police Constable Ray Farringdon groaned as the jangling telephone rudely interrupted his reverie. He detested night duty, finding the greatest difficulty in keeping himself awake as the long hours dragged on interminably. He was a tall gawky-looking young man and if his uniform appeared ill-fitting this came as no surprise to his circle of friends, who knew full well that no cloth on earth could be made to fit his awkward frame. Reared from solid country stock, many said that he would best be employed as a scarecrow in the fields of his native Norfolk. Despite his skinny appearance, PC Farringdon put away copious helpings of food with no apparent effect on his physique. Prior to commencing this night duty, he had slightly altered his usual pre-duty schedule.

On past occasions he had fortified himself with a visit to the local chippy to order his usual two large cod and a double helping of chips smothered in curry sauce. On this occasion, however, acting on the advice of his colleague, PC Amrit Singh, he had opted for a visit to Rajah's Emporium, a top-rated Indian restaurant located only yards from the police station. Rising to the challenge, he had asked for 'the hottest curry in the shop', and he had not been disappointed. The fiery meal, though enjoyable at the time, had not settled at all well on his notorious cast-iron stomach.

As a consequence his tour of duty had proved most uncomfortable. He had made frequent visits to the toilet and his insides felt as if they were on fire. Despite the fact that his colleagues teased him unmercifully, his naive country yokel ways and untidy appearance making him an easy target, he did not react in any way. He was a very easy-going, good-natured man and took the baiting in good spirit with no hint of retaliation or anger.

During his stint at the front desk he had coped manfully with the usual nightly flotsam which flowed into the inner city police station. There was the usual collection of drunks, brawling youths and a couple of minor muggers arrested soon after their crime had been committed.

Two hours after midnight things had quietened down and an unnatural stillness descended upon the police station. The jangling telephone soon put a stop to that and Farringdon struggled manfully to write down the muffled message delivered by Bo Dawson.

"Would you repeat that, caller?" asked Farringdon, sighing as he heard the click signalling the termination of the call.

Reading through the message, he did not at first realise its full significance, but any call relating to the prostitute murders had to be taken seriously. For a brief moment he wondered whether he should contact Mulraney at this ungodly hour but concluded that he would he in deeper trouble if he didn't. His call to Mulraney's home took an interminable time to be answered, by an exasperated Caroline Mulraney. She had been rudely awoken from a deep sleep induced by a mixture of booze and sleeping pills, and she wasn't at all happy.

"No, he isn't here! You ought to bloody know where he is. He's supposed to be on duty! ...What! ...Then I suppose he's been lying to me as per bloody usual! ...I suggest you contact that blonde whore's house – he's bound to be sleeping with her! ...Who do I mean? How long have you been on the force, sonny? ...When you do contact the bastard, tell him he needn't bother coming home!"

Caroline slammed down the receiver in anger, leaving Farringdon staring bleakly at his. 'Blimey, what a can of worms I've opened,' he pondered in reflective mood. So it was true about Brian Mulraney and Jackie Harper. 'Lucky old sarge – I wouldn't mind giving her one myself. Huh, fat chance of that! His wife sounded a right old harridan, but why tell her he was on duty when he wasn't? He was bound to be found out eventually. What was it the lads used to say? Never shit on your own doorstep. How very true!'

Turning these thoughts over in his mind, he was joined at the desk by the portly figure of Sergeant Don Whittle. The sergeant was just two years from retirement, and though, in common with his younger colleague, he shared a dislike of night duty, he was experienced enough to delegate and had spent most of the night asleep in a disused cell, taking care first of all to instruct his young staff to waken him in an emergency situation. For once, however, he had struggled to get off to sleep and after a couple of hours of restlessly tossing and turning he found that still sleep eluded him and he felt in need of a strong brew of tea.

"What are you looking so worried about, you dozy-looking country bumpkin?" he asked Farringdon.

"I've just had an urgent telephone message for Detective Sergeant Mulraney and when I rang his house his wife answered and gave me a right mouthful as apparently he had told her he was on duty and she screamed that if I wanted to speak to him I would find him at Jackie Harper's house."

"Oh no!" groaned Whittle. "You bloody young fool! I told all of you that any message for Detective Sergeant Mulraney was to be referred to me and that his home number not to be contacted under any circumstances."

Farringdon's pink cheeks turned an instant shade of red. "Oh, er, sorry, Sarge. With the call being about the murders I clean forgot. I'm sorry, I really am."

"You will be bloody sorry, young fella, when Mulraney hears about it. Now give me the details of the message and God help you when I tell him who rang his wife!"

Brian Mulraney's arm emerged from the covers of the warm bed and reached out to still the nagging *buzz-buzz* of the bedside telephone. Though still in the hazy warm afterglow of deep sleep, he handled his rude awakening with practised ease, born of many a past interruption of his slumbers and a bone of contention with wife Caroline. But this night had been different. His sleep had been all the nicer due to two delicious hours of lovemaking with the highly desirable Jackie. This was the first time they had spent the whole night together, their previous couplings being snatched furtively on the back seats of cars. Though pleasurable, these moments could not match the intensity and sheer joy they had both experienced in this night of love in Jackie's flat. Though she doubted the wisdom of her partner's impetuosity, Jackie had finally relaxed, sure in the knowledge that Caroline knew nothing of their night of illicit passion. She gave herself to her partner with an ardour that matched his own. Finally, their passion spent, they had succumbed, bodies entwined, to sleep.

Mulraney cleared his head with alacrity as Sergeant Whittle's words brought home to him the possibility of a break in the murder hunt.

"Yeah, okay, Don, I'll be at the station in about twenty minutes. Thanks for letting me know."

He was about to replace the receiver when Sergeant Whittle's next words hit him with the sting of ice-cold water.

"One more thing, Brian. I, er, don't quite know how to put this but I'm afraid young Farringdon rang your missus by mistake before I could stop him and of course she now knows you are not on duty."

"What!" roared Mulraney, by now wide awake. "Where the bloody hell were you when that idiot rang Caroline? I've got a bloody good idea though – I bet you were kipping in your usual cell."

He slammed down the receiver and slipped reluctantly from his warm love nest, for once wishing that he was anything but a policeman. He struggled to insert his long limbs into his rather too tight casual trousers, sitting on the bed to facilitate the process. Jackie, by now awake, her blonde hair falling attractively over her face, reached out for her lover, grasping Mulraney by his neck and pulling him down to her. She covered his face with kisses and, though protesting half-heartedly, he soon become aroused. Unable to resist her, he gave up the struggle with his trousers and, kicking them off, he rejoined his blonde paramour under the covers. They made love once more and in the warm afterglow Jackie nibbled his ear, whispering, "I heard most of the gory details of your early morning call, lover, so I suppose you'll have to go back in."

"Yeah," groaned Mulraney. "'Fraid so, darling. I mean, it might, just might be the lead we have been looking for to nail this murdering bastard. On the other hand it will probably lead to nothing. But I won't find out lying in bed with you, so, much as I hate to do so, I'm afraid I'll have to love you and leave you."

"Oh yes please, one more time!" said a smiling Jackie.

"You'll bloody wear me out!" said Mulraney as he reluctantly pushed her away and resumed his struggle with his trousers.

Fifteen minutes later, after a breakneck drive through the deserted city streets, he arrived at the police station.

Sergeant Whittle, ever-anxious to repair damaged bridges, had despatched young Farringdon to the small kitchen to hastily prepare a bacon sandwich and make the strong coffee so beloved of Mulraney.

The detective sergeant, his burly frame encased in a loose-fitting thick fisherman's sweater pulled well down over his tight trousers, burst through the main entrance of the police station. His cheeks were tingling red with the effect of the keen early morning air, making him feel refreshed and eager for the challenge of a new day. He snatched up the sandwich offered him by an anxious-looking Farringdon. He took a large bite out of it before he reached for the steaming cup of coffee, recoiling instantly as the hot liquid burnt his throat.

"By God that's hot!" he gasped, turning towards the office door from which Sergeant Whittle had emerged. "I'll take young Farringdon and Singh with me to St Ann's. Rustle up some replacements to cover their station duties. Oh, and you had better let Inspector Hutchinson know exactly what is happening."

Police Constables Farringdon and Singh sat tentatively in the back sent of Mulraney's Escort en route to St Ann's. Neither officer attempted to engage Mulraney in conversation, both equally aware that any trite remark could trigger off his notorious anger.

The silence was eventually broken by PC Amrit Singh. The tall well-built Sikh was a rarity in the police as he was one of only two Asians in the city force. He was popular with both his superiors and his colleagues and was a credit to the force, already earmarked for promotion. He was well aware of the tension between Mulraney and the gawky Farringdon. Mulraney had restrained himself, not without some difficulty, from venting his feelings on the young constable, instead concentrating his mind on the current investigation. Unable to endure the awkward silence any longer, Singh leaned over the seat and addressed Mulraney.

"This tip-off is intriguing, Sarge. Trouble is, we are not sure exactly who phoned it in."

Mulraney glanced in his rear view mirror before replying. "Perhaps our country bumpkin friend could enlighten us further on that subject. That's if he can remember taking the call," he added with heavy sarcasm.

Farringdon blushed furiously before replying.

"The caller sounded very muffled, as if he was deliberately disguising his voice, but I did detect a trace of West Indian accent."

"Great!" said Mulraney. "That narrows the field down to the odd five thousand or so!"

Halfway down the Woodborough Road, Mulraney drove the Escort over the rough ground towards the deserted church, the tyres crunching over glass, broken bricks and assorted debris. He brought the car to a halt directly in front of the main door of the church. The door gaped open, slightly askew on its hinges.

"Okay," said Mulraney quietly, "let's take this place apart."

It became obvious to the trio that somebody had done that very thing even before they had commenced their search. They entered the church and were met by a scene of devastation. The interior was littered with the remains of broken wooden chairs, the interiors of cupboards were exposed and stripped of their contents, their doors ripped off their hinges, hanging forlornly. Most of the wooden floorboards were ripped asunder.

At the far end of the church, the remains of church pews were flung haphazardly around, whilst in the corner a large tarpaulin covered others. The two constables teamed up in an effort to remove the large tarpaulin.

Mulraney grunted in disgust. "It looks like some bastard has beaten us to it, unless of course we were deliberately given a bum steer."

"I don't think so, Sarge," said Singh. "Look at this."

Mulraney joined the Asian, who pointed out oil stains under the tarpaulin and the marks of tyre tracks which could clearly be seen snaking through the dust leading to the rear door of the church.

"That oil looks fresh," observed Mulraney. "So there could have been two bikes stowed in here. Do we know who uses this place?"

"I reckon it could only be Rasta Alexander, Sarge," said Singh. "I mean, this is his territory and the tip-off was apparently from a West Indian."

"Yeah, but whoever it was meant to harm Alexander and it would hardly be one of his own kind. It's got to be someone with a grudge and that's pretty obvious when you think about it. It's just got to be Bo Dawson, especially as the two thugs who beat up Charlie Reid escaped on motorbikes."

"But, Sarge, we have no proof that these machines were Kawasaki," said Farringdon nervously.

Mulraney glared at him for a moment, his anger rising again, but he calmed himself before replying, "Yes, you're quite right for once. Use your handset, get back to the station and find out the address of Alexander and we'll pay that gentleman an early morning call."

Office Gossip

Mrs Eunice Pilkington frowned at the excited chatter emanating from the main office. She glanced at her watch which showed 11.30 a.m., this being well past the time allowed for mid-morning break.

She sighed as she rose to her feet. She would just have to have a sharp word with those wretched girls again.

Oh my, how standards had slipped since she was a young office girl. She found to her chagrin lately that she frequently allowed her mind to slip back to those halcyon days of her youth.

Eunice's present position was senior clerk of the office staff of the Birmingham and Nottingham Assurance Company. She bore her seniority with pride and dignity and attempted to enforce her strict code of correct office procedure on the clerical staff, and she was regarded as a bit of a harridan by the younger members.

She had been only seventeen years old when she first joined the ranks of the firm as an office junior. She was now fifty-one years of age and a lonely widow, her husband having died some five years ago after a long illness. Eunice's life had been drab and uninteresting. She had married at the age of thirty, the marriage being childless, and for the last five years of his life husband Reg had been virtually bedridden, shunted in and out of hospital, suffering from the stomach cancer which had eventually claimed his life.

Eunice had, however, experienced moments of rare happiness and she constantly rued the day she had spurned the opportunity of marriage to Frederick Coombs. Thirty-one years ago, whilst she was an office junior, he had joined the firm as a raw but enthusiastic young agent. They had met, fallen instantly in love and embarked on a passionate affair. For the young shy Eunice these were the happiest days of her entire life. Never again would she experience these moments of rapturous bliss found in her tempestuous romance with the young Coombs. There was, however, a black cloud hanging over them: Frederick Coombs had been married for a year and had a wife and baby son at home in nearby Mansfield. He was very much in love with Eunice, however, and was quite prepared to abandon his new wife and child to live with Eunice and eventually to marry her. But, to her lifelong regret, Eunice had followed her conscience and, ignoring her strong feelings for him, she had ended the affair, tearfully ordering him back to his wife and child. After fierce and bitter recriminations, they went their separate ways. Eunice threw herself into her work and it soon became her driving passion. She became extremely proficient and had reached her present position after a series of unspectacular but steady promotions.

Husband Reg was a life assurance inspector and their romance had taken off after the annual staff get-together, held at the Palais de Dance. He was a smooth-talking, extremely affable young man, and after a brief courtship they had married.

Reg's health soon took a turn for the worse and the inadequate snacks he snatched between appointments took their toll on his stomach. He was constantly in and out of hospital under the care of various specialists. His stomach ulcers were treated but he seemed to get worse not better. Eventually, after a series of X-rays, he was diagnosed to be suffering from stomach cancer. His already thin frame became even thinner until he began to resemble an inmate of the infamous Belsen horror camp.

The ever-faithful Eunice coped magnificently with the dual burdens of looking after Reg and maintaining a high standard of efficiency in her work. She even procured the services of a private nurse to look after Reg during her time at the office, at considerable expense to her income. Soon Reg's condition worsened and the doctor advised immediate hospital admission. Reg begged and pleaded with Eunice to let him spend his last days in his own bed. Eunice took special leave of absence from her work and nursed him to the end.

After the funeral, Eunice had stoically resumed work with an even greater degree of effort in an attempt to ease the pain of her loss. Exactly one month after Reg's funeral Eunice's emotions received another jolt as a certain Frederick Coombs arrived at the Nottingham office in his new role as area manager.

After their brief affair he had moved to Derby and from then onwards his career had taken off spectacularly. His first promotion was to senior agent and after a brief spell as a life assurance inspector he had been given his first district manager appointment at Burton upon Trent. After transforming the Burton office, he was transferred to the much larger district of Wolverhampton as area sales manager. Whilst in Wolverhampton, his barnstorming sales technique ensured that the district held the national cup for the highest sales for three years running. It came as no surprise to anyone when he was eventually promoted to his present position of high office as the area manager for the entire Midlands region.

He had not forgotten Eunice but neither had he forgiven her. She was shocked by his severe manner and coldness towards her, especially as she discovered that the passage of time had not dimmed her love for him. After the stark realisation that her feelings were not reciprocated, Eunice became very bitter and her whole personality changed from that moment on. Her co-workers were the first to notice the change when she adapted a carping manner towards them. Even her features seemed to change, the softness being replaced by a harsh steely glare. Her once long brown hair changed almost overnight to iron grey and was gathered in an unattractive bun atop her head. She presented a sad figure as a lonely widow and even sadder was the fact that she was the subject of derisory gossip amongst the younger clerks as they become aware of her unrequited love for Frederick Coombs.

Eunice opened the inner door of the main office and saw that Marilyn Watkins, Janet Compton and Patsy Bowers were gathered round the main reception desk, which was manned by Jane Milford. The bubbly Jane was in her element as the main centre of attention after recounting the events of Thursday evening in lurid and exaggerated detail. The conversation had then turned to animated discussion of the prostitute murders and the increasing vulnerability of women on the streets. The chatter died away abruptly as Eunice entered the office and stared angrily at the group.

"Come along, girls. This really is too bad. Your break finished twenty minutes ago. This is no way to run an office. Will you all please return to your desks immediately. If Mr Coombs were to hear about this, you will all be in serious trouble and I'm very surprised that Mr Malone hasn't complained about all the noise you are making."

"Oh, come on, Eunice, we're only having a good old natter, now where's the harm in that?" said Janet Compton.

Eunice, her face now flushed with anger, replied, "Mrs Pilkington to you, Mrs Compton, and, while we are on the subject, you in particular ought to be setting an example to your younger colleagues."

She angrily turned on her heel and stalked out of the office. Janet, stung by her criticism, gained a degree of revenge by mimicking Eunice's mannerisms as she minced out of the office, imitating Eunice's high-pitched voice. "Come along now, girls, get back to your desks. Mr Coombs won't like it, you know!"

The two younger girls were convulsed with fits of giggling at Janet's amusing satire.

As Janet opened her office door, she found the phone was ringing. On answering it, she was surprised to find that the call was from the reception desk.

"Oh, Janet, there are two policemen here to see Mr Malone. I thought I had better check with you first," said Jane Milford.

"Hang on, Jane," said Janet as she pressed the intercom button. "Mr Malone, there are two policemen in reception wanting a word with you. Shall I send them up?"

Malone's heart skipped a beat as he answered the intercom, but he quelled his fear replying in a firm voice, "Yes, Janet, send them up right away."

He gripped the arms of his chair tightly while his mind raced with terrifying thoughts. Were the police on to him? Had they already checked on his movements? Had his blackmailer informed the police that he had been in the company of the murdered girl on that night? He heard the sound of approaching footsteps and with a supreme effort he banished these negative thoughts as he opened the door of his office, forcing an oily smile as he greeted his visitors.

"Come in, gentlemen, please take a seat. What can I do for you? I hope I haven't parked my car in the wrong place."

"No, sir, nothing like that," replied the suave-looking Sergeant John Mabbutt.

The vice squad policeman, though in uniform, didn't really look like a policeman. His swarthy Latin features, combined with his oily swept-back hair, brought to mind an image of a Forties style gangster. This was in sharp contrast to his companion, PC Harry Broughton, whose large frame was unsuited to uniform. His red chubby cheeks, large hands and feet were typical of the public's conception of PC Plod.

Mabbutt's sharp eyes took in the over-polite Malone and sensed the unease of the corpulent manager.

"We are making inquiries regarding owners of blue Rover saloons of recent origin. According to records I see that you own a two year old car of that make and colour."

"Yes, I do indeed own a Rover," replied Malone, feeling strangely calmed by the routine questions. But all his old fears returned at Mabbutt's next question.

"In that case could you recall your movements last Wednesday night? Let's say from 8 p.m. until midnight."

"Wednesday night you say." Malone glanced briefly at his desk diary, aware that his hand had started shaking. He forced a smile. "Yes, of course, I was working that evening with my young agent Mark Daley in and around the Bestwood Park area. We commenced our calls at 6 p.m. and finished about 8 p.m. We then called in at The Vale public house in Daybrook for a few drinks and left about 11.15 p.m., when I drove home."

Mabbutt looked searchingly at Malone, sensing that his replies were too pat, as if they had been rehearsed.

"I see, sir. Rather a long session in the pub. I do hope you weren't over the limit for driving?"

Realising his error, Malone replied hastily, "Oh no, indeed not. I only had two shandies all night. I'm not much of a drinker actually. You see, we had had such a good night as regards sales that I thought the lad deserved a few beers by way of recompense for his efforts."

"Very well, sir," said Mabbutt, apparently satisfied by Malone's explanation. "Thank you for your assistance. You will probably have realised that our inquiries are in connection with the murder of a young woman in Radford on Wednesday evening. There is one more piece of information I require of you and that is the address of your agent Mark Daley. We do not disbelieve your account of events, sir, but we must, as a matter of routine, confirm your version."

Malone's eyes avoided those of the sergeant as he replied, "Yes of course. He lives in Hereford Road in Woodthorpe. Just a second and I'll give you his telephone number." Malone located the details from his office register, scribbled them down on a piece of paper which he handed to Mabbutt.

"Thank you once again for your co-operation in this matter," said Mabbutt. "That will be all for the moment but we will require a close look at your car in the near future. We'll be in touch about that. Cheerio sir."

Malone closed the door on his visitors, his body now shaking uncontrollably. He was finished: once they contacted Daley they would realise his lies. He must get to Daley without delay. He hastily perused his register of the agents' daily schedules and found to his relief that Daley's collecting today centred on a private housing estate to the north of the city. He checked his watch. With luck he could intercept him on the course of his collection round before he returned home to lunch. There was not a moment to lose. Donning his coat, he hastily vacated his office and left the insurance building via the rear stairs, avoiding the main office in a deliberate attempt to hide his whereabouts.

During the lunch break the office was buzzing with rumours concerning the police visit. Eunice could not resist informing Frederick Coombs of Malone's visitors. Up to this point he had been blissfully unaware of events. Curious to discover more, he pressed his intercom buzzer to summon Malone to his office. The call went unanswered because, for once, the usually punctilious Malone had been found wanting and had informed no one in the office of his intentions.

Malone's Ill-Fated Encounter

Malone drove along the Mansfield Road towards the north of the city with one thing paramount in his mind: that of the absolute necessity of reaching Mark Daley before the police. He had one prime advantage over them in that he knew with a degree of near certainty that Mark would not return to his home for lunch until he had completed his collections, usually round about 2.30 p.m.

He was confident that he could persuade young Mark to go along with his version of events and that, once his story was confirmed by the police, his worries would be over. There was of course the little matter of the examination of his car but he was well-nigh certain that they would find no trace of the murdered girl. He turned off the Mansfield Road at Daybrook and sped up the hill towards the Plains Estate where he was confident that he would find Mark.

Four minutes later his search was rewarded and he parked his car behind Mark's distinctive green Mini. Inside a nearby house Mark was enjoying a second cup of tea with one of his favourite customers, a Mrs Edna Humphreys. She had developed quite a soft spot for Mark as he reminded her of her own son, who had been tragically killed in the Falklands. She looked forward to Mark's weekly visit to collect her insurance premiums. He always arrived with clockwork precision at exactly the same time every Tuesday. He was such a polite young man and so easy to talk to. She tended to mother him and would always prepare a small snack for him to eat and he usually drank two cups of tea from her large brown teapot.

The sound of Malone's car drew Mrs Humphreys to the window. She pulled aside the net curtain exclaiming, "Now who is that in that big blue car? I'm not expecting any visitors."

Mark put down his half finished cup of tea and joined her at the window.

"Crikey, that's old Mooney, my manager. I wonder what he wants?"

"Tell him to come indoors. I'll make another pot of tea."

Mark grimaced. "Er, no, Mrs Humphreys, he's not a very nice man and I don't think you would like him. Thanks very much for the tea and sandwiches. I'd better go and see what he wants."

He picked up his collecting book and left the house to join his manager.

Malone, seeing him approach, wound down his car window. "Ah, Daley, just the man. Pop inside the car a minute, I just want a quick word."

Mark opened the passenger door and slid alongside Malone. A look of slight apprehension appeared on his face.

"I have a little favour to ask of you, Daley," said Malone, looking as if all the troubles of the world were heaped on his shoulders. He continued, "I'm afraid I have got myself into a bit of a mess. You see, the police came to see me this morning. Seems they are checking up on the drivers of all Rover cars. They were particularly asking me about last Wednesday night. You remember that was the night we went out canvassing?"

Mark nodded. He was curious about the favour Malone required of him. He certainly wasn't himself: he was usually so superior and domineering but now he seemed almost meek in comparison. The old bastard certainly had something on his mind.

Malone continued, "The police always make me nervous, so when they asked me what time I left The Vale, I told them I had been in there since 8 p.m. and didn't leave until

11.15 p.m., and then I rather foolishly gave your name as a witness. So when they contact you I want you to confirm my version of events. Now you will do this, won't you, Daley? You see, I don't want my wife to find out about it."

Mark looked at Malone askance. "You surely don't think the police suspect you of being involved with this girl's murder?"

"No of course not! They are just making routine enquiries. I expect that dozens of other Rover drivers are being asked to account for their movements."

Mark frowned in bewilderment. "So why don't you tell them the true version of events? Surely your wife doesn't object to your being outside a pub? I mean, you didn't even go inside, did you?"

Malone squirmed in his seat and Mark revelled in the sight of his manager almost grovelling as he replied, "You see, Daley, I did actually go seeking pleasure from the ladies of the night on that particular evening, and if my wife found out... Well, need I say more. So please, Mark, I would be eternally grateful to you if you backed up my story on this one occasion."

Mark was really beginning to enjoy himself now. This was really something. 'The lads will be amazed when I tell them about the day old Mooney begged and pleaded with me to lie for him – and he actually called me by my Christian name!' He took his time before replying.

"I hope you realise exactly what it is you are asking me to do for you, Mr Malone? I mean, I will be committing perjury and that's a lot to ask. However, I am prepared to do it just this once. However..." He paused, observing the look of sheer relief on his manager's face. "I hope that in return you would reciprocate my favour to you by allowing me to freely take my half day each Wednesday in future and to adopt a kinder attitude towards me and my fellow agents."

"Of course, Daley. Anything you ask. I'm most grateful, I really am. Well, I had better get back to work now. I'll see you in the office tomorrow, Daley. Let me know how you get on."

Mark stood deep in thought on the pavement turning over Malone's startling admission in his mind. He realised that he was in a bit of a quandary: if Malone really was involved in this girl's murder, he was laying himself wide open to charges of perjury; on the other hand he had promised the old bastard that he would back his story and for that Malone had promised to be eternally grateful – but would he be?

He drove slowly home still unsure of his course of action.

Malone, feeling a little better now, drove slowly back to the city, he still felt strangely out of sorts with himself and was not in the mood for returning to work. He parked his car in the Victoria Shopping Centre Car Park and wandered aimlessly amongst the crowds in the shopping complex.

He didn't feel really hungry but decided to have a cup of tea and a hamburger at a tea kiosk in the Victoria Market. The hamburger was greasy, the tea too milky and both lay heavily on his stomach. At a loss as to quite what to do next, he returned to his car and sat deep in thought for several minutes.

On a sudden whim he reached under the dashboard and pulled out his wig, placing it carefully on top of his bald head, then he completed his disguise by the addition of his horn-rimmed spectacles. He glanced with considerable satisfaction at his reflection in the car mirror. What a difference these adjustments made to his appearance! He began to feel his old self again.

Mindful of his work commitments, he found a telephone kiosk and phoned the office. His call was answered by Janet Compton and he explained to her that he would not be returning to the office today due to two urgent appointments. Janet replied that Mr Coombs was anxious to see him but Malone said that he would see him first thing in the morning and hung up.

He really was indispensable, he reflected, still, let the buggers wait – surely he was entitled to the odd afternoon off considering all the hard work he put in.

In rebellious mood he left the confines of the Victoria Centre and wandered aimlessly up Shakespeare Street. He felt in dire need of a drink, if only to get that taste of greasy hamburger out of his mouth.

Opposite the fire station he entered the doors of the first public house that he came upon. He was somewhat surprised to see a man seated at a table barring his further progress. The man, deep in his perusal of the sports page of *The Evening Post*, didn't even glance up at him as he spoke.

"You 'ere for the lunchtime strippers, mate? They are a bit late today but they'll be 'ere shortly. It'll cost you a quid if you want to see the show."

Malone began to wonder if this really was a pub but bemusedly paid his entrance fee and entered the main hall.

He peered through the smoky atmosphere at a scene not unlike a small theatre, with the seats lined up row by row; the front row was already fully occupied. Behind the semicircular bar counter was a small stage bedecked with velvety blue curtains. An incandescent blue light illuminated the whole scene, reflecting off the bald pate of the rotund barman, who, recognising a creature of similar ilk, greeted Malone cheerfully.

"What's your pleasure, mate?"

"A pint of bitter please," answered Malone.

The barman busied himself manipulating the old-fashioned pump and continued in cheerful vein. "Strippers are on in five minutes, mate. Allus worth a look, some better'n others a course. The first one is an absolute dog, but the second one is worth a look, especially if you're into black velvet."

He glanced up at Malone before continuing, "First time 'ere, ain't it? I've got a good memory for faces. I'd advise you to get yourself a good speck as the students will be in soon. Bloody 'ell, 'ere they come now!"

He broke off his conversation as the bar was suddenly engulfed by a crowd of excited chattering students, their garish attire contrasting with that of the bar's regulars, who were rather tired-looking middle-aged or older men.

Malone thanked the barman, picked up his drink and hastily took up one of the few seats not yet occupied by the students. He glanced at the occupant of the seat alongside him and wrinkled his nose in disgust at the distinct body odour emanating from a rather scruffy-looking man with a pronounced beer belly. The man grinned at Malone.

"Sit yersen down, mate. I see you've got a pint of Shippo's. Good ale that, mate, 'specially if you're constipated. If not it'll mek yer shit through the eye of a needle!"

He guffawed loudly at this last remark, slapping Malone jocularly on the thigh.

Malone groaned inwardly; it was just his luck to sit next to such an uncouth individual. He began to doubt his own sanity in entering such a place. He consoled himself with the thought of the oncoming show and chose to ignore Beer Belly's comments.

The hum of conversation in the bar faded a little as the dimming of the lights heralded the arrival of the first stripper, announced euphemistically by the barman as hailing, "Direct from the Casbah!"

The fleshy stripper, who had lank greasy black hair, pendulous breasts and crude tattoos on each shoulders, seemed well past her 'sell by' date.

Beer Belly nudged Malone. "I don't know about the Casbah – this one looks as if she's direct from Hyson Green!"

The stripper's taped musical accompaniment came over in a series of spasmodic sounds indicating a fault with either the music system or the tape. She stopped her act in mid-strip, stuck out her posterior towards the audience and angrily berated the barman.

"Adjust the bloody tape, Sam, it's all over the place."

This provoked howls of laughter from the students who yelled, "Play it again Sam!"

Further adjustments to the sound system failed to produce any improvement. The exasperated stripper, now down to a skimpy G-string, halted proceedings once more to berate the barman in very strong language. This action provoked the students to howls of derision.

Malone's companion rose unsteadily to his feet and shouted, "Listen 'ere, darling, bugger the tape, we'll 'um it, you just ge' 'em off!"

This remark was greeted with a huge roar of approval from the students. In something of an anticlimax the stripper divested herself of her last article of clothing and strode off the stage in disgust to the roars, whistles and catcalls of the audience.

Malone was beginning to enjoy himself and as he sipped his pint he failed to notice the arrival of several black youths and a tall black girl.

After an interval of ten minutes the rotund barman clutched his microphone and announced, "Now, gents, by public demand, we are proud to present for your delight the return of the Black Angel!"

To the musical accompaniment of Tina Turner's *Simply the Best* there appeared the lithe figure of Angie McPherson onstage, provoking roars of approval and appreciative wolf whistles from both the students and the older regulars. As she commenced her act, as if by magic an immediate hush developed.

Angie glided across the stage. She certainly knew her stuff, dancing provocatively in perfect time to the music. The eyes of the audience stared unblinking as she wriggled seductively out of her costume. This was a different class from the previous act, and by the time she had disposed of her last garment Angie had her audience completely mesmerised. She stood defiantly proud on stage with an almost haughty expression, bowing slightly in acknowledgement of the ecstatic applause. She claimed her robe and, with a final wave to her delighted fans, she exited the stage.

Malone, swept along with the rest of the audience, was entranced by her performance. He mopped his brow and decided to order another drink but changed his mind on seeing the crowded bar.

Meanwhile Angie had changed back into her street clothes and had joined Bo and his entourage for a drink at the bar. Malone, pushing his way through the throng, was on his way out when his eyes met those of Angie's. He gasped and stared in fascination as recognition dawned on him.

Angie stared back at him. She was used to the stares of men but there was something familiar about this bloke. She turned to Bo exclaiming excitedly, "Hey, Bo, that bloke just going out of the door, I'm sure it is the same bastard that drove off with Jacqui."

She ran across the bar after Malone. "Hey you, come back here!" she shouted.

Malone, realising he had been spotted, hurried through the doorway barging past the throng of students and causing drinks to be spilt in his headlong rush to get away.

Exiting the premises he turned left into Shakespeare Street and ran as fast as he could, anxious to disappear amongst the city crowds. Out of breath but still moving, he half turned to check on the proximity of his pursuers and ran straight into a patrolling policeman.

"Oops, steady, sir. Where are we going in such a hurry?" said the policeman, restraining the gasping Malone whose look of horror was made worse by his wig, now slightly askew.

Malone Is Detained

Angie led the pursuers in the rush towards Malone, who made no attempt whatsoever to shake off the policeman. Truth to tell, he was not the fittest of men and his terrified dash at breakneck speed had taken its toll on his unfit body. He was ashen-faced, gulping for air and unable to control his shaking limbs.

Angie confronted him and pointed at him, screaming, "That's him, that's definitely the bloke that done Jacqui! Hey, copper, arrest the bastard!"

The policeman put out a calming hand towards Angie. "Just a minute, miss. Let's not be too hasty, shall we? Why don't we all go across the road to the Central Police Station and sort this out?"

By this time Bo and his two companions had caught up to the group and Bo raised both his fists in a menacing attitude towards Malone. The policeman, sensing trouble, put a protective arm across Malone, who stared wide-eyed in horror at his pursuers. A crowd of curious onlookers joined the scene and the policeman repeated his previous suggestion to Bo as he shepherded Malone across the road, making their way past the fire station and rounding the corner before entering the Central Police Station. Bo's enthusiasm waned as the group approached the desk. He had been inside too many police stations of late.

The constable explained to the desk sergeant exactly what had occurred on Shakespeare Street. After taking particulars, the sergeant realised that the incident could be of interest to the murder squad and he contacted Radford Road, where a rather weary Mulraney took the call. His mind cleared miraculously as he realised the significance of the incident and he instructed the sergeant to detain the suspect for questioning by Detective Chief Inspector Hutchinson.

After a few brief questions, the desk sergeant directed Malone to one interview room and Angie to a separate one. Bo and his two companions were told that their presence would no longer be required and they left the building with feelings of both relief and disgust.

Some fifteen minutes later a fresh-looking Hutchinson and a tired-looking Mulraney arrived together at the Central Police Station. They checked the location of the interviewees and first entered the room containing Angie. Mulraney switched on the tape recorder and Hutchinson commenced the questioning.

"Now, Angie, I'm going to ask you a few questions and I want you to think very carefully before you answer. I shall be recording everything you say."

"Bloody get on with it! You coppers are too long-winded."

"Now, Angie, think carefully. Do you recognise the man you pointed out in Shakespeare Street this afternoon?"

"I don't know his bloody name, but I'll never forget his face!"

"Where and when did you last see him?"

"Forest Road on Wednesday night. I've told you all this before!"

"Patience, Angie, what time exactly did you see him?"

"Round about half past eight."

"Was he in the company of Jacqui Reid?"

"Yeah, she got in his car."

"Did you see Jacqui Reid again that night?"

"No I bloody didn't, and we all know why, don't we?"

"Thank you, Angie, that will be all for now but we will be in touch with you again shortly."

"Is that all? Are you going to do him, Inspector? I reckon he should be strung up by his balls!"

"Come on, Angie, no more talk like that," said Hutchinson as he gently steered Angie out of the interview room.

The policemen made their way towards Malone's interview room, Mulraney remarking, "This should be interesting, Pete. I've got a feeling about this one – it's about time we had some luck."

"Let's wait and see, shall we?" replied Hutchinson.

They entered the interview room containing Malone and both looked him over as they settled themselves into chairs opposite him. A pale-looking Malone stared straight ahead as he strived manfully to appear calm although he still found difficulty in controlling his shaking limbs.

Hutchinson began.

"I would advise you that you are not under caution at this time and any statement you give is entirely voluntary on your part. Do you understand this?"

Malone nodded assent and replied, "Yes," in a barely audible tone.

"Would you confirm that you are Reginald Alfred Malone of 25 Harlaxton Crescent, Wollaton, Nottingham?"

"Yes."

"Could you tell me the reason why you were running down Shakespeare Street this afternoon?"

"I was afraid of being assaulted by a group of youths."

"Was there a girl with this group of youths?"

"Er, yes there was."

"Do you know this girl and have you ever seen her before today?"

"No, I do not know her, but I did see her performing a striptease act in a public house this afternoon."

"Do you know or have you ever been in contact with a girl called Jacqui Reid."

"No, never."

"The girl I referred to previously is called Angie McPherson and she alleges that you were the driver of a blue Rover car in which you picked up Jacqui Reid for immoral purposes and then drove off with her last Wednesday night. Do you confirm or deny this allegation?"

"I deny that allegation entirely."

"You have previously been questioned about your movements on Wednesday night. Do you stand by that statement?"

".Yes, I do."

"You named a witness to corroborate your statement. I would advise you that we are now seeking the whereabouts of this witness as I speak."

Hutchinson referred to his notes.

"I see that you are the owner of a blue Rover saloon. Will you tell me the present location of this vehicle?"

"The Victoria Centre Car Park."

"Have you the keys of this vehicle on your person?"

"Yes."

"Would you please therefore give me the keys as we need to carry out a thorough examination of your vehicle in connection with this investigation. Do you have any objection to this?"

"No."

"I note that you are wearing a wig. Is there any particular reason for this?"

"Er. No." Malone reached up rather self-consciously and removed both his wig and glasses.

Hutchinson and Mulraney exchanged meaningful glances and the uniformed constable at the door suppressed a snigger.

At this point an attractive woman constable entered the room and passed a note to Hutchinson. He read the contents and spoke to Malone.

"Excuse me, Mr Malone, I am wanted on the telephone."

Hutchinson then left the room and Mulraney eagerly resumed the questioning. He stared directly into Malone's eyes.

"Are you in the habit of consorting with prostitutes, Mr Malone?"

"No, definitely not."

"Do you regularly visit striptease shows?"

"Not as a rule, no."

"I see that you have admitted to watching a striptease show this afternoon. Do you attend that particular venue on a regular basis?"

"No, that was the first time – in fact I didn't even realise it was one of those places at first. When I went in I thought it was just an ordinary pub. Anyway, it's not a crime, is it?"

"No, of course it isn't. It's also not a crime to consort with prostitutes except, of course, if you are caught kerb-crawling. Do you ever kerb-crawl, Mr Malone?"

"No, never."

The door of the interview room was opened and an expressionless Hutchinson took up his seat. Ignoring the quizzical look from his colleague, he continued the questioning of Malone.

"Mr Malone, in an earlier statement which you gave to one of our officers, you mentioned a Mr Mark Daley, who you said would confirm your whereabouts on Wednesday night last. Do you still stand by your account of these events?"

"Yes."

"In that case, Mr Malone, I have to inform you that I have just been speaking on the telephone to an officer who interviewed Mr Mark Daley earlier today, who, when questioned, did *not* confirm your version of events. In fact he stated that you left the car park of The Vale Hotel at 8.15 p.m. on Wednesday last, and, furthermore, he stated that you did not even enter the premises."

Malone gripped his chair tightly in a supreme effort to shake off the rising tide of panic that engulfed him.

"But he can't have said that! If he did, he's deliberately lying!"

"Now why should he do that?"

"Well, er, perhaps he wants to get me into trouble."

"I think you are enough trouble already, Mr Malone. Now think again and tell me the true version of the events of that night."

"I've already told you what happened. Now, look here, I'm not answering any more questions. I want to see my solicitor."

"You have an absolute right to see a solicitor, but I am obliged to inform you that at this point I intend to detain you in this police station for further questioning as I have reason to suspect that you are involved in the murder of Jacqui Reid. You have a right to inform a relative or close friend that you are being detained. You also have the right to examine the code of practice for the procedure, detention, treatment and questioning by police officers, if you so wish."

Malone swallowed, finding this very difficult as his throat was so dry.

"Please can I have a drink of water? And I request that you contact my solicitor Mr Brian Beddowes now."

Mulraney rose from his chair.

"Yes, of course, Mr Malone. I'll see to both of those things for you."

Hutchinson collected his papers and left the room with his second in command, leaving Malone in the charge of the uniformed constable at the door.

"Fancy a quick cuppa, Pete?" said Mulraney. "I don't know about you but I'm bloody parched."

"You've also been on continuous duty for nearly twenty-four hours so I suggest you go home and get your head down," replied Hutchinson.

"What and miss homing in on the killer? Not bloody likely! I want to see this bastard well and truly nailed to the mast."

"That's if he is the right man, and besides, we haven't nailed him yet. I've had dealings with this Beddowes before. He's so good he could make the Yorkshire Ripper appear innocent. And I am not one hundred per cent clear in my own mind that this Malone is the guilty party."

"Oh, come on, Pete, of course he's guilty! It's written all over him! Look at the way he was sweating! I was watching him whilst you were questioning him and his legs were trembling and he kept clenching up his hands."

"Let's wait and see, shall we?" said Hutchinson, pushing open the door of the canteen.

The nearby offices of *The Evening Post* were soon informed of Malone's detention, but his name was not released at this point. The late afternoon edition did a brisk trade as the billboards proclaimed VICE GIRL MURDER LATEST – SUSPECT HELD FOR QUESTIONING.

The Noose Tightens

The call for the services of Mr Brian Beddowes was some seven hours too late, as he had departed from Nottingham's Midland Station that very morning on the 'businessmen's special' to St Pancras to attend to urgent business in the capital. An urgent telex message was then relayed to his London hotel urgently requesting that he return to Nottingham. He replied that he would cut short most of his business in London and would return by the first available train the following morning, estimating that he would arrive at the Central Police Station by 11 a.m., or 11.30 a.m. at the latest. This message was relayed to Malone, who had earlier refused to select an alternative solicitor or one available to the police on a temporary basis, insisting that only his close friend Mr Beddowes was capable of representing him.

Hutchinson meanwhile had located Malone's Rover and arranged for it to be driven the short distance back to the Central Police Station garage. With Hutchinson and Mulraney as interested spectators, a team of four white-overalled police specialists prepared the car for a thorough investigation. Mulraney took a brief look around the interior of the car and his keen eye observed that the carpets had recently undergone a very thorough cleaning, which further enhanced his suspicions of Malone.

The first action of the examiners was to completely remove the two front seats of the car. On turning over the passenger seat, they struck gold immediately. They discovered a piece of chewing gum with a faint trace of red which could be either lipstick or blood; only laboratory testing would determine that.

The gum was found adhered towards the centre of the base of the seat, and attached to the gum was a long black hair. The examiner very carefully removed the gum with a pair of tweezers and deposited it into a plastic evidence bag.

He handed this to a jubilant Mulraney who could barely contain his excitement.

"Bingo!" he exclaimed to Hutchinson. "I'll bet a pound to a penny that the lab boys will trace this gum back to Jacqui Reid and I reckon that black hair is one of hers too. These two bits of evidence alone will prove without any doubt that she was in Malone's car. I'll take this bag to the lab myself."

Malone, unaware of this latest piece of damning evidence, was deep in thought as he sat dejectedly in his cell. He couldn't quite believe how quickly his whole world had turned upside down within a matter of hours. His initial feelings of despair had now turned to anger at his predicament and he was furious at what he considered to be a deliberate betrayal by Mark Daley. He vowed that if he ever got out of this terrible mess he would make life hell for the young whippersnapper.

At 6 p.m. that evening a bewildered Betty Malone arrived at Central Police Station. She was placed in a police interview room and Malone was brought in to see her.

This still slim-looking middle-aged woman was on the brink of tears at the sight of her husband. The change in his appearance frightened her. He looked dishevelled and crestfallen; gone was the cocky, self-assured and at times arrogant man who was her husband. Despite his faults and his womanising, she still loved him and could not bear to see him in this state. She reached out to him and suddenly her distress overcame her and she burst into the tears which were never far away.

Malone patted her gently. "Come on, Betty, you're supposed to be cheering me up."

"Oh Reggie, what is happening? What have they done to you? I don't believe all those horrible things they are saying about you. Why isn't Brian here? I'll get him immediately, he'll know what to do."

"Don't worry, dear, it's all in hand. Brian is in London but he'll be back first thing in the morning," said Malone.

"But what's all this about a murdered girl? Surely there must be a terrible mistake?"

"There is, there is. Brian will sort it all out. In the meantime I don't want you to tell the girls anything yet and I want you to phone Coombs after you have left here."

"Oh, don't worry about work now, but yes I'll do as you ask. The main thing is to get you out of here as soon as possible. They haven't actually charged you with anything yet, have they?"

Cups of tea were brought in for Malone and Betty and produced a soothing effect, on her at least.

The minute examination of Malone's car continued and the entire interior was removed piece by piece. Despite the thorough search, only three further black hairs were discovered and these were despatched to the laboratory. A scientific analysis of the chewing gum revealed traces of saliva and lipstick which were compared to samples from the dead girl and positively matched. Similarly two out of the four black hairs were found to be from the scalp of the dead girl whilst the other two were from her pudenda.

These scientific examinations were conducted throughout the night and into the early hours. The results were conveyed to a bleary-eyed Hutchinson at 5 a.m. on Wednesday morning. He had spent the night more awake than asleep on a bunk bed inside one of the cells with instructions that he be woken if there was any news from the laboratory. Though hoping for a positive result, he was still not entirely convinced of Malone's guilt. One good thing to come out of it would be that he would get Chief Super Maudsley off his back. He was aware of the Chief Super's dislike of him and that he had not helped his chances when he had stoutly defended Brian Mulraney against charges of committing a sexual act with a colleague in a public place, i.e. the back of a police car. 'God help us,' reflected Hutchinson. 'The jury is still out on that one!'

While he gulped down a hot cup of reviving tea, his spirits visibly brightened on reading the computer sheet containing the positive results on the hair and chewing gum samples. His first telephone call was to Maudsley and he took great delight in his grumpy response on being awakened at such an early hour, but was disappointed though not surprised by the grudging 'well done, I suppose' from his superior. His next call was to the Hucknall home of Brian Mulraney and produced a much more positive response.

"Yippee, bloody told you so!" exclaimed a delighted Mulraney, adding, "I'm on my way."

The detective sergeant had fallen asleep early from sheer exhaustion after being harangued continually by wife Caroline almost from the first minute he stepped through the front door.

"Where have you been all this time? Don't tell me you been on continuous duty! I don't believe a word you say any more. You've been with that blonde tart again, haven't you? Don't bother denying it – I don't believe you! You do realise I've told the Chief Super all about you? You can get your own bloody supper. I've had it with you! Why do you bother coming home at all? That's right, walk away like you always do. Why don't you bloody hit me? Then I'll really have something to go on! Open this bloody door! I'll make sure you get no sleep!"

Mulraney had finally locked himself in the bedroom and collapsed into exhausted sleep despite Caroline's turning on the stereo full blast. Forty-five minutes after receiving his telephone call from Hutchinson he arrived at Central Police Station in buoyant mood, glad to be away from his shrewish wife.

Armed with the successful findings, the two detectives prepared a dossier of more searching questions to present to Malone.

"I reckon we have enough evidence now to charge him with murder," said Mulraney.

"Yes," agreed Hutchinson. "We can definitely prove that Jacqui Reid was in his car and that he deliberately lied as to his whereabouts that Wednesday night, but if he is guilty then I hope he confesses because, quite frankly, we can't actually prove he did it – and with Mr Brian Beddowes to deal with we'd better be damned sure of our facts. The only thing that puzzles me is what exactly his motive was."

"But unlike you I'm damned sure he did it," said Mulraney.

"Well, if you are right that rules out either Dawson or Alexander. Talking of which, how did you get on with your early morning visit to Alexander? I take it the bird had flown?"

"Yes, you could say that," replied Mulraney. "There was no sign of him at his flat and as usual his neighbours didn't know anything, but we did strike lucky when PC Singh went for a morning paper. The local newsagent, a fellow Sikh who didn't like Alexander one bit, said that he had unexpectedly cancelled his papers for a week due to a sudden urge to visit his dear old mum in Manchester."

"I didn't know his sort had mothers!" said Hutchinson.

"True, he should have been strangled at birth," laughed Mulraney. "But seriously, I reckon we ought to keep an eye open for when he returns. That anonymous call intrigues me. I mean, suppose it was true and those missing bikes were Kawasakis. Then that could tie in Alexander to the Janice Longman murder. In any event I think we ought to have another word with him when he gets back."

"I take your point," replied Hutchinson. "We may be looking at two separate killers of these girls but somehow I don't think so." He looked at his watch. "It's nearly half six. Why don't you kip down in the cells for an hour or two? I'll wake you before Malone's solicitor arrives at eleven. I don't suppose it's worth you going home. How are things on the domestic front?"

"Don't ask," said Mulraney. "Caroline gets worse. I'm dreading the do on Saturday. But thanks for the offer; I could do with some extra kip."

Too Late for Help?

Mr Brian Beddowes settled himself comfortably on the rear seat of the hackney cab as it sped away from the Midland British Rail Station en route to the Central Police Station. He was a well-built, sturdy-looking man, whose aquiline nose, bushy dark eyebrows and slicked-back dark hair gave him a Slavonic appearance. He presented a picture of smooth elegance in his light grey suit and handmade Gucci shoes. He was a little annoyed at the curtailment of his London visit, as he had meticulously planned it to mix his business appointments with a few nights of romantic dalliance with the wife of a business colleague who was conveniently in Brussels for that particular week. He ruefully reflected on what might have been, but the pull of duty was undeniable, in this case especially, as it concerned one of his friends.

Though not one of his closest friends, he felt as if he had a bounden duty to help Malone due to the close friendship between Betty Malone and his own wife Madeleine. The two met up in town on a regular weekly basis and enjoyed a wander round the shops and a good old womanly gossip. Whilst recognising Malone's undoubted prowess as a businessman, he disliked him as an individual. Though sharing his love of women and the odd indiscreet fling, he was aware of Malone's visits to the red-light district and had voiced his disapproval with a warning of the consequences to be faced should he be caught.

Though he had been only given brief preliminary details as to the reason for Malone's detention, he was concerned at the threat of an impending murder charge.

Shortly after his arrival at Central Police Station Beddowes was soon in close discussion of the case with Hutchinson, who brought him up to date with all the relevant facts. He then requested an immediate meeting with Malone before proceedings could be taken further.

The relief on Malone's face was clear for all to see as Beddowes entered the interview room, and he greeted his solicitor with great enthusiasm. Beddowes calmed him down and then questioned him closely on his version of the events. Malone related to him more or less the same version he had given to the police until halted by the solicitor.

"Look, Reg, I'm your friend as well as your solicitor, so please tell me what really happened and leave nothing out. Just answer me one important question – I think I already know the answer, but I want to hear it from you. Did you kill that girl?"

"No, of course I didn't, Brian."

"Okay then, start again, slowly, from the beginning, I'll take it all down and we'll prepare a statement for the police."

Forty-five minutes later, Beddowes collected up his papers and gave Malone a reassuring pat on the back.

"Now try not to worry, Reg. What you did was bloody stupid and to try and deny it to the police was even worse. They will probably have to charge you with murder but the important thing is *you didn't do it* and, if it has to go to court, I'll prove you didn't."

Beddowes gave the prepared statement to Hutchinson, who perused it thoroughly before arranging for it to be typed up. The two men engaged in a close discussion which lasted some fifteen minutes.

Hutchinson retrieved the typed statement and both men re-entered Malone's interview room. Hutchinson resumed his original seat directly opposite Malone whilst Beddowes drew up a chair alongside his friend.

Looking directly at Malone, Hutchinson began, "I have here a statement prepared by your solicitor Mr Brian

Beddowes which purports to be your account of the events of last Wednesday night. I will now read out to you the statement and if you consider it to be correct, then you are obliged to sign it. The statement is as follows:

"'On Wednesday 16th February 1987 I left The Vale Hotel at approximately ten minutes past eight in the evening. I proceeded to Forest Road in my car where I picked up a young woman I now know to be Jacqui Reid for immoral purposes. I took her to some waste ground off Hartley Road and paid her £40 for sex. After sex there was a disagreement over the price she charged and she got out of the car. I did not assault her; in fact she assaulted me. Whilst I was recovering from the assault on me, she snatched my wallet and left the car. I did not follow her – I was in no position to – so I am unable to say where she went and I did not see her again. I then returned to my home in Wollaton. The next day I reported the loss of my bank and credit cards to the companies concerned.

"'At my office I received a telephone call from an anonymous caller requesting payment of £5,000 in cash for the return of my wallet. I was by this time aware that the girl I had consorted with on Wednesday night was the same girl later found murdered. I totally panicked and paid the £5,000 to the anonymous caller. I realise that my actions appear suspicious, I bitterly regret them and protest my complete innocence of this crime.'"

Hutchinson put down the statement and pushed it towards Malone.

"If you consider this to be a true version of events, then please sign where indicated."

Without even bothering to look at the statement Malone took the pen proffered by his solicitor and signed the statement.

Hutchinson cleared his throat and stared directly at Malone.

"Reginald Alfred Malone, I am formally charging you with the murder of Jacqui Reid on the night of Wednesday 16th February 1987. I have received and accepted a signed statement of your account of the events of that night. This statement differs greatly from your previous statement of events and this, together with forensic evidence, leaves me no option but to charge you with murder. Have you anything further to add to your statement? I must caution you that anything you do say will be used in evidence against you."

Malone, eyes downcast, replied, "No, I have nothing further to say."

Hutchinson flicked over the typed statement and looked again at Malone.

"I would like you to tell me a little bit more about this anonymous caller who you claim contacted you. I take it you didn't recognise his voice in any way?"

Malone frowned slightly. "Well, I have gone over it again and again in my mind and I thought at the time that there was something vaguely familiar about that voice, but I just can't put a name to it."

"Could it be someone you currently work with?"

"No, definitely not."

"Someone you used to work with?"

"No, I don't think so."

"Have you any enemies or do you know of anyone with a grudge against you, or even perhaps someone you have upset in your business dealings?"

"Well, now you mention it there are a few people with whom I have had disagreements with in business but they don't sound anything like the voice I heard."

"Okay, well look, write down all the names of the people you can remember having disagreements with, and we will proceed with our own inquiries into the matter. I must now inform you that you will be brought before the Guildhall Magistrates' Court tomorrow morning for a preliminary hearing of the charges against you. You will of course be detained here for a further night but I understand from your solicitor that he will be requesting bail for you at the hearing. In the meantime I will allow you further time with your solicitor."

He left the room leaving a uniformed constable to guard the door.

Beddowes placed a reassuring hand on Malone's shoulder. "Now I know it looks a bit grim, Reg, but I can assure you that there is nothing for you to get too worried about. You are not a killer and your only crime is giving a false statement to the police. I strongly suspect that Inspector Hutchinson has a seed of doubt in his mind, and he appears not to doubt the validity of your anonymous caller. Once the police find out who he is then I suspect they will find their murderer. He either committed the murder himself or knows who did it. Try and keep your spirits up. In the meantime I shall be working hard to obtain bail for you at tomorrow's hearing, so hopefully this will be your last night in custody."

Beddowes left the room deep in thought and pushed his way through the throng of pressmen gathered outside Central Police Station, ignoring several requests for information. He hailed a passing taxi, relieved to escape the drizzling rain and the persistent reporters.

The billboards of *The Evening Post* were already displaying the headlines of the latest edition: LOCAL BUSINESSMAN CHARGED WITH VICE GIRL'S MURDER.

Hutchinson's Growing Doubts

A large crowd of curious onlookers, including the morbid and the just plain nosy, attracted by the lurid press coverage of the murders, assembled outside the Guildhall Magistrates' Court on Wednesday morning. The usual local press representation was enlarged by a number of reporters from the tabloid dailies. There was also a bigger than average police presence, encircling Malone as he was bundled into the court, his head covered by the obligatory blanket. His appearance provoked a few angry shouts and boos from the crowd who surged forward only to be stopped by the police, who hastily linked arms.

Inside the court were gathered members of Malone's family, including his wife and two daughters, who had both travelled up overnight despite Betty's protestations. She was both pleased that they had made the effort to rally round their father in his hour of need but worried that he would consider she had ignored his wishes.

The large figure of Frederick Coombs represented the company and already he was mentally preparing his address to the company chairman regarding the serious consequences of Malone's involvement in a major crime. One thing for sure was that Malone's immediate future with the company looked decidedly bleak.

The object of all this attention, though pale, appeared calm in the dock and his face did not reflect his inner turmoil. He confirmed his name and address and, when the charge of murder was put to him, he replied, "Not guilty," in a clear voice.

Representing the accused, Brian Beddowes put in a persuasive appeal for bail for his client on the grounds of his previous unblemished record and his full co-operation with the police, a point fully endorsed by Hutchinson. After some minutes of earnest consultation the chairman of the magistrates announced that they had to also take into account the serious nature of the charge and, on the advice of the police, they had to take into account the safe custody of the accused and therefore they reluctantly concluded that bail was inappropriate at this time. The magistrates remanded Malone into police custody pending further investigations into the crime.

Brian Beddowes seized upon this last point as an optimistic sign as he consoled Malone's weeping family. He put his arm round Betty Malone as he gently explained, "Don't you see, Betty, even the police themselves aren't convinced that Reg is guilty. If they were he would have been committed for trial at the crown court."

This was, alas, little comfort to Malone's family as they had confidently expected him to be released on bail.

The whole court procedure lasted five minutes less than an hour, and, on the advice of the police, Malone was ushered out of court via a rear entrance in order not to provoke the mainly hostile crowd at the front of the building.

Hutchinson returned from court directly to Radford Road Police Station where his first act was to scan the entries in the daily occurrence book for the previous week. There was now a growing doubt in his mind whether the case against Malone would stand up to a full crown court trial, especially with the formidable Brian Beddowes presenting the defence case.

He was well aware of the fact that most guilty men attempt to lie their way out of their complicity in a crime and Malone, on his own admission, had lied, although he had, eventually, admitted to his meeting with Jacqui Reid. Yet despite all this irrefutable evidence, Hutchinson's gut instinct told him there was far more to this case than seemed apparent. The first thing he must do was investigate the truth or otherwise of Malone's alleged blackmailing. He had already checked with Malone's bank, which confirmed that he had made a substantial withdrawal on the day in question.

Unfortunately his perusal of the occurrence book proved fruitless, as the only recorded incident of the afternoon in question in the Arboretum area was the apprehending of two prostitutes in Waverley Street. Undaunted, Hutchinson next studied the duty patrol roster and found that the area had been patrolled on that particular day by PC Amrit Singh.

He found the turbaned officer enjoying a meal break in the canteen after his morning shift. Hutchinson asked him to recall his patrol of the Arboretum area on the day in question, especially between the hours of one and two in the afternoon, and whether he could recall anything unusual occurring. PC Singh recalled being on patrol in the Arboretum at that time and yes, there had been a small incident but it was so trifling that it did not merit recording.

He remembered that there had been a young mother feeding the ducks in the pond and reprimanding her son Jamie from playing too near the water. The child had run away and begun rummaging in a nearby litter bin. As she went to drag her son away from the bin, the mother had been startled by the sudden appearance of a man, clad in black leathers. He had pushed her young son roughly out of the way, snatched something out of the bin and run off towards the park gates. Her young son had been very upset and had run crying to his mother. PC Singh had been patrolling near the bandstand at the time of the incident and did not personally witness it. He came upon the young mother comforting her son and she had related the details to him. It appeared that, as the child was not hurt in any way and there was no sign of the man, he felt there was no point in pursuing the matter further. He had, however, noted down the name and address of the mother, an action for which Hutchinson was grateful. Hutchinson thanked the constable for his assistance and transmitted the details of the address from the constable's notebook to his own. The incident, though appearing trivial, was to prove of some significance to the case.

Hutchinson enlisted the services of Mulraney and the pair proceeded to the Raleigh Street address of the young mother. Her name was Marie Stokes and she lived in a small bedsit near the Arboretum. She clearly recalled the incident. She hadn't, however, got a very good look at the leather-clad man as he had been running away in the opposite direction. Pressed further, she recalled that he was of medium build and had worn a green crash helmet, his leathers were all black with a distinctive green flash. No, he didn't harm young Jamie in any way, he had just pushed him to one side. He had been more shocked than hurt. Like all little boys he was very nosy but he did remember things, so when she asked him what the man had taken from the bin he recalled that it was a big brown envelope. Hutchinson thanked Ms Stokes and pressed a pound coin into her hand to buy some sweets for young Jamie.

Mulraney remarked to Hutchinson on their way back to Radford Road that it appeared as if his boss was right again, and he grudgingly admitted that even he was having doubts as to Malone's guilt and was surprised that his story of the blackmailer seemed to be true.

Once back in the police station, Hutchinson consulted the computer to check the details of the unsolved murder of Janice Longman, some three months previously. There were only two main witnesses, whose statements tallied in that they had both seen a leather-clad, helmeted motorcyclist astride a green motorbike. The first witness had parked his car in the darkened car park near Colwick Racecourse for the purposes of a romantic interlude with his girlfriend, this particular spot being popular with local courting couples. His girlfriend had brought to his attention the presence of a helmeted motorcyclist who was sitting astride his machine and seemed to be staring directly at them. She was very disturbed as she thought he was a peeping Tom. Her angry boyfriend had been restrained by her from seeking a confrontation with the man as she "didn't like the look of him, there was something sinister about him". They had driven off and didn't realise the incident was of any significance until they read the next day's papers.

The second witness recalled that he had been forced to pull up sharply to avoid a collision with a green motorbike that had suddenly cut across the road in front of him, coming from the entrance of the car park. The bike had roared off in the direction of the city, and had been closely followed by a light blue Ford Escort but he couldn't recall what the driver looked like, only that they had both appeared to be in one hell of a hurry.

Hutchinson jabbed his finger at the computer screen. "Two men involved in that murder, one in a car, the other on a green motorcycle. Two men involved in the attack on Charlie Reid, both escaping on green motorcycles. We can't connect them with Jacqui Reid's murder, except of course via this blackmailer, who we confirmed today does exist. I think that those two men are the ones we should be looking for. As from Monday next I want the whole team to concentrate our efforts in an all-out hunt for these two."

"We haven't got that much to go on," said Mulraney. "But why wait until next Monday? What's wrong with right now?"

"I want everyone's minds one hundred per cent on the job in hand," replied Hutchinson. "And there is the little matter of the annual do to be surmounted before then."

"Yeah," said Mulraney. "That reminds me, please arrange for me to be on duty that night – I don't want Caroline causing a scene, especially with all the bigwigs there."

"Consider it done," said Hutchinson. "Though I reckon you'll be missing out on a good night."

The Policeman's Ball

Pamela Hutchinson struggled manfully with the stud fastening the highly starched white shirt of her husband's evening dress.

"Keep still, darling! You really will have to get a bigger collar size for next year – your neck seems to swell annually!"

"Nonsense!" replied Hutchinson, planting a kiss on his wife's forehead in a sudden moment of tenderness. He looked down on her scarcely lined features, reflecting that she had hardly changed since he had married her twenty-six long years ago. Pamela had certainly retained her vivacious red hair and attractive green eyes; her figure had filled out a little and she could hardly be described as slim but her wholesome womanly curves attracted many an envious male glance, to the secret delight of her husband.

He never felt the slightest pang of jealousy since Pamela adored her husband and was as much in love with him now as when they had first met. He had been a good-looking ambitious young constable and she the daughter of a chief superintendent. They had fallen madly in love and married despite the fierce disapproval of her parents. Hutchinson was a born detective but his promotion was slow in arriving due to internal pressure exerted by Pamela's father. She bore him two children, a daughter, now a practising solicitor, and a son safely ensconced at university hoping to forge a career as a scientist.

Pamela was now an experienced veteran in the art of being a wife to a highly successful detective. Throughout their years of marriage she had stoically borne the long periods of virtual separation, the call-outs at night, the interruption and sometimes complete cancellations of holidays. She understood fully the vagaries of her husband's job, and, unlike many police wives, never complained.

On the few occasions they did manage an evening out together, she endeavoured to make sure that they both enjoyed themselves. Such an evening was this, the annual get-together of the city force, held in the large ballroom of a city centre hotel. Commonly known as 'The Policeman's Ball', it was an event of some significance in the local social calendar and was host to many local bigwigs including the mayor and mayoress. With a bar extension until two in the morning, it was an occasion for the policemen to let their hair down and in this aim they did not disappoint. Every year there was an incident, usually brought on by an excess of alcohol, and this year was to prove no exception. Dire warnings of the consequences to be expected by any member of the force misbehaving himself had been issued by Chief Superintendent Maudsley and had filtered down through the ranks. Past events at occasions of this nature had been seized upon eagerly by the local press, who were well aware that scandal in the police force made good reading.

Pamela, having at last succeeded with her husband's collar, found time to indulge herself with a last-minute check of her own appearance in the long mirror of the bedroom wardrobe.

"Come on, Pam," said Hutchinson, "it's high time we were on our way. I don't want to give Maudsley anything more to moan about – I've been in enough trouble lately as it is."

"You're quite sure that Caroline Mulraney isn't coming?" queried Pam.

"Well, seeing as Brian is on duty, I can't see her coming without him. I mean, she has no friends whatsoever in the force among the wives, which is hardly surprising."

"You really are a little hard on her," said Pam, who scarcely had a bad word to say about anybody.

Thirty minutes later they entered the spacious ballroom of the hotel hosting the event. As at the commencement of all such occasions, small groups of people gathered somewhat self-consciously around the bar. The obvious hangers-on, or "arse lickers" as Brian Mulraney crudely called them, were already toadying to the senior ranks.

Peter Hutchinson ignored such groups and steered Pamela towards a table occupied by Jackie Harper and her friend, fellow WPC Audrey Benning, and Constables Farringdon and Singh.

"Right, lads and lasses," said a smiling Hutchinson as he warmly greeted the group, "what are we all drinking then?"

Ray Farringdon leapt to his feet and endeavoured to pull out a chair for Pamela to sit on. True to his clumsy image he slipped on the polished floor and clutched at the table to prevent his fall. Unfortunately for him, he succeeded only in tipping over the entire table and its contents, several of the glasses breaking as they hit the floor. The group roared with laughter as poor Farringdon rose to his feet, blushing furiously while he stammered out his apologies. The table was soon righted and the glass fragments swept up by the bar staff. Pamela Hutchinson consoled the unhappy Farringdon, who was secretly flattered by her attentions. He had long had a crush on his boss's wife but regarded her as akin to a goddess from afar.

Hutchinson soon returned with a tray of drinks and steadfastly refused to allow the constables from returning the compliment, insisting that any further rounds were on him. Fortified by the drinks, the young constables soon relaxed and engaged in animated conversation with their popular boss and his friendly attractive wife.

At the other end of the bar, Chief Superintendent Maudsley paused in a long tedious conversation with the lord mayor and frowned when he observed Hutchinson's group. He nudged his wife Fiona, whispering in her ear, "Look at that Hutchinson and his wife, consorting with the lower ranks again. The man has no style whatsoever yet he expects promotion."

A brief announcement that dinner was about to be served momentarily stilled the animated conversation as drinks were hastily consumed and the main body of people converged on the swing doors to gain access to the dining room.

They were all soon tucking into a meal of consummate perfection, washed down by many bottles of house red and white wine.

At the end of the dinner came what was officially regarded as the high spot of the evening, speeches from the lord mayor, the chairman of the local business group and, finally, the chief constable. To the lower ranks this represented the nadir of the evening, which had to be stoically endured before the dancing commenced.

After the lord mayor's speech the imposing figure of Frederick Coombs rose to his feet to deliver his speech in his temporary role as chairman of the local business group. He had had to alter his intended speech at the very last minute as the arrest of Malone had put him in a slightly embarrassing position. His original speech had contained an intended sideswipe at the police for their apparent failure to apprehend the prostitute killer. His hastily rearranged speech contained much praise for the local force but was of undue length and quite boring to the majority of his captive audience. The speeches ended with a surprisingly humorous oration delivered by the chief constable.

The speeches over, the gathering engulfed the ballroom once more and took to the floor enthusiastically to the sounds of a well-known local group. Jackie Harper was really enjoying herself, unhampered by the presence of Mulraney, a fact not unnoticed by a few young policeman, who, emboldened by a few drinks, pursued her remorselessly for dances. Laughing and thoroughly enjoying the evening, Jackie obliged them all.

Taking advantage of a 'ladies' excuse me', Pam Hutchinson rescued her husband from the clutches of a large-bosomed lady of ample proportions who in fact was the lady mayoress.

"Alone at last," gasped Hutchinson in his wife's ear. "Thank God you rescued me from that overbearing woman. She happened to be perspiring profusely and reeked to high heaven!"

"Peter!" said his wife in mock horror. "Do mind what you are saying about the lady mayoress."

Laughing, Hutchinson spun his wife around in time with a lively tune and glanced towards the swing doors.

"Oh no!" he groaned, halting his step in mid-stride and causing Pam to crash into him. "Don't look now but guess who has come through the door."

Pam's attention was caught by the sight of a wild-eyed Caroline Mulraney, who, though suitably dressed for the occasion in a low-cut evening dress, presented a bizarre figure as she clutched drunkenly at the door, her eyes sweeping across the floor.

Pam, quickly assessing the situation, squeezed her husband's arm, whispering to him, "Don't worry, I'll have a quick word with her and see if I can persuade her to leave before she causes any trouble."

She hurried across the floor to confront Caroline, who had staggered a few hesitant steps into the ballroom and was still glancing left and right at the dancers and those at nearby tables. Jackie Harper was at one of them, engaged in conversation with two young constables, glad of a break from the non-stop dancing but beginning to tire of the constant attention of the young men who were intent on chatting her up.

Before Pam could reach her, Caroline espied the object motivating her startling entry and her eyes lit up as she confronted a surprised Jackie.

"Ah, there you are, you blonde whore!" she screeched in a raucous voice. "True to form, throwing yourself at all the men. Tired of my Brian, are you? Or are you looking around for another marriage to break up! I hate you, you tart!"

With that she snatched a three-quarters full pint glass from the grasp of a startled constable and threw the contents in Jackie's face.

Jackie gasped with shock at the cold beer streaming down her face, rubbed her eyes and stared in amazement at Caroline. This was the first time she had encountered her face-to-face and she was dismayed by what she saw. Caroline, encouraged by her initial attack, smashed the beer glass on the side of the table and advanced menacingly towards Jackie, waving the glass from side to side.

"Come on, bitch, let's see how your face will look after a few strokes of this!"

She lunged suddenly at Jackie, who nimbly sidestepped her, clutched her wrist and expertly twisted her arm, causing Caroline to drop the glass on the floor as she gasped with pain.

"Let me go, you bitch!" she cried.

Jackie forced Caroline's arm behind her back and forced her to walk, protesting, out of the ballroom with three of the young constables in close attendance followed by Pam Hutchinson, who, in common with those who had witnessed it, was amazed by the young policewoman's cool reaction to a dangerous situation.

The incident had not gone unnoticed by Chief Superintendant Maudsley, who was extremely angry about an occurrence which threatened to spoil a delightful evening. He strode across the floor and angrily confronted Hutchinson, seizing him by the arm and demanding his attention.

"Really, Hutchinson, this is too bad. I hold you totally responsible for that incident. You obviously have no control over your staff. You should never have allowed the situation to reach this stage. You should have nipped it in the bud when you first heard about it. I want to see you in my office first thing Monday morning and I would advise you to warn both Detective Sergeant Mulraney and WPC Harper that I will be taking steps to arrange their *separate* transfer to another division."

Before Hutchinson could reply to this tirade, the chief constable turned on his heel and strode angrily away. Hutchinson, looking somewhat shaken, rejoined Pam who had returned through the swing doors after seeing Caroline safely placed in a police car to be returned home.

"Will she be charged?" she asked her husband.

"She bloody well ought to be," said Hutchinson. "But I'll get hold of Brian before I take any positive action. In the meantime, darling, are you up to playing nursemaid to her?"

A disappointed Mulraney joined Hutchinson and Pam at his home. The police doctor had been called out and he had given Caroline a mild tranquilliser which had effectively put her to sleep. He had advised against giving her a strong sedative due to the large amount of alcohol she had obviously consumed. Mulraney was more concerned for Jackie than his wife but was reassured when she told him jokingly that the incident would cost him a new dress.

Hutchinson decided to keep quiet his encounter with the chief constable until Monday morning, reasoning that Mulraney and Jackie had enough to worry about already.

Later that night he did confide his fears to Pam, who reassured him by suggesting that perhaps the chief constable had been hasty in his judgement and would reassess his decision in the cool light of day, reasoning that the two officers were indispensable to the solving of the current crimes.

'Good point,' mused Hutchinson. 'I'll bring that up on Monday.' He sighed contentedly as Pam snuggled up alongside him.

It certainly had been an eventful policeman's ball.

A Pleasant Surprise for Luke

There would be no prizes for guessing the main topic of conversation in the offices of the Birmingham and Nottingham Assurance Company following Malone's arrest. The sudden loss of the district manager had thrown the office routine into temporary chaos, causing the regular 'paying-in' day to be hastily put forward to Friday whilst a frantic search for a stand-in manager ensued.

On Friday all the agents were in the office at nine sharp, an unusual event in itself. They all crowded round the main reception desk in earnest conversation with the three female clerks, Jane Milford, Patsy Bowers and Marilyn Watkins. Area manager Frederick Coombs had been away in Birmingham directly after his attendance at Malone's court appearance, having been summoned to head office to explain the extraordinary events leading up to the arrest of his manager. He had telephoned Edith Pilkington late the previous evening with a full list of instructions to followed in his absence. Edith, proud of her extra responsibility, was enthroned at the desk of the area manager, and was soon busily engaged in dealing with a series of non-stop telephone calls from curious policyholders.

One floor below, the industrious Janet Compton was equally busy handling the calls from Malone's extension. On the ground floor Malone's arrest and retention in police custody was discussed with fevered interest. Mark Daley unwittingly became the main focus of attention when he casually remarked that he had been interviewed by detectives on Monday afternoon. He became embarrassed by all the attention but was secretly pleased when Jane insisted that he sit beside her. He recounted Malone's clumsy attempt at persuading him to back up his story and provide him with an alibi, which had at first confused him to such an extent that he had reluctantly agreed to go along with it, though he was far from happy. On his return home his mother had informed him that two police officers had called earlier to interview him and were returning within the hour. Mark, though fearful of the repercussions, decided to refute Malone's story and to tell the truth.

"Ooh, I'm sure you did the right thing," said Jane. "He's just a dirty old man. He was always brushing past me in the office and looking down my blouse. He tried it on with all the girls, except old Eunice of course! The very fact that he tried to persuade you to lie for him proves he must have done it."

"Now we don't know that for sure, Jane," said Marilyn. "We all know how he treats women but I really don't think he would go so far as to commit murder."

"Oh, I don't know about that," said a grinning Luke. "I reckon we are all capable of murder – there's many a time when I have felt like putting the old bastard away! Anyway, look on the bright side, we may never see the evil old git again in this office. I mean, even if he gets off I can't see the company keeping him on. Bad for the image, you know!"

"Yeah, that's a point," said Matthew. "Hey fellas, do you realise we haven't got a manager any more? Old Coombs is away in Birmingham so who is taking the accounts?"

"You had better ask Mrs Pilkington about that," said Marilyn. "She is in overall charge at the moment, even if it's only temporary."

During these conversations the occasional policyholder entered the office to pay premiums or to submit a query. One of these required managerial expertise, so Jane contacted Eunice Pilkington via the intercom. Whilst answering the query, Eunice detected the hum of excited conversation in the background. Mindful of the importance of office discipline, she decided to investigate further. Putting the telephone on hold, she descended the two flights of stairs to the main office.

On opening the door she was horrified to find the agents either sitting or leaning on the reception desk. Mark Daley occupied Jane's chair and she was perched on his lap. Teacups, both full and empty, were all over the office. Two members of the public were waiting patiently to be attended to. Everybody seemed to be talking at once and the subject was certainly not insurance. Eunice strode angrily into the office, picked up a tea tray and banged it down on the nearest desk. This had the desired effect for the chattering ceased abruptly and they all stared at Eunice.

"Now that I have your attention, would all the district agents kindly assemble in Mr Coombs's office? I have an announcement to make. As for you ladies, will you all get back to work immediately! This is the second time within a week that I have had to reprimand you. It's simply not good enough, especially so in the present circumstances. From now and until further notice, you will all be required to take your lunch breaks in the office – no desk must be unattended. You will arrange for one of your number to order and convey refreshments for the rest on a daily basis. Now, gentlemen, be so kind as to follow me."

Somewhat chastened, the agents picked up their briefcases and followed Eunice upstairs, standing in a semicircle in the area manager's office. Eunice, seated at her former lover's desk, felt an immense feeling of power and satisfaction. She looked around the assembled agents and felt akin to a general addressing his troops prior to battle.

"Gentlemen, it does not need me to remind you that we have a crisis on our hands, and that in such times we all have to pull together. I would remind you all not to discuss the unfortunate Mr Malone. The publicity associated with this case does the image of the company no good at all. Mr Coombs has instructed me to inform you that until a replacement manager is appointed Mr George Allis, the company auditor, will be your temporary manager."

"Oh no," groaned Luke. "The bloody Ferret! Talk about out of the frying pan into the fire!"

"Bring back old Mooney," said Matthew.

"Gentlemen, do you mind?" said Eunice, frowning at the interruption. "As I said, Mr Allis will be your new manager for the time being and you will present your accounts to him in exactly the same order you did for Mr Malone. Now, as time is pressing, I suggest we make a start. Mr Tomey, will you kindly proceed to Mr Malone's office where Mr Allis awaits you? Thank you for your attention, gentlemen."

Luke retrieved his briefcase and followed a grinning Matthew out of the office.

Matthew turned to his old friend. "Lucky old you! Mind the Ferret doesn't bite!"

Luke gave a muttered greeting to George Allis who was seated in Malone's chair. The company auditor was the very antithesis of Malone. His angular, hawk-like features were dominated by a beak-like nose. A loose flap of skin below his chin resembled the crop of a chicken. But his strange appearance belied a sharp computer brain and an aptitude for figures which made the use of a calculator superfluous.

He peered at Luke through the thick lenses on his 'John Lennon' spectacles.

"Sit yourself down, Tomey. Though Mr Malone has already arranged an audit for you, I propose to bring the date forward due to the present circumstances, so I would like to accompany you on your debit tomorrow morning."

Luke groaned. 'That's all I need!' he thought. He still had to see Bo to make arrangements for the drug deliveries and now he was saddled with the Ferret. Was there no justice in this lousy world?

He spent another uncomfortable hour in the company of Allis, who scoured his collecting book, his beady little eyes devouring the pages and instantly spotting the slightest

168

discrepancy. Soon Luke's book was filled with entries in green ink denoting queries and possible discrepancies to be checked out on the forthcoming audit.

The following morning he was conveyed to his debit round in the modest Skoda belonging to George Allis. The interior of the car was a true reflection of his personality. Adhered to the dashboard was a large notice which proclaimed *Passengers are expected to refrain from smoking whilst in this vehicle.* The inside of the car was devoid of any creature comforts and the seats were covered with old blankets to protect the upholstery. Luke bemoaned the fact that he had not offered Allis the use of his own car.

The morning round covered streets in the Forest Fields area and the close proximity of the Hyson Green flats worried Luke, fearful lest they bumped into Bo.

George Allis was very meticulous and painstaking in his work and each of the policyholders' books was compared to Luke's collecting book entries. In several cases the arrears of premiums exceeded the company's limits but, surprisingly, Allis did not terminate the policies, tactfully pointing out ways to reduce the arrears. His conversations with the policyholders were conducted in a very friendly manner. Much to Luke's surprise. he displayed his considerable knowledge on the subjects of gardening and cooking, impressing both husbands and wives alike with his enthusiasm. Once he had gained their confidence, he very adroitly turned the conversation towards insurance and converted his slick sales patter into new business. As he collected ten new policies, Luke concluded there was more to the dry old Ferret than he had assumed.

As lunchtime approached, Luke tactfully broached the subject of food by bringing to Allis's attention the proximity of a quaint old public house. Expecting an instant refusal, he was surprised when Allis agreed, adding that he knew the establishment very well indeed.

They were soon seated on a red leather bench seat and enjoying some excellent roast beef sandwiches, washed down with a pint – a half pint for Allis – of excellent local ale. Suitably refreshed, Allis began to relax and recount to Luke his intimate knowledge of the area and of this particular public house. It transpired that he had commenced his company career some twenty years previously in this very area. Luke was beginning to enjoy the company of The Ferret and volunteered buying a second round of drinks. Whilst waiting to be served at the bar he became aware of the entry of an attractive, buxom woman in her early forties who greeted him with the hint of a Scots accent.

"Hello hin, it's Luke isn't it? I haven't seen you in here before."

Luke turned towards the woman, instantly recognising her as Agnes McPherson, the mother of Angie.

"Hello Mrs McPherson, nice to see you. Actually I'm due to call on you next week. Don't the months fly by? Can I get you something to drink?"

"Now that's what I call a gentleman. Yes, Luke, I'll have a brandy and Babycham. Are you on your own? If not I'll join you; that's if you don't mind an old biddy like me for company."

"Well, actually I'm sorry, I'm not alone. Unfortunately my manager is with me."

"Not that old Malone surely. I thought he was locked up."

"Oh no, not him, this bloke is just temporary – he is really the company auditor, by the name of George Allis."

"Did you say George Allis?"

"Yeah, that's him over there," said Luke pointing to Allis.

Luke ordered the drinks and was startled by a delighted whoop from Agnes, whose eyes lit up when she espied Allis.

Allis peered at her through his thick lenses, a puzzled frown on his face. Agnes minced across the floor of the lounge bar in her high heels and tight skirt and reached for Allis, embraced him and planted a firm kiss on his forehead.

"Well, if it isn't old Georgie boy! How are you after all these years? I'd like to say you haven't aged a bit, but you have!" laughed Agnes.

Allis was a picture. Face flushed with embarrassment, he desperately tried to compose himself but he remembered his manners and pulled out a chair for Agnes.

"Agnes, how nice to see after all this time. Please sit down."

Luke arrived with the drinks, amazed at this startling reunion. "So you two know each other then?"

"Oh yes, me and Georgie go back a long way. Don't we, petal?"

She tweaked the ear of Allis, who blushed furiously.

"We first met when I came down here from Glasgow over twenty years ago. I was just starting out on the game then. He was a smart young fellow in them days, good at his job, but he liked his bit of totty now and again, didn't you, George?"

Luke could hardly suppress the urge to burst out laughing. The old Ferret was certainly full of surprises! The mere thought of the lifeless old dodderer cavorting in bed with the buxom Agnes was indeed one to savour; if nothing else it provided a marvellous story to amuse the lads with next week.

Agnes chattered away non-stop to Allis, who warmed to her company, and insisted on buying another round of drinks. Luke looked on in fascination as Agnes recounted past times and revealed startling facts about her experiences on the street. A bemused Allis bought yet another round of drinks while Agnes continued her endless reminiscing.

They finally left the pub at 3.30 p.m., all a little the worse for wear. Agnes insisted that they accompany her back to her house for tea, an offer they daren't refuse. As they neared Noel Street, their ears were assailed by the *nee-naw* of police sirens and they watched four police cars pass in quick succession, followed by the flashing blue lights of an emergency ambulance.

An Unpleasant Surprise for Bo

The minority of the inhabitants of the vast Hyson Green Flats Complex fortunate enough to have a job and wealthy enough to own a car were entitled to use one of a warren of garages situated in the shadow of the tower blocks. But those who availed themselves of this facility invariably had their car stolen, not surprising due to the fact that few of the garages had even their door intact. The garages had been practically gutted by vandals and were dark, damp, rubbish-strewn hell-holes. Lewd graffiti covered the walls and discarded needles from drug addicts littered the floors, together with empty glue canisters abandoned by young glue sniffers who held nightly sessions amid the rotting garbage. The garages were put to use by the rougher prostitutes, none too choosy where they took their clients. The dark recesses provided a haven where muggers could lure their unsuspecting victims. Unfortunately they were also used by local children, who played quite happily amid the filth and squalor despite warnings from their parents.

Among the lines of doorless garages, one stood out from the rest like a beacon. It was fronted by bright silver aluminium doors and was immune from vandals. Woe betide any foolish youth attempting to enter this particular garage, which was the personal property of one Bo Dangles Dawson. Outside his criminal activities Bo liked to tinker around in the engines of old cars. His present passion was for American cars from the Fifties and Sixties. He bought such models, improved them and sold them when he tired of them. The present occupant of Bo's garage was a massive white

Studebaker, vintage 1958, which he was lovingly restoring to its original former glory.

Bo loved Sunday mornings, as this was the particular time of the week he devoted to his hobby. He did not seek any sort of company at this time, happy to be up to his elbows in grease in the entrails of one of his old cars. This particular Sunday morning was no exception and Bo, attired in blue overalls, lay on his back beneath the Studebaker. He was endeavouring to remove one of the elongated headlights with the aid of a long screwdriver. It was very quiet in the complex and Bo was alone save for a small group of children playing quietly in one of the garages near Noel Street.

Suddenly the stillness of the early Sunday morning was ripped asunder by the sharp ripping roar of a high-powered motorcycle, which entered the complex at high speed and halted in a cloud of dust outside Bo's garage.

The motorbike was a green Kawasaki 750cc whose rider sat astride the machine, arms folded, staring at the garage. Bo could not fail to hear the bike and, though he sensed it had pulled up outside his garage, he ignored it and carried on with his work beneath the car.

"Okay, Rasta, what's your problem?" he asked of the rider, whose identity he seemed to know.

Silence greeted his remark.

Bo, now somewhat puzzled, hauled himself up from under the car and spoke again to the rider. "You fucking deaf or something?"

The rider remained motionless and did not reply.

Becoming a little irritated, Bo rose to his feet and, clutching a long screwdriver in his right hand, he approached the rider. He stopped directly in front of him, leant forward and peered into the rider's visor.

"Hey, you're not Rasta! Who the fucking hell are you?"

Suddenly the rider straightened his fingers inside leather gauntlets and thrust his right hand at Bo's throat in a chopping motion. The unexpected blow surprised Bo and caused him to gasp and stagger backwards. In one swift motion, the rider dismounted and kicked Bo viciously between the legs, following this up with a blow to the head. This sudden attack completely felled Bo who crumpled to the ground, releasing his hold on the screwdriver as he did so. The motorcyclist snatched up the screwdriver and sat astride Bo, pinning his arms with his knees. Dazed, and with all the breath knocked out of him, Bo screwed up his eyes in an effort to see who his attacker was.

"Who are you?" he gasped.

The motorcyclist grasped the screwdriver with both hands and, raising them above his head, he brought the screwdriver down with crushing force on Bo's chest. Bo's strangled scream was stifled when the stranger delivered a similar blow with even greater force. The force of this blow was such that the handle was only some two inches from Bo's chest after entry. The rider pulled out the screwdriver and tossed it to one side. He raised his visor and leant towards Bo

"How do you like that, you bastard?"

He thrust his face right up to Bo's.

"Remember me now, do you? I always said I'd get you in the end."

Bo was now making a horrible gurgling sound, blood frothing from his lips as his life slowly ebbed away. His eyes dimmed as he belatedly recognised the stranger. He tried to speak but all he could manage was a mumbled, "Oh yuh," as a fresh surge of blood filled his throat.

The rider applied both of his hands around Bo's throat, about to administer the *coup de grâce* but stopped on hearing the cries of children.

The small group of children playing near the entrance of the garages had halted their game when they heard the motorbike and had witnessed the attack on Bo, gazing in horrified fascination, not daring to move. After a while they cautiously approached the scene of the struggle but stopped in fright when the rider looked at them. He swiftly pushed down his visor, mounted his machine and roared away from the garages into a deserted Noel Street.

The children rushed towards the stricken figure of Bo and gathered curiously around him. Though frightened, they stared at him with horrified awe, quite unable to speak as they looked down on Bo whose glazed eyes stared fixedly upwards, the blood frothing from his mouth and trickling slowly down his throat.

The largest of the group of children, a thin red-haired boy, tentatively prodded Bo with his foot and said knowledgeably, "Reckon 'e's dead, or at least not far from it."

A smaller black child peered at Bo and pointed. "Bloody 'ell, that's Bo Dawson! We'd better get 'elp quick."

The children ran out of the garages shouting and screaming, glad to be away from the horrific scene. They ran up Noel Street and nearly bowled over a patrolling policeman, who with outstretched arms stopped the leading pair. The excited children gabbled their story all together and it took the startled policeman some minutes before he could make sense of their garbled version of events. He immediately radioed for an ambulance and alerted his station.

The arrival of the ambulance to the scene was pre-empted by four police cars from Radford Road. Hutchinson and Mulraney were amongst the group of policemen crowded round Bo. Two paramedics alighted from the ambulance and pushed their way through the policemen to reach Bo. The frothy blood from Bo's mouth was now a mere trickle. The first paramedic wiped the blood away and quickly checked Bo for signs of life. The second paramedic sought the emergency resuscitation equipment from the interior of the ambulance and was about to assemble it when his colleague shook his head and waved him away.

To an enquiry from one of the policeman the paramedic replied, "I'm afraid he's gone. There's no point in pumping his lungs – they are badly punctured, judging by the frothy blood. I'm afraid he wouldn't have stood a chance even if we had got to him earlier."

A screen had been hastily erected around Bo's body and the police taped off the entrance to the garages to keep away any onlookers. The blood-stained long-bladed screwdriver was quickly found, placed in a cellophane bag and tagged as the murder weapon. The position of the body was marked out in chalk before the corpse was removed and taken away for the post-mortem.

Hutchinson was anxious that the police should comb the area thoroughly for clues whilst at the same time he was anxious to clear the scene as soon as possible since he feared that this particular incident could fuel the simmering discontent of the local populace.

Two policewomen had rounded up the group of children who were the only witnesses to the horrific crime. After first contacting their parents, most of whom were found with some difficulty, the children were conveyed via transit van to the police station.

Once ensconced in the safe confines of the police station, Hutchinson arranged for the children to be royally entertained in the police canteen, plied with glasses of Coke and fed sticky buns. Two policewomen, Jackie Harper and Lisa Harris, recently relieved of her onerous vigil at the Queen's Medical Centre, were assigned the delicate task of extracting clear and concise information from the children. The interviewing was to be conducted in the relaxed atmosphere of the canteen rather than the close confines of the normal interview rooms, which might make the children nervous.

The two policewomen split the children into small groups and began their task using their communicative skills. They found the children either too excited or too quiet but with patience they elicited a broad outline of what exactly what occurred. The one fact on which all the child witnesses concurred was that the crime had been committed by a helmeted rider clad in black leathers riding a green Kawasaki motorbike. Two of the young boys, both motorbike fans, were quite specific on the make of the motorcycle. However, closely questioned for a description of the rider, the children's replies were very vague.

The two policewomen relayed their findings to Hutchinson who decided that he would question the children further on the vital question of the rider's description. He arranged all the children in a semicircle around him and put them at their ease by giving them each a chocolate bar. Having once gained their attention, he began to ask them some very basic observation questions.

"Now children, I want you to try and remember a few things about the motorcycle rider. For instance, how many of you can remember how tall he was?"

The replies he elicited from the children varied wildly from four foot six to six foot but the majority did agree that he was of medium height and of slim build.

Hutchinson scanned the faces of the children before he posed what he considered to be a crucial question.

"I want you all to think back to the time the rider had the other fellow on the ground. You all rushed up and got as close as you dared and there was a split second when he turned and looked right at you. Now" – Hutchinson paused dramatically – "can any of you tell me if he was a white man or a black man?"

There was complete silence as the children screwed up their faces in their efforts at recollection, then, rather hesitantly, a small black boy piped up, "'E was definitely a honky. Same as you." He pointed at Hutchinson.

"You're absolutely sure?"

"Yeah," said the boy.

The other children weren't even sure that they had seen the rider's face but this one small boy remained adamant.

Later Hutchinson relayed his findings to Mulraney.

"Well, there's your answer, Brian. I know it hangs on the word of one small boy, but it confirms that the killer is white."

Mulraney's creased features broke into a grin.

"Sorry boss, but I can't agree with you. I still reckon we should pull in our friend Alexander. I reckon drugs are behind this whole business. I know children can be very unreliable witnesses, but surely there should be corroboration of this lad's story?"

"Well, while I disagree with your theory, I do agree with you that we should haul Alexander in. I'll get on to Ted Jenkins at Manchester and see if they can round him up. In the meantime I should warn you that old Maudsley is on the warpath after the disturbance at the do. There is talk of transfers in the air and I'm due for a Monday morning meeting with him in his office. But don't worry too much, Brian. I'll try my level best to talk him out of it. After all, I can't lose my two best officers at such a crucial time in the investigation," said Hutchinson.

"I'm sorry about all this, boss," said Mulraney. "It may even get worse I'm afraid. I've decided to leave Caroline for good. We just can't go on like this."

"Have you told her yet?" asked Hutchinson.

"No," replied Mulraney. "But I'm going to do it today, I've made my mind up. So stand by for further fireworks!"

"Do you want Pam and me to come round for some moral support?" asked Hutchinson.

"No," replied Mulraney. "This is one thing I have got to do on my own."

The Aftermath

The after-effect of Bo's murder could be likened to a slow-burning fuse as word spread like wildfire amongst the ethnic community of Hyson Green. There was a feeling of simmering unease prevalent not previously experienced in the area since the riot in 1981. There was a feeling of anger at what was considered to have been the deliberate execution of a notorious local criminal. Rumours abounded as to who exactly was responsible but, apart from the obvious fear of a war between rival drug barons, the main focus of the community's anger was the police.

The first incident occurred at an off-licence in Hyson Green when a group of youths began an argument with the Asian shopkeeper. There was a scuffle during which the Asian was knocked to the ground and kicked about the head and body. The youths then systematically looted the shop. His terrified wife locked herself in a back room and telephoned the police.

Radford Road despatched a van containing six constables suitably equipped with batons and riot shields. The van was stoned even before it reached its destination. A crowd had already gathered outside the off-licence and an ugly situation was developing. Hutchinson, directing operations from Radford Road, quickly despatched further vans of riot police to the area, concentrating mainly on the flats complex. This move effectively sealed off the area, preventing further reinforcements from joining the confrontation outside the off-licence. The police had learnt from their 1981 experience and Hutchinson was anxious to quell any potential bushfire situation before it could spread further and spark off a riot. The gloves were off and the no-nonsense riot police waded into the off-licence mob with flying batons. There were quite a few casualties on both sides and many arrests.

Despite a considerable police presence in the flats area, the emergency ambulances transporting the night's casualties and the police vans containing those arrested at the scene were stoned as they passed the flats complex. Gangs of youths leaning over the walkways pelted the vehicles with anything they could lay their hands on, oblivious to the fact that their own friends or even relatives could be inside them. Their anger was directed at their common enemy, the police, whom they considered responsible for Bo's demise. The situation remained tense into the early hours of Monday morning and as dawn approached several of the bleary-eyed riot police were stood down.

Hutchinson had been up all night and, though pleased with the initial success of his operation, was well aware that the simmering situation could boil over again. News from Manchester of the detention of Rasta Alexander came through during the night and also confirmation that he would be driven to Nottingham early on Monday morning. Of more immediate concern to Hutchinson was his forthcoming confrontation with Chief Maudsley who had asked to be regularly apprised of the current situation in Hyson Green.

After a reviving cup of black coffee and a bacon sandwich, Hutchinson prepared himself for what he already knew was going to be a very busy day. He assembled his close-knit team and brought them up to date with the night's events before allotting them their various daily tasks. He assigned Mulraney to the task of questioning Rasta Alexander as soon as he arrived from Manchester. He sent Sergeant Mabbutt, together with Constables Singh and Farringdon, to the St Ann's area of the city with specific instructions to carry out discreet house-to-house enquiries. The two policewomen were despatched to Hyson Green on a similar mission, with WPC Lisa Harris assigned to interview Angie McPherson.

She drew a blank at Angie's flat, where apparently the distraught Angie had not been seen since Saturday night. Neighbours advised Lisa to try at her mother's house in Noel Street. As Lisa drove there in her police panda car she became aware of the tension on the streets. Although it was still relatively early small knots of youths were congregated on street corners; this was despite the still considerable presence of blue-helmeted riot police. Lisa was no stranger to violent confrontation, having survived two incidents in which she had been outnumbered whilst on vice patrol. In one such incident she had been assaulted by several youths, but received only superficial injuries. Though appearing outwardly calm, she recalled that at the time she had been terrified.

Ever since that incident, after which she had received special counselling, she had felt very nervous when patrolling alone. Fortunately such occasions were rare in the vice squad, as she was usually accompanied by at least one male colleague. She took comfort in the fact that help was close at hand in the form of the increased police presence on the streets and her radio, with which she could summon help in seconds.

She drew up outside Agnes's house and as she got out of the car she was disconcerted to see a number of black youths lounging on a wall directly opposite. As she walked towards Agnes's door they shouted obscene comments at her.

Lisa pointedly ignored the jibes of the youths and pressed Agnes's doorbell. The door was opened by a scowling Agnes, who greeted Lisa with undisguised hostility, recognising her as an officer who had frequent contact with Angie. With a flick of her head she reluctantly allowed the policewoman to enter.

"Now don't you go upsetting my daughter! She's got quite enough to put up with lately without you lot making it worse. She is ever so upset about Bo being stabbed. She actually loved the bastard! Can you credit that? He treated her like dirt, but she won't hear a word against him. You wait here and I'll see if she wants to see you. I had to give her a sleeping tablet to get her off last night, poor darling."

Lisa waited outside the door of the living room whilst Agnes shook the sleeping figure of Angie on the couch. Angie rubbed her eyes in protest at being aroused from her drug-induced sleep. As her consciousness returned, she burst into a fit of uncontrollable sobbing.

Agnes cradled her head.

"Come on, my darling. There, there," said Agnes while she stroked the hair of her unhappy daughter. She allowed Angie to cry out her grief for several moments then gently told her of the policewoman's presence.

"You have a visitor, my darling. It's that vice squad girl, Lisa something or other. You know, the one that pulled you in last time. She's not all that bad really. Anyway she wants a word with you. Perhaps you'd better, eh? Then we'll get rid of her, all right, my darling?"

In reply Angie released a fresh wave of sobbing, then, rubbing tearstained red eyes, she turned to her mother.

"Okay Mum, I suppose I'd better speak to the cow. Send her in."

Angie propped herself up between two cushions and glowered at the policewoman as she entered. Lisa sat down gingerly on the couch and smiled sympathetically at Angie.

"I'm very sorry to hear about Bo."

"Don't give me that, you cow – you couldn't give a monkey's really. In fact I bet you're bloody delighted to be rid of him! Anyway, why aren't you out with the rest of the pigs looking for the bastard that did for Bo?"

"Well, that's precisely why I am here, Angie. We want to catch this man and we will, with a little help from you. For instance who do you know who rides a green motorbike?"

Angie scratched her head before replying, "Yeah, well I reckon the only bloke I know who rides a green bike is that queer zombie Alexander, and I certainly wouldn't put it past him to have a go at Bo. He used to send his boys round to scare us off the streets. He didn't like Bo one bit – in fact he bloody hated his guts, and the feeling was mutual."

Before the policewoman could reply there was a sound of breaking glass from outside. Lisa rushed to the widow and saw that the youths from across the road had armed themselves with bricks and were systematically smashing in the windows of her police panda car. She radioed in immediately for assistance and made for the door.

"Don't be a bloody fool! Don't go out there!" said Angie. "You'll get your head kicked in."

Lisa opened the front door to find that the youths were attempting to overturn her car, pushing and pulling at it in uncontrolled fury.

"Stop that immediately or you'll be arrested!" said Lisa.

The youths howled with laughter and two of their number ceased their exertions and walked towards the policewoman.

They encircled Lisa and were joined by the rest of the group, numbering eight in all. The leading youth, sporting long Afro-style locks, crouched down and made a beckoning motion with his hands.

"Come on, little policewoman. How'd you like to feel a black man inside you?"

"In your dreams, sunshine," said Lisa as icy cold fear gripped her.

The youth made a sudden lunge at Lisa, who nimbly stepped to one side. The other youths rushed towards her as Lisa belatedly made for Agnes's front door. Her hand was actually on the door handle when she was seized roughly from behind in an armlock. Other hands clutched at her blouse and skirt as she fought desperately to free herself. The arm encircling her throat tightened and, as she gasped for air, her eyes bulged and she began to lapse into unconsciousness.

Suddenly the front door was opened and the tall figure of Angie stood proudly, eyes flashing, as she shouted at the youths.

"Stop! What the bloody hell do you think you're doing! Trying to prove yourselves men? You're bloody pathetic! Eight of you on one poor cow. Let her go right now!"

Before the youths could respond there came the sound of fast-approaching police cars.

"Fucking 'ell, the cops! Let's scarper!" said the youth with the Afro locks.

They dropped the now unconscious Lisa in an undignified heap and ran away in different directions from the scene. Angie, helped by Agnes, dragged Lisa inside and carried her to the couch. By the time the first policeman entered the living room, Lisa was slowly coming round.

"Here comes the cavalry, late as bloody usual," said Angie as the first policeman gaped in astonishment at her all too revealing dressing gown.

"Are you all right, duck?" the policeman asked Lisa, who smiled weakly.

"Yeah, not too bad, but I've got to thank this lady here for saving me from being raped."

Angie gasped in delight.

"Lady huh? That makes a change from some of the things you usually call me. I'll remind you about this next time you pull me over for soliciting. Remember you owe me one."

Soon the room was filled with policemen and Agnes provided all of them with mugs of steaming tea protesting, "All you bloody coppers will get me a bad name!"

Though she protested, Lisa was despatched to the city hospital for a check-up and by midday seven of the eight youths were arrested and charged with assault, though Angie declined to make a statement, saying, "I never saw a bloody thing!"

Hutchinson's Problems Mount

The expected early morning meeting with Chief Maudsley was postponed until the afternoon, giving the beleaguered Hutchinson a brief respite. The reason for the postponement was that the chief super had become alarmed by the intense media pressure over the prostitute murders, heightened by the brutal murder of Bo and the near-riots that had followed. He set up a hastily convened press conference at which he attempted to convey the positive police response to the situation and their successful arrest of a strong suspect for the prostitute murder. He praised his officers for their efficient handling of a potentially explosive situation following the latest murder.

Maudsley bristled with annoyance when *The Sun* representative put a contentious question to him.

"What is your reaction to the strong rumour that you have arrested the wrong man and that these murders are drug-related?"

"I do not react in any way to rumours," replied Maudsley testily.

Undaunted, *The Sun* reporter continued, "Furthermore I understand that your local police force is actually completely baffled both by the motive and the exact identity of the person responsible for these crimes. In view of this would it not be better for all concerned if you enlisted the help of a special investigative unit from outside the area?"

"Certainly not," snapped Maudsley. "I have every confidence in my officers and I have already outlined their success to date in my statement."

Then he added rashly, "In fact I would not be at all surprised if there were not more arrests in the next few days."

Pressed further on this point, he refused to elaborate but, bringing the meeting to an end, promised there would be another statement later in the week.

Whilst the press conference was taking place at Central Police Station, events had moved on apace at Radford Road. A much chastened Rasta Alexander had arrived under escort from Manchester in mid-morning and, without so much as a cup of tea, had been hastily installed in an interview room.

Mulraney's hurry to begin the interview was all in vain because Rasta insisted that a solicitor was present before he would allow any questions to be put. This infuriated the impatient Mulraney who paced up and down in annoyance. When the balding solicitor Arthur Sornsen arrived at Radford Road he insisted on a few minutes alone with his client before he would allow him to be questioned. Rasta was a frightened man. He had been horrified to hear of Bo's brutal murder but was more concerned that the anger of the locals would be directed at him and he feared for his life.

Mulraney grilled him remorselessly but, though at times nervous in his replies and prompted by his solicitor, Rasta had an unshakeable alibi for he had been in Manchester at the time of the murders. Furthermore his main associates had all given unshakeable alibis when questioned by the officers covering St Ann's. He denied ever owning any Kawasaki motorcycles and, though he seemed a little unsure and hesitant on this point, Mulraney could find no chink in his armour despite incessant probing. After an hour of questioning, Mulraney reluctantly admitted that he was free to go.

"I trust you won't be wasting any more of my client's valuable time, let alone mine," sneered Sornsen.

Mulraney smiled politely, inwardly fuming that once again he had been thwarted by this scrawny solicitor, with whom he had crossed swords on numerous occasions. Mulraney was certain that Alexander knew a lot more than he would admit about the motorcycles and felt that, if only he could get him on his own, he could force the truth out of him.

Hutchinson arrived for the afternoon meeting with his chief fully prepared to do everything in his power to prevent the transfer of his two officers. In the event the meeting proved to be an anticlimax. Using the well-known tactic that attack is the best form of defence, he launched into articulating his strong conviction that to lose these two officers at such a crucial stage in the investigation would be detrimental to the case's successful conclusion and would affect the morale of the rest of the team. The chief super listened patiently to Hutchinson's stout defence of his colleagues, pausing only to draw on the slim cheroot he smoked continuously in times of stress.

Hutchinson reflected that his chief was not his usual fiery self, though whether this was a good or bad thing remained to be seen. Halfway through his lengthy argument Mulraney was stopped by Maudsley with a wave of his hand.

"All right, Peter, there's no need to go on. You'll be pleased to know I have reconsidered my decision and will not be transferring either Mulraney or the Harper girl. I admire your loyalty to them and hope they are worth it. To tell you the truth, I have had a very stressful morning at the press briefing. Those damned reporters seem to know almost as much as we do – it's bloody uncanny. I've come to the conclusion that somebody is feeding them information and that means we've got a spy in the camp. I want you to have a quiet sniff around and let me know what you come up with. In the meantime keep me up to date as usual with the investigation. As for that incident the other night, try and keep a lid on it. God knows what the press would make of that!"

Brian Mulraney, still smarting from the outcome of his unsuccessful morning, slipped out of the police station to meet Jackie Harper at a prearranged rendezvous. Their frequent clandestine meetings took place at an old-fashioned backstreet pub not a stone's throw from Slab Square. The battered exterior of the premises belied the warm cosy atmosphere found inside an establishment well-used by the business fraternity and which was the favourite haunt of many a discreet couple.

Jackie, having arrived some thirty minutes early, had found herself a corner table. She was casually dressed for the occasion in baggy white sweater and black jeans, and her long blonde hair, released from the confines of its bun, hung loosely down her back. She studied the menu while she sipped her lager and received admiring glances from the businessmen seated at the bar. Her eyes lit up when Mulraney entered the bar, ordering himself a pint and two beef rolls before joining her at the corner table.

Jackie glanced up at her lover, noting that he looked rather drawn as if from lack of sleep, his darkened jowls indicating a hasty morning shave.

He planted a kiss on her forehead remarking, "Hello darling, you look good enough to eat!"

Jackie smiled. "You just stick to your beef rolls – talking of things to eat, where's mine?"

"Oh sorry, darling, I just didn't think." Mulraney rose to his feet. "What would you like?"

Jackie smilingly put a hand on his shoulder. "Sit down, lover boy, and eat your rolls. I'll have a quiche and I'll order it myself."

She rejoined him after ordering and didn't speak until he had wolfed down the two beef rolls.

"Wow, you look as if you needed them. Now I'm dying to know what happened with Caroline last night. Did you tell her? And when are you moving in with me for good?"

"Questions, questions," laughed Mulraney rolling up his eyes in mock horror. Then he frowned slightly as he recalled his confrontation with Caroline.

"Yeah, I did tell her in the end, though it was well into the evening when I got round to it. I got the ice-cold shoulder treatment for most of the day even though I served her breakfast cum lunch in bed. She was in one hell of a state after last night, as you can imagine. Anyway by the time I got my call-out to the murder scene, she hadn't uttered one word to me. It was a different story when I got back though. She really launched into me. All the familiar old stuff of course."

"I bet she said blonde whore a few times!" said Jackie.

"Oh that, and the fact that I was a baby snatcher and old enough to be your granddad. Anyway I let her rant and rave and get it all out of her system before I mentioned divorce."

"And then the balloon went up?" asked Jackie.

"And how! She hit the bloody roof as expected, then all of a sudden she calmed down and spoke very quietly but with a great deal of menace. She said she would never divorce me, that she'd ruin my career and make sure you would never attract another man."

"Well, that's good, isn't it? I mean, she's made all these threats before and nothing's come of it. I know she had a go at me on Saturday night but I can handle her. In any case I'm sure she won't try that again."

"I'm not so sure," said Mulraney. "She can be one vicious bitch when she sets her mind to it. Anyway she took a sleeping pill last night. In the morning I packed a few belongings, which I've left at the station in a locker, and told her that I wouldn't be coming back. She just stared at me with a really nasty look in her eyes but didn't say anything at all. I told her that I would arrange to have a financial allowance for her, which I was sure would rouse her to speak, but no, not a flicker – she just kept staring at me, so I turned on my heel and left her."

"Great!" exclaimed Jackie. "At long last I've got you all to myself. Come round to my place straight after work tonight and I'll have something really tasty all prepared for you."

Mulraney reached under the table and caressed her knee.

"I can think of something I'd rather have right now," he said with a grin.

"Not now, lover boy," said Jackie. "Unless you want to risk skiving off this afternoon? You know, we really must try and have our days off together."

"Easier said than done," said Mulraney. "But no, I daren't risk skiving. It wouldn't be fair to the rest of them. Talking of which, I really ought to be heading back."

"I'll walk with you as far as the square," said Jackie, draining the dregs from her glass.

Outside of the pub they walked up the narrow street, arms entwined and gazing at each other in the manner of all lovers, failing to notice the muffled figure of Caroline Mulraney waiting opposite in a shop doorway. She shuffled out into the narrow street and began to follow the couple, making sure she kept a distance of about twelve yards behind them. She paused as Mulraney halted at the taxi rank in the square, speaking briefly to the driver before kissing Jackie and getting into the taxi. Jackie made her way across the square and Caroline, blending well into the crowds, decreased the distance between them. Jackie made her way up King Street and joined the queue of people near the post office waiting for a bus to the park and ride site.

Caroline paused and turned blindly into a shop doorway to avoid being seen by Jackie who was now facing in her direction. The park and ride bus soon pulled up at the stop and the passengers began to board. Caroline peered round the corner of the shop doorway, choosing her moment with care. As soon as Jackie boarded the bus, she ran forward bumping into a scruffily-dressed man in her headlong dash to the bus. She didn't stop to apologise to him and he hawked a blob of spittle on to the pavement as he turned away in disgust.

There were two people in the queue behind Jackie and both had got on to the bus by the time Caroline reached the stop. In fact the bus was about to pull away when the breathless Caroline hauled herself on to the step.

"Cutting it fine, meduck," said the cheerful driver. "Ticket please."

Caroline gasped in dismay, realising that she should have purchased a ticket at the park and ride site as she had done on past occasions.

"Oh, sorry, I'm afraid I've lost it," she said to the driver.

She found a pound coin in her handbag and gave it to the driver. She kept her head down as she searched for a seat, then realised with some relief that Jackie must have boarded the upper deck. After a short ten minute journey the bus pulled into the Forest Recreation Ground and the passengers alighted and hurried off in search of their cars. Caroline remained in her seat until Jackie descended the stairs from the upper deck and set off across the tarmac along the lines of cars neatly drawn up in the car park.

Caroline was the last passenger to leave the bus, half smiling as the bus driver remarked, "Next time remember your ticket, missus, and you won't have to fork out twice!"

She hurried off in pursuit of Jackie who was setting a fair pace. Caroline began to wonder what she was going to do next. She had intended to set off on an act of revenge. She was determined to harm the object of her hatred but realised that she would have to have some plan of action. Physically she was no match for the fit young policewoman, so whatever she planned to do had to have at least the element of surprise.

She quickly stepped between two cars as Jackie opened the door of her maroon Fiat Uno. Caroline began to panic. She realised that she must do something quickly or her prey would soon be gone. She ran towards the car but stopped suddenly as Jackie got out and walked to the rear.

She had obviously forgotten something, and she opened the boot of the car, bent over as if in search of something. Caroline approached the rear of the car, her eyes searching for an object with which to hit Jackie. She snatched up a loose half brick in desperation and swung it in arc towards Jackie's head. Jackie half turned in a swift second of awareness as the brick crashed down on the side of her head. She cried out in pain and weakly put up a hand to ward off further blows. Caroline followed up the first blow with an even harder blow to Jackie's forehead. There was a flow of blood down her face as the young woman lost consciousness and slumped forward.

Caroline glanced in desperation left and right, suddenly fearful that her attack had been observed. She bent down, clasped Jackie's legs and bundled the unconscious policewoman unceremoniously into the boot. She quickly snapped shut the boot lid, took out the keys and got into the Fiat. She had never driven this particular model before but soon acquainted herself with the controls. She drove out of the car park still uncertain of her next move.

She drove automatically while her unsound mind devised a means of disposing of Jackie. She negotiated the busy roundabout on Mansfield Road and headed northwards, ignoring the filter light as she swung the Fiat left and accelerated up Hucknall Road. In a sidestreet two streets from the traffic lights there was a stationary police patrol car in which sat PCs Singh and Farringdon, enjoying their recently purchased takeaways and snatching an unofficial lunch-break. As the maroon Fiat roared past PC Singh said, "Bloody hell, that thing's moving! Come on."

His companion groaned as he tossed his half-eaten takeaway out of the window. "No peace for the wicked!"

The white police patrol car set off in pursuit of the speeding Fiat which was already fast disappearing into the distance.

The lights changed at the next junction on Hucknall Road but Caroline ignored them and continued straight across, causing a near collision as two drivers braked frantically, cursing as they did so. PC Singh switched on his blue flashing lights and warning siren as he slowed momentarily. The powerful engine of the police Escort narrowed the distance between the two speeding vehicles while PC Farringdon radioed into Radford Road.

"Am in pursuit of maroon Fiat Uno, registration number Monkey 189 Tango Tango Victor. This car is being driven at speeds in excess of ninety miles per hour and has driven through two sets of red traffic lights."

"Bloody joyriders I bet!" said the police controller as he keyed in the registration letters on the computer. He gasped when he saw the result. "That's got to be a mistake! According to this, the car belongs to our own WPC Harper."

He radioed back his findings to the patrol car. Both officers were shocked at the news. PC Singh peered forward as they closed on the Fiat.

"It certainly looks like a woman driving but I don't reckon it's Jackie."

Caroline had been aware of her pursuers for some time and was angry at her own recklessness which had drawn them to her. She suddenly swung the car violently left, causing a screech of tyres as she desperately tried to shake off her pursuers. Unfortunately for her the street she had chosen was one-way and the street ended in a cul-de-sac of houses. Caroline snorted in exasperation as she engaged in a hasty three point turn and drove back up the street, noting with dismay that she had not fooled her pursuers with her sudden move. The white Escort, blue lights flashing, was slewed across the entrance to the street effectively blocking any exit or entry.

Caroline banged her fists in frustration on the steering wheel and for a brief moment she considered making a dash from the car, but discarded the thought instantly as she realised the futility of it. She folded her arms in a despairing gesture and, head down, awaited her fate.

The two police officers approached the car very carefully, one on either side. As they neared the Fiat Farringdon cried out to his companion, "Christ, it's Mrs Mulraney!"

The officers visibly relaxed and strode more confidently towards the car in the realisation that its occupant was neither a criminal nor a joyrider. Farringdon smiled nervously as he tapped on the side window. Caroline, expressionless, wound down the window. Farringdon bent down, his eyes scanning the interior of the vehicle.

He saw nothing untoward and spoke to Caroline rather hesitantly, "Er, Mrs Mulraney, can I ask you first of all why you are driving WPC Harper's car, and why you did not stop the vehicle when you realised we were pursuing you?"

Caroline smiled coldly at the young constable. "Oh, I recognise you, it's young Farringdon, isn't it?"

Without waiting for a reply she continued, "You had better get my husband. I am not answering any questions until he arrives."

Farringdon, taken aback by Caroline's response and unsure as to what to do next, looked at his fellow officer for help. PC Singh was equally baffled by the situation but used his radio to request Mulraney's presence at the scene with some urgency. He walked around the vehicle but could detect nothing out of place. He spoke to Caroline through the open window.

"Mrs Mulraney, would you mind getting out of the vehicle?"

Caroline placed her hands on the steering wheel and glared at him.

"No, I will not. I'm not going to move or answer any questions until my husband is present."

Singh shrugged his shoulders in a despairing gesture to his colleague and answered his radio as a call came in requesting more details of the incident.

He was interrupted halfway through his reply by the sound of a muffled cry and a thumping noise emanating from the boot of the car.

Farringdon leaned into the car. "Mrs Mulraney, do you mind handing me the keys to the boot?"

Caroline stared fixedly ahead and completely ignored his request. Farringdon then reached into the car and removed the keys dangling from the ignition. Singh joined him at the rear of the car as he tried each key from the bunch in turn. He was rewarded with the third key and both policemen gasped in astonishment when the raised boot lid revealed a dazed, bedraggled-looking Jackie. The side of her head was caked with blood and she struggled to raise herself on one elbow. She looked up at her two rescuers with glazed eyes.

"Hello boys, am I glad to see you!"

She struggled to get out of the boot but Singh restrained her gently.

"Easy, Jackie. Don't try and move just yet. I'll radio for an ambulance and they'll sort you out. What the hell happened anyway?"

"I don't remember too much. I was getting into my car when I sensed somebody was behind me. I half turned round when I noticed a woman then everything went black."

The sound of approaching footsteps announced the arrival of a breathless Mulraney.

"Move that bloody patrol car!" he snapped at Farringdon. "What the bloody hell has been happening here?"

He rounded the car and gasped with alarm as he saw Jackie.

"Oh my God! Are you all right, darling?"

"All the better for seeing you," smiled Jackie weakly.

He cradled her in his arms oblivious of the startled looks of the two policemen. Caroline sat through all this, stony-faced but inwardly seething that her husband had completely ignored her presence.

Fifteen minutes later the ambulance arrived and Mulraney accompanied Jackie to the city hospital. Caroline was eventually persuaded to leave the Fiat and was then taken into custody and conveyed to Radford Road by the two young constables, who were given specific instructions to detain her but not to process any charges until Mulraney's return from the hospital. Jackie's skull was X-rayed and fortunately there was no trace of even a hairline fracture but she was to be kept in under observation overnight at least.

Mulraney returned to Radford Road to find a grim-looking Hutchinson waiting for him.

"My office, pronto," he said as Mulraney came into the operations room. Knowing looks were exchanged by the staff as the two officers left the room.

Hutchinson produced a half bottle of Teacher's from his desk and took a reviving swig from it. Without a word he handed it to Mulraney, who gratefully followed suit. Hutchinson motioned for him to sit down.

"Okay, Brian, I don't want to know anything from you except of course how Jackie is. While you were at the hospital I got a pretty fair idea as to what happened. I've decided to keep the lid on things for now. If the press get on to this they'll have a field day. I've briefed all the staff to keep shtum."

"What about Caroline – what have you done with her?"

"I'm coming to that. I got old Munro to take a look at her and he confirms what we all suspected – that she's mentally unstable and unfit to be detained. Anyway, surprisingly she has voluntarily agreed to be admitted to Mapperley Hospital for a few days at least, then we'll review our options."

"Thank God for that," said Mulraney. "Though I'm surprised she agreed so readily, at least it gives us time to think."

"Yeah, but we are not out of the woods yet," said Hutchinson. "Practically the whole station knows about this latest occurrence and I reckon our unknown press informant won't be able to resist this latest tasty offering."

"I wish I knew who the bastard was," said Mulraney. "Any ideas?"

"No," said Hutchinson. "But I have my suspicions and this latest bit of gossip might just be his undoing."

"Tell me more," said Mulraney.

Hutchinson laughed. "I can't say any more just yet, Brian, but hopefully all will be revealed soon. You still haven't told me the extent of Jackie's injuries."

"She'll live," said Mulraney. "The bash on the head fortunately didn't do any serious damage but she's being kept in for a day or so."

"Good," said Hutchinson. "Now, my old friend, I think you had better get yourself over to Mapperley to see Caroline. She wasn't exactly singing your praises the last time I saw her."

Mulraney grinned ruefully. "Yeah, I bet. Anyway thanks for keeping a lid on things, Pete."

The Raid

John Rawson opened the main door of the Briars Garden Centre for what he hoped would be another Saturday of brisk business. He had his doubts as he looked upwards at the grey scurrying clouds, a sure sign of unsettled weather to come. The weekend usually produced an influx of customers into the centre, resulting in brisk business but bad weather reduced the numbers. John, ever the optimist, braced himself for a busy day; his only regret was that once again he would miss the Saturday afternoon football match with his friends.

As a consolation he was able to attend the midweek matches, except that on these occasions he had to go alone as his friends in the insurance business were invariably working. On rare occasions he was accompanied by his fiancée Marilyn, but she wasn't at all keen on football.

His thoughts turned to Marilyn. Truth to tell, she was rarely out of his mind. They made a handsome couple: he, tall, good-looking, with piercing blue eyes and black, slicked down hair; she, equally tall with a slim figure, gorgeous brown eyes and bubbly personality. They were so content in each other's company, and for this John was truly thankful. So many times in the past he had got it all wrong in matters of the heart. His last disastrous affair with a married woman had caused him to leave his job with the insurance company.

John was extremely proficient at his present job. As a very small boy he had developed an interest in gardening when he grew cress on a wet sponge in the kitchen window. Whilst other boys of his age kicked footballs around, the young John helped his father on his allotment and soon began to cultivate a plot of his own. He had left school early and attended a horticultural college where he passed his exams with satisfactory results.

Much to his dissatisfaction, he was disappointed in his search for a suitable opening for his talents. Becoming bored with waiting and anxious to earn a living, he reluctantly took a clerical job in the offices of the Birmingham and Nottingham Assurance Company. It was here that he had developed his lasting friendship with Matthew and Luke, after which they became known as 'The Disciples'. But he didn't enjoy his working environment and soon embarked on the disastrous affair with a married woman, which had resulted in two broken hearts and the termination of his employment.

By one of those odd quirks of fate which characterise life, it was at this point that an opening cropped up for a nurseryman at the Briars. John seized the heaven-sent opportunity and threw himself enthusiastically into his new job, partly from relief after a boring job and partly to relieve the misery of a broken heart. His keenness and natural aptitude for the work ensured his rapid progress and after two promotions he had attained his present post as senior sales and administration manager, with special emphasis on retailing.

John normally looked forward to the hustle and bustle associated with the Saturday crowd and relished the challenge. This particular Saturday, however, proved an exception. For some strange reason which he couldn't fathom, he felt jaded and out of sorts with himself and he found it difficult to summon up his usual enthusiasm. He felt a curious sense of unease, as if something was about to happen over which he had no control. John threw himself into his work in an effort to throw off his lethargy. A steady stream of customers throughout the morning kept the staff on their toes without quite reaching the sales figures of the previous Saturday.

Just before midday John took a call from Cashguard Security informing him that their van would be calling at the centre at 5.30 p.m., this being closing time and the latest possible time for cash collection. Cashguard varied their collection times for security reasons and never confirmed their arrival time until the actual day of collection.

John found time for a hurried lunch of sandwiches and coffee taken in his office at one o'clock. His right-hand man Lee Harrison came in the office and handed him the lunchtime edition of *The Post*. He skimmed the front, whose main story was about the police questioning of the latest suspect held in connection with Bo's murder. This subject had intrigued the staff at the garden centre and had been the main topic of conversation over the past few days. John was dying to meet up with his old pal Luke, who he knew was related to Bo and he hoped that he could provide him with the latest inside information on a topic which was currently the talk of the city.

The expected rain arrived for the afternoon but the predicted showers turned into a continuous heavy downpour. This had a disastrous effect on the number of visitors to the garden centre and the expected flood turned into a mere trickle. John found that the afternoon was dragging on interminably and his despondent mood of the morning returned.

At half past four he called Lee Harrison into his office.

"We might as well cash up now, Lee. This rain looks as if it's here for the day."

John's office was situated at the rear of the main building of the centre and, as the main outer door was already secure, Lee Harrison bolted the inner door whilst the pair completed the bagging up of the cash prior to the arrival of the Cashguard Security van.

The dark skies hastened the oncoming winter evening and car headlights were turned on well before the official lighting up time. By 5 p.m. there was only a handful of vehicles left in the garden centre car park and most of those belonged to the staff.

A battered blue transit van pulled into the car park and halted behind the row of vehicles nearest the rear entrance of the centre. The two occupants of the van sat motionless, staring out at the desolate scene through the van's rain-spattered windows. Any casual observer would assume that their reluctance to vacate the vehicle was due to the fact that they simply didn't want to get wet. Not that anyone even noticed their presence in the vehicle, as only the occasional glow of a cigarette indicated their presence.

At precisely 5.25 p.m. the black and silver Cashguard Security van entered the garden centre car park and drove slowly round to the rear entrance of the main building. It backed slowly up to the rear door which was opened on a prearranged signal by Lee Harrison. The appearance of the security van galvanised the occupants of the blue van. Both were young men although they differed slightly in appearance in that one was of stocky build, whilst the other was slim, though both were of roughly the same height. They had identical crew-cut hairstyles and both wore blue boiler suits. Before leaving their van, they donned gaudy 'Mickey Mouse' type masks.

One security guard remained in the van whilst the other went through the green outer door to assist John in loading the cash. The two masked men, both now carrying ominous-looking sawn-off shotguns, approached the security van on the run. The leading raider brandished his shotgun menacingly at the driver's window and ordered him to leave the van. His companion raced through the open green door shouting a warning to those inside John's office. The speed and unexpectedness of the attack ensured its success, aided by the inclement weather which ensured that there were no witnesses to the attack in the area of the car park.

John was the first to react as he looked up in surprise at the unexpected entry of the masked intruder. The gunman brandished his shotgun in an arc as he threatened the three occupants of John's office. He shouted in a grating tone:

"Face the wall and put your hands behind your backs! If any of you utters a sound it will be your last."

His menacing tone left them in no doubt that he meant what he said and they all complied with his instructions. His companion entered the building behind the driver of the security van, who, arms behind his head, had the shotgun rammed in his back while he was marched in unceremoniously to join the others. All four captives were then placed facing the wall, whilst the slimmer of the two raiders produced lengths of nylon role from his pocket and swiftly and expertly bound together the hands and feet of the captives. Next he produced a roll of black sticky tape which he cut into lengths and applied to the mouths of all four men, which left them all in extreme discomfort

With their unfortunate victims now rendered helpless, the two raiders gathered up the already neatly prepared bundles of notes and bags of cash and carried them out to their own transit van. They next entered the security van and emerged with armsful of cash and notes. They even made a second visit to the security van and the slimmer of the two made a final check on their victims. He walked over to John and punched him viciously in the ribs. John gasped in pain and half turned to look at his attacker. Without a word the gunman pushed his head so that it struck the wall, causing John further pain. As the man backed away John could barely discern the sound of a quiet chuckle.

The whole raid had taken just under ten minutes from start to finish by the time the blue transit van roared out of the garden centre. The only witness to their departure was sales assistant Jo Wilson, engaged on her final task of the day, that of brushing the front entrance of the centre. She wondered why the security van was taking so long, particularly in view of the fact that she was anxious to finish on time this particular Saturday night. She had arranged to meet a new boyfriend and was anxious to get home in time in order to make preparations to look her best to impress him. She decided that she would go to the office, knock on the door and ask her boss if she could leave right away. She knocked on the door and, as there was no answer she tried the door, which, as she expected it to be, was locked. Next she shouted through the keyhole but elicited no reply. Puzzled, she became alarmed and decided to summon the help of two young but strong male assistants who accompanied her to the rear of the building. As soon as they espied the gaping doors of the security van and the open rear door of the centre, they knew that something was very wrong.

They cautiously entered the office and were shocked by what they found. John Rawson had managed to move himself alongside a table supporting a telephone by a series of rolling movements. When they found him, he was engaged in attempting to knock the telephone on to the floor, hoping to raise the alarm. The two lads were unable to untie the skilfully fixed knots but freed the captives of their bonds with the aid of a pruning knife. Next they ripped off the black tape, which, although painful, was a great relief to all four men. The police were immediately alerted whilst the two security men contacted their depot.

Soon the car park was swamped with police cars and the rain continued its relentless onslaught, providing a sullen background to the drama. Jo Wilson was the only witness to the fugitives' getaway vehicle but she could provide only a sketchy description because, as she explained to the police, she had had other things on her mind and hardly noticed it. All four men gave more or less similar descriptions of the two masked raiders. The police questioned John more than the others as they were curious why he had been singled out for assault. John could not enlighten them on this point and was equally curious. The message relayed to all police patrol cars was to be on the lookout for a blue Ford transit van, registration number unknown, containing two men last seen wearing blue boiler suits.

The Getaway

When the blue transit van exited the garden centre it turned left and mingled with the steady stream of traffic moving away from the city. The two occupants removed their hideous cartoon masks, opened the sliding door of the van and hurled them away into the night. The slimmer of the two punched the air in triumph and slapped his companion on the back.

"We did it, we bloody well did it, Don!"

The other man smiled at his younger companion. "I told you it'd be a piece of cake! It went like clockwork and we didn't need any violence."

"Yeah and think of all that lovely lolly!"

"Just you concentrate on driving, my lad, and remember we want the Calverton turning, so don't miss it."

The van sped towards the busy main road linking Nottingham with Doncaster but slowed at the second road junction and turned right towards Calverton village. The road twisted left and right before descending a steep hill. The constant rain and the dark moonless night made driving very hazardous. The van driver was bent forward peering through his windscreen and then suddenly doused his lights prior to turning abruptly right across a sharp bend just below the summit of the hill, the purpose of this dangerous manoeuvre being to reach a bridleway on the other side of the road.

Unfortunately, without the benefit of lights, he failed to notice an oncoming red bus ascending the hill from Calverton. Likewise the bus driver failed to see the unlit vehicle until the very second it suddenly appeared in front of him. He cursed and braked sharply, turning his steering wheel in a vain effort

to avoid the transit van. A collision was inevitable. The bus
struck the van a glancing blow to its nearside, causing the van
to lurch to the right as the driver struggled frantically with the
steering wheel.   The force of the impact pushed the van
towards a barred gate, which, although open, did not prevent
the van from striking the gatepost with some force.

Miraculously the van remained upright but it had been
badly damaged by the two impacts, with both sides bent
inwards. Though badly shaken, the driver stuck manfully at
his task and the van bumped and slithered its way along the
muddy farm track, the tyres battling to maintain purchase in
the mud.

The stouter of the two men was grim-faced as he rebuked
his companion. "You fucking idiot, I told you to watch where
you were going! A blind man could have seen that bus! The
cops will soon be on our trail so we'll have to rush the next
part thanks to you, you cretin!"

"Sorry Don," said the driver. "I must have got carried
away with all the excitement but I swear to God I didn't see
that bastard bus until it was too late."

Eventually the van slithered to a halt alongside a small
wood, the lights of Calverton twinkling in the valley below.
Being unable to open either of the sliding doors, so badly
damaged by the impact, the men were forced to use the rear
door of the van to get out.

They secured the doors and first removed from the van two
motorcycles which had been roped together to prevent them
from sliding around. Both machines were green Kawasaki
750cc models and had two large pannier bags strapped either
side of their rear wheels. The two men quickly cut the rope
freeing the two machines and began hastily stuffing the
proceeds of the robbery into the pannier bags.   They
performed this task at lightning speed, with the result that two
of the heavier bags containing coins were dropped on the
ground, but were ignored by the two men in their haste to
complete the task. The last part of their well-rehearsed plan

was to remove from the van a five gallon drum of petrol and liberally douse the entire vehicle with it. The final act was to toss a lighted match at the van.

The two men stepped sharply back and grinned at one another as the flames consumed the stricken vehicle.

Then they calmly wheeled their machines through a farm gate, and, without switching on their lights, freewheeled down the steep incline of a field. They entered a small copse at the bottom of the hill and could not resist turning and looking upwards at the funeral pyre they had created. It illuminated the night sky like a beacon and there was a *whoosh* and a *bang* as the petrol tank exploded.

The stouter of the two men nudged his companion.

"Come on, mate, no time to admire the fireworks. Time we weren't here. This place will soon be swarming with coppers and fire engines. Let's get the hell out."

The men pushed their bikes along a rough path which skirted the trees and led to a lane alongside a darkened farm from which a dog barked continuously. They stopped for a minute, peering cautiously up at the windows of the farmhouse, fearful lest they were spotted, but there was no sign of life.

Breathing a little easier, they pushed their bikes further down the lane, which widened and became firmer as they progressed. They could now make out the lights of a pub at the end of the lane and across a road. The two men halted and divested themselves of their blue overalls, which they rolled up and tied to their saddles. Underneath their overalls they wore identical black leather motorcycle gear and completed the transition to innocent motorcyclists by donning green crash helmets.

Up to now the raid had proceeded without a hitch, with the exception of the slight collision with the bus. But fate now took a hand in the guise of a small boy who was playing action games on his computer in the farmhouse they had just passed. He was alone in the house, his parents not too far away in the pub across the road. The barking of the farm dog had alerted the boy, who ran to the rear window of the house and looked out to see the glow of the burning van atop the hill.

He was startled by the sudden explosion and, in the brief instant created by the flash, he saw the silhouettes of the two men leaning on their motorcycles. Standing back from the window to avoid being seen, he cleverly switched off the only light and watched their progress down the lane. Once they had passed the farm, he took a small torch and slipped quietly out of the front entrance, pausing only to fondle and reassure the collie dog who ceased barking. He carefully followed the two men, keeping a safe distance from them in case he was seen. When they stopped to remove their overalls, the boy, using the hedge as cover, crept up until he was almost level with them.

The men wheeled their bikes to the very entrance of the lane, before kick-starting their machines into life and roaring off in different directions. The observant boy was able to make out the registration letters of the number plate of the nearest of the two machines, and, repeating the numbers continuously out loud to himself, he ran back to the farm. Once inside the farm he snatched a pencil and pad from the telephone table and wrote down the registration number of the motorcycle.

At the summit of the hill, the driver of the bus had pulled in his vehicle to the side of the road and was surveying the damage incurred in collision with the van. He was extremely angry and then relieved to see the flashing blue lights of a police car approaching from the direction of Nottingham. As the police car screeched to a halt alongside the damaged bus, the bus driver angrily gesticulated towards his damaged vehicle.

"Bloody maniac van driver did this! He shot straight across the road on a blind bend with no bloody lights on! I swerved and did the best I could, but he hit the bus, bounced off that gate and carried on up the lane."

"Can you describe the vehicle?" asked the police officer.

"Mucky old van, couldn't tell the colour. Maybe a Ford transit but I couldn't be sure as the bugger had no lights."

At that moment there was a violent explosion and the night sky lit up.

"What the bloody hell was that?" exclaimed the bus driver.

"I don't know but we'll sure as hell find out," said the police officer.

The officers immediately jumped in their car and set off down the muddy lane in the direction of the blazing vehicle. Very soon two more police cars drew up near the bus and a third drove down the hill towards Calverton.

By the time the first police car had arrived at the scene of the blaze, the initial fury had all but died down. The charred remains of the van presented a sombre picture to the officers, who conducted a thorough search of the area, stumbling almost immediately upon the two bags of coins dropped by the raiders in their haste to get away.

Confident that they were now hot on the trail of the security van raiders, the police directed a spotlight around the immediate area surrounding the burnt-out van. The spotlight illuminated clear sets of tyre tracks through the mud, which petered out at the entrance to the field. The police officers knew now that the two men had fled the scene and proceeded downhill through the fields to Calverton. They radioed in their findings and the main focus of police attention now switched to the village of Calverton.

Police cars were despatched from the nearby County Police Headquarters at Epperstone to converge on Calverton. All exit roads from the village were blocked by police cars and no traffic was allowed to move in or out; indeed the whole village was a scene of intensive police activity.

The small boy from the farm, ten year old Tommy Watkinson, was soon the centre of attraction. Immediately after writing down the registration number of the bike, he had run all the way to the pub to confront his surprised parents. A police car was positioned in the pub yard and soon Tommy was passing on his story to a grateful police patrolman.

Realising the significance of Tommy's alertness, the policeman swiftly relayed the message to police HQ. Within minutes an urgent all-points bulletin was relayed to police cars in the county ordering them to stop and detain the rider of a Kawasaki 750cc machine, registration number F789WIL.

The two police patrol vehicles positioned at Redhill roundabout checked all vehicles entering the city from the north. Little did they realise that the two men they so badly wanted to detain had preceded them by only five minutes and were already speeding through the streets of the city to their unknown lair, where they planned to lie low for a few days before carrying out their next plan of action.

A Question of Identity

The intensive police search for the security van robbers was now beginning to show signs of definite progress. The big break in the case was undoubtedly the recording of the registration number of one of the bikes used in the getaway. The police computer revealed the Kawasaki owner to be one Donald James Newton, whose last known address was Albert Road, Retford, Notts. Another police computer showed that he had a criminal record commencing at age fifteen when he had been sent to an approved school after being found guilty of serious assault. A further spell at a Borstal institution followed after he escaped from the approved school and was found guilty of aggravated burglary. Shortly after his seventeenth birthday he had joined the army as an apprentice and served two years with the Royal Corps of Signals with an unblemished record. Next he had undertaken an arduous course at Hereford, which he successfully passed to become a member of the SAS.

As a member of this elite group he had served tours of duty in Cyprus, Oman and Northern Ireland. He proved to be an excellent soldier with exemplary conduct until, on a second tour of Northern Ireland, he had involved himself in an unsavoury bar-room brawl in which a member of the public was badly scarred after a vicious attack with a beer glass.

Newton was identified as the assailant by a number of witnesses and was committed for trial by an army court Martial. He was found guilty, awarded a dishonourable discharge and given six months' detention at the notorious Colchester Detention Centre.

He had returned to civilian life at the age of twenty-two and then had lived with his parents at their home near Chesterfield. Nothing further was heard of him for the next three years, except that he had a number of part-time jobs as a security guard with little-known firms. He was, however, from time to time observed in the company of known criminals and was suspected of being involved in several robberies, though this was never proved. In July 1986 he had formed a small private security company with a Jonathan Hopkins as a co-partner. This firm was registered as Steel Lock Security, and employed at various times up to six part-time security guards. No further information was available on him beyond this.

Hutchinson was delighted with this latest information and was anxious to link it with his murder investigations, the Kawasaki motorbike being the obvious connection. He felt that he needed still more information on Newton and to this end he contacted his old friend Detective Inspector Len McCardle of the Sheffield force. The two men had joined the police at the same time and their friendship had proved lasting as their careers pursued remarkably similar courses.

Hutchinson left Nottingham on Monday morning and the two old friends met up at a delightful olde worlde pub in the village of Hathersage amid the Derbyshire hills. They exchanged pleasantries and soon re-established the natural warmth and intimacy enjoyed by two old friends. They hadn't seen one another for over a year and had a lot to catch up on. Their conversation soon returned to their daily work and McCardle expressed a keen interest in Hutchinson's theories on the murders.

After an appetising meal of homemade steak and kidney pie washed down with two pints of strong local bitter, they settled down to the business in hand. Len McCardle lit his briar pipe and settled back on the comfortable red leather seat. Then he glanced around the near empty lounge bar before he began to converse in a low tone with Hutchinson.

"So you want to know a bit more about Donald James Newton? Well, my old mate, you're not alone on that score. I for one would like to know a lot more about him. I have a strong feeling – in fact I'm bloody well certain that he was involved in a string of armed robberies on my patch, but we can't prove a damned thing. He is one clever bastard! But I'll tell you everything I do know about him. I have interviewed him twice and I can assure you, Pete, he is one very cool customer. He answered all my questions with ease, his alibis were watertight and I couldn't get to him. But I felt uncomfortable in his presence. I couldn't even scratch the surface to find out what he was really like.

"Now, as you know, he served in the SAS and I reckon that's where he learned all his skills. I mean, take their interrogation technique – they send their men on survival exercises and when they catch up with them, they really put them through the mill. They treat them as if they were the real enemy – they beat them up and even torture them – so it's no bloody wonder I can't get a damned thing out of him! But, you know, Pete, I am absolutely convinced that this security set-up is really a front for arranging and carrying out armed robberies. I have actually visited his so-called premises, which consist of a small office above a butcher's shop and two lock-up garages containing a car and a transit van."

"Did you say transit van?" interrupted Hutchinson.

"Yes, a battered old thing it was too, just about roadworthy; I couldn't even nail him on that, more's the pity!"

"Do you remember what colour it was?"

"Why is that important? As far as I can remember it was a mucky shade of blue!"

"I'll bet that was the very same van they torched on Saturday night."

"Well yes, I suppose it could be."

"Talking about the robbery, I'm very anxious to find out the identity of the man with Newton. Could it be one of his employees?"

"Well, I can tell you who it isn't, and that is his partner Jonathan Hopkins, as that gentleman is currently a guest of Her Majesty's, serving a five year stretch at Strangeways for armed robbery. He was one of a gang of four men we caught after a tip-off. I was convinced at the time, and still am, that our old friend Newton was heavily involved in this one. As usual he had an unshakeable alibi, but I reckon that he gave us the tip as a means of ditching Hopkins.

"Two months after we nailed Hopkins there was an armed raid on an off-licence on the Worksop Road. Our cars gave chase and the robbers' car hit a wall. We caught two of the buggers but the third got away, and I'm sure that bloke was Newton. I detained him a couple of hours after the incident but as usual his alibi was faultless and he answered all my questions cool as a cucumber. According to him he was having a drink with his girlfriend at the time of the robbery and he produced eight people allegedly present in the pub at the time."

"I take it you checked up on his whereabouts for last Saturday?" asked Hutchinson.

"Yes. Apparently he's currently on a business trip to the Midlands according to his company secretary, who also happens to be his girlfriend."

"Yes, I see what you mean about his being a cool customer. But this so-called business trip to the Midlands could mean that he is in Nottingham at this very moment."

"Agreed, but when I asked his secretary exactly where he was in the Midlands she maintained that she was not privy to that information, which was a polite way of saying mind your own bloody business. However, if he does have the nerve to return to either his home or business premises, then we'll nab him, as I have got both of them under round-the-clock observation. But one thing puzzles me, Pete, and that is I can't quite see Newton fitting into your investigation. I mean, where is the motive? We know he's into armed robberies but drugs and prostitution? Sorry, Pete, but I just can't see the connection."

"Well, Len, it's just a feeling I've got. I agree with you that there doesn't appear to be any motive or clear evidence linking him to the murders, but what about this second bloke? The whole thing hinges on these two motorbikes. We know for certain that Newton owns one and I reckon once we identify the second owner we'll have our killer."

"But surely you've already arrested and charged a man with one murder."

"I'm wholly convinced he didn't do it. He certainly didn't kill Janice Longman and he sure as hell didn't kill Dawson."

"Okay, Pete, I'll start the ball rolling from this end. For a start I'll check up on all staff employed at Steel Lock Security for the past couple of years. I've actually got a current list which I obtained from Newton's secretary on my last visit, so I'll soon see if it is authentic or not. Next I will have a word with Newton's parents. I've met them before. Quiet, respectable retired couple – how they managed to produce one like him is beyond me! Don't worry, Pete, we'll nail this bastard in the end!"

The two old friends had a final drink and shook hands before returning to their respective police stations, each of them promising not to leave it so long before meeting up again. McCardle assured Hutchinson that he would fax through any information gleaned as a result of his investigations. Before returning to his home Hutchinson called in at Radford Road to monitor the very latest information on the hunt for the security van raiders. A public appeal for information on the owners of Kawasaki 750cc motorcycles had produced a staggering response. Teams of policemen had been checking out addresses throughout the day but as yet with no positive sighting of the wanted bikes.

Hutchinson entered his office and made straight for a tall cupboard behind his desk. He opened it with a key and removed a small tape recorder from a shelf. He put the tape recorder on his desk, rewound the tape and played it back for several minutes, three times in all before he was satisfied. He next used his internal phone to the vice office to request that Sergeant Mabbutt come to his office immediately. Two minutes later the tall figure of John Mabbutt entered his office after knocking politely. Hutchinson motioned him to sit down, staring intently at him. Mabbutt seemed puzzled by Hutchinson's request.

"Er, you wanted to see me, sir? Is it about the vice murders? I've had several of the girls questioned today already and—"

He paused as Hutchinson held up his hand. "No, John, it's nothing to do with the current investigation. Now you say you have been questioning prostitutes today – would that be in your office or outside the station?"

Mabbutt screwed up his thin features in some surprise and scratched his thinning hair before answering.

"Well, both really, sir. I called round to see Angie McPherson at her mother's house this morning and I interviewed a couple of Dawson's younger girls in the office this afternoon. May I ask the relevance of all this, sir?"

Hutchinson ignored his question. "Okay then, answer me this: did you at any time use this office to make a phone call?"

Mabbutt's face reddened as he replied angrily, "Certainly not, I would never dare to come into your office without you being there."

Hutchinson's face was grim as he replied, "I think that you are a bloody liar, Sergeant! Listen to this."

He switched on the tape recorder. There was a slight hiss then the unmistakable sound of Mabbutt's voice.

"Hello, is that Michael? Okay, listen and take this down, I haven't got time to repeat it and I'll have to talk quietly because I'm in the chief's office again – no, no chance. The bugger is away in Sheffield for the day... Anyway further to the scandal story I gave you last time, which incidentally I'm still waiting to be paid for. Anyway I digress, last Monday Sergeant Mulraney's dypso wife really went over the top. She followed him downtown where he had arranged to meet the blonde WPC Harper. Harper goes back to the Forest to collect her car and the dypso clobbers her with a brick, stuffs her into the boot of her car and drives off...

"It gets better! One of our patrol cars spots her and after a chase they corner her and the game's up. But it's not – you see, our beloved boss Hutchinson decides to hush it all up. The dypso is bundled off to Mapperley and our randy blonde recovers in hospital. How do you like it so far? ...Great, I'm bloody certain *The Sun* will be very interested in this little lot ...So we're talking how much? ...Well, let's say substantially more than the last lot. By the way any more inside info on the murders? ...All in good time, Michael, but what about the last payment you owe me? ...Okay, listen meet me at The Bell tonight round about seven o'clock. ...Okay, bye for now, Michael."

Hutchinson switched off the tape and Mabbutt, who had listened in stunned silence, looked sick with apprehension.

"Nothing to say eh, Sergeant?" said Hutchinson. "I think Chief Superintendent Maudsley will have quite a lot to say when he listens to this tape in the morning. I don't know how long this has been going on but we will find that out later. As from now you are formally suspended from duty. I would ask you to hand over all relevant items belonging to the force before you leave this station. You will report here in the morning to assist in further inquiries into this matter. I suggest you go home and consider your future, which after this must inevitably be outside the police force. You are dismissed."

An ashen-faced Mabbutt slowly rose from his chair and walked at a leaden pace from the office.

The Funeral

The day of Bo's funeral dawned almost reluctantly. Black clouds scurried over a grey sky and there was a hint of rain in the air. The wind was from the north-east, a biting chill wind that stung the faces of the early morning workers. It sent paper cups and trays containing the remains of the previous day's takeaway meals bouncing along the pavements. Flurries of dust blew into the eyes of those brave souls defiant enough to brave the elements by cycling to work along the city's roads.

The residents of Radford and Hyson Green rose with some reluctance from their warm beds to be confronted by the breezy chill of an unwelcoming winter morning. This day was of significance to most of them as this was to be the day local villain Bo Dawson would finally be laid to rest. For some of them Bo had appeared indestructible and they genuinely felt a sorrow and sense of loss at his passing and some even felt that life would be poorer without him. But to the majority it was to be a day of rejoicing because their life would now be free from threats and violence.

To the local police force it was to be a day of vigilance, as they realised full well that with such a large attendance expected at the funeral there was every possibility of trouble erupting. The death of Bo had created an inevitable shift of power in the local criminal fraternity. There was a power vacuum and whoever filled it would be able to do so only after a hard struggle and not without some bloodshed.

Hutchinson made a point of attending the funeral service in company with Mulraney whilst ordering a discreet police presence to be on hand in case of trouble.

The funeral service was to be held at the evangelical church in Radford to be followed by a cremation at Bramcote Crematorium. Afterwards mourners and selected friends of the deceased were invited to a wake at The Cricketers' public house, which had been wholly reserved for the entire evening. Luke Tomey was one of those who were secretly delighted at Bo's demise, particularly so as it freed him from any obligation to distribute drugs. He had taken a day off work in order to attend the funeral. His wife Myra, who as Bo's cousin was included in the list of close family mourners, had warned Luke not to express any deprecatory thoughts on Bo in the presence of his family, although she too was not exactly unhappy at his passing, she would never admit this to anyone. She had purchased a new all-black outfit especially for the occasion. Luke too looked the part in his charcoal grey suit, worn for only the second time since his wedding.

Angie McPherson, though still red-eyed with grief, presented a picture of poignant elegance attired in an expensive black suit, with a silken veil covering her face and a small hat, which, though perched at an angle on her head, nevertheless matched perfectly the rest of her attire. She was prominent amidst the group of close female mourners, clinging on to the arm of her mother Agnes, a tall dignified figure.

There was a large group of Bo's loyal aides, almost indistinguishable in their identical dreadlocked hair. A posse of street girls were in attendance, belying their usual garish appearance in staid black outfits, displaying little or no make-up, some of them openly weeping.

Surprisingly there were members of local religious groups mingling with the mourners, together with several local shopkeepers and even a local councillor. The church was not large enough to contain the number of people attending the funeral and those unable to gain entrance stood in dignified groups on the pavements outside.

The arrival of the funeral cortège was greeted with mournful wailing by the female members of the family. Bo's expensive white coffin with gold handles was carried into the church by six of his closest friends and a calm descended on the gathering as the procession slowly made its way up the aisle. The funeral service itself was anything but quiet, as the wailing of the women intensified but broke off to allow the enthusiastic singing of hymns which included *The Old Rugged Cross*, *Nearer Thy God To Thee* and finally *Amazing Grace*, the last-named being the signal for the wailing to recommence.

The words of an address to the assembled gathering were heard by only a few due to the lack of acoustics and the continuous wailing. Eventually the long service came to an end, to the relief of Luke and his friends, to name but a few. Amid much weeping and wailing the white coffin was carried aloft to the waiting hearse and conveyed to Bramcote.

Only a small immediate family group attended the short cremation service as Bo departed to meet his maker. As the purple curtains finally closed over the white coffin, Angie collapsed to the floor, inconsolable in her grief. A chill wind and driving rain hurried the mourners back to their waiting cars and they were soon homeward bound to ready themselves for the forthcoming wake.

Luke and Myra returned to their Mapperley home to change into more informal outfits. Luke had obtained permission to allow his two workmates and John to accompany himself and Myra to the wake, which was scheduled to start at 5 p.m.

Matthew was unable to come with them at that time due to his large collection round, but hoped to join them round about half past eight. John had taken a day off from work as he had spent most of the morning at the Central Police Station making a statement and helping the police after Saturday's robbery.

The office staff at the Birmingham and Nottingham Assurance Company had been granted a surprise day off by temporary manager George Allis, who had been invited to the funeral wake by Agnes McPherson. Marilyn Watkins was invited to accompany fiancé John and she had persuaded Jane Milford to come along to make up the numbers, to the delight of Mark Daley. They all arranged to meet up at Luke's house and share a taxi cab both to and from the venue.

By the time they arrived at The Cricketers at 6 p.m., the crowd of people was almost to the door. The atmosphere was more akin to a wedding reception than a funeral wake. Luke's group pushed and jostled their way through the throng and eventually claimed a space alongside the raised stage but conveniently near the bar. Luke struggled to get to the bar to order a round of drinks but was stopped in his tracks by the arm of a Bo lookalike. "Hey, Lukey boy, where are you going?"

"Er, to fetch a round of drinks in for my friends," said Luke.

"No way man, you just tell me what you want and the drinks will be brought to you. After all, that's the way Bo would have wanted it."

A surprised Luke mumbled his thanks and returned to his friends. The tray of drinks soon arrived as promised, to be followed by two further rounds and a tray of delicious sandwiches and sausage rolls. As soon as the group had consumed one round of drinks, another was thrust upon them, prompting John to remark that if you had to go this was the best way to do it. Conversation soon became well-nigh impossible due to the amplified booming sound of the group directly above them on the stage. The group belted out a reggae version of the Rolling Stones' hit *Walking the Dog*. Accompanied by a pulsating rhythm, the diminutive black vocalist crouched over the microphone grinding out the words in a curiously high-pitched voice which sounded out of tune and yet was strangely rhythmic and hypnotic in its effect on the gyrating dancers.

Jane Milford was hugely enjoying herself and found the rhythm irresistible. Unable to contain herself, she dragged a bemused Mark on to the dance floor. As the evening wore on the drinks kept arriving and Jane's inhibitions dissolved in a haze of drink; she was soon draped around Mark, shuffling in a slow dance. Mark was delighted by this turn of events and was thoroughly enjoying himself.

John nudged Marilyn.

"Jane is certainly coming on to Mark, and he certainly seems to be enjoying himself. They make a nice couple, don't they?"

"Yes," said Marilyn nodding agreement. "But she is going to hate herself in the morning."

Luke remarked on the non-appearance of Matthew but presumed that he was working later than expected.

Around half past eleven, with the whole place literally throbbing with noise, the first hint of trouble arrived. A group of youths from the St Ann's area had unsuccessfully attempted to gatecrash earlier but had been prevented by the bouncers deployed in large numbers at the main entrance. Determined to gain entry, they smashed a toilet window and had actually managed to make their way to the bar before they were spotted. A small scuffle ensued which soon escalated into violent fighting as blows were freely exchanged. Beer glasses began to fly through the air and soon wholesale violence erupted as more groups of youths engaged the bouncers in another confrontation at the main entrance.

Jane screamed in terror as a beer glass smashed near her, showering the group with shards of broken glass. Marilyn clung to John and Myra urged Luke to do something. Luke didn't need any prompting and was already anxious for the safety of the women. Linking arms with John and Mark, they attempted to form a protective barrier around the three women as they carefully made their way through the throng of people, taking a circuitous route in an effort to avoid the worst of the fighting. Using a side entrance, the doors of which had been forced open by frightened people anxious to flee the scene, they gulped in the cold night air and huddled protectively together whilst Luke sought out a taxi. As they drove along Radford Boulevard in the taxi, two police cars passed them in the opposite direction prompting Luke to remark, "Here comes the cavalry, late as bloody usual!"

Revelations Part 1

Matthew Haines delayed picking up his cup of tea for a last sip before venturing out into the cold winter evening. He recalled the words of his late departed father: "Allus was a nesh bogger, our Matthew."

He had returned to his house for a quick bite to eat and a refreshing cuppa in a welcome break from his long collection round. As this was the last week in the month, it meant that he had an extra twenty-five calls to add to his usual round.

Matthew's wife, a homely girl, was settling herself down on the couch in company with three year old son Tommy and baby daughter Trudie to view the children's TV programmes. Matthew had changed out of his workday clothes into his trendy gear as he planned to join his friends at the wake later in the evening.

The rain spattered on the window and the door rattled with the force of the wind. Matthew shuddered at the thought of having to go out again on such an unfriendly night. He looked longingly at his wife and children huddled together on the couch.

"I envy you, Liz, all warm and snug with the kids for company. What a night to have to go out in!"

"Oh poor old you," said Elizabeth mockingly. "You know you don't really have to go to that wretched wake. Why on earth do you want to anyway? It's not as if you even knew the deceased. And as for celebrating someone's death, I really do think that is in very poor taste."

"Well yeah, I agree in a way," admitted Matthew. "But I can hardly let Luke and the rest of the lads down, now can I? I shouldn't be too late getting home, so don't wait up for me."

"Famous last words!" said Elizabeth. "Oh, that reminds me, Mrs Warburton from Ebury Road rang this morning just after you'd left and said to tell you that she will be away until the weekend, but she will leave the books and money with her two lodgers and that you should walk straight in through the back door as usual."

Matthew nodded in acquiescence, donned his raincoat and hat, picked up his briefcase and kissed his wife and children goodbye. The weather failed to improve during the next two hours, and Matthew felt a sense of relief when he parked his Toyota outside Mrs Warburton's house in Ebury Road, for it was his last call of the day.

Mrs Warburton was a widow whose large family of six children were all married and lived away. Her home was a large, rambling old-fashioned house situated just off Hucknall Road on the edge of the city. To supplement her income, she took in lodgers to a maximum of four. The lodgers were mainly students or young working men.

Mrs Warburton was a warm-hearted motherly type who worked hard on the maintenance of her large house. The rooms were basic but spotlessly clean and there was an aroma of old-fashioned carbolic soap and lavender polish reminiscent of houses of a previous era. She cooked excellent lavish meals and her lodgers were grossly overfed. Indeed she looked after them a little too well and fussed over them like a mother hen; so popular was her board and lodging package that there was seldom a vacancy. The rent provided her with a reasonable living as well as contributing to the not inconsiderable upkeep of the house. Every couple of months, to give her a break from her chores, she visited her various offspring, on a rota basis to avoid arguments.

Matthew always ensured that Mrs Warburton was his last call of the day; for one thing he could rely on a warm welcome and for another he could look forward to a large cup of steaming brew from Mrs Warburton's king-sized teapot, for, even if she herself was not present, she never failed to instruct her current lodgers to provide for Matthew. As he alighted from his car he noticed that the street light directly outside the house was unlit, making it difficult to see the latch on the wooden gate of the passageway leading to the house.

After a deal of fumbling he eventually located the latch, admonishing himself for forgetting his pocket torch, an absolute must on these dark cold winter nights. Blinking in the gloom, he forged ahead down the dark passageway at the side of the house, relying on his memory to guide him along. He gasped in pain as his right knee encountered a sharp solid object. His momentum carried him forward and his hands encountered what seemed like a wet tarpaulin covering two motorcycles. He fell on top of the motorcycles, dislodging one of them, which crashed sideways on to the ground, Matthew following in an untidy heap, cursing as he did so.

The clatter of the fallen machine made a loud noise and within seconds a figure with a torch had appeared from the rear of the house and trained the beam directly on Matthew. He was by now very wet and dishevelled and rose painfully to his feet, shielding his eyes from the glare of the torch.

"Who the hell are you and what are you up to?" shouted the man holding the torch.

"I'm the insurance man for Mrs Warburton," said Matthew, holding on to the wall to steady himself and wishing that his knee didn't hurt so much.

The man took a pace forward and trained his torch on to Matthew's face then suddenly exclaimed, "Good grief, it's Matthew! I'd no idea you were the landlady's insurance man. How are you, Matty old son?"

Matthew peered at the man, who, laughing, turned the torch on his own face.

"Blimey O'Reilly!" gasped Matthew. "It's Ginger Tomlinson! We meet again for the second time in ten days.

How's it going, mate? I thought you said you lived in Worksop now?"

"Yeah that's right," said Ginger. "But I'm staying here with my mate for a few days whilst we finish a job. Anyway, come on inside and sit yourself down and get warm. I'll organise a brew but first of all I'd better prop the bikes up."

Matthew didn't need a second invitation. He hurried inside the back door and made a beeline for the large Aga cooker, enjoying its warming glow. Mrs Warburton's old-fashioned kitchen was a large high-ceilinged room, dominated by a scrubbed white wooden table surrounded by six wooden chairs. On either side of the Aga cooker were two well-worn but very comfortable leather armchairs. Her insurance books were neatly laid out in the centre of the table, the first book containing a twenty pound note. Matthew marked and signed the premium receipt books, pocketed the twenty pound note and left the relevant change at the side of the books. By the time he had completed this transaction Ginger had returned from his task, and he grinned at Matthew.

"Quite like old times, eh Matt? Where are the other two tonight?"

"Well, believe it or not, they have been to a funeral today and I am meeting up with them as soon as I leave here, at The Cricketers – for a wake of all things!"

A surprised Ginger replied, "Oh yeah, who has died then?"

"Oh, I don't suppose you have heard of him. It's Bo Dawson, local black pimp, drug dealer the lot – no great loss to society! But they reckon it should turn out to be a good do, and you know me, any excuse for a piss-up! Talking of which, reminds me that I'm busting! This cold weather certainly has a drastic effect on the old waterworks."

Ginger grinned. "Help yourself, Matty, you know where it is."

Matthew made his way to the downstairs toilet through the long corridor from the kitchen. He found the toilet chilly due to the window's being slightly open. He reached over to close the window and noticed the rear end of one of the motorcycles positioned directly underneath the window. The wind had blown the tarpaulin to one side and the light from the toilet was just sufficient to allow him to see that the machine was green in colour. He thrust his head out of the window and, turning it to one side, he was able to make out the number plate, which read F789WIL.

Matthew felt a cold chill sweep through his body as he realised the significance of his discovery. He recalled that, earlier that evening, whilst enjoying his cup of tea at home he had read the lead story in *The Post* which had contained a police appeal to the public to look out for a green Kawasaki motorbike, and he distinctly remembered the registration number, which tallied with the one outside the toilet window.

He returned to the kitchen with a feeling of apprehension. This must mean that the Kawasaki owner must be one of Mrs Warburton's lodgers; perhaps Ginger would know his name.

A sudden thought struck him as he reached for the steaming mug of tea proffered by Ginger, who said, "You look a bit pale, Matt! Get this cuppa down you, you'll soon feel better."

Matthew took the cup and nodded his thanks to Ginger. He didn't quite know what to say, so he sipped his tea slowly before speaking a little hesitantly to Ginger.

"Those two motorbikes outside?" He paused, unsure. "Er, do you, er, own one of them? No, I mean do you know who owns them?"

Ginger looked strangely at his friend before replying.

"Yes, one of them belongs to me. They are both bloody good Jap bikes, none better in my opinion. What do you want to know for, anyway?"

"Oh, just curious, you know, Ginge," said Matthew, anxious now to change the subject, but he felt his face beginning to redden under Ginger's glare.

Ginger looked hard at Matthew.

"You know, don't you?"

"Er, know what, Ginge?"

Ginger sighed and pushed back his chair, putting his feet on the table.

"Oh, don't kid me, mate, it's written all over your face. Yeah, one of those bikes belongs to me and the other is my mate's, Don Newton. You are a good mate too, Matt, so I might as well tell you: we did the security van together and I did the murders."

There was a stunned silence for a moment before the astonished Matthew reacted.

"What! For Chrissake, Ginge, you must be having me on! Did you say murders plural? How many for God's sake?"

Ginger smiled at the reaction to his admission.

"Yeah, well, I suppose it is a little hard to take in. But I can assure you, my friend, it's true! You have every right to be surprised. You remember the old Ginger – he wouldn't hurt a fly, would he? Never stood up for himself; in fact a right bloody wimp! But the worm has turned, my friend, you see before you a different Ginger, a killer if you want. Yes, I strangled Janice Longman and Jacqui Reid and I bashed in that miserable worm of a husband of hers, but best of all I stabbed that bastard Dawson with his own screwdriver! And yes, I did have a quiet chuckle to myself when I heard you and the lads were attending his wake. I've half a mind to join you. But I can't really because I have one more job to do before I leave town."

Matthew, still in a state of shock, replied, "I just can't take in what I'm hearing! You've changed so much!" He added weakly, "Dare I ask what your pending job is?"

Ginger was now beginning to enjoy himself, particularly when he looked at the shocked expression on his friend's face.

"Yeah, of course you may. The last name on my hit list is Dawson's girlfriend, that black bitch, Angie McPherson."

"But why Ginge, for Chrissake why? There must be a reason for all this?"

"Oh, there is, my friend, a very good reason," said Ginger smugly. "Are you quite sure you want to hear it?"

"Yes, I think you had better tell me all about it," said Matthew gravely.

Ginger looked at the half sipped mug of tea in front of Matthew and collected it up.

"Oh dear, Matty, you haven't drunk your tea, you've let it go cold. I'll brew us a fresh cuppa before I start. You look as if you're in a state of shock, so you'll need one more than me!"

He calmly poured fresh water in the kettle and returned it to heat up on the Aga hotplate, humming softly to himself as he did so.

Matthew stared at his old friend. He still couldn't comprehend what he had heard, but one thing was for sure: Ginger was deadly serious and he felt genuine fear at the thought that one of his close friends was a serial killer. Ginger handed him his second mug of hot tea and this time he sipped steadily at the hot liquid, finding some small degree of comfort in its warming effect on his insides.

Ginger leant back in his chair and resumed his comfortable position, feet on the table, one foot crossed over the other.

"Right, well, I'll start at the beginning which was, I suppose, nearly four years ago. You remember me getting married to Karen? She was one sweet kid, at least I thought so at the time. Extremely pretty she was; well, you know that, don't you? 'Course I fell for her hook, line and sinker and I couldn't wait to get married. I was so very much in love with her I couldn't see her faults – everybody else could, but not me! I was blind! Looking back in the cold light of day, I can see now that she was shallow, a real flirt always looking for a good time. Nothing too much wrong with that, I suppose, but there were too many sharks around looking to take advantage. Even before we got married she was seeing John Rawson behind my back. That was the start of it all, but it wasn't just the flirting – she wanted money and lots of it.

After we got married I was working all hours God sent to earn enough money to keep things going.

"We bought the house in Basford with an endowment mortgage from the company, and even though I got a staff discount, those repayments were pretty hefty. Karen wanted more and more money. She was always going out, saying she wanted the money for a good time, she was young and she was going to enjoy herself. John Rawson must have finally seen through her, because he soon chucked her, not that I knew anything about it at the time.

"She drifted into very bad company when she met up with Janice Longman at a nightclub in town. She was soon introduced to wild rave parties in the Hyson Green flats. Sometimes she stopped out all night, but I still didn't twig. God, I was so bloody naive and trusting! She told me she had spent the night with friends – and I believed her! But Janice Longman had done a good job on her. She introduced her to that evil pimp Dawson who encouraged her into taking drugs down the usual route, marijuana cigarettes rapidly progressing to heroin, and in no time at all she was well and truly hooked. In order to support her habit, Dawson proposed that she go on the game. Janice Longman, Jacqui Reid and the McPherson bitch all combined to teach her the ropes and soon she was a fully-fledged working girl. It wasn't until much later that I learnt Dawson took practically all her earnings off her in exchange for regular supplies of heroin. She was completely hooked by this time and would do anything to support her habit. Dawson took full advantage and used her for group sex, pornographic photos, the lot.

"By this time even I realised there was something going on. She was hardly ever at home. Her appearance changed almost overnight from the sweet-faced attractive girl I married. Instead she looked haggard and pasty-faced, her hair grimy and unwashed; she had lost weight and her eyes were bloodshot and prominent. When she did come home, all she talked about was money, which she continually asked for, and about having a good time. Eventually even my patience snapped and we had a blazing row when she staggered in one breakfast time. She blurted out everything, what she was doing, who she had been with – the lot! You can imagine how I felt. My whole world had collapsed: I was devastated. I refused point-blank to give her any more money and she erupted in rage. She ranted and raved and even threatened to tell Dawson to set his boys on me to teach me a lesson.

"I just didn't know which way to turn. I was at a complete loss. I slammed the door of the house and drove off aimlessly in my car. I can't even remember the journey but I ended up in Matlock Bath, where I went into a pub, downed a few drinks and drove home. It was a Tuesday night, I remember that clearly, so I knew I had better do my account. I went straight to the desk safe to count out my collection monies. When I opened the cash box it was empty. Of course Karen had taken the lot, though where she got the key to the safe from God only knows. I felt so desperate. I didn't know what to do. I spent a sleepless night trying to find a way of replacing the monies.

"The next morning I went to the bank and drew out every penny from our account, which didn't amount to much. I stalled the office by phoning through to say I didn't feel too good but I would endeavour to be in on Friday to pay in my account. I had in my possession three cash surrender cheques due to be paid to clients, so I forged the signatures on these and used the monies raised to replace the missing collection money. I never saw Karen again after that day. I did hear a rumour that she left the area for London about six months ago. If that's true I expect she ended up in King's Cross, that is of course if she is still alive. To tell you the truth I couldn't care less. I have absolutely no feelings left for her now.

"I tried to keep everything on a normal footing at work by robbing Peter to pay Paul. I managed it for about three weeks, but of course Malone spotted there was something amiss. He made my life absolute hell did that bastard. Very ironic him being banged up – I had a great laugh when I heard about that I can tell you..."

He broke off at the sound of footsteps from the passageway at the side of the house. The back door opened and a man wearing an anorak entered the kitchen, the hood of the anorak obscuring his face. The man pulled back the hood to reveal rounded unshaven features, a shaven head and dark slightly slanted eyes which gave him a sinister appearance. He was a squat muscular-looking man and Matthew realised that he was looking at one Donald James Newton.

Revelations Part 2

Newton stared fixedly at Matthew with an uncompromising glare of deep suspicion. He thrust out an accusing finger.

"Who the hell is this, Pete?"

Ginger smiled at Newton reassuringly.

"Don't worry, Don, this is an old pal of mine. He's from my old firm and he's actually Mrs Warburton's insurance man."

Matthew got to his feet and proffered a hand in greeting to Newton, who pointedly ignored it and spoke gruffly to Ginger.

"I'm going to have a hot bath now before I catch my death of cold, then we'll have a bite to eat."

He took off his wet anorak, draped it over a wooden chair near the Aga and shuffled off through the kitchen door.

Matthew moved to collect his own coat.

"I think I had better be making tracks, Ginge. Your friend is obviously not too keen on my being here."

Ginger put a restraining hand on Matthew's shoulder, gently pushing him back towards his chair.

"Nonsense, Matt! Don't take any notice of Don, he's fine once you get to know him. Besides I haven't finished telling you everything yet."

"But I really should be going. They will be expecting me to turn up soon, especially as I promised to be there the minute I finished work," protested Matthew.

Ginger shook his head and patted the back of the chair.

"Sit yoursen down, Matt. There's no rush, stay a while. You really must hear the rest of the story, then everything will be much clearer to you."

Matthew relented and sat down. "Okay, I'll stay another ten minutes or so, then I really must go."

Ginger settled himself back in his chair before resuming.

"Right, now where were we before Don came in? Talking of Don, I met up with him shortly after I arrived in Worksop. I suppose you remember only too well when I got the sack?"

Matthew nodded.

Ginger continued.

"I knew then of course that there was nothing left for me in Nottingham, so I had to sell the house and take whatever was offered. It was the lowest point of my life. My wife had left me, I was sacked in disgrace from my job and branded a thief. Every time I left the house, even when going to the shops, I felt as if people were talking about me behind my back. I felt as though I *had* to get away from it all – there were too many bad memories. I was lucky with the house, in that the very first couple who looked round it decided to buy it there and then, and, what's more, they didn't need a mortgage.

"I moved in at my sister's house in Worksop as a temporary measure whilst I got sorted out. I felt suicidal and for several weeks I wandered aimlessly about, drifting in and out of pubs to relieve the monotony. After six weeks I was able to claim dole money and at least give my sister a pittance for my board and lodging. When I look back on it I'm surprised she didn't chuck me out – I must have been diabolical company. I hadn't even bothered looking for a job; I had absolutely no interest in anything, let alone ambition. However, everything changed when I met Don. I was slumped over a bar one night, feeling sorry for myself as usual, when this stocky guy comes in and knocks my pint on the floor with his elbow. It looked and was deliberate on his part, but I ignored him and ordered another drink. He stared at me in amazement before asking me why I didn't retaliate. I replied what for, as I didn't think he had done anything wrong. He said I was a wimp and should stand up for myself. I agreed with him that I was a wimp, but that I couldn't care less and made to leave the bar. He bought me another drink and persuaded me to stay.

"Soon, relaxed by the many drinks I had consumed, I poured out my whole sorry story. If I was hoping for a sympathetic response from him, I certainly didn't get it. He said I was stupid for allowing a few unfortunate events to dominate my life. He told me to stand up for myself and hit back. I asked how the hell was I expected to do that? I mean, I had no job, no prospects and no money. Come and work for me, he said, I'll give you a chance. But a word of warning, I must do everything he told me – screw up and you're out, he warned me. I asked him what sort of work he was engaged in and he replied vaguely security. I didn't need much persuading. I mean, what had I got to lose? I didn't have anything to start with!

"For a start he concentrated on making me physically fit by embarking on long runs in the Derbyshire hills. He taught me how to look after myself in a fight and a little of the martial arts. He toughened me up mentally by making me adopt a positive attitude towards life.

"'You take what you can get out of life,' he said. 'There's only winners and losers.' It was my choice. He told me all about his own life in the SAS and how he had used the knowledge gained from that to develop his present lifestyle. You see, he set up this security firm with the help of another guy, who incidentally is now in jail, but no matter. There were six of us altogether working in the security firm. On the surface it was all above board: we would go to inspect business premises and private houses to advise on the best way to make them secure. Quite legitimately we would make a nominal charge for the installation of burglar alarms and security lights etc. But the real purpose of the exercise was to suss out the premises for future robberies. Of course we didn't raid them all, just a select few. Sure the police suspected us but they couldn't prove a damned thing. Don really did his homework and we did have one narrow squeak, but to tell you the truth the risk factor gave me a real buzz. Don convinced me that as part of my healing process I should seek revenge on those who had caused me such misery.

"I drew up a hit list. Number one was Dawson, followed by the three prostitutes and Charlie Reid. I also included Malone, but, as things turned out, I had no need to top him. We planned it all very carefully. We travelled to Nottingham leaving word that we were on a business trip to the Midlands. Don drove the old transit van containing the two bikes whilst I followed in the Ford Escort.

"We toured the red-light district and found out exactly where and when the girls operated. Don picked up Janice Longman and drove her out to Colwick Park for a session with a 'kinky' client. I was waiting there on the Kawasaki posing as the kinky client. Don got her nicely spread out on the back seat of the car, then I took over and strangled her. It was so bloody easy. There was a bit of a hue and cry after this first murder, so we lay low for a bit. In fact we actually returned to Sheffield for a short time to carry out a raid to keep the finances ticking over.

"We returned to Nottingham and one night, whilst we were deciding on the next killing, a heaven-sent opportunity cropped up. I had intended Angie McPherson to be the next victim and I was actually watching her from across the road when out of the blue Malone appeared. He picked up Jacqui Reid, not Angie, so we followed him in the Escort. They went to some waste ground and we followed but doused the lights and waited. After a few minutes, Jacqui Reid got out of the car in a great hurry and ran towards the road. I took my chance and followed her. I took her completely by surprise, overpowered her and strangled her. She was clutching Malone's wallet in her hand, so I put it in my pocket. Don reckoned I should blackmail the old bastard – it was a unique opportunity. I took full advantage and phoned him a couple of times. I disguised my voice by placing a handkerchief over the mouthpiece, so he hadn't a bloody clue who I was.

"I persuaded him to hand over five thousand in used notes in a waste bin in the Arboretum. Both Don and I used Kawasakis that day to fool the police and I think it worked. I was amazed and delighted to read about Malone's arrest and about him being charged with Jacqui Reid's murder. Like Don said, it was even better than our original plan.

"Next we followed Jacqui Reid's husband Charlie one night after he had broken into a doctor's to steal some drugs. We tailed him back to his house and I clobbered him, but I didn't have time to finish the job because we were interrupted and had to scarper quick.

"Then at long last I finally got my chance to nail Dawson. We had tracked him for weeks in the hope of catching him alone but there was always at least one of his hangers-on around. We struck lucky early on a Sunday morning when he went alone to the garages near the flat complex. I took him completely by surprise but I let him know exactly who I was when I stabbed him with his own screwdriver. That really was one sweet moment. I felt really good after it. I remembered the time that bastard had me doffed up by two of his goons, when he had stood over me and taunted me by saying what he had got up to with Karen. Yeah, I enjoyed doing 'em all but that one was the best!"

Matthew had listened with growing horror to his old friend's long account and could contain himself no longer.

"For pity's sake, Ginge, you must give yourself up to the police! You have murdered three people, left another for dead. Whatever these people did to you, you can't go around murdering them."

Ginger grinned at his friend and Matthew realised that he didn't really know him at all. Gone was the shy conscientious young man he had known four years ago, replaced by a laughing, cold-hearted killer. The sound of running water from the bathroom had not been heard for the last ten minutes when Don Newton came into the kitchen. He had changed into a fresh pair of jeans, thick checked shirt and leather jacket.

He spoke directly to Matthew.

"Is that your car outside?"

Matthew nodded.

Newton held out his hand. "Give me the keys."

Matthew frowned. "Why?"

"Because I say so," snapped Newton.

"Look here, I don't like your attitude," said Matthew, rising to his feet.

Newton pushed him back in the chair and slapped Matthew's face viciously with the back of his hand.

"Sit down, pal, you're going bloody nowhere!" he sneered.

Ginger remonstrated with Newton. "Easy, Don! Matt's all right. We had better let him go, he won't say anything. After all, we're old mates and he's certainly no dobber."

"Are you mad?" screeched Newton. "I thought I taught you better than that. You don't trust nobody in this game. Especially so after you have been shooting your mouth off to him – and don't deny it because I have been listening at the door for the last five minutes. Truss him up, blindfold him and put him in the cellar. I'll take his car and put it away in the lock-up garage. We'll have another couple of days before the old dear comes back."

Matthew, becoming increasingly alarmed at the turn of events, leapt to his feet and made a dash to the door. Newton thrust out a foot to send Matthew tumbling to the floor, and he struck his head on the stout leg of the table, leaving him dazed and unable to get up off the floor. Newton strode over to the broom cupboard from which he produced a length of clothes line. He swiftly pinioned Matthew's arms to his side and bound both his arms and legs with the rope. He went through Matthew's pockets and relieved him of his car keys.

He turned to Ginger.

"I'll go now and get rid of his car. We can't afford any loose ends so once I'm out the door, put his bloody lights out."

With this last callous instruction he hurried through the door into the night.

Ginger picked up Matthew from the floor and propped him up in the fireside chair. "Now just you keep nice and quiet, old son. You have upset Don, so I don't suppose you will be going home tonight. But don't worry too much, I'll have a word with him when he gets back. In the meantime we'll relax and watch a bit of telly."

He crossed to the corner of the room and switched on the small portable television. The local news programme was drawing to a close.

"Finally the local headlines again. Police forces throughout the Midlands are searching for Donald James Newton, aged twenty-seven, of Retford, Notts. He is wanted on armed robbery and suspicion of murder."

Newton's picture then appeared on the screen. The announcer continued, "The public are warned not to approach Newton, who may be accompanied by another man of similar appearance, but whose identity is as yet unknown, as both men are armed and dangerous. Members of the public are warned not to approach them but to report their whereabouts to the nearest police station."

Ginger grinned at Matthew.

"Fame at last, Matt, eh! It's a nice feeling to be wanted!"

A flash of light suddenly appeared at the kitchen window. Matthew's head jerked up when he saw it. Ginger's reaction was instantaneous,: he flicked off the kitchen light, pulled the plug from the television and rushed out of the kitchen and up the stairs and into the front bedroom, peering cautiously on to the street. He saw with alarm the figure of a policeman shining his torch down the passageway on to the two motorbikes. He watched with growing horror as the policeman advanced down the passageway and flung back the tarpaulin covering the bikes. When he pulled out his police radio and began speaking into it, Ginger had seen enough. He descended the stairs in a great hurry, snatched up a roll of sticking plaster from the kitchen drawer, cut off a strip and attached it over Matthew's mouth.

"Sorry about this, Matt, but needs must! There is a copper outside and he's spotted the bikes, so it's time I went. I'm afraid I'll have to put you in the cellar for now, but it shouldn't be too long before they find you. No hard feelings, eh!"

Matthew's heart beat faster as Ginger opened the cellar door and dragged him down the steps. He felt a pang of fear as he recalled Newton's last chilling barb, to "put his bloody lights out".

Ginger had killed three times: was he to become the fourth victim? He needn't have worried. Ginger propped him against the wall, ruffled his hair by way of a farewell and rushed back up the stairs, locking the cellar door on his way out.

He snatched up his coat and left the house via the kitchen door. Adopting a running crouch, he raced up to the garden wall, scarcely pausing before he scaled it in true military fashion to reach the neighbouring garden. Without pausing for breath he scaled the wall of the next garden and the next until he reached the garden of the first house on the street, which was on the corner of the main Hucknall Road. Gasping for breath from his exertions, he crouched beneath a large shrub and considered his next move.

The Hunt Is On

Things were certainly starting to happen outside the house Ginger had left in such a hurry. As Ginger had rightly discerned, the patrolling policeman had spotted the Kawasaki bikes and had immediately radioed in his sighting to Radford Road. The controller had ordered the policeman to take up a position opposite the house and maintain a watching brief until the arrival of reinforcements, for he was on no account to approach the house on his own.

Radford Road Police Station was soon a scene of hectic activity as a long-planned plan of action was put into practice. Within minutes of the policeman's call three police cars screeched out of the station yard, closely followed by two police vans. One police car pulled up outside Mrs Warburton's house and trained a searchlight on the side passage. The two police vans disgorged their cargo of blue-capped, armed response officers, who took up positions around the house. The other two police cars sealed off each end of the street.

Hutchinson, accompanied by Mulraney, was in the lead police car and was soon conversing with Inspector Richard Wardle, the commander of the armed response unit. Before any action was initiated, several of the immediate neighbours were quizzed as to the inhabitants of Mrs Warburton's house. They soon discovered that the landlady was away and that the only known inhabitants were two young men, presumed to be working men as they were invariably attired in blue overalls. They had been lodging at Mrs Warburton's for at least the last ten days. They kept very much to themselves and didn't appear to have much of a social life. One neighbour recalled that they were similar looking, both having close-cropped hair.

One appeared surly, "the stocky one," said the neighbour, but the ginger-haired one spoke politely and smiled a lot. "I wouldn't mind taking him home to bed!" joked the buxom middle-aged neighbour.

Hutchinson and Mulraney exchanged meaningful glances. When they were out of earshot of the neighbour, Hutchinson, rubbing his hands together with a growing feeling of excitement, said, "At last this looks like our men, Brian."

Mulraney nodded and the two officers relayed their findings to Wardle, who immediately ordered his men to move in on the house with extreme caution and detain the two suspects. Two of the men crept up the passageway and, one either side, cautiously peered through the kitchen window. They saw two unwashed cups on the kitchen table, but there were no obvious signs of occupancy.

Two more of the armed officers tried the back door, which they found unlocked. Six men then entered the kitchen at a rush. Soon the entire house was systematically searched room by room, one officer covering another as they burst through the doors. Various items suspected of belonging to the two wanted men were bagged up and removed for forensic examination. There was only one door found to be locked in the entire house and that was the cellar door. This proved to be no problem whatsoever for the two burly policemen who tackled it with the aid of a sledgehammer. One blow was sufficient to shatter the lock and gain entry to the dark and dank cellar. The powerful beam of the officer's torch picked out the trussed-up figure of Matthew propped up in the corner.

Hutchinson was summoned to the scene and was surprised and little amused at what he saw. He bent over Matthew and grasped a corner of the sticking plaster.

"I'll say sorry in advance of pulling this off," he said, "because I warn you, it will hurt!"

With one sharp tug he tore away the plaster. Matthew gasped involuntarily, first with pain then relief at finding that he was able to breathe through his mouth as well as his nose.

"Thank God for that!" he gasped. "It didn't take you blokes long. I thought I would be down here for days."

Hutchinson smiled as he cut through the ropes binding Matthew.

"Glad to be of service, now perhaps you will return the compliment by answering some questions."

Matthew began to feel normal, aided by a cup of tea, brewed by one of the two policewomen who had joined the numerous policemen now swarming all over the house. Matthew then related to Hutchinson his account of the extraordinary events which had led to his being found in the cellar. Hutchinson listened intently, particularly when Matthew revealed the identity and extraordinary confession of Peter Tomlinson.

Whilst the drama was enfolding at one end of Ebury Road, Ginger was making good his escape at the other. He realised that he couldn't remain in the garden any longer because Don Newton was due to return to Ebury Road any minute and would unwittingly drive straight into the hands of the police. He must warn him. He knew that Don had driven Matthew's car to the lock-up garage they rented at Rise Park, to the north-west of the city. The journey time was about fifteen minutes, so if he was lucky he should be able to intercept Don somewhere along the Hucknall Road, unless he took a different route. He pulled his coat round him, vaulted the wall and strode up Hucknall Road in confident fashion, even though he was feeling rather nervous. His anxiety increased when a series of police cars, blue lights flashing, passed him and all turned into Ebury Road. He pulled up his collar and slightly averted his head as the police cars passed him. Oh God, he had stirred up a hornet's nest – the house must be swarming with cops. They would find the bikes and they would also find Matthew, who would tell the cops everything.

'Why couldn't I have kept my big mouth shut? But, there again,' he reflected, 'I had to tell somebody. It was sheer bad luck that that copper had spotted the bikes. The main thing now is to find Don and go to ground until the rumpus dies down.'

There was sleet falling from the sky as he neared a set of traffic signals with a long line of traffic waiting either side of the lights. They changed to green and it was then that Ginger spotted Don's blue Ford Escort pulling away from the lights. He dashed across the road, frantically waving down the Escort as it increased speed. Newton spotted him in the nick of time and fiercely applied his brakes, bringing the car to a halt within inches of Ginger. He wound down his window and glared furiously at him.

"What the hell are you playing at? I nearly ran you down."

Ginger didn't waste any time. He opened the passenger door and got in.

"Quick, Don! Turn the car round and go back to the lock-up! The whole place is swarming with cops!"

Newton didn't argue; he turned the car into a side road, waited for a gap in the traffic and swung the car in the direction from whence it had come. As the car sped back towards the lock-up, Ginger brought Newton up to date with what had happened. Newton listened in grim silence until Ginger had finished then he exploded.

"You fucking stupid idiot! I told you to trust nobody and still you go and blurt everything out to your so-called pal, then instead of remedying your mistake by knocking him off, you leave him to tell the cops all about us. You realise you have probably done for the pair of us! We'll be hunted down like rats!"

They remained in the lock-up garage throughout the night, arguing into the small hours as to what they should do next. Newton was all for leaving the area immediately and hiding up in the Yorkshire Moors. Ginger argued that the police would expect them to do that and would be armed with details of both the Escort and Matthew's Toyota. He also reminded Newton that he had one more task to fulfil before he left the city for good.

After the long argument left them both drained and exhausted they lapsed into uneasy sleep. They awoke at 5 a.m. stiff, cold and uncomfortable on the leather seats of the Escort.

They felt curiously unrefreshed by their sleep, thirsty and hungry, and knowing that the entire city was being combed for their whereabouts didn't make them feel any better. Spurred on by the increasing desperation of their situation, they decided upon a new plan. They knew it was imperative that they abandoned the lock-up and the cars, as it would be only a matter of time before the police stumbled on them. Newton finally conceded the point that the police would expect them to flee the city and as a consequence would be covering all exit points. So why not steal a beat-up car, preferably a van, and drive around the city in the guise of workmen? They reasoned that the police would not expect them to brazenly hang around the city, let alone carry out the final part of Ginger's plan to murder Angie, but that was exactly what they intended to do. They decided to deposit the robbery monies, together with the £5000 obtained from Malone, in the left luggage office at the Midland Station. In the event of either one of them being captured by the police, they would each have a ticket to reclaim the money from the luggage office. Other than that, they both planned to travel to London after the murder and lie low. Newton knew a man he had met in the army who would put them up, for a price.

They donned their familiar blue overalls and pulled woollen hats over their heads to look like ordinary workmen. They crammed the proceeds of the robbery and the extra £5000 into two battered suitcases and reluctantly left the lock-up garage and the two vehicles to their fate.

They shivered in the chill morning air as they walked through the deserted streets of Rise Park. Soon the modern houses of the private estate were replaced by the council houses of the Bestwood Estate. Here there was an abundance of battered second-hand vehicles either side of the street. They were spoilt for choice but finally selected a begrimed transit van. Breaking into it was child's play for Newton, who quickly located the ignition wires, touched them together and they were off.

The filthy blue transit van didn't warrant a second glance as it sped through streets now showing signs of life on its way to the city. The normally ice-cool Newton felt on edge and cast nervous glances at the oncoming traffic. Not so Ginger, who whistled as he drove on confidently, a mood of optimism engulfing him. He felt as if his confession to his old friend Matthew had somehow justified his actions. He knew deep down that Matthew would be honour-bound to tell the police all he knew, but no matter – he was famous now and, besides, they would never catch him.

Police were everywhere, especially at road junctions, but Ginger soon merged the transit van into a solid stream of early-morning commuter traffic which increased as they neared the city centre. He pulled off the main Mansfield Road and joined a queue of cars awaiting entry to the Forest Park and Ride site. They parked the van along one of the neat lines of cars on the recreation ground before paying a pound for their bus journey into the city centre.

Adopting a low profile, they mingled with the early morning shoppers and entered McDonalds, where they wolfed down cheeseburgers and lingered over their coffee. They ambled through the crowds on Slab Square, even pausing to feed the pigeons. They spent the remainder of the morning scanning the morning papers for news of themselves. They were disappointed that there was no mention of them in the dailies. But they got rather a shock when they stared at two large photo-fits of themselves on the front mid-morning edition of *The Post*. They felt a little unnerved at the remarkably good photo-fits and read the banner headlines: POLICE COMB CITY FOR WANTED MEN.

Full descriptions followed and Ginger found his name in print for the first time. Both men cast furtive glances around the library reading room.

Newton nudged Ginger and whispered in his ear, "So much for trusting your old mate!"

Ginger ignored the jibe and continued reading his newspaper. After all, he couldn't really blame Matthew. He supposed that he would have done exactly the same thing in his position. It had never even crossed Ginger's mind to carry out Newton's suggestion of disposing of Matthew.

Feeling increasingly conspicuous in the reading room, they left the library anxious to mingle unnoticed with the city crowds. In mid-afternoon they returned to the park and ride site and drove off in their van, skirting the city centre, towards the Midland Station. After parking the van they took a suitcase each and entered the left luggage office independently of each other by five minutes. In line with their prearranged plan each man retained a separate ticket to reclaim the luggage. They returned once more to the park and ride site and waited there, with some impatience, for the onset of darkness prior to their embarking on what they hoped was their final crime, the killing of Angie.

A Trap Is Set

The fugitives were blissfully unaware of the elaborate plan about to be put into operation to ensnare them. Up to now they had been very lucky and felt almost blasé about their chances of ever being captured by the police. But all that was about to change. Throughout the day Hutchinson had been putting together an audacious plot involving the deployment of a large number of personnel, including the armed response unit. He was aware that his plan would need the explicit approval of the top brass and, after hammering out the main details of the plan with his subordinates, he arranged a lunchtime meeting with Chief Maudsley.

The police chief was highly sceptical of Hutchinson's plan at first, pointing out that its main flaw was the tying up of a significant number of policemen, therefore leaving an absence of cover on the streets. Hutchinson's original idea had been for the plan to be implemented over a period of three nights, which Maudsley scotched immediately. Hutchinson put his case for a compromise and reluctantly the chief agreed that he could deploy the required numbers for one night only. Hutchinson decided there and then to gamble as to when the best time would be, and obtained permission to put the plan into operation that very same night.

Earlier that morning the Rise Park lock-up garage had been discovered and Hutchinson assumed, based on Matthew's evidence, that the two men were still in the city and intended to carry out the final part of their plan. Hutchinson estimated, rightly as it turned out, that they would waste no time in its execution, so why not tonight?

After the long hours of discussion and dissemination of Matthew's crucial statement, Hutchinson concluded that he was dealing with a very dangerous psychopath whose orgy of killing, on his own admission, had not ended. It was of paramount importance that he was caught before he got the chance of achieving his aim.

Hutchinson knew that great care must be exercised in the manner of his arrest, as there was a distinct possibility of further killings if he was cornered in the manner of the proverbial sewer rat. The fact that he was teamed up with Newton would make his capture that bit more difficult. Newton was an experienced and hardened criminal well-versed in the skills of evading capture. The crux or centrepiece of Hutchinson's plan was to lure the two men into the open and box them in, leaving no escape route whatsoever. To tempt the men into breaking cover, suitable bait was required, and that was to be Ginger's intended victim, Angie McPherson.

After a hurried lunch, Hutchinson gathered together his close-knit team of Mulraney, the two policewomen Jackie and Lisa and a specially selected member of the ARU, PC James Amrowalla. They set off in two cars for the Noel Street home of Agnes McPherson, their mission to persuade Angie to act as a decoy.

Hutchinson's bold plan was fraught with danger and, though loyal to his boss, Mulraney had grave doubts as to its feasibility, considering that the risk factor was too great. He feared that things would go seriously wrong if, for instance, Tomlinson got to Angie first. Hutchinson's plan was to virtually eliminate the risk factor by ensuring that three police officers, two female and one male, would be in close attendance of Angie and that one would be armed.

They would all be carrying personal radios and would maintain contact with their operational commander and with each other at all times. As an extra precaution a microscopic tracking device was to be placed in Angie's handbag ensuring that her every movement was traced. On the surface the plan appeared to cover every contingency.

The biggest hurdle for the team was convincing Angie to act as a decoy. She remained in a highly emotional state after the funeral. She did not attend the wake and had remained closeted in her mother's house ever since. Hutchinson decided that they could best persuade Angie by informing her that they had identified her boyfriend's killer and uncovered a plot to kill her. This was a risk, as she might well be terrified by this disclosure, but Hutchinson reasoned that her volatile temper would explode and that she would grasp the chance for vengeance.

The police entourage was received at the door by a sceptical-looking Agnes.

"What, you lot again! Why can't you keep away and leave my daughter to grieve in peace?"

Hutchinson used his considerable charm to persuade a reluctant Agnes to allow them to speak to her daughter. Entering the living room, they confronted the sullen-looking Angie lying full length on the couch. She truculently made room for the two policewomen to perch themselves either side of her.

Hutchinson decided, as time was pressing, not to beat about the bush, but to tell her the full facts of the situation. Angie sat for a short time in stunned silence as Hutchinson recounted all he knew about the identity and actions of Peter Tomlinson, then she suddenly erupted.

"The murdering callous bastard!" she cried. "Just let me get my hands on him! I'll tear his bloody heart from his body! I'll gouge his bloody eyes out!"

She turned scornfully to Hutchinson. "And as for you, conniving crafty bastard – I won't do it! Why the hell should I? Why don't you do your own dirty work?"

She collapsed into the arms of Lisa Harris, sobbing uncontrollably, Hutchinson wisely not intervening but allowing her emotions to run their full course. As Angie's vitriolic outburst subsided, Agnes came into the room bearing a tray of tea and biscuits. Angie wiped her tearstained eyes and an air of normality was resumed.

Hutchinson quietly outlined his plan of action to the two women, assuring them of the close surveillance proposed for Angie, as her safety was of paramount importance.

Hutchinson used every method of psychological know-how in an effort to persuade Angie to co-operate in his plan. He praised her courage in advance of her accepting the role. He hinted, albeit light-heartedly, of the celebrity status she would attain if she helped to arrest a notorious killer. Finally he appealed to her basic instinct of revenge and the satisfaction she would feel at participating in the capture of her boyfriend's killer. Finally the logic of Hutchinson's argument won her over, as it had Chief Maudsley earlier in the day. Then the two policewomen took over and began reassuring and instilling confidence in her.

Lisa Harris briefed her on the exact details of the operation as it affected her. Lisa herself would be at Angie's side at all times. Jackie Harper would be a few feet behind her. On the opposite side of the road, PC Amrowalla, in plain clothes, would keep her in sight at all times. The two women officers would be effectively attired to resemble members of Angie's profession.

With Angie reasonably happy about her part in the operation, the two policewomen left Agnes's house to return to Radford Road to change into their street attire. To test the effectiveness of their new disguises they decided to walk the relatively short distance back to Agnes's house. They had already received appreciative wolf whistles from their uniformed colleagues, and were amused at the reaction of a stout middle-aged woman who stared in disgust at them and turned to her companion, saying in a loud voice, "Bloody tarts, they seem to be everywhere these days. Why can't they make a living on their two feet instead of on their back!"

After arriving back at Agnes's Noel Street home, they were flattered by the praise and admiring comments from the police officers but brought down to earth by a biting comment from Angie. Hutchinson gave a final briefing to the whole team and proposed that the operation commence immediately, there being only one hour to go before official lighting-up time.

Angie was encouraged to resume her normal nightly route in search of punters, with the surveillance team in close attendance. Everything was to appear normal, and she was to be allowed to converse with each prospective client, except that she was on no account to go with them or to get into their vehicles. The surveillance team would carefully scrutinise every prospective punter in the hope that he was the wanted man.

Immediately either or both of the men were identified then the trap would begin to close, roadblocks would be mounted in the immediate vicinity, and the fugitives hemmed in before being forced to surrender.

Shortly after the group left the house an untoward event occurred which very nearly put the whole operation in jeopardy. Two black youths suddenly appeared from an alleyway strolling nonchalantly, hands in pockets, towards Angie. As they neared her, they suddenly rushed forward, one either side of her. The first youth lashed out with his fist, striking Angie across her chest and causing her to cry out in pain. The second youth snatched her shoulder bag and began to run away.

He almost ran directly into Lisa Harris, who was only just behind Angie. Lisa reacted immediately by bringing the surprised youth crashing to the ground in a rugby tackle. The other youth panicked and ran straight across the road, directly into the waiting arms of PC Amrowalla, who handled him none too gently. Within seconds, a police van screeched to a halt at the side of the road and the two youths were dumped without ceremony into the back. They regarded one another in stunned silence, amazed at the lightning turn of events.

Hutchinson hoped that after such a disastrous start his plan could only get better. Angie's bag was restored to her fully intact, and, apart from hurt pride, she had suffered nothing other than shock and a slight bruising on her chest. She would never admit it but she had been secretly impressed by the swift reaction of the police and the incident was useful in that it gave her added confidence.

With her unusual escorts in close attendance she eventually reached her usual much prized spot on Forest Road. She was stopped twice on her way there by enquiring punters, whom she dissuaded by quoting a ridiculously high price for her favours. Two of her prostitute friends attempted to converse with Angie but changed their minds at the last minute, recognising the policewomen despite their elaborate disguise.

A steady stream of punters approached Angie and even the two policewomen were propositioned, much to their amusement. Two men actually agreed to the high price quoted by Angie, but Angie walked away, to the amazement of the bemused punters.

After seven o'clock there was a lull in the activity and the cold northerly wind was having an effect on the girls, their scanty attire being inadequate protection on such a cold night.

Angie spoke to Lisa Harris. "I'm bloody fed up! I'm cold and I'm dying for a pee, I haven't earned a single penny all night and I've even turned down a couple a hundred quid. There is no sign of them bloody fellas, so let's call it a night!"

Lisa looked at her watch.

"Hang on, love, let's give it a bit more time. Have a pee up that alleyway, I'll keep watch."

Angie reluctantly agreed and, squatting down, noisily relieved herself in the porchway of a nearby house.

Fifteen minutes later their boredom was relieved by the appearance of a van being driven very slowly down the road as if the driver was searching for something. Lisa noticed the van first and shouted to Angie, who emerged from the doorway where she had been sheltering from the wind. She began a slow trudge down the road with Lisa only two yards behind her. The van followed her at a snail's pace.

Lisa risked a glance and noted that the van was in an appallingly filthy condition, with the windows all steamed up. The van finally overtook Angie and halted some three yards in front of her.

As Angie neared the van, the window was slowly wound down. Angie bent down to converse with the driver, the two policewomen rapidly closing on her. As the dirty, steamed-up window was only half wound down, Angie had difficulty in seeing the occupant. She could quite clearly see that he was wearing blue overalls but she was unable to perceive his features as he had a woollen cap pulled well down over his head. She didn't know the man but he aroused her suspicions enough for her to alert the two policewomen by using the prearranged signal of scratching her head.

She spoke directly to the man.

"Looking for business, duck?"

"Yeah," replied the man. "How much?"

Angie smiled. "Bit out of your range, matey. One hundred quid!"

"Bollocks," replied the man, who reacted quickly, though not in the way that Angie had anticipated. He opened the sliding door of the van and thrust out an arm, almost crushing Angie's head in the crook of his arm.

Maintaining a vice-like grip, with one almighty heave he pulled the screaming girl into the van. Inside the van a second man took over. He pulled the terrified girl into the interior of the van. He pushed her face to the floor and twisted her arms behind her back, making any movement impossible.

Lisa Harris bravely threw herself at the rapidly closing door of the van, outstretched fingers seeking to grasp the handle. The van began to pull away with her arm trapped in the door. Mercifully the driver released the door, causing her to fall in a heap at the side of the road.

Jackie Harper dashed to the aid of her injured colleague and PC Amrowalla spoke urgently into his handset.

Soon the crackle of police messages dominated the night's airwaves as the police contingency plan swung into action. The speeding van headed towards Alfreton Road but its progress was halted by the positioning of two police patrol cars at the junction with Forest Road.

Don Newton reversed the van and drove back up Forest Road, passing PC Amrowalla, who hurled his baton at the windscreen. He scored a direct hit, but though the windscreen cracked it did not shatter.

At the next traffic lights the van's further progress was blocked by the presence of two police cars, forcing it to turn left down Noel Street.

Inside the van, Newton was quietly pleased that thus far he had avoided the police, unaware that he had taken the route pre-planned for him. In the back of the van Angie's initial anger had evaporated and she now felt terrified and in fear for her life. She knew, though she was unable to see him, since her face was thrust down on the filthy floor of the van, that the man holding her was the man she abhorred, the killer of Bo.

She knew full well that this man intended her to be his next victim. This thought spurred her into a desperate effort to save her life.

Summoning up every ounce of strength in her body, she wriggled and twisted from side to side in an attempt to dislodge the vice-like grip employed on her by Ginger. She freed one of her shoulders and managed at last to raise her head from the dirt-encrusted floor. She twisted her head and looked up at her captor, seeing him for the first time.

She swore at him, "Let me up, you bastard, you're hurting me."

Ginger grinned malevolently at her as he released one of her arms then grabbed her hair, jerking her head upwards.

"Shuttup bitch and eat dirt – that's all you're fit for!"

With that he slammed her face to the floor of the van, causing Angie to cry out in pain.

Newton drove the van at speed down the hill and was through the traffic lights on Radford Boulevard before he suddenly realised that he had reached the end of the line. As he passed the huge flats complex on his left-hand side he saw that further progress was effectively blocked. At the end of Noel Street there was a phalanx of police vehicles. With a sudden feeling of apprehension he glanced into his rear view mirror and his worst fears were confirmed when he saw more police cars sealing off his retreat. He brought the van to a sudden stop at the entrance to the flats complex, and turned in his seat.

"We're trapped, Pete – the bastards have boxed us in. Leave the girl and we'll make a dash through the flats."

Ginger pulled Angie to her feet and produced a knife from his pocket, placing it across her throat.

"No way, Don. The bitch comes with us – she could be our passport out of this. Here, grab the shotgun."

He kicked over the sacking-wrapped sawn-off shotgun towards Newton. As soon as the two men and their hostage got out of the van they were surrounded by at least twenty policemen, including three blue-capped members of the armed response unit.

The trio backed slowly towards the concourse entrance, Ginger to the rear, his knife pressed so close against Angie's throat that it broke the skin, causing a small trickle of blood to seep slowly down her neck.

At the forefront Newton raised his shotgun to shoulder height, swinging it menacingly from side to side in an arc towards the policemen. The three members of the ARU trained their weapons on Newton. One of their number shouted at Newton, "*Stop!* Armed police! Throw down your weapon immediately and release your hostage or we will shoot!"

Ginger pressed the knife with even more force to Angie's throat, producing more blood.

"Stay where you are! One move, copper and I'll slit her throat!"

The leading policeman hesitated, glancing back at his commander for guidance. The commander slowly shook his head at the marksman, who remained where he was. The trio began to walk slowly backwards up the concrete ramp of the concourse, encouraged in the realisation that Ginger's threat was being taken seriously by the police.

Ginger suppressed the urge to run for he didn't dare risk turning his back on the police. He was alerted to a presence to his rear by the low murmur of approaching voices. A large group of some twenty youths came into view at the top of the concourse. Suddenly the leading bunch rushed forward towards the trio. Ginger's arm was pulled to one side and Angie was first jostled then pulled to one side by the youths.

Two of their number rained blows and kicks at Ginger. He staggered sideways, surprised by the suddenness and ferocity of the attack. But he retained his grip on the knife and lashed out, slashing the arm of one youth who clutched the wound as blood gushed through his fingers. Ginger waved the knife in a threatening fashion and the youths retreated warily. Other youths attempted to overpower Newton by jumping on his back. He turned to shake off his assailants, amid a furious onslaught of kicks and blows to his head. In the ensuing mêlée he was forced to drop the shotgun and use his fists to defend himself.

He had floored two of the youths and was about to stamp on the head of a third when the first of the police marksmen arrived on the scene. He jabbed his gun hard into Newton's ribs and shouted, "Armed police! Put your hands in the air!"

The youths backed away to the walls of the concourse as the two other blue-capped policeman joined their colleague, who continued to shout orders to Newton.

"Lie face down on the ground and put your hands behind your back!"

Newton did exactly as he was ordered and his hands were roughly seized and secured with handcuffs, the policeman kneeling none too gently on his back while he secured the cuffs.

Meanwhile Ginger, taking advantage of the commotion around Newton, rushed headlong up the walkway anxious to lose himself in the rabbit warren of passageways in the vast flats complex. Several of the youths began to pursue him but were stopped by a police officer who bellowed instructions with the aid of a bullhorn.

"This is the police! Do not follow that man. He is a dangerous criminal. Please return to your homes immediately. Please assist the police by keeping these walkways clear."

The police commander monitoring the operation from a police van on Noel Street ordered an instant curfew of the flats complex with all entrances and exits to be manned by police officers to check the identity of anyone leaving.

The unfortunate Angie was given immediate first aid on the nasty gash to her neck and then taken to her mother's nearby house. Although very badly shaken and bruised and in deep shock, she was thankfully still alive. Ginger's desperate sprint had gained him a good lead on his pursuers, who were now wholly policemen. He had reached the end of the first walkway and was about to turn right and dash down the next one when he noticed an open door at the head of a flight of six steps leading to a flat.

Framed in the doorway was a small girl, earnestly sucking her thumb and staring quizzically at Ginger. He saw that she was a very pretty little girl, with light coffee-coloured skin, dark curly hair and large brown eyes. Ginger gripped the stair rail, leaning forward and gasping for breath.

"Are you coming to our 'ouse?" asked the child in a piping voice.

Ginger glanced over his shoulder, the thudding footsteps of his pursuers sounding ever nearer. He didn't need any further persuasion. He ran up the short flight of stairs, lifted the child inside and snapped shut the latched door. He put down the child and raised his finger to his lips.

"Let's play a game, okay?" he asked.

The child smiled and nodded enthusiastically.

Ginger bent down and looked into her eyes, still with his finger to his lips. "Shusssh," he said.

The child smiled delightedly and raised her finger to her lips in imitation, whispering, "Shussh."

The sound of footsteps was now a crescendo, then they halted. Ginger could hear the sound of voices.

"Which sodding way has he gone?"

"Dunno for sure, but that set of steps leads straight down to the street so he must have gone right down the next walkway."

Another voice then. "Take your time, lads, there's no way this bugger gets away. We've cornered him like a rat, every exit is sealed – it's only a matter of time."

The sound of many footsteps, now at walking pace, slowly receded.

Ginger strained his ears for signs of occupation in the flat. He looked down on the little girl.

"Where's your mummy and daddy?" he asked the child.

"Ain't got no daddy and me Mam's gone to bingo. Come on in and watch the telly wi' me."

The little girl trustingly proffered her tiny hand to Ginger and, clutching it gently, Ginger allowed himself to be led into the oblong-shaped sitting room whose windows looked directly down on Noel Street. He stepped towards the window and, placing his body to one side, pulled back the net curtain and risked a look. There were large numbers of police everywhere. Two large vans blocked off either end of the street and searchlights illuminated the concourse.

On the opposite side of the street two lines of blue tape were stretched from one end of the street to the other, behind which was a large crowd of curious onlookers. The scene was further enhanced by the arrival of a television crew from Central TV who soon began setting up arc lights and cameras.

Ginger had seen enough. He released the curtain and pondered his situation. He felt like a cat with nine lives who had reached the ninth. There was no doubt in his mind that up to now he had been extremely lucky but he felt that his luck was about to run out. He was trapped like the proverbial rat and there didn't seem to be a way out.

He looked at the little girl sprawled contentedly on the floor, large brown eyes taking in a lurid film on the television.

"What's your name, sweetie?"

The small girl delicately picked her nose but kept her eyes riveted on the screen. "Nat Lee. What's yours, mistah?"

"Natalie. Hmm, that's a nice name. You had better call me Mr Man," said Ginger.

He decided to explore the flat further. He left Natalie fully engrossed in her lurid film and discovered a small kitchen next to the living room. A narrow corridor led to two bedrooms, the smaller of the two being Natalie's judging by the wallpaper.

He entered the larger of the bedrooms, which was dominated by a large double bed covered by a pink quilt. Two wardrobes covered the entire wall facing the bed. The first of the wardrobes contained the clothes of Natalie's mother but the second wardrobe interested Ginger. There were a number of shirts, three pairs of jeans and two smart-looking leather jackets of good quality, complete with matching leather caps.

On a sudden impulse Ginger decided, what the hell, he might as well help himself. He stripped off his blue overalls and selected for himself a red check shirt, blue jersey and jeans from the wardrobe. They were a good fit and, after checking his appearance in the wardrobe mirror, he decided to complete the picture by donning one of the leather jackets. Placing the leather cap on his head, he added a final touch to his disguise by wearing a pair of dark glasses that he found in the inner pocket of the jacket.

He went back into the living room where a giggling Natalie looked up at him, saying, "Are you our Mam's new boyfriend then?"

"Well, I don't know about that," said Ginger, forced to smile. "And who is Mammy's boyfriend?"

"He's called Colin. But Mam sez 'e's gone on holiday to Lincoln and 'e won't be back for six months. I'm glad really cos I don't like 'im."

"Why don't you like him, Natalie?"

"'Cos 'e 'its me and keeps telling me I'm naughty."

Before Ginger could reply there was the sound of footsteps outside the flat followed by a loud banging on the door.

Ginger's heart began to beat faster, and he turned towards Natalie, placing his finger to his lips in a familiar gesture.

"Shuuuussssh."

Natalie grinned, remembered the game and repeated the gesture. The knocking ceased and the letterbox flap was raised. A voice shouted, "Anyone at home?"

There was a pause as the voice continued, "This is the police. Please do not leave your home until further notice. There is a dangerous man at large in the immediate area. If you see or hear anything suspicious please let us know directly or by dialling 999. Thank you."

As Ginger listened intently, hardly daring to breathe, the footsteps faded, to be followed by more knocking next door. Ginger exhaled deeply, Natalie giggled and resumed her viewing, happy in the sweet innocence of her youth.

Ginger paced back and forth, nervous at the proximity of the police and unsure of his next move. At the moment he was safer staying put but what if Natalie's mother were to return? Another hour elapsed before a police van mounted by a loudspeaker announced the end of the curfew but advised residents to report anything suspicious to any of the police officers on duty in the immediate vicinity of the flats. Ginger had devised a sketchy plan of action and decided that now was the time to put it to the test. He extended his hand to Natalie.

"Come on, sweetheart, let's get your coat on and go for a little walk."

Natalie looked up at him. "Where are we going, Mr Man? And what will me Mam say?"

Ginger smiled reassuringly.

"Somewhere nice, Natalie, I promise you'll like it. It will be a surprise. Don't worry about Mummy. She won't mind one bit."

Natalie struggled into her purple anorak and trustingly placed her hand in Ginger's. Ginger lifted the Yale latch, pausing momentarily as he considered the huge risk he was taking. Reaching the bottom of the steps, he picked up Natalie and swung her on to his shoulders.

Taking a deep breath, he strode purposefully down the walkway whistling a tune with Natalie's chubby legs astride each of his shoulders, swinging them to and fro shouting, "We're going for a ride!"

The flats were rapidly returning to life after the curfew, people appearing in small groups hurrying along the walkways. Ginger's heartbeat increased as two uniformed policemen approached him from the opposite direction; desperately trying to maintain a nonchalant air, he continued whistling.

The first of the policemen smiled at the sight of Natalie atop his shoulders.

"Can't keep the kiddies in for long, can you, sir? But mind how you go. We haven't caught this bleeder yet!"

Ginger mumbled an incoherent reply and continued walking, his apparent unconcern masking his thumping heart. As he neared the end of the concourse he saw with growing dismay that there was a group of four policemen deep in conversation whose purpose, he assumed, was to check on people leaving the complex.

Ginger slowed his pace as a chattering group of young women emerged from a flat door directly in front of him. His heart almost stopped when one of the young women turned around and spoke directly to Natalie.

"Hullo Natalie darling, are you going to meet your mum?"

Natalie giggled and beat her fists up and down on Ginger's head.

The woman spoke to her companions.

"I reckon that must be Mary's latest – she never could go long wi' out it!"

The women burst into peals of laughter and bunched together as they passed the policemen.

Ginger slightly increased his pace and tagged on to the end of the women as if he were with them. Natalie, thoroughly enjoying herself, tugged at his left ear, causing him to slightly avert his head. As he passed the policemen, out of the corner of his eye he could see one of their number, a uniformed sergeant, break off his conversation and glance at the group leaving the concourse. Ginger felt the tension at the back of his neck as his muscles tightened. He expected to hear a challenging shout at any minute.

He walked slowly down the walkway into Noel Street resisting the almost overwhelming urge to run. The crowds of some two hours ago had dispersed but there were plenty of people about. Ginger strode on feeling ever more confident, even when he passed more policemen patrolling singly up and down Noel Street. Reaching Gregory Boulevard, he crossed the road and joined a long queue of people waiting for a city-bound bus.

Boarding the bus, he put Natalie down and paid his fare to the driver. Natalie tugged at his coat.

"Can we ride on top, Mr Man?" she asked.

"Okay sweetheart," replied Ginger, gently lifting her up the first two steps of the stairway.

The bus driver and some of the passengers smiled at the nice young man and his charming daughter enjoying the simple pleasures of life.

The happy pair alighted from the bus in the city centre and, after a short walk, Natalie's eyes lit up when Ginger took her into McDonalds restaurant. Ginger bought himself a Big Mac and Natalie devoured a cheeseburger and a large strawberry milkshake. He noticed that Natalie had finished her cheeseburger before he himself had finished his Big Mac.

"Would you like another cheeseburger, Natalie?" he enquired.

"Yeah!" said Natalie, brown eyes bulging, giggling contentedly.

Ginger purchased a second milkshake along with the cheeseburger and paid £35 for a large yellow teddy bear on special offer.

Natalie's delight overflowed when Ginger returned to the table. She wolfed down her second cheeseburger and sipped happily on her milkshake, one arm clutching the large yellow teddy bear. Ginger sighed contentedly as he finished his meal. He hadn't felt this happy for a long time. He glanced at Natalie, whose eyelids were beginning to flicker. If only things had worked out differently, how proud he would feel to have a daughter like Natalie. The child's head began to droop. He leant over the table.

"Are you tired, sweetheart?"

"Yeah, Mr Man. Time for Nat Lee to go bed."

Ginger turned over the menu card and wrote a short note in pencil on it, folded it up and placed it in Natalie's pocket. "Time to go now, pet. Make sure Mummy gets that note."

As they left the restaurant together, Ginger scooped up the little girl, who fell asleep in his arms clutching her teddy bear.

He hailed a passing taxi cab and gently placed the sleeping child on the back seat, planting a farewell kiss on her forehead. He slipped the driver a £20 note and requested that Natalie be delivered to 107 Tenby Walk.

"That's in the Hyson Green flats," he added.

"Yeah, I know it well, mate," replied the driver. "But listen, how—"

His words were lost in the roar of passing traffic as Ginger merged swiftly into the night.

Twenty minutes later the midnight St Pancras express glided out of Nottingham's Midland Station en route to the capital. As the train passed beneath the floodlit outline of the castle, Ginger, reclining luxuriously in the seat of a first-class compartment, wondered if he would ever see his home town again.

Recriminations

Mary Paterson was in a happy mood as she left Yates' Wine Lodge after celebrating a modest £150 'house' win at the city centre bingo hall she patronised so frequently. In carefree mood she hired a taxi to return to her Hyson Green home. Poor Mary was blissfully unaware of the night's dramatic events and the part her only daughter had played in them. She was paying off the taxi cab in Noel Street when she was hailed by a plump girl, one of the group of women who had encountered Ginger and Natalie some two hours earlier. She tugged excitedly at Mary's sleeve.

"Ey up, Mary duck! I seen your new boyfriend tonight – you certainly don't waste much time do you, duck! Still, Natalie seemed to like him. You're well shot of that bugger doing time in Lincoln. Best bloody place for the likes of him!"

The astonished Mary pressed the girl for more details and then the full horror of the situation became glaringly apparent. She ran home in a panic, dropping her key in her anxiety to open her flat door. She rushed from room to room shouting out Natalie's name. On the bitter realisation that her daughter was missing, she collapsed in a heap on the sofa, sobbing uncontrollably. She always felt guilty when she left Natalie alone on the one night a week she visited her favourite bingo hall. She knew that the neighbours talked about her behind her back and more than one had been quick to condemn her for leaving the child alone. All very well for them to talk, they didn't know the full facts. Babysitters were like gold dust and they charged the earth. Besides, Natalie was a good kid: she wouldn't go out, or answer the door.

Mary was on the verge of ringing the police when there was a knock on her door. She opened the door and snatched the sleeping Natalie from the arms of the taxi driver. She repeatedly kissed the sleeping child, who opened one eye.

"Why are you crying, Mam? Where's Mr Man?"

The taxi driver turned to leave, but Mary grabbed his arm and thanked him profusely, pressing him to reveal exactly how he had found Natalie. The taxi driver told Mary of his encounter with Ginger, which alarmed Mary who thought that Natalie had probably been abducted and maybe, God forbid, sexually interfered with. Panic-stricken she grabbed the half awake child by the shoulders.

"Natalie, tell Mam, what happened with this strange man? Did he hurt you, darling?"

Natalie shook her head vigorously. "No, Mam. 'E was a nice man. 'E said to read a note in my coat pocket."

Mary thrust her hand inside Natalie's anorak and found the McDonalds menu. On the reverse side was written:

> *To the mother of Natalie,*
> *Thank you for the loan of your smashing kid.*
> *Don't worry, no harm has come to her. You*
> *should be proud of her but also ashamed for*
> *leaving her on her own. Please get her something*
> *nice with the attached. My love to Natalie*
> *Signed Mr Man*

Mary found a folded £20 note attached with a pin to the menu card. She gasped with shocked indignation when she read the note.

"The cheeky bleeder! Who the hell does he think he is! He breaks in here and snatches Natalie and then has the cheek to criticise me. Right, I'm going to get the police round here right away."

The taxi driver put a restraining hand on Mary's arm.

"Just a minute, my duck, don't be too hasty. I reckon your little girl was abducted by the man the cops are looking for."

Mary's eyes widened with alarm.

"All the more reason to call the police in then."

The taxi driver shook his head.

"No, me duck. Let me put a call through to one of the papers first – you'll make a packet out of a story like this."

Mary looked doubtful. "Ooh, I dunno, I mean all that publicity, the neighbours will chit-chat. Still, as you say, there's the money to consider. How much do you reckon then?"

"Well, I reckon a story like this should bring in a few thousand at least, especially as he apparently got away right under the noses of the police."

"Yeah, you're right there," said Mary, now definitely warming to the idea. "Will you ring the papers then? I'm not very good on the phone."

"It'll be a pleasure, my duck!" said the taxi driver, smiling broadly. "Of course I shall expect a little remuneration to be coming my way!"

"Okay," said Mary returning his smile, "I'll show you where the phone is."

The taxi driver contacted several of the tabloids and unashamedly hawked the story around for the most lucrative offer. Very soon Mary's small flat was engulfed by reporters but the main story was entrusted to *The Sun*. The following morning the banner headline proclaimed CHILD LEADS KILLER TO SAFETY.

The text continued:

> Five year old Natalie Paterson trustingly placed her hand in that of Britain's most wanted man, triple killer Peter Tomlinson. She unwittingly helped Tomlinson evade a police dragnet thrown around the Hyson Green flats in Nottingham. The cool killer treated Natalie to a

meal at McDonalds in the city centre, then calmly
ordered a taxi for her to be returned to her home.
The inevitable question must be posed. What the
hell were the police doing to allow this to happen?

This and similar stories in the tabloids made sorry reading
for Hutchinson and his colleagues. Mary Paterson belatedly
informed the police of her daughter's involvement with the
wanted man but their questioning of Natalie was fruitless, as
the exhausted child was not up to answering any more
question, having been kept up half the night with the posse of
pressmen. Despite the capture of Newton, Hutchinson's
daring plan was considered an abject failure. The
overwhelmingly hostile criticism from the media demanded
that heads should roll, so things looked ominous for
Hutchinson when Maudsley requested an early meeting with
him.

However, all was not lost for Hutchinson, thanks mainly to
a sharp-eyed desk sergeant. The police had lost no time in
questioning Newton, who had been quizzed throughout the
early hours of the morning. Not surprisingly, despite astute
questioning by both Hutchinson and Mulraney, he had
remained stoical throughout.

An exasperated Mulraney thumped the table in annoyance.

Newton smiled cynically and said, "Stop wasting your
time, copper, you'll get nothing out of me. I've been
questioned by experts and you're not in the same league."

Five minutes later Mulraney drew heavily on his cigarette
as he leant against the wall of the interview room whilst
enjoying a well-earned break.

"We're getting bloody nowhere, Pete," admitted
Mulraney. "This bastard is admitting nothing and not giving
us a clue where his oppo has gone."

Hutchinson nodded dolefully in agreement. They
desperately needed that little bit of luck so vital to the solving
of all murder cases.

It was at this moment that the missing luck was provided by the unlikely figure of portly Sergeant Don Whittle, who squeezed his bulk through the narrow door leading from the main office.

"Ah, there you are, sir," he said to Hutchinson. "I think I have found something that might interest you."

He handed Hutchinson a folded piece of paper.

"I was searching through Newton's anorak, which I found in the back of the van, when I noticed there was a tear in the lining of one of the pockets and that's where I found this left luggage ticket."

Hutchinson unfolded it.

"Of course! Well done Don! Midland bloody Station, today's date! The buggers have stashed the robbery money there and hope to pick it up later I'll bet. But what's more, I'll bet that's where Tomlinson headed."

He turned to Whittle.

"Get on to the Midland now. Tell them on the highest authority to halt the London train."

They were very fortunate. Due to a points failure the five minutes past midnight express had been stationary for just over an hour some eight miles out of Nottingham.

A Fugitive's Luck Runs Out

Ginger yawned and stretched out his legs. His previous good spirits had been replaced by feelings of frustration. He had lapsed into blissful sleep minutes after the train pulled out of the Midland Station but his sleep had been disturbed when the train jerked to a stop some eight miles further down the line. Ginger disregarded the temporary halt. He remembered travelling on the train years ago as a schoolboy and they were always being held up at some point or other; nothing changes, least of all on British Rail.

The only other occupant of Ginger's compartment was a stout, very disgruntled businessman, who complained in loud tones about the delay.

"Bloody British Rail," he mumbled to no one in particular. "Always late, never on time. What is it this time? Bloody cow on the line probably!"

Ginger ignored him, closed his eyes once more and tried to return to his slumber. Despite his efforts he found it impossible. The long wait dragged on and seemed interminable. Fully awake by now and only feeling half refreshed by his short sleep, he ventured into the corridor and pulled down the window, peering into the night to find the cause of the delay.

As his eyes traversed the length of the train his attention was caught by the sight of a flashing blue light. The train had halted some thirty yards from a level crossing and there was a police car on the right-hand side of the crossing. Ginger noticed that all the signals were red. As he watched, another police car appeared and he could detect the sound of shouts clearly in the night air. There was a sudden shudder and with a jerk the train began to move, except that it was now moving backwards.

Ginger returned to his compartment to find the irritable businessman in a better mood.

"We're on the move at last," he said to Ginger. "About bloody time. I'm for the bar. Fancy taking a snifter with me?"

"No thanks," said Ginger. "Besides, I think you'll find we're moving backwards not forwards."

The businessman exploded in a plethora of oaths and stamped out of the compartment in search of a British Rail official. "And when I find him I'll wring his bloody neck!"

Ginger, though becoming increasingly irritated by the delay, was not at this stage alarmed. The police cars worried him but perhaps there had been an accident at the crossing. The train appeared to lurch, then with a squeal and a clanging of metal it stopped again. Ginger ventured out into the corridor once more to find it full of chattering passengers.

"What the bloody hell is going on? Why have we stopped again?" he enquired of a youth sporting a purple punk hairstyle.

"It's all to do with the coppers, mate," said the youth. "Seems as if they are looking for some bloke or other. We've pulled into a siding so as they can search the train."

Ginger's heart skipped a beat.

"How do you know all this?" he asked the youth.

"Ah well, you see, it depends who you know," replied the youth. "It just so happens that my brother-in-law is the guard. Matter of fact, I've just this minute left him. The coppers have already started at the front of the train. They'll soon be here, then at last we can get moving I hope."

Ginger was thoroughly alarmed by now and he returned to his compartment and considered his next move. He had only two options open to him: either he bluffed it out and hoped he wasn't recognised; or he would have to make a run for it. He looked up at the rack, at his suitcase. He groaned inwardly. That was going to be bloody awkward if he did make a run for it. He was feeling desperate in his indecision when the stout businessman reappeared.

"Can you believe it?" he said to Ginger. "The bloody police are on the train now looking for a bloody criminal. They are in the next carriage so they should soon be here."

Ginger made his mind up fast as the police neared. He pulled down his suitcase from the rack and, keeping his back to the businessman, took out four bundles of notes and stuffed them into his pockets. He pushed hurriedly past the businessman.

"'Scuse me, mate, when you gotta go you gotta go."

He turned right down the corridor towards the toilet, and as he neared the end of the carriage he glanced back to see the blue uniform of a policeman sliding back the door of the first compartment. Ginger hurried through to the next carriage. He had to get off the train and he had better do it now.

He wrestled with the door handle but it was either stiff or locked, and he could not budge it. Somebody was coming down the corridor towards him. Grunting with the effort, he pulled down on the handle, pushing against the door with his knee for extra leverage. Suddenly the door burst open and Ginger almost fell out on to the track, so fierce was his forward momentum. He clung desperately to the door, swung out his legs and landed in an untidy heap between two clumps of blackened grass at the side of the track.

His fall was witnessed by a startled passenger who had appeared at the open door.

"Are you all right, mate?" he shouted to Ginger.

Ginger glanced up in alarm and rose hurriedly to his feet. He declined to reply to the man's question and scrambled up a grassy bank, anxious to get away from the train before the police realised what was happening. At the top of the grassy bank there was a hedge and behind that Ginger could detect the rusty strands of a barbed wire fence. He hesitated for a moment, glancing right and left, unsure as to which way to go. Shouts from the train made up his mind for him.

Not daring to take a backward glance, he plunged through the hedge, and, lifting one strand of the barbed wire, he crouched down in an effort to force his way through the barrier. The barbs tore at his brown leather jacket. He snatched at his leather cap, which was wrenched off his head as he plunged headlong. The wire ripped at his flesh, drawing blood, and he caught his leg on the rusty barbs of the fence, tearing a hole in his jeans. Ginger didn't feel any pain and ignored the damage to his clothes in his haste to put as much distance between himself and the train as possible.

The businessman in Ginger's compartment had been questioned by the police and had given the police a full description of him.

"Hope you catch the blighter," he added.

The police were now confident that they were hot on the heels of the wanted man, the opened carriage door and the witness confirming their suspicions. In minutes several uniformed officers had scrambled up the bank, and police radios crackled in the night air. A helicopter with searchlight was commissioned to sweep the nearby fields for the fugitive, and a call went out for tracker dogs to be brought in. Officers soon found Ginger's suitcase on the luggage rack. They opened it and recovered a little over three thousand pounds in used notes. Hutchinson was informed that the hunt for Ginger was gaining momentum and, together with Mulraney, sped through the night towards the scene, anxious to be present at the capture of their quarry.

Ginger sped across the field with the desperation of a hunted man. He tore through similar barriers of barbed wire fences and hedges through field after field. Without pausing for breath and not even daring to check on his pursuers, he plunged recklessly on, scattering a herd of startled cows in one field before his progress was slowed slightly in another, his shoes becoming clogged by the glutinous mud of a recently-ploughed field.

Despite his rapid progress, Ginger was fast losing the race as the police dragnet closed inexorably around him. He could see in the distance the converging lights of cars and as he looked skywards he could even see the red and blue lights of an approaching helicopter. His slow progress across the muddy ploughed field ended when he reached the edge of a small copse, an island of trees among the fields.

Its skeleton-like trees, shorn of their leaves, provided scant cover for Ginger as he sank despairingly down on his knees on a bed of moisture-sodden decayed leaves, his lungs heaving as he gasped for breath after his non-stop flight.

The drone of the helicopter neared, bringing with it a fresh source of worry for the fugitive as its powerful searchlight was suddenly switched on, its beam sweeping the fields.

Ginger threw himself forward into the sparse cover of tangled brambles, his arms and face receiving yet more tears from the sharp spikes of the brambles. He gasped with alarm as the beam of the searchlight lit up the adjoining field. The noise of the rotor blades seemed almost on top of him. Ginger pushed his face into the earth as the beam swept the small wood. He pressed his body into the earth and closed his eyes. Surely the beam would pick him out. The helicopter seemed to be hovering over him for an interminable length of time while the searchlight probed back and forth through the trees. Ginger remained motionless expecting to hear the triumphant shouts of his pursuers any minute.

Slowly, ever so slowly it seemed to Ginger, the sound of the helicopter receded and he raised his head. He watched the beam of the searchlight as it picked out the outline of a small farm some six hundred yards to the north of the copse. Ginger listened intently. He could now hear the nearing shouts of his pursuers. Looking back, his eyes now accustomed to the darkness, he could make out a line of figures in the next field but one.

He rose to his feet and, skirting the edge of the copse, broke into a trot towards the small farm, a plan of action already forming in his mind. He had already discarded the idea of forcing an entry to the farm cottage, far too risky in the circumstances, especially as he had no weapon with him. He decided instead to seek shelter in one of the outbuildings. He knew that this was a risk in itself but really he had no alternative. He approached the farm with care, fully aware that most farms had a dog whose barking would alert the occupants to his presence. The first building he came to housed pigs but the second larger building was more promising, because it was open at the front and inside, behind a tractor and two rusting ploughs, were stacked several bales of straw, four deep, piled twelve feet high almost to the roof. Ginger at first listened intently for sounds of his pursuers, but he could hear nothing so he climbed carefully up the bales of straw.

Reaching the top, he carefully lifted two bales and made a hole for himself, replacing the bales over him. He was glad of the rest but after some ten minutes or so he began to feel uncomfortable. He itched and it felt as if myriads of insects were entering his body from the straw.

He was about to move when he heard voices. A light was flashed inside the entrance to the barn, and voices seemed to be nearby. Straining, he could even make out the words. Someone, it could only be a policeman, was saying, "We'll search all your outbuildings, if you don't mind. He is definitely in the area. Lock everything up after we have gone. We'll call again after it's got light. If you see or hear anything suspicious be sure to call us. Don't tackle this blighter on your own. He may or may not be armed, we aren't sure, but he *is* dangerous, so don't approach him."

Another childish voice said, "Will we be on the telly, Dad?"

Another voice, "Shurrup and get back to bed! You've got school in the morning, remember!"

Ginger could plainly hear the sounds of two men searching the very barn he was in, and his dislike of his cramped uncomfortable hideaway evaporated as fear of discovery gripped him. He heard the sounds of nearby bales being removed and held his breath.

"There's nowt here but bloody straw, George," said a voice.

"Keep looking," said another voice. "The bugger might be behind them."

Ginger felt the bales near him begin to move and thought, 'This is it!' He tensed his muscles, prepared for a do or die rush at the policeman.

It never happened. He heard another voice, "Come on, lads, back to the mobile. Sarge reckons there is a much bigger farm down the road. The dogs never barked according to the farmer, so he can't be here – them buggers never miss a trick."

Ginger breathed more easily as he heard sounds of the police departing. 'Phew, that was a little too close for comfort.' Still, care was needed, as there were two farm dogs about, and he was lucky they hadn't heard him before. He waited another ten minutes before he removed the bale covering him and carefully eased his cramped limbs until he was on top of the bales.

The amount of light was increasing as dawn approached and Ginger realised that he must find somewhere else to lie low. So far he had been incredibly lucky but it surely couldn't last. He peered cautiously out of the building, and across the farmyard he could make out the outline of a small lorry. He immediately considered driving it away but discarded the thought almost as soon as it entered his mind. If he wasn't discovered in the act of stealing it then he would not get very far with police swarming all over the area. No, better to try and hide away in the lorry in the hope that he would unknowingly be driven somewhere well outside the immediate search area. He trod almost on tiptoe towards the lorry, his ears alert for the sound of the farm dogs.

The trouble was that the slightest noise would betray his presence and the lorry was within yards of the door of the farmhouse, in the middle of open ground. Ginger glanced anxiously around, mentally assessing an escape route in the event of his being heard approaching the lorry. The direct route was through the farm gate, down a muddy lane which led to a road. The only other escape route was via a walled garden at the side of the house leading to an orchard at the rear.

Ginger crouched as he neared the lorry. He cautiously tried the nearside door, which was locked; no surprise there. The tailgate was hanging down and he could see that the back of the lorry contained rusting machine parts. A dirt-encrusted tarpaulin was draped unceremoniously towards the back of the machine parts. Ginger, one hand on the tailgate, considered his next move. Should he take a chance and hide away in the lorry and hope that it would be driven out of the farm in the morning? But if the lorry was standing idle, how long would he remain undiscovered in the vehicle? He glanced up at the house as a light appeared in the kitchen window. This, after all, was the country and farm workers were early risers.

Ginger made his mind up. He crawled into the back of the lorry, lifted the filthy tarpaulin and eased his way under it, curling his body into a ball and making himself as small as possible. He lay there for over an hour as hurrying grey clouds were replaced by black clouds and another day began with sharp lashing showers of icy rain. Ginger shivered under the tarpaulin. At least he was dry, but he felt cold, hungry and cramped, breathing in the odour of filthy oil.

He tensed his body as he heard a door slam and approaching feet, a guttural command and the sharp excited barking of dogs. A voice within feet of him said, "I'll turn the engine over, Frank. It might take some starting seeing as how it's been laid idle for a week."

Ginger felt a slight vibration as somebody entered the driver's cab, followed by the rasping sounds of a reluctant engine being turned over. After four or five tries the engine spluttered into life and Ginger could smell the acrid exhaust fumes. The engine was allowed to run for two or three minutes, the rumbling noise now seeming quieter as the warming-up process had its desired effect. The man left the cab and returned to the house, allowing Ginger to stretch his cramped limbs. Ten minutes later the second man returned with the dogs. Ginger could hear their snuffling and panting at close range and he felt anxious lest they sniffed out his presence. The danger receded when he heard the excited shouts of a small boy, then the *thud-thud* of a ball followed by the yelling and barking of the dogs as they raced after him.

There was another agonising period for Ginger, in which he dared not move from his cramped position, before he heard the sound he was longing to hear, that of the motor being started up again and he felt almost exultant as the lorry began to move out of the farmyard.

After a short journey, the lorry stopped and Ginger strained to hear a conversation between two men.

"Do you want this lot unloaded right away?" enquired an unknown voice.

"Well yes, but I'll need a hand, some of this stuff is heavier than it looks," said a voice that Ginger recognised as being from the farm.

"Can't help you for about half an hour," said the first man. "Go and get yourself a cuppa in the station canteen – it's too bloody cold to wait about here."

'Amen to that' thought Ginger, relieved that the unloading was not to take place immediately.

As the sound of the men's footsteps receded, he knew that once again he had to make a move before he was discovered. Cautiously he raised the tarpaulin and risked a peep over the side of the lorry. From what he could see, he surmised that he was in a railway goods yard. Only feet from the lorry was a line of railway trucks, to his right were two large black loading sheds. He risked a second peep, not daring to raise his head above the sides of the lorry as he could hear the sound of scurrying feet, and his second look around confirmed that there were numerous workmen walking across the goods yard.

Ginger decided, not for the first time, to throw caution to the winds and risk being seen. He threw back the tarpaulin and clambered over the rusting machine parts, sliding thankfully on to the ground. Pins and needles shot up his cramped limbs as he tried to walk, almost falling over.

He made for the line of railway trucks as two railwaymen appeared from near the guard's van. Ginger ducked underneath the couplings of the trucks and waited until they had passed. Then he heaved himself up the side of the truck and dropped down into an empty container, which, judging by the coal dust, had recently been emptied of its load.

Ginger waited for what seemed endless hours but was actually only three before he was thrown to the side of the truck when the line of trucks gave a sudden judder. With a crank and a grind, the line of trucks began to move. Ginger could see the backs of houses as he peered through a crack in the side of the truck. He was on the move again, he knew not where, but he didn't really care so long as it was away from the police.

Manhunt

At about the same time Ginger was hiding away in the railway truck, Hutchinson and Mulraney returned to Long Eaton Police Station, which had been temporarily designated headquarters for the search team. They bit hungrily into their favourite bacon rolls and discussed the events of the last few hours. Mulraney ruefully scratched his unshaven jowls.

"It's uncanny, Pete, how this bastard always seems to be one jump ahead of us. I really thought we'd nailed him when we flushed him off that train. But still, it can surely be only a matter of time before his luck runs out, can't it?"

Hutchinson smiled wryly. Though he had been up all night with Mulraney, his smooth features appeared virtually unaffected.

"I wouldn't put money on it, Brian! But we have got to work out his next move. Somehow, I don't quite know how, he has got through our net. We have got to work out which direction he is heading. Now I reckon he'll head straight back to town. After all, it's what he knows best and the country is too open for him. I've been thinking that he might just be heading back to his old mates in the insurance business. I'll contact the chief and get him to assign a man to watch each of their homes."

By lunchtime, the intensity of the search for Ginger had subsided and Hutchinson and Mulraney returned to the Central Police Station for a tactical discussion with Chief Maudsley. As a direct result of this, the search for Ginger was now concentrated on the city of Nottingham and its suburbs.

Ginger's photo and description appeared in the local press as well as on the local television news programmes. Copies of his picture were distributed to all hotels and lodging houses, and even the local homeless night shelters were checked by uniformed policemen. A police car was positioned outside each of the four Disciples' homes, much to the chagrin of their wives and loved ones. Angie's home too was guarded round the clock, so there really seemed nowhere for Ginger to head for.

The object of all this attention was pondering his next move. The goods train on which he was travelling had finally reached its destination in a siding just north of the Midland Station, where it was to remain overnight prior to its being loaded with coal. Ginger was awaiting the cover of darkness before attempting to leave the railway truck. He was a really sorry sight. His jeans and jacket were little more than torn rags. His face, legs and arms were matted with dried blood and jagged scratches. Coal dust covered his hands and face. His physical condition had deteriorated rapidly: he was very cold and shivering constantly. He was both hungry and thirsty as he had not eaten or drunk anything for twenty-four hours.

He was badly dehydrated and felt weak and light-headed. Slumped in the corner of the truck, he dropped off into a troubled sleep, awaking with a start when the truck suddenly rumbled and jerked forward, the result of the guard's van being uncoupled. With an effort he pulled himself up the side of the truck, resting his battered body uncomfortably on the rim whilst he fought to regain his breath. He tried to slide slowly over the side but, in his weakened state, he released his hold on the truck and ended up in an untidy heap between two lines of trucks. He lay there for a full minute, his left elbow badly grazed from the impact with the hard ground. He felt dreadful: his mouth was dry, his throat parched, his need for a drink overwhelming.

So great was his craving for water that he even contemplated scooping rainwater out of a dirty puddle. He staggered blindly on through the lines of trucks, unsure of his direction. His tired brain tried to recall the geography of the area around the Midland Station. Then he remembered the canal and the bridge underneath Carrington Street, a favourite haunt of down-and-outs. Yes, that was it! He could mingle unnoticed amongst them; after all, he must be looking and smelling like one of them by now.

On the edge of the goods yard was an area of rough grass which led down to the towpath at the side of the canal. Ginger made his way unsteadily through the tufts of grass. Reaching the towpath, he glanced to his right and saw a huddled figure beneath the bridge. On closer inspection, he found an old tramp lying amidst a pile of cardboard boxes. A loose, shabby tweed overcoat enveloped his body, beneath which was a layer of newspaper to keep out the cold. Head back, he drank from a plastic bottle, contents unknown, and a further unopened plastic bottle lay by his side. He looked up suspiciously at Ginger.

"Whaddya want?" he asked in a slurred voice.

Ginger sank to his knees alongside him.

"Nothing from you, mate. I've got to sleep, I'm so very tired."

His head lolled to one side, his whole body ached and his limbs shook uncontrollably.

The tramp mistook him for an alcoholic.

"'Ere, you look in a bad way, mate. 'Ave a swig of this." He thrust the unopened bottle at Ginger. "Get that down your throat. You can pay me back tomorrow."

Ginger took the bottle from the tramp and, easing off the plastic stopper, he raised the bottle to his mouth and took a large gulp. He gasped and almost retched as the fiery liquid hit his throat. He paused, then took another swig; though not entirely quenching his thirst, the liquid warmed his stomach with a comforting glow. He turned to his benefactor.

"Thanks mate. I don't know what this is, but it's bloody good stuff."

The tramp's eyes gleamed as his wizened features creased into a broad grin. "Just the usual, mate, meths and cheap sherry, but that's the last bottle so make the most of it."

Ginger swigged contentedly from the plastic bottle. He felt a little warmer now and his brain was beginning to clear. With a start he remembered the money in his pocket. He was hungry and still a little thirsty, but dare he risk going to a shop? He rejected the idea as too dangerous but then another thought struck him. He glanced at his companion, who had lapsed into a drunken slumber, and nudged him none too gently. The tramp's eyes flickered open.

"Woss marrer, what's up?" he mumbled.

"Easy, mate," said Ginger. "Listen, you helped me, so one good turn deserves another. I've got a twenty quid note here, so how about you go to the nearest shop and get us something to eat and a decent bottle of booze to drink."

The tramp licked his dry lips at the thought of more booze. He thrust out a grubby hand to Ginger. "Giz it then, mate!" A sudden thought struck him. "'Ere, 'ow come you want me to go to the shop? Why can't you go yourself?"

Ginger shook his head. "No, mate, let's just say it wouldn't be too healthy for me if certain people saw me."

The tramp grinned. "Yeah, know just what you mean, mate, but you'll have to trust me, you know. I mean, I can get mesef two or three bottles a booze with the twenty note."

"I trust you," said Ginger as he turned away from the tramp easing a bundle of notes from his pocket. He selected a twenty pound note and handed it to the tramp.

"My name's Pete by the way, what's yours?"

The tramp seized the note and got to his feet. "Ta, mate. The name's George. See you soon."

As the tramp shuffled off up the towpath Ginger wondered if he would ever see him again. He took yet another swig from the plastic bottle. He felt really light-headed now as the strong alcoholic mixture coursed through his veins. He had no idea what the time was, but he could hear the constant roar of traffic over the bridge above him and the scuffing of many feet. His head began to droop and sleep soon claimed him.

He woke with a start to find that he was being vigorously shaken by George. The tramp had purchased a loaf of bread, two Mars bars, three bottles of cheap sherry and half a bottle of whiskey. He broke the loaf of bread in two and handed half to Ginger.

"Get that down yer gullet, mate," he said, taking a huge bite out of his portion. He nudged Ginger. "'Ere, I know who you are. You're that fellow the police are after. I must say though, that you don't look much like a killer to me."

Ginger paused in his demolition of the half loaf of bread. "Yeah, I'm him all right, so what do you plan to do about it?"

George raised his hands in mock surrender. "Don't you worry, mate, not a bloody thing. I've nothing to thank the coppers for. They 'ate our guts and the feeling's mutual. Stick wi' me, mate, you'll be all right."

Ginger nodded his thanks and the pair of them eased their hunger pains and then attacked the bottles of sherry, taking turns to swig from the whiskey bottle. Soon the pair of them were overcome by the excess of alcohol in their bodies and, oblivious of the cold night, lapsed into drunken slumber. They would probably have passed the entire night in a state of soporific abandonment were it not for the drunken youths who appeared unexpectedly on the scene.

The youths had staggered out of a nearby nightclub in an ugly mood, ejected by muscular bouncers for attempting to cause an affray. They made their way unsteadily along the side of the canal and saw what looked like two bundles of rags underneath the bridge. The first of the youths peered at the sleeping pair more closely, then turned to his companions.

"Hey, look what we have here! A pair of old dossers. Let's give them a good doing-over!"

Another of the youths yelled enthusiastically, "Yeah, let's kick the fuck out of the useless pair of tossers!"

The sleeping pair had no chance whatsoever as the six yobs closed in on them. They laid into the unfortunate pair with demonic glee, lashing out with their feet, kicking both men about the head. Two of their number dragged old George to his feet and held him whilst two more used him as a punchbag, raining blows with their fists to his head and body. The other two laid into Ginger, who somehow managed to stagger to his feet and began to fight back.

One of the youths turned from attacking the old man and picked up a half brick. He came to the aid of his two companions by hurling the half brick at Ginger. It struck the back of his head, causing him to collapse in a heap on the ground. His two assailants stamped and kicked at his unconscious body. Pausing for breath, one of the youths bent down and rifled through the pockets of Ginger's leather jacket.

"Look at this bloody lot!" he exclaimed. He held up the bundles of notes triumphantly.

"Bloody 'ell!" said one of his mates. "'E must 'ave won the pools or summat!"

"Robbed a bloody bank more like," said another of the youths.

The leading youth, sporting a gold earring and punk style haircut, shouted to his companions, "It's our lucky night! Let's make sure these two dossers don't live to tell tales."

"And how are you going to do that?" asked the only black youth in the group.

The punk youth grinned. "Set fire to the bastards," he said, sniffing the contents of the half full plastic bottle. "There's bloody meths in this. I'll chuck it all over them and put a match to it and we'll have ourselves a nice little blaze."

He began to pour the contents over the crumpled figure of the old tramp.

"Bloody hell, Rob," said the black youth. "That's going too far! We'll all get done for murder – that's a life sentence don't forget!"

"Bollocks!" said the punk youth. "These old dossers don't count. I mean, they are hardly human, now are they?"

He threw the empty bottle into the river. "That's finished that bottle. Have a look around for another one while I light up this old bugger."

He took a pack of matches from his pocket, struck one and threw it on the prone figure of George. It flickered briefly and went out. Undaunted, he struck a second match and reapplied it to the tramp, this time with more success. The meths ignited and within seconds blue flames enveloped the body, licking greedily at his clothes. There was a sickly sweet stench in the air.

The punk youth, arms folded, stood back in triumph grinning maliciously. "Just look at the old bastard burn! If we're lucky he should soon start screaming!"

"You mad prat," said the black youth, moving towards the flames. He turned to the others. "Come on, let's push the old bloke in the river before someone sees us. We'll all get done otherwise."

The other youths must have realised the logic in his reasoning because they all rushed forward to help him. They kicked and prodded at the burning body of George in an effort to move him towards the water. One of their number found a large piece of wood on the far side of the bridge and they used this to propel the body by pushing it underneath George and levering him towards the bank. It was slow progress and they couldn't get too close because of the flames. But they finally achieved their objective and emitted a small cheer when the body entered the water with a splash that doused the flames.

"Lets get the fuck out of here," said the black youth breaking into a run; the others followed suit. The punk youth glanced down at the prone form of Ginger, seemingly reluctant to join the others. Finally, with an oath, he gave Ginger a final kick and hurried to rejoin his friends.

The charred remains of George sank slowly to the bottom of the canal, where they remained undiscovered for a couple of days. Ginger, deeply unconscious, remained sprawled underneath the bridge for another hour before he was discovered by two Irish 'travellers' returning from a foraging expedition.

"Hey Patrick," said the tall tousle-haired Irishman. "Will you look at the state of this poor bloke?"

"Jesus, Michael," said Patrick. "He looks in a bad way. Some bastard has done him over. Do you think maybe we should inform the cops?"

"Not bloody likely, Pat," said Michael. "We don't want to get mixed up in whatever has been happening to this fellow. Besides, the cops will be sure to blame us. Best to leave well alone, I say."

"Ah, come on, Michael, we can hardly leave the poor bastard here to die, now can we?"

They found an old tweed overcoat lying alongside Ginger. They wrapped this around him and between them they carried him up the canal bank in the direction of Lenton.

Fate Takes a Hand

Ginger blinked his eyes on awakening. There was a shaft of winter sunshine winking through a nearby window and he wondered where he was. He attempted to raise his head but a series of sharp stabbing pains dissuaded him from any further movement. His arms and legs ached and his entire body seemed a mass of pain. He groaned with frustration because he couldn't remember how he had got in this state. He looked upwards at a rounded arched ceiling; to his left there appeared to he a plastic wall. His mind slowly cleared and then it dawned on him that he was in a caravan! He flicked his eyes to the right as he sensed movement. There was a dark-haired woman peering down at him. She was not exactly what you call pretty but she had nice brown eyes and rosy cheeks. Her nose was too long and she wore no make-up but her expression was kind and caring.

"So you've woke up at last," she said to Ginger in a soft lilting voice with a noticeable Irish accent. "Sure, I thought for a time that we'd lost you last night."

Ginger wore a puzzled expression. "I, er, I'm sorry but I don't quite know what you mean."

The woman smiled down at him. "No, I don't suppose you do, but don't worry, stay right where you are. You should be on the mend in a day or two. Somebody must really have disliked you to give you such a beating. I'll get you a cup of tea."

Ginger was still puzzling over her last remark when the recollection of the previous night's events came flooding back. He remembered the violence of the attack by the youths, which had certainly surprised him. But he recalled fighting back and the satisfaction he had felt when he punched one of them in the face and headbutted another, then everything seemed to go blank. How the hell had he arrived in this caravan and who was the mysterious woman? What had happened to poor old George? He remembered that he had taken one hell of a beating. Again he attempted to move his head but the pains were still there. He recalled the woman's words: "Someone must have really disliked you to give you such a beating."

So the youths must have knocked him unconscious and laid into him. Still, at least he was still here to tell the tale.

Further thoughts were dispelled by the arrival of the dark-haired woman carrying a large mug of tea. She gently pulled up his pillows and he attempted to rise but she restrained him.

"Easy now," she said. "Don't try and get up yourself, I'll pull you up."

She leant over him, then, pushing her hands under his armpits, she gently propped up his body so he was in a sitting position. Ginger's pain was nullified a little by the pleasant feel of the soft flesh of her generous breasts pressed against his face.

Propped up against the pillows, he could now see more of his surroundings. He was in a large old-fashioned caravan. The furnishings were basic but the interior had a homely feel about it. His bed folded out from the side of the caravan, the bed-coverings consisted of a thick blanket over which was a brightly coloured shawl of diverse colours. Extending each side of the long caravan up to the door was a long covered bench seat. The two identical bench seats were draped with covers of the same gaudy colours as those atop Ginger's bed.

The woman handed Ginger the mug of tea and sat herself down on the bed at the side of him. Ginger took a sip of the tea which was hot, strong and sweet-tasting. He looked at the woman and liked what he saw. She was wearing a tight pink sweater which emphasised her large but firm breasts. Her legs were encased in tight jeans and her figure, though full, was very feminine. She remained silent for a while, allowing Ginger to drink his tea, then she spoke to him.

"I expect you're wondering how you got here. My man Michael and his brother Patrick found you by the side of the canal last night. You were unconscious so they brought you back here. My name is Dolores by the way. When they got you here, you were in a right state and I was all for calling an ambulance and getting you to hospital. But Michael said no, he seemed to think you might be in trouble with the police or something. Anyway, I cleaned you up as best I could. We were going to try and get some whiskey down you, but by the smell of your breath you'd plenty of that already! So we just left you to sleep it off."

"Where is your husband and his friend now?" asked Ginger.

Dolores laughed. "He's not me husband, he's me boyfriend. They have gone out on the scrounge as usual. You see, we are what was used to be called tinkers, now we're known as travellers. We make our living by buying odds and ends, sometimes doing them up and selling them. The boys also make a bob or two turning their hand to a bit of busking in the Market Square. But enough about us. Tell me something about yourself."

Ginger was in something of a quandary – he was warming to this warm-hearted attractive woman, indeed he rather fancied her, and was disappointed to learn that she was already spoken for. He felt an affinity with her and was sorely tempted to tell her everything about himself. But part of him rejected the idea; after all, these people were only gypsies and were obviously short of money. There must be a tidy reward for information on him, so what was to stop them from handing him over to the police?

In the end he compromised with himself, and said to Dolores, "Yeah, you are right in a way – I am wanted by the police but I'd rather not say why for the minute. I'd like to thank your boyfriend and his brother for bringing me in last night, and your good self of course for looking after me. I'd like to repay you all with some money but unfortunately the muggers who did me over took all my money. But one thing I can promise you is that as soon as I get back on my feet, I will repay you all."

Dolores smiled indulgently. "Well, we'll have to see about that but for the moment are you up to eating a sausage sandwich?"

"Er, yes please," replied Ginger, his gastric juices churning in his stomach at the thought. Apart from the half loaf of bread and a Mars bar, he had not eaten for nearly thirty-six hours.

Dolores busied herself with the frying pan and the delicious aroma of the frying sausages whetted Ginger's appetite. He wolfed down the thick-breaded sandwiches as soon as they arrived. Dolores told him that she was going out for a short while to do some shopping. She would lock him in and warned him not to answer any knocking on the door.

'She needn't have worried on that score,' thought Ginger as he lapsed into a contented sleep. After what seemed like only a few minutes the sound of voices just outside the caravan awakened him. He strained to overhear what was being said. He recognised the voices as belonging to his two rescuers.

"Will you no' get it into your thick skull, Michael, that we'll make a packet if we tell the police about this fellow?"

"I couldn't do it, Patrick, I really couldn't. Besides we're not one hundred per cent certain that this is the same man as the one in the paper."

"You must be bloody blind, Michael! Take another look! It's him, it's got to be!"

"Ah well, mebbe you're right but even if it is, there is no way I am going to turn him in. For one thing Dolores is dead against, she likes him."

"Huh, fancies him more like! Never trust a woman, Michael. Still, that's always been your downfall, hasn't it?"

"You're just bloody jealous as usual! You've always fancied Dolores and it sticks in your gullet that she prefers me."

"Oh, don't come that old baloney! You know fine well I sampled her before you got your mitts on her!"

"You lying bastard!"

There was the sound of fisticuffs and blows being exchanged and landed.

Ginger became quite alarmed. He didn't like the sound of this. Fortunately the arrival of Dolores put a stop to the brawling and Ginger's respect for her grew as she roundly berated both men. All three entered the caravan some minutes later and the two men seemed chastened and subdued.

Ginger spent the next two days recuperating and his strength returned gradually. He talked with the two men and offered to help them out as soon as he was well enough. Of the two Patrick appeared more uncomfortable in his presence and spoke abruptly to him. Michael seemed pleasant enough but Ginger detected an underlying element of hostility within him.

At night-time the sleeping arrangements were that Ginger slept at one end of the caravan and Patrick at the other. Dolores and Michael slept on a mattress in the middle of the floor. Ginger felt uncomfortable at the sound of their lovemaking and shut his ears to it. In the circumstances he could well understand why Patrick felt jealous.

Ginger reviewed his situation and decided that it would be beneficial to both himself and his rescuers if they parted company. He made up his mind to tell them of his decision on the third morning after his arrival at the caravan. He got out of his makeshift bed and stood unsteadily on his feet despite the protestations of Dolores. He looked at himself in the small mirror, hardly recognising the battered creature he found reflected in it. His whole body was a mass of yellowing bruises, his left eye was nearly shut, there were gashes on his face and neck and he was badly in need of a shave. He cleaned himself up as best he could and with a borrowed razor he scraped at his face. Although he scraped off most of his beard, he opened up some barely healed wounds and he had to dab at his face with swabs of cotton wool to stem the blood.

At breakfast he announced his intentions to his rescuers. Their reaction was mixed. Patrick didn't say a word but Ginger sensed that he was pleased to be rid of him. Dolores, on the other hand, was very upset, and insisted that he was not nearly well enough to set out on his own. Besides, she argued, he would be picked up by the police if he showed his face in public.

Ginger was unsure how Michael felt. He had expressed some concern at first but his weak protestations didn't appear to be sincere. They argued for some time, but could find no common agreement and eventually reached a compromise which satisfied them all with the exception of Dolores. Ginger would remain with them for a further two days, but, to test the water so to speak, he would accompany the two brothers, suitably disguised, on a busking trip to the old Market Square that same afternoon.

The two brothers rummaged through their wardrobe to provide some suitable clothes for Ginger's disguise. They had decided to clothe Ginger in the garb of a tramp and to achieve this effect he was given an overlarge T-shirt, baggy torn trousers and a loose-fitting tatty jersey. Finally the whole ill-fitting outfit was enveloped in the voluminous folds of the late departed George's tattered, filthy tweed overcoat. Ginger studied his reflection in the mirror and scarcely recognised himself in the garb of an extremely scruffy tramp. As a final touch he pulled over his head a blue knitted balaclava, on top of which was a torn cap.

The strange looking trio left the caravan just after 2 p.m. Ginger was touched and secretly pleased by Dolores's farewell gesture as she planted a kiss on his forehead and wished him good luck. Michael carried a battered old case containing his fiddle, whilst Patrick carried his flute under his arm. The brothers walked a little in front of Ginger but had to slow their pace to accommodate him. Ginger was still a little wobbly on his feet after his ordeal.

As they made their way along Castle Boulevard, Ginger felt conspicuous, but he needn't have worried for he scarcely received a second glance. His worst moment came on passing a newsagent's, when he glanced at the outside display and was shocked at the large picture of himself prominently displayed on the front of most of the dailies.

The crowds and the traffic increased the nearer they got to the city centre. The two brothers had not exchanged a single word with Ginger during the journey and he sensed that they would disown him should he be challenged by the law. They did pass several policemen en route but there was no hint of a challenge and Ginger became more confident. Michael chose their prime busking spot with care, selecting a point midway between The Bell Inn and the Odeon Cinema.

A ragged blanket was spread on the pavement and Michael motioned Ginger over, speaking quietly in his ear.

"Sit yourself down on this," he said, patting the blanket. "We'll play a few tunes and the punters will chuck their coins on the blanket. We'll more than likely get moved on by the law, but don't panic if a copper approaches. Don't talk to him. I'll do all the talking if it should become necessary. Okay?"

Ginger nodded his assent and squatted down cross-legged on the blanket. Michael adjusted the strings on his fiddle as Patrick launched into a lively Irish air on his flute. Michael joined in and they were soon into their familiar repertoire of Irish country songs.

Ginger stared straight ahead, occasionally flicking his eyes to the left and right, scanning the crowds of people for a familiar face. Though anxious to test his new disguise, he was still fearful of being recognised.

The lively Irish music seemed incongruous set against the hustle and bustle of the city crowds and in competition with the constant roar of the non-stop traffic. But the brothers' act was very popular, of that there was no doubt judging by the flow of coins tossed on to the blanket. Occasionally people stopped to listen and pass words of encouragement. One nasty moment occurred for Ginger when he spotted his assailants from the incident of two nights previous. They emerged from Yates' Wine Lodge directly across the road and linked arms, shouting and swearing at passers-by. Ginger's body tensed as it appeared for one moment that they intended to cross the road. Michael and Patrick played on, oblivious to the imminent possibility of a violent confrontation. But the moment passed thankfully without incident when the group became impatient at waiting for a gap in the traffic and chose instead to stagger off up Market Street, to the annoyance of those nearby.

Ginger gathered up the coins and as he stuffed them into his pockets he was startled to hear a familiar voice. Three young women had paused to look at a display in a nearby shop window. One of them clutched the hand of a bored-looking little girl. The youngster released her hand from her mother's and approached the musical group, wide-eyed with curiosity. Sucking her thumb, she stared upwards in that strangely challenging manner of all small children at the flute player. On his knees, Ginger turned from picking up the coins, his face at eye level with the youngster's.

Recognition suddenly dawned on the little girl's face, and her brown eyes lit up.

"Mr Man!" she cried, reaching out to grab hold of Ginger's balaclava. She pulled it down on one side, shrieking, "Take off that funny old hat, Mr Man! Why are you wearing that mucky old coat?"

Ginger recoiled and hastily pulled back the balaclava. His heart sank as he recognised Natalie. Michael abruptly stopped playing his fiddle and looked on with dismay. Natalie's mother Mary suddenly realised that her daughter was no longer holding her hand and looked hurriedly around for her. As she caught sight of her she ran forward and grabbed her hand.

"Come along, Natalie!   What on earth are you doing? leave that poor man alone."

"But, Mam, it's my friend, Mr Man," protested Natalie.

"Come along you silly girl," said Mary, dragging Natalie with her prior to crossing the road with her friends.   But Natalie was not yet ready to desert her old friend just yet, and petulantly she jerked at her mother's arm yelling, "I want to talk to my friend, Mr Man."

"Don't be silly!" said Mary.   "That's a dirty old tramp, you don't know him."

"I do, I do!" shrieked Natalie.   "I'm not going with you! He's not an old tramp!"   She stamped her foot in defiant anger.

Mary lost her temper with the recalcitrant child, first slapping her very hard on the back of her thighs, then, picking her up, she thrust her under her arm and carried her daughter across the road.   Natalie screamed and kicked her chubby legs, protesting long and noisily.

When they reached the other side of the road Mary put Natalie back on her feet and wagged a finger at her, warning her of the dire consequences should she further misbehave. Natalie ignored her mother and stared defiantly back across the road.

Michael had seen enough.   He nudged Patrick and they began to gather up the blanket and make preparations for their departure.   Ginger became even more apprehensive when he espied the approach of a uniformed policeman.   He pulled up his coat collar and began to walk away, then glanced across the road and was horrified to see Natalie start to run across the road, arms outstretched, to meet him.

To his left Ginger could see a green city transport bus fast approaching from the direction of the Odeon Cinema.

"Natalie, stay where you are!" he shouted with rising alarm.

Ignoring Ginger's warning shout, the little girl continued her mad dash but suddenly became aware of the approaching bus and froze in horror. What happened next would require the use of a slow motion, frame by frame sequence to take in every detail. In reality it was all over in seconds, to the horror of the many people who witnessed it.

Ginger seized up the situation in a split second: Natalie was about to be hit by the bus; in all probability she would be killed; at best she would be seriously injured. Ginger didn't hesitate. He ran across the road and flung himself full length at Natalie. He pushed the terrified child forward as he fell directly under the wheels of the bus. Natalie's mother rushed after her child and caught the youngster as she landed at the side of the road. Sobbing with relief, she clutched Natalie to her and frantically kissed her.

The bus driver saw the child frozen with fear in front of him. He desperately applied his brakes though he knew that he could not stop in time. At the last second before impact he saw the blurred form of Ginger and felt the jolt as the offside front wheel passed over his body. He brought the bus to a juddering halt with a squeal of protesting brakes. For a few seconds there was a ghastly silence as the horrified onlookers gathered their thoughts.

The silence was broken by the static crackle of a police radio as the police officer Ginger had seen summoned the emergency services. Several passers-by crouched on their hands and knees peering under the bus, shaking their heads at what they saw. It seemed a long time but it was actually only four minutes by the time an ambulance reached the scene. The patrolling policeman had rustled up the help of three more colleagues, including a police sergeant who assumed control of the scene. Traffic was halted and the police set up a protective barrier around the bus to prevent any further incursions by the large number of curious onlookers who revel in gawking at the misfortunes of others.

Alighting from the ambulance, the green-and-white-coated paramedic quickly assessed the situation after looking underneath the bus. He shook his head grimly at the police sergeant.

"No need for first aid, I'm afraid," he said. "That poor bloke is beyond our help. His head is crushed and the bus will have to be moved before we can get the body out."

Eventually an emergency repair truck arrived from a nearby bus depot and a king-sized jack hoisted up the bus to reveal the crumpled body of Ginger. Now they were able to see the full extent of his injuries. The offside front wheel had passed directly over his head, crushing it in the manner of an egg. A few of the curious spectators saw more than they had bargained for, judging by the evidence of their pale shocked faces. It was all too much for one man who vomited his recently consumed four course lunch into the gutter.

The two Irish brothers had looked on in amazement at Ginger's suicidal dash towards the bus and then melted swiftly into the crowds in their rush to avoid the inevitable questions they were bound to be asked.

Whilst the body of Ginger was gently removed from the scene, the police began to take witness statements. Mary was in a state of shock and couldn't really take in all that had occurred. Her statement was confused and faltering, constantly interrupted by the childish ramblings of Natalie, who was herself trembling with shock. Despite her protests, it was considered advisable that both Mary and Natalie be taken to hospital to be treated for shock before answering any more questions.

The police sergeant assisted Mary and Natalie into the ambulance. The little girl was made to lie down and the sergeant placed a blanket around her. He spoke quietly to Mary.

"Keep the child warm. It's always advisable in cases of shock."

The sergeant left the ambulance and was closing the doors when Mary spoke to him.

"That bloke's a bloody hero! He may be the bloke you're all looking for but he saved my little girl's life!"

The sergeant stood open-mouthed in amazement as the ambulance moved swiftly away, then recovered his composure as he contacted Central Police Station on his radio.

By the time Ginger's body arrived at the mortuary, Hutchinson and Mulraney were already awaiting its arrival with increasing excitement. Draped in a sheet, the body of Ginger was wheeled into the mortuary by a white-coated attendant. He carefully pulled back the sheet to reveal the bloodied, crushed head. Hutchinson screwed up his eyes in disgust and restrained himself from uttering an oath. Grim-faced, he walked out of the building followed by Mulraney.

"It's *got* to be him, Brian – but how can we be certain? The face on that body is crushed beyond recognition."

Mulraney nodded ruefully in agreement.

"Yes, Pete. It's uncanny, isn't it, how that bastard always seems to have the last laugh, even in death!"